INFIDELITY'S FOOL

by

Mannie L. Magid

Strategic Book Publishing
New York, NewYork

Strategic Book Publishing
An imprint of AEG Publishing Group
845 Third Avenue, 6th Floor - 6016
New York, NY 10022
www.StrategicBookPublishing.com

ISBN: 978-1-60693-779-2   1-60693-779-0

Printed in the United States of America

Book Design: SP

TABLE OF CONTENTS

CHAPTER ONE

2005

"I'm not sick, Doc. I only need something to help me get a little sleep."

In the seven by ten examination room, Dr. Len Darshan glanced suspiciously at this patient who, he thought, might be trying to wangle some sedatives, either for recreational use or perhaps to sell at a profit on the street. The medical chart was thin, but it was not new; the man had been into the office before. Still, Len could not readily recognize him.

Surreptitiously, the doctor turned to the summary on the chart: the patient, forty-three year old Mr. Ralph Carter, had last been in eleven months ago with a severe and neglected foot infection. And before that visit, going back four years, he had seen Len on only two occasions. Either Ralph was consulting more than one physician or he was your typical stoic male, unwilling to submit to minor, inevitable ailments that would bring the average person in for medical care.

Len thumbed back to the personal information on Ralph's chart: wife, Elaine Carter, and one daughter, eleven-year-old Missy.

That's right. Now I remember. Len looked up from the chart in recollection. *Elaine is that attractive and well-groomed petite blonde who works as a secretary in some local law firm. Missy comes in frequently because of her bothersome allergies, always smiling, about as cooperative and as brave as can be expected of a pediatric patient.*

No, with this family and this medical history, Ralph was not a drug seeker. What is more, with his open request, he probably had a significant new illness or, more likely, a sizeable problem weighing heavily on his mind.

Len briefly studied Ralph sitting on the end of the examination couch, his legs dangling down to the retractable step.

Ralph could not face the doctor. Grinning nervously, he chose to stare straight ahead, only daring the occasional glimpse Len's way.

"Something bothering you?" Len asked.

Ralph wore a maroon college cap with the visor respectfully forward to shade his brow. With a sickly smile pulling firmly upon his lips, he did not speak. He merely nodded gently and turned an embarrassed gaze down and into his lap.

"Is it something at work?" Len guessed. Then, looking once more at the chart, he added, "Remind me. What do you do for a living?"

Ralph turned to Len, who was swiveling gently on a stool next to a small counter to the patient's right. "That's another thing I been wanting to speak to you about, Doc. I meant to, but I just never seemed to get round to it."

Len noticed how the tension in Ralph's face and shoulders was beginning to waver. The patient seemed relieved to turn the conversation away from the major problem, which gave the doctor some inkling of the magnitude of this man's anguish.

"What is it?" Len jumped at the opportunity to start his patient talking. *Once the conversation begins to flow, Ralph will get to his real problem*, Len thought. *All he needs is a sympathetic ear and a comfortable milieu. He'll soon want to tell me what's really on his mind . . . I see this all the time.*

Ralph thought for a moment, removed his maroon cap, briefly contemplated the inside lining and size tag, and then spoke. "I've been in this job ten years." His prominent larynx bobbed, the awkward smile softened, and his voice was mellower and deeper than expected of a man with his slight frame. "I work in a factory," he said. "We make a range of plastic containers. I earn okay, but I should do better. My wife, Elaine, brings home a bit more than I do. The thing is that I didn't do too good when I was a kid at

7

school. I had a hard time learning." He ran a hand over his straight dark hair and his constant smile actually found a hint of geniality. "I heard about this *Attention Deficit Disorder* thing, and I've been thinking that that's what I got. I had problems studying when I was a kid, and I don't seem to remember things now. If I could concentrate better, maybe I could get a better job. What you think, Doc? You think maybe I got it?"

Len did not want to digress from the patient's major concern. Nor did he want to overlook a condition that could indeed be contributory. "You may be right, Mr. Carter. Your self-diagnosis may be spot on the money, and treatment may make a difference to your life. Let me set you up for a psychological evaluation. That will help clear up the matter, and we'll take it from there."

"Good. Yes. Thanks, Doc. Let's get it done." The glimmer of hope seemed to lift the burden that had brought the patient to the doctor.

But Ralph's ailment had not been cured; it had not even been addressed. So, one slow word at a time, Len said, "It's not the *ADD*, Attention Deficit Disorder, that brought you in today . . . is it, Mr. Carter?"

"If I can think better and get a little smarter, then everything is going to be okay." He looked Len squarely in the eyes and, with newfound trust, blurted, "Hell, Doc! My wife has been with another guy."

This is a no-brainer, Len thought. *If she's cheating, why doesn't he tell her to take a hike, like most men would do?*

8

But this was not the doctor's decision; it was the patient's, and separation and divorce did not seem Ralph's solution of choice.

As he stared at his patient's pitiful posture, questions began to flood Len's mind, and foremost in his thoughts was, *what is Ralph's connection between his possible ADD and his wife fooling around?*

Len stood from his stool, placed a comforting hand on his patient's shoulder, and then backed up to perch on the edge of the writing counter. "Are you certain?" he asked. "How did you find out?"

"The guy's wife told me, Doctor. I would never have found out for myself."

"Well, is she certain? How does she know?"

"Yeah," Ralph sneered. "How does she know; how does everyone know?"

"What do you mean?" Len asked. "Do you believe the woman? How long have you known her?"

"The guy is my friend, Doc. Or, at least, I thought he was my friend. And his wife was a friend, too. We've been hanging out with the same bunch of guys for years, ever since high school."

I would have bet that Elaine Carter cheated on her husband with one of her suave lawyer employers, Len thought. Then, for the umpteenth time, he had to admit to himself that he would find any opportunity to judge lawyers with a tainted eye, as did most of his colleagues—especially those currently named in malpractice suites. Standing up straight and folding his arms high across his chest, Len cautiously inquired, "What do mean by 'everyone knows?' and who is everyone?"

"She, my friend's wife, told me that all our other friends know. They speak about it behind my back. And my wife has been with at least two other guys."

And probably one or two suave lawyer employers too, Len once more thought to himself. He dropped his folded arms and whispered, "I'm sorry, Ralph. What is going to happen? What are you going to do?"

"I been thinking about it, Doc. I don't know how long it's been going on, but I'm sure it's a long time now. I've spoken to Elaine. I was pretty cut up at first, but she was crying about it, and she doesn't want a divorce. We're going to have to move away. I can't stay here, not where everyone knows."

"How do you know?" Len asked, unable to control his curiosity. "How do you know it has been going on a long time?"

"Elaine didn't exactly tell me, but she cries when I ask. My friend's wife—you know her; she's also a patient here—told me. And it's been going on for some time now. I thought about speaking to the guys who have been with her, but I'm not going to. It'll only end up in a fight and won't do any good." He thought for a moment and then added, "Or maybe it would. Maybe if I beat the hell out of one of the miserable bastards, then I could get some rest. But I didn't come here to trouble you with my personal problems, Doc. I really need something to sleep."

"I understand, Ralph. And of course I'll give you a sedative. You probably could use some anti-depressants, too. But I must tell you that it's the uncertainty that is keeping you awake. I know you don't want to speak to your so-called friends who have stabbed you in the back, and I can't blame your wife for being too embarrassed to discuss it fully. And yet, learning the unknown is an important step toward putting this or any other unpleasant matter behind you." Len rolled the small stool back to his desk, sat, and began writing the prescription.

"I know how long, Doc. When I think about it now, I know real well. And it's also the knowing that gets me angry and keeps me awake."

Len again looked up at Ralph, inviting him to continue.

"Those nights when she said she was working late. I might not be too smart, but I see now what was going on. And there were lots of other times when she was gone longer than I expected. She would go to buy groceries alone, and come home with a couple of items two hours later. Then, there were the nights that she didn't want to be with me, sometimes for months at a time. I even spoke to some of our friends about it. We all laughed together, and I believed it was normal. We thought it was *hormonal imbalance* and that it happened to most women. I was a fool, Doc. I was a fool, and it hurts real bad."

11

"You're right in one way, Ralph," Len said. "I can't do much to help your situation. But you are no fool; you have a much rarer condition: you are trusting. And if it helps any, I admire you for the way in which you're handling your problem. I am sorry and I certainly hope you and Elaine can make a fresh start. If you want me to have a word with her, I'll do my best. I don't think she realizes what a catch she has in you. Or, if you prefer me to say nothing, then I'll honor your request. I'll do whatever I can to help." Len handed Ralph the prescription. "The capsules that you take in the mornings are anti-depressants. They'll kick in slowly over about three to four weeks. We may need to increase the dosage at that time. There will probably be no side effects, but they may cause a slight increase in weight." Len smiled a friendly smile at Ralph and added, "Maybe that wouldn't be such a bad thing in your case." He then quickly calculated the risk of mentioning the other possible unwanted effect of the medication and went ahead anyway. "They may also decrease your sex drive. If that becomes a problem, let me know and we'll either change the medication or adjust the dosage. The other tablet you can take as needed to sleep at night. It can be habit forming, so I'm hoping that as the anti-depressant takes effect, you won't need the sedative. Set an appointment to see me four weeks from today, and we'll review the medications. Meanwhile, go slow on making big decisions. When you're feeling better, you'll be thinking better. Also, if you need an ear, I'll be only a call away."

Len meant every kind word he said to his patient. He wished he could utter *abracadabra* and make all Ralph's woes disappear. He felt that this gentle soul certainly deserved a rapid and complete cure, but he also realized that Ralph's condition was about as hopeless as any case of widespread malignancy with systemic

12

manifestations. With little else to offer, the doctor still did the best he could; he allocated the Ralph Carter case to that exclusive holding area in his mind, the corner where he kept the histories of a few select patients that he deemed deserving of special consideration at any time, day or night.

Len moved toward the door, but Ralph remained seated and spun on his haunches to face the doctor. "I've known Elaine since we were kids at school," he said." I can't imagine life without her, Dr. Darshan . . . I need her . . . I love her, and I know she loves me. She told me." His voice spluttered with uncertainty, and his eyes shone with stubborn tears, refusing to well into droplets, but he did not lose his poise. "It's just that . . . you know . . . I'm not as sophisticated as other men. When we were young, I was popular, but since we have grown up and come into the real world, I've changed. I let her down. I try, but I'm not the man she once knew and then married. The friends that we mix with are mostly the same as the ones we had back at school, and all the guys seem to be doing better than I am. Sometimes, I can't blame Elaine. I know that what she's done is wrong, but I also know that it's largely my fault, too." He hopped off the edge of the examination couch and placed the maroon cap squarely on his head using both hands. "Actually, it's mostly the men's fault. You know how some guys can be. Always chasing beautiful women and tempting them with money and gifts." He again removed his cap and once more asked, "Do you think I'll do better if I can get treatment for ADD, Dr. Darshan?"

All Len could do was nod feebly, but what Ralph saw was a gesture of agreement and a gateway of hope from his broken life.

The time was ten minutes to one. Ralph had scheduled a return visit for four weeks, and the office referral specialist had set him up with an appointment for psychological testing.

Across the corridor from the checkout desk, Len's medical assistant, Mary, a fifty-something, fattish blonde in green scrubs, looked over the high counter of the nurses' station. "That's it for the morning, Dr. Darshan." She pointed toward the doctors' lounge at the far corner of the suite and whispered, as though revealing some dark secret, "The drug reps brought a kosher lunch."

Hungry and ready for a break, Len gave Mary a thumbs up and made his way toward his sanctuary, the doctors' lounge, a small triangular shaped room with an oval mahogany table surrounded by six comfortable chairs. As he ambled down the hallway, Len's shoulders began to slump. He had not lost any of his six-foot-three height, but posture and gradual portliness made him seem no taller than average. His brown hair, always neatly parted to the right, was graying and thinning, yet his face had few creases and had hardly aged.

Rex Gooding and Angela Smith, two good-looking young Pharmaceutical representatives were sitting opposite Dr. Terrance Stein, Len's associate of twenty-seven years and best friend for an additional eleven years.

"Hello, Dr. Darshan." Angela looked up, brushed back a few fallen strands of jet-black hair, and offered the doctor a perfect white smile.

14

"Hi, guys." Len took the seat between Dr. Stein and Rex. "Thanks for bringing lunch again."

"It's really not necessary. It's nice of you, but you don't have to bring lunch," Dr. Stein said to Angela and Rex while chomping away at his turkey sandwich.

"You don't have to, but I appreciate it," Len argued, and then turned to his associate and said, "That's how they get our ear. They know what they're doing. It makes good business sense, and it adds nothing to the cost of drugs."

"Exciting news!" interrupted Angela. "We got a great new drug. I mentioned it to you last time I was here. Now it's approved and available."

"Remind me," said Len, pouring a diet soda into the waiting Styrofoam cup, half-filled with ice.

"We were telling Dr. Stein about our new, long acting, selective *phosphodiesterase inhibitor*, for *erectile dysfunction*," said Angela.

"What's the advantage?" asked Len.

"This one lasts thirty-six hours, compared to the other product's four hours."

"Who on earth needs more than four hours?" asked Dr. Stein.

"It brings back spontaneity into a relationship," offered Angela. "When a couple goes out on a date, the man doesn't have to watch the clock and think, *when will I have to be ready to perform?* If they go to dinner and a show, and if the man takes the other company's pill before going out, then the effectiveness may wear off by the time they return home. You agree that an evening out can last more than four hours, don't you?"

"So why can't the guy just take the pill with the meal?" asked Dr. Stein.

"That's the other thing," Rex interrupted eagerly. "You shouldn't take the other product with a fatty meal. Ours, you can take at any time."

"The other product works pretty well," said Len. "Let's take a look at your studies. Do you have a head to head comparison between the two drugs?"

"We have a seven minute video," Angela said, leaning over to retrieve a laptop from the briefcase at her feet. "Have a look at it, and then we'll try to answer any questions."

She positioned the computer opposite the doctors, switched it on, and, while the screen slowly lit up, she offered them each a glossy green invitation to a dinner-lecture by a prominent Academic Urologist, hired to help launch their new product.

The program went into the causes and the pathology of erectile dysfunction, the related psychological and social problems, and the available forms of treatment; and towards the end, it

16

focused on the ever-increasing sexual problems in the aging male population.

Switching off the computer, Angela casually asked, "Are you seeing more patients with erectile dysfunction in your practice?"

Dr. Stein nodded tentatively. His hair was completely gray and much sparser than Len's. His face, too, had aged, with deep creases between the nose and the cheeks and loose skin hanging from the neck. Still, his green eyes had not lost their luster, and he remained a handsome man, handsomer than his long time friend, Len Darshan.

"How are you recognizing the condition?" she continued. "Do patients volunteer the information, or do you have to ask?"

"Both," replied Dr. Stein. "With all the media exposure, men are beginning to realize how widespread the problem has become, and I try to remember to ask my diabetics and hypertensives if they're having any problems."

"Some of my other doctors tell me that wives are coming in to look for help for their husbands. Have you seen that?"

"Yes."

"Do you think that's because some men are still too embarrassed to speak about it?"

"Probably."

Angela then skillfully left a moment for contemplative silence before asking, "How do you think your patients would respond if you were to routinely inquire whether they had erectile problems?"

"Well, sometimes we do ask," Dr. Stein replied. "Those who don't have the problem are quick to let us know. They seem to laugh the question off." He leaned haughtily back in his chair, drummed his fingers on the table, and agreed with Angela's implication. "It's true, though. Most men who have the problem seem relieved when we ask."

"Do you think you should be asking more often? Do you think you may be missing many cases?"

"The question about ED doesn't always come to mind. If a man comes in with an acute respiratory infection or a broken toe, we might feel stupid asking about his sex life. He'd probably think we were perverted or something. We could ask during routine physicals. But you're right; we are probably missing some cases. We should fine-tune our awareness of the condition, especially when the patient has any clinical problem that may be connected."

Like Ralph Carter's problem, thought Len. "I just saw a guy who was extremely upset because he found out that his wife was cheating. Pitiful fellow. I really felt bad for him."

"Did he have ED?" asked Rex, the ex-college wide receiver with the rust-colored and well-gelled crew cut.

"I didn't ask."

Angela did not have to say a word. Merely throwing up both hands, ten fingers spread wide, with her head tilted sharply to the left stated clearly, *now there's a typical case that needed asking.*

"I didn't ask, but I actually think he was okay. He said that his wife was the one who wasn't responsive."

Dr. Stein turned to Len. "You reckon she was cheating and he wasn't. We seem to be seeing more of that."

"At first blush, men seem less faithful than women, but when you think about it, the numbers must be about the same. Every time a man is cheating, a woman is cheating, too."

"Not really. It is possible that fewer women are cheating, but much more often and with many more partners."

"Funny you should say that. My patient said that his wife was cheating with quite a few other men."

"So why doesn't he leave, or tell her to leave?"

"He doesn't want to. He seems a little inadequate in the self-sufficiency department. That's probably why I feel so sorry for him."

"It's woman's lib that is to blame," said Dr. Stein. "I know that it's politically incorrect to say so, but twenty years ago, things were different."

"Oh, so men were cheating and women weren't, and that was acceptable," said Angela.

"For every man cheating, there still has to be a woman," Dr. Darshan repeated.

"Maybe I'm wrong," Dr. Stein argued. "But it seems like it was married men having affairs with unmarried women."

"That's still happening today," said a smiling Rex. "That's one of the reasons for the higher divorce rate. Older successful men are leaving their wives for their younger secretaries."

"That's women's lib's fault again," said Dr. Stein. "Women in the work place are becoming just as sexually aggressive as the men. I think the birth control pill is largely to blame. Now they feel free to fool around, too." He turned to Angela with apologetic wide eyes forcing deep wrinkles into his forehead and added, "It's not the individual woman's fault. Women seem trapped in the new messed up world order, and they have no choice. Twenty or thirty years ago, most mothers would stay home. Today, people are greedier and need two incomes, so women must go out to work."

"You're such a chauvinist, Terry," said Len. "I'm not one hundred percent sure, but in this patient's case, his wife's infidelity had nothing to do with the work place. She was fooling around with her husband's friends."

Terrance Stein pushed back from the table and turned his chair to face Len. "You have to admit that the world order has changed, Len."

20

"What exactly do you mean by 'world order,' Terry? Do you mean the chase?"

"Exactly. 'The chase.' The roles of man and woman. Years ago, man was the pursuer, and woman the pursued. Today, who knows who is chasing whom? It's open house for anyone to pursue anyone else. In fact, with all these sexual harassment fears, it seems the roles—at least in the work place—have been reversed. It's easier and less dangerous for a woman to approach a man. I know there have been movies in which the pursuing woman has ended up with legal problems, but in the real world of today, it's the man who had better watch his step."

"Maybe roles have been modified rather than changed, Terry. Women have always lured men. Just like in the animal world, where the female puts out her scent, which turns the male wild with desire, so, too, do human females put out their lures. Their clothes, their perfumes, their jewelry, their constant dieting and exercising to stay trim. Retailers would starve without women. They don't need men . . . except to pay the bills, after the men have been lured."

"That may be so. But, with women's liberation, women not only lure, they pursue, as well. That's what women's liberation is all about, Len. That's what women's libbers are fighting for. They want to be liberated in every walk of life. And make no mistake, liberated means assuming man's role in each of those walks: in business, in politics, in academics, in religion, and in the social setting, which includes the world of sex."

"I don't know how right or wrong you are, Terry, but most people still view male-female roles in the traditional light. That patient I was telling you about assumed and accepted that his wife fell victim to preying men. He thinks she is so beautiful that the men couldn't keep their hands off her. He blames them . . . not her." Len wistfully stroked his clean-shaven chin. "She's not bad looking, and she always seems well groomed. I suppose men are attracted to her."

"And she was in the work place. Right?"

"Right, but she had her flings or affairs with friends, not co-workers or bosses."

"How do you know? If she was seeing social friends more than socially, who knows what was going on at work?"

Dr. Darshan shrugged his shoulders.

"And you said that your patient was challenged in his top story. He didn't know about his wife's goings on. I can understand why you feel sorry for him."

"Naïve! Terry, the guy is naïve. I don't think he's a fool." *Although Ralph views himself as a fool*, Dr Darshan recalled.

"A fool! Naïve! It's all the same when it comes to affairs of the heart. Women usually can't believe that their husbands are cheating, and men never believe it of their wives. Men are really naïve. It's always the same. The husband is always last to find out."

22

Dr. Darshan smiled genially. "That's exactly what my patient said, that he was the last to find out."

"They never see it coming, and then when it smacks them right between the eyes, they wonder how they could have been so blind."

"Isn't that the truth?" agreed Len Darshan as he took the final sip of soda, set the Styrofoam cup on the table, and stood to leave.

"Do you think you'll be able to make the dinner program next week?" Angela quickly asked before Dr. Darshan made his way to the door.

"What day is it?"

"Thursday. Eight o'clock."

"I don't know. I'll go if Dr. Stein goes."

Angela turned to Dr. Stein. "Will you be able to make it? It's going to be a really good program."

"Are wives invited?"

Angela looked embarrassed. She turned to Rex, who smiled mischievously and, attempting to draw Dr. Stein into a deceptive response, suggested, "The invitation is extended to medical staff. Your wife does help in the office, doesn't she?"

Dr. Stein too stood up and replied, "No, I don't think she'll feel comfortable."

"I'm sorry," Angela said. "You know we'd love to have you and your wives, but we have to comply with the new *Pharmaceutical Research and Manufacturers of America Code*. The Pharmaceutical companies have to keep their noses clean with the *FDA*."

"I know," replied Dr. Stein. "But you also understand that we spend our whole day here, at the office, and when we go somewhere at night, it's nicer to go together with our wives."

Angela shrugged her disappointed shoulders as she watched the two doctors leave the lounge.

Dr. Stein was anxious to get back to his desk to review his patients' x-ray and laboratory reports.

Dr. Darshan, too, would return to his paper work before the afternoon batch of patients made their way into the consulting rooms, but his mind was not on clinical matters; he was pondering Terry's attitude towards the Pharmaceutical Company's invitation. *Did Terry really only want to go to the dinner meeting if his wife, Melinda, was also invited, or was he just using the spousal exclusion as an excuse? Terry knows the Major Pharmaceutical Companies agreed to limit their educational programs to practitioners only. I'm indifferent about the dinner program. I've been to thousands of those meetings during my years in practice. The lectures are useful but not essential. I'll come across all the information I need about their new product, either in my journals or by word of mouth from my colleagues. My wife doesn't care one way or the other if I go to a medical meeting without her, and it makes very little difference to me whether she tags along or not.*

At the intersection in the corridor, Dr. Stein branched off to his side of the suite. Len Darshan stared for a moment at his associate's back and continued to wonder about him. *Terry does have more insight than I do*, he thought. *We come across the same spectrum of patients, we have the same window to view all trends in our community, and yet, Terry is more in tune with changing behaviors. We both know that promiscuity is on the rise, especially among the younger population of today, but that's not breaking news; the topic is covered in every popular TV and radio talk show . . . and yet, I seem to have needed Terry's insight to help me realize that we have been seeing more infidelity among wives.*

Len Darshan arrived at his desk and began opening junk mail, but his thoughts could not leave the events of the morning. *Why am I so shocked to discover that Elaine Carter has been fooling around?* he wondered. *What is it about Ralph that's tugging so pathetically at my heartstrings?* He placed the envelope knife onto the desktop, gazed into open air, and focused on the real question, the matter most curious of all: *why all of a sudden now; why has this kind of thing never really bothered me before?*

CHAPTER TWO

Driving home from work that day, Len Darshan at last began to imagine one possible reason for his obsession with the Ralph Carter case, a reason that required a great deal of introspection, both honest and modest. Although Ralph believed in his own popularity as a youngster Len thought this might have been a wishful figment of the patient's imagination. Conversely, when Len himself looked back over his own life, he had to admit that he likewise had overestimated his popularity, and he assumed this shared and pitiful trait probably lent him empathy for his patient.

By the time Len parked the car in the garage and came through the laundry and into the kitchen, his wife had gone out for the evening. Len found a neatly laid out table setting, bread on a cutting board, freshly shredded lettuce, a sliced tomato, salami, condiments, a small bucket of ice beginning to fuse into a single block, and a note from his wife:

Hi Len,

Why didn't you call to say you would be late? I have gone to play bridge. See you when I get back.

Alone and happy to be alone, Len enjoyed his simple dinner while watching the evening news on the thirteen-inch kitchen television. He then took a shower and, although it was still early, put on boxer shorts, comfortable slippers, and a fluffy, black, cotton gown that his wife had given him for his last birthday.

He poured a tall diet soda and settled into his favorite den armchair with his aging and spoiled cat, Juliet, purring contently on his lap. Juliet's playmate, Romeo, had died a young and violent death when he had wandered into the next-door yard and into Rex the Rottweiler's domain. Len was upset at first. He foresaw the two cats living happily ever after in each other's company. Since that time, however, Len had changed his mind and claimed that it was better to have only one pet, because, being alone, Juliet drew closer to people and hence seemed more a part of the family. Although Len intended reading the latest medical journals, his mind continued to wander. And with all the component parts tugging at his memory, he could not avoid traveling back thirty-four years to the most carefree time of his life.

***

The summer of 1971

Marvin Cohen swam the one-ten and two-twenty butterfly for his college, Jacobsburg State. He stood six-foot-five, and whether in a Speedo or in street clothes, his broad shoulders and narrow waist remained ever evident. Then, when Marvin graduated magna cum laude, his proud parents bought him a basic but brand spanking new Volvo, right off the showroom floor. Of course, all Marvin wanted was to stare at his car and drive it as often and as far as possible. On the third night after receiving the gift, as he stood in a gown on the sidewalk at three a.m., admiring his precious new possession, he had an idea. Then and there, he put through a call to his swim teammate, Terrance Stein.

"This had better be urgent," Terry warned.

"It surpasses urgent," Marvin said, fervor whizzing across the telephone lines and into Terry's receptive cerebrum. "The weather is great, we have a trustworthy set of wheels, and we are currently jobless. What do you say we pack a swimsuit and head for a place where the sun shines brightly, the surf meets the sand, and beautiful young women run around sparsely clad?"

"Do you prefer that to studying for finals?" Terry teased. "What exactly do you have in mind?"

"Just what I said. We get into my car and head for the coast."

"It's 680 miles to the nearest beach," Terry said. "When do we leave?"

"Crack of dawn."

"Sounds sensible to me."

"I'll pick you up in the morning. It's a little more than 680 miles, but Seaview is the place to be. That's where the major players from Jacobsburg State are going this year."

"Great!" Terry suddenly remembered that he had arrangements to meet Len Darshan the next day. He did not want to put a damper on the plans, nor did want to let Len down. "Should we ask Len to come along?" he asked, without much consideration.

After a brief but sobering silence, Marvin replied, "The more the merrier. Will you give him a call?"

A series of urgent last minute responsibilities disrupted the plans to get off to an early start, and it was not until shortly after midnight that the three young men were on the outskirts of the city of Jacobsburg, singing along with the Beatles on the radio and heading toward the highway that would take them to Seaview.

As the radio stations turned faint and sparse, gusto waned and eyelids began to droop. Although they changed the driver every thirty minutes, by six a.m., they decided to pull over for a power nap, which lasted over three hours—two-and-a-half more than planned.

After pancakes and coffee at a truck stop, they again sped along the highway, Marvin at the wheel. The sky was clear and blue, the distant mountains purple and tall, and the nearby shrubbery sparse and dry.

Within an hour, the summer air felt sticky and thick, and their backs began to cling to the seats. With all four windows open, still the breeze could not cool the car, and the heat rising lazily off the blacktop up ahead promised a scorcher with no respite.

To their right, a stream began to follow the road. Clear water lay calmly below huge willows. For a while, the river flowed disappointingly further away, only to return and rush closer and closer, until the road itself had to be protected by a low concrete wall. Marvin maintained a watchful eye on the route ahead, while Len and Terry looked onto the stream, splashing against protruding rocks and sending refreshing sprays to cool the sweltering air.

Sitting in the front passenger seat, Terry leaned left and shouted into Marvin's ear, "Let's pull over at the first opportunity."

"What?" Marvin yelled back and then rolled up his window to cut down the billowing noise. "What did you say?"

Turning halfway toward the back seat, Terry suggested to Marvin and to Len, "Let's stop the car and cool off in that river."

Two miles further, they found a suitable shoulder to park. Here, the river had again veered about one hundred yards away from the road, but this did not bother the three friends. Their zest revived, they ran toward a flat rock on the bank, where they took off all their clothes and waded into the refreshing stream to cool off and cavort.

Len was the first out of the water. No towel available and not wanting to wet his clothing, he stood on the flat rock and began jumping up and down to dry himself off.

They were not as far from the road as they thought, and traffic was growing thicker. Two cars sped by, but the third and fourth honked their horns at the naked man on the rock. Then, as though the commuters could actually communicate, everyone began noticing Len. Hands began to wave out of open car windows, and screams of approval were heard all the way down to the river.

Swimming towards the shore and laughing along with the spectators from the road, Marvin called out, "Len, put something on!"

Remote from the responsibilities of home, drunk with joy, and completely out of character, Len was savoring the attention and the commotion. "Okay," he called back to Marvin, and picked up his watch to strap onto his wrist.

Marvin and Terry swam to the rock, but hesitated before climbing out of the river; they both still had a modicum of modesty. Terry actually waded into shallower water where he crouched forward to hide his nudity and asked Len to throw him a shirt.

When Len picked up on Terry's shyness, and when he saw that Marvin, too, did not want to expose himself to the motorists on the road, he strolled over to the three piles of clothing, lifted them all into a bundle against his chest, and slowly started walking back toward the road.

Marvin remained in the water and shouting at Len, but Terry, anxious to regain his clothing as soon as possible, and as distant from the road as possible, scampered onto the land and immediately gave chase. Marvin did not relish the idea of being left alone without a stitch of clothing, so he, too, pulled himself out the water and ran after the other two. As the gap closed, Len of course quickened the pace.

Four women in a shining red convertible screeched with delight. Two other cars actually pulled over to the side to witness the nude chase.

The three laughing friends scampered into the safety of their waiting Volvo. They quickly dressed and Marvin pulled out from the parking spot and onto the main road once more.

With the oppressive heat a distant memory and the nude swimming adventure fresh in their thoughts, they again sang along with the crackling radio, discussed the likelihood of finding decent accommodations in the resort town of Seaview, and every once in a while burst into spontaneous fits of laughter.

Their camaraderie was sealed; they were a team of three, and Len never did discover that Marvin had felt a subliminal twinge of disappointment when Terry first asked if Len could come along.

At four o'clock in the afternoon, after a short driving tour of the beachfront, the team stopped in front of the *Ritz*, an aging and affordable looking hotel situated in what appeared to be the hub of Seaview.

Opposite the reception desk, the hexagonal lobby opened into a dimly lit and spacious hall, from which emanated voices, laughter, and the music of a local band attempting to reproduce the sound of The Rolling Stones. And in and out of the hall wandered young adults, all around college student age and appearing as scruffy and as weary as the three newcomers.

Terry led the way to the reception desk. "Have you got a room for three?" he asked the receptionist, a skinny blonde student who managed to secure this coveted temporary job.

She wore her hair in a ponytail and had on the informal hotel uniform, blue jeans and a yellow T-shirt with *Ritz* written in dark blue on the pocket. She smiled affably at Terry, a handsome young man with striking green eyes and wavy sand-colored hair that was charmingly disheveled. "Sorry," she said. "We're full. We have accommodation for the day after tomorrow. Would you like to make a reservation?"

Terry shook his incredulous head, while Len stepped forward to explain. "We actually need a place to sleep tonight."

"Sorry," she repeated. "Why didn't you book ahead? It's the busy season. We're fully occupied."

Len looked at his watch. "Have all the guests arrived?" he asked. "Maybe you'll have a no-show."

Surprised at the novel suggestion, the receptionist answered, "That's a good idea. Sometimes people book and don't show." She took a moment to inspect the register lying open faced on the countertop. "The guests for 214 have not yet arrived. Let me ask my manager if I can let you have the room."

She turned to go through a door marked *Private* in the corner of the reception area.

"Good thinking," Marvin said, placing a congratulatory hand onto Len's shoulder.

"Yeah, that was a pretty smart idea," Terry agreed, looking up at his two taller friends.

Coming out of the music hall were two young men. The stocky one, with a bodybuilder's biceps and a boxer's nose, beamed cheerily and called across the lobby, "Hey, Marvin! Marvin, my buddy, when did you get into town? I didn't know you were coming."

"Hi, Rick," Marvin answered with equal delight. "Nor did we. We decided yesterday and got into my car to drive down."

"Hi, Terry" Rick said, recognizing a second member of the trio.

Terry shot out a hand to greet Rick and asked, "Do you know Len Darshan?"

"Pleased to meet you, Len," Rick replied. "This is Bennie," he added, introducing his companion, a dumpy young fellow with a round face and a premature potbelly protruding beneath a baggy but short T-shirt.

"What's this hotel like?" Len asked Rick. "It seems vibrant."

"Yeah," Rick agreed. "Pretty vibrant. This whole town is vibrant. It's amazing how many kids from Jacobsburg State College have hit this resort. Are you guys checking in?"

"We hope so," Marvin answered. "The receptionist is trying to organize us a room."

"That's terrific. Listen, there's a shindig tomorrow night at the *Chateau*, a hotel at the other end of the main street. You're all invited."

A balding man in his early forties came out of the room marked *Private*, together with the pony-tailed receptionist. "Good afternoon, gentlemen." He smiled disingenuously. "My assistant may have led you to believe that we might have accommodations. I apologize. Unfortunately, we *are* fully booked; we cannot let out a room that has been reserved. And in the case of the room she mentioned, the guests have informed us that they might be arriving late."

"Excuse me, Mr. Ritz." Bennie came forward to the counter. "Maybe somebody is checking out today, and my friends can have that room."

The manager was not wearing the hotel's yellow T-shirt. He had on a formal white shirt, a yellow tie, and black blazer. Pinned to his lapel, however, was a large badge with the hotel logo, *Ritz*, in dark blue. He glanced down at his lapel and chuckled. "My name is actually Mr. Franklin." Then, looking at the group standing at the counter, he said, "It's going to be difficult to find accommodations in this town tonight, but let me put through a call to the Chateau, our sister hotel. Perhaps they can help. Come this way."

While Mr. Franklin used the phone at the end of the reception counter, the five young men stood around in a semi-circle speaking about the resort and hoping for accommodation.

"There are three beaches," Rick explained. "North, Central, and South. Central beach is for families, not for you; college kids, including everyone from Jacobsburg State College, dominate the South. If you want something a little quieter, go up to the North, and if you're into surfing, go to the far end of North—that's where the local surfers go."

Mr. Franklin replaced the receiver, but lifted it again to make another call.

Len stepped closer to the counter. He heard Mr. Franklin throw about the names of a number of hotels, and he heard a few "tomorrows," "two nights," and "three nights," but no "vacancies for today."

Eventually, Mr. Franklin lifted his head and spoke to Len. "I can't find a single available hotel room in all of Seaview. We're really having a boom season. Good for us, but unlucky for you. Do you have a car?"

"Yes."

"The best I can suggest is that you drive down the coast about fifteen or twenty miles to Rockview. Do you know it?

"No."

"It's also a resort town, similar to Seaview. I'm sure you'll enjoy it. I don't know why everyone wants to come to Seaview this season. Try the *Vacationer's Inn*. It's also popular with college kids. If you want, I'll call ahead and ask them to hold a room for you. That is, if they have a vacancy"

Mr. Franklin looked at the five confused and disappointed faces surrounding him. "Otherwise, you can head north for about thirty miles and stay in San Martin. It's a growing city, but the beaches are well kept, and there's lots to do. More than here."

"Nothing in Seaview, at all?" Len asked.

Mr. Franklin glanced at this watch. "The only other thing I can suggest is that you go two streets up to Green Street. In line with this hotel, you'll find Green Street Realtor's. They sometimes have furnished apartments that they'll let you have for a short term. But you'd better hurry. They close at five."

"On the beachfront?" Len asked. "Do you think they'll have something on the beachfront?"

"Probably not," Mr. Franklin answered, apologetically.

38

Len thought it was time to discuss the problem with Marvin and Terry, but after brief contemplation, he changed his mind, turned back to Mr. Franklin, and said, "Your receptionist mentioned that you have an opening for the day after tomorrow. Can we have that room?"

"Certainly." Mr. Franklin moved along the counter to get the register. Examining the date in question, he grimaced and explained, "You can have that room, but it's available for one day only."

"Come on, Len," Marvin said. "Let's get going to that Realtor. It's probably our best bet."

Len, Marvin, and Terry felt dejected and concerned. Rick and his friend Bennie felt sympathetic and helpless.

The hotel phone rang; the pony-tailed assistant answered and put the call through to Mr. Franklin.

Marvin was in a hurry to leave. He was already making his way to the door. Terry took time to shake hands with Benny and say, "It's nice meeting you." Len smiled and said to Rick, "Looks like we may not be seeing you on the beach after all. I'm kind of sorry."

Len and Terry were halfway to the exit, close behind Marvin, when Mr. Franklin caught Bennie's attention. "Tell your friends to wait."

The call was from the receptionist at the Chateau. The hotel had a cancellation, a room available the next day.

Five faces once again crowded around the counter, this time smiling and eagerly telling Mr. Franklin to grab the accommodation.

In the hall across the way from the reception area, the five friends sat drinking beers to celebrate the newly found hotel accommodation.

"Meanwhile," Len asked soberly, "where should we sleep tonight, in the car or on the beach?"

"The car was pretty cozy last night," Terry answered, and raised a beer bottle to propose a toast to Marvin's comfortable car.

Rick and Bennie, too, raised their bottles, but they shared a knowing glance, and Bennie said, "Bullshit! You guys can crash on our floor tonight."

"No. We'll be fine in the car," Marvin protested feebly.

Before Bennie or Rick could answer, Terry said, "Thanks, Bennie." He turned to Marvin and continued, "You can sleep in the car if you really want, but Len and I are sleeping on the hotel room floor." Then, raising his bottle again, he offered, "We'll bring all the beer you guys can drink."

Rick and Bennie were sharing a family suite with two other friends from Jacobsburg– Bernie, a pale faced, curly haired, young man who had already completed one year of medical school, and Bernie's best friend, Colin, a skinny dark fellow who had elected to forgo college and enter into business for himself. Although Colin was already making money hand over fist in his stereo store, he repeatedly threatened to sell the company and gain admission to college while his mind was still young and alert. Besides business acumen, Colin had another talent: he was the man with the guitar, the voice, and the repertoire of popular sing-along-folksongs.

In appreciation for the hospitality, Len, Marvin, and Terry bought the pizza and, as promised, four dozen beers, which they estimated would cover all the beer they and their four hosts could drink.

Colin reclined on the upper level of the bunk bed in the corner of the room, a beer by his side and strumming a string of Joan Baez songs on his guitar, one after another. After two or three beers each, the group gradually sung along with Colin, softly and shyly at first, but, as they entered the appropriate frame of mind, lyrics and tunes became unimportant obstacles, easily overcome by loud humming or substitute wording that often unhinged the melody's tempo.

They barely heard the thumping on the wall as the neighboring guests protested the racket.

Bennie, a little tipsy, stood up, raised his hands high above his head and shouted, "Quiet down! What was that?"

They all listened carefully, but after a moment's silence, Colin once more began strumming his guitar.

41

Terry also thought he heard the thumping, so he opened the door and looked into the corridor to try discover what had caused the intrusive noise.

At first, the hallway was empty. He looked up and down and stayed there a while, enjoying the less stuffy air and the respite from the droning within.

Then, the door directly across the hallway opened and a girl in her late teens or early twenties, carrying an empty ice bucket, came out. She left the door open, smiled amiably at Terry, and walked down the corridor toward the ice machine, certain that Terry was watching not the swinging silver bucket in her graceful long fingers or her shining brunette hair flowing stylishly to her shoulders, but rather her wiggling trim behind in her tight blue jeans.

She was right. Terry watched until she stood over the machine, ice pummeling into the bucket.

Terry now looked through the open door and into the girl's hotel room. It was far smaller than the one in which he and his friends were going to spend the night—smaller, yet plusher and definitely much neater. He saw a second girl, reclining against a mountain of pillows on a twin bed, sipping a glass of something and watching the television. This girl had long red hair falling about her shoulders, and she was almost as attractive as the ice-fetcher who had caught his eye seconds earlier.

Anxious to meet the two young women, searching for an opening line, envious of their plush accommodation, and egged on by a comfortable blood alcohol level, Terry marched across the corridor, knocked politely on the door, stepped into the room, and announced, "Management. The hotel is completely full, and we have made a miscalculation with the linen distribution. I am afraid that we will have to remove three pillows from this room."

"What nonsense," she answered. "You're from the noisy room across the hallway. You can't have our pillows."

"We need them. We're short and you have too many."

"Call housekeeping. They'll get you what you need."

Terry considered her suggestion, but decided it would be easier and more fun to just confiscate three pillows from the girls. He dashed into the room, swiped two pillows from the other twin bed, and then a third that was supporting the redhead's left arm.

The girl screeched with delight rather than fear and jumped off the bed to give chase. At that moment, the brunette in the tight jeans returned with the bucket full of ice. Terry barged past her and into the refuge of the larger and stuffier room across the corridor. But he had neither the time nor the inclination to slam the door closed, and the two girls chased him past the two twin beds to his right, with the seascape pictures over their headboards, and into the corner of the room where he dived onto the bottom level of the bunk bed and partially hid behind Rick and Marvin.

The two girls stopped short of the bunk bed. Smiles all around, the redhead shouted, "You can't just come into our room and take our things," while the brunette held a piece of ice up high, threatening to hurl it at Terry.

Marvin stood placidly, raised his arms to calm down the girls, and said, "Let us try to settle this dispute peacefully. What the hell is going on?"

"He stole our pillows," said the brunette, jerking her ice cube bearing hand in readiness, pretending that only her tenuous self-control was protecting Terry from the severe beating he deserved.

Most eyes in the room were fixed on the brunette, not only because of her compelling stance, but also because of her striking good looks. She had high cheekbones, almond-shaped green eyes, and an unfaultable figure.

The redhead too was a beautiful young woman. Her nose might have been a smidgen too long and her chin a tad too sharp, perhaps her dark brown eyes a little too small and her lips too thin, but her stunning attribute was her grace. Approaching six feet in height, with a head poised proud, she had the elegance of an exclusive and much sought after fashion model.

At this time, no one in the room focused on the redhead, but as *she* took in the towering figure of Marvin, she thought, *Tall, handsome, diplomatic, and amusing. I hope this one will notice me. He may turn out to be a jerk, but I sure would like to find out. If he were to date me, I could wear high heels and we would look good together. But he's smiling at Joyce, my pal. He's probably more attracted to her. A pity. She can go out with any man she wants, while I have difficulty finding good-looking men who are taller than I am. I'm sure she won't mind if I make a move on this Adonis. If he goes for me, good . . . if not, tough.*

"Perhaps we can negotiate for the pillows," Marvin said. "Three of us have to sleep on the floor, and unless you let us use your pillows, we're going to have a tough time dozing off. Do you have two pillows for tonight, one for each of you? Because if you do, then it's only fair and reasonable that you at least enter into negations with us."

Dropping the melting cube into the ice bucket and drying her hand on her jeans, Joyce answered, "Sure, those pillows are for sale." She turned to her redhead friend and asked, "What do you think, Gertrude? How much are they worth?"

Smiling an unmistakable "come hither" smile at Marvin, a gesture visible only to Marvin, and a gesture that made him nervous, she asked, "What have you got to offer?"

With a noticeable melting of confidence, Marvin suggested, "How about a beer for each pillow?"

Gertrude and Joyce glanced deliberately at each other and Gertrude said, "And what else?"

"Two beers for each pillow. We only need to lease them for one night."

"Why?" Joyce asked. "Are you going home tomorrow?"

"No. We only arrived today, and we don't have a hotel room for tonight. Tomorrow, we're moving out to the Chateau." He looked from Joyce to Gertrude, back to Joyce again, and said, "How about two beers for each pillow and an invitation to a party tomorrow night at the Chateau."

"What makes you think we want your beer?" Gertrude asked.

Before anyone could answer, Len fished a beer out of the cooler, popped off the lid with a bottle opener, and handed it to Gertrude. "Here. Try one and see."

Who is this guy? Where did he come from? Gertrude thought. *He's also tall, but not nearly as good-looking as the other one. Besides, does he really believe that we are negotiating seriously? He must be the nerd of the bunch.* She took a sip of the beer, grimaced, covered her mouth with one hand, and stretched her bottle-bearing arm back toward Len, beckoning him to retrieve the evil brew he had handed her.

She's making me look stupid in front of all these guys, Len thought. He stared at the beer in his hand and, attempting to regain some dignity, said to Gertrude, "Well, if you want to come to the party, we're going to have to keep the pillows."

Again belittling Len, this time by ignoring him, Gertrude looked around at all the young men in the room, five of whom were too short for her liking, and turned back to Marvin and asked, "Are all seven of you going to sleep here tonight?"

"Sure. Len, Terry, and I are going to have to spend the night on the floor," he said, pointing to the other two, Len standing in the middle of the room and Terry hugging the pillows on the bunk bed. "So we're not going to return your pillows." He walked across the room and sat on the edge of one of the twin beds, next to Bennie. "And that's final."

Gertrude smiled, thinking to herself, *The thief, the nerd, and the Adonis have come to stay with the four dwarfs.* Then, deciding on a tactical change in the bantering, she said, "Okay, you can have the pillows. You guys are a bunch of bullies." She flung her head high and said, "Come on, Joyce."

As the two girls turned to leave, Terry chased after them. "Here," he said. "Take your pillows."

Joyce accepted the three pillows in a bundle against her chest, and as she and Gertrude marched across the room toward the door, Terry said, "You are still invited to the party."

"Thank you," Gertrude replied. "Where did you say the party is?"

"The Chateau," Terry answered.

"Where's that?"

"At the other end of the beachfront."

"Is it far? Can you give us a ride?"

"Sure. We can arrange a ride for you," Terry said, smiling broadly. "Don't you have a car?" Then, realizing that they did not know where the girls came from, Terry asked, "How far do you live from Seaview? How did you get here?"

"I think we come from the same place as you do," Joyce answered. "Jacobsburg."

"How did you know?" Terry asked, surprised.

Joyce pointed to Rick, sitting on the lower level of the bunk bed, partially hidden behind Colin's legs, straggling from the upper bunk. "I think I've seen you on campus, at Jacobsburg State."

"Right," Rick replied with an air of pride at being noticed on a campus of over fifty thousand students. "So how did you girls get here? By plane?"

"By bus," Joyce answered. "It was a long ride."

"At least you had air conditioning," said Terry.

"Sure," Joyce answered.

"We drove down and hit a real scorcher in the stretch across the desert," Terry said. He looked at Len and then Marvin, and the three burst into unexpected fits of laughter.

Colin, guitar in hand, was on the top bunk, Rick in the bottom bunk, Bennie on one twin bed, and Bernie, the medical student, on the other. Gertrude and Joyce were standing close to the door, while Len, Marvin, and Terry came together in the middle of the room to offer high fives and to share their amusement. Everyone stared curiously. Only Gertrude shook her head in feigned pity.

Standing between Marvin and Len, Terry said, "I'll explain why we're laughing," and he went on to tell the story about their naked swim in the river. As he spoke, Marvin added a little exaggerated color to the story. Everyone smiled and chuckled when Terry came to the part about Len jumping on the rock to dry off. Marvin took great pleasure in describing how Len's tallywacker had bobbed up and down, completely out of sync with the rest of his body.

Len left the storytelling to his two friends and climbed up onto the upper level of the bunk bed next to Colin, from where he had a bird's eye view of Terry on the center stage.

Gertrude sat at the foot of the twin bed next to Bennie.

Joyce dropped the pillows and sat on them Indian style.

Colin squinted at Len and then strummed and sang a few lines from a ditty about a certain Jim Bob's tallywacker, and although both Joyce and Gertrude gazed graciously down to the floor, they could not contain a pair of naughty little giggles.

Terry told about Len choosing a wristwatch as the first article to wear. He described how Len gathered all the clothing into a bundle and forced the others to chase him toward the busy freeway.

Although Len reveled in the attention, he remained as nonchalant as he could, pretending that this event was just another in a long line of exciting adventures dotting the path of his thrilling life.

Along with everyone else in the room, Gertrude enjoyed the mirth. She was not formulating any new opinions, but the image of Len as a bore did gradually fade, until she took a second look at him and saw him as a reasonable second choice in this fun-loving, albeit immature, collection of neo-college-graduates.

Conversation continued late into the night. At first, only the young men drank beer, but as Gertrude completed a story about the time she and the boy next door invaded her father's liquor cabinet, she casually stood and helped herself to a bottle from the ice chest.

At this, Len caught her eye, sneered, letting her know he had not forgotten her earlier rudeness, and shook his head.

She, in response, shrugged her self-assured so-what shoulders, took a generous what-are-you-going-to-do-about-it gulp, and proposed an I-got-you-good toast across the room to Len, who was still sitting on the upper level of the bunk bed.

In the early morning, Joyce and Gertrude decided to return to their own room. They said their goodnights and made their way to the door, but before they actually stepped into the hallway, they whispered something to each other, then turned around and hurled the three pillows back into the room with all the force they could muster. One hit Colin, who had not budged from his top bunk, the second knocked over a bedside lamp on a pedestal between the two twin beds, and the third Bernie managed to catch before it could do any damage.

They had not arranged to meet the next day, nor had they discussed the party to be held at the Chateau the following night. Gertrude and Joyce had mentioned, in passing, that they enjoyed the South beach, the one nearest to the hotel. And Bennie was quick to point out that South beach was probably the best in Seaview, with its steep back-wall that eliminated the view of the street and the noise of the traffic, and the smooth boulders that offered bathers refuge from the gritty sand.

Len, Marvin, and Terry slept well on the floor but woke early as the sun shone through the crack in the drapes over the small corner window. They thanked their friends for the loan of their hotel room floor and made tentative arrangements to meet them at the party that night at the Chateau.

The hallway was quiet. As they hesitated in front of Joyce and Gertrude's room, they all had the same thought, that they should knock on the door, return the pillows, and get a casual conversation started, something that would lead to a rendezvous later in the day. Yet, they also realized that making a noise at this early hour may not engender a kind response from these two oh-so-fair members of the opposite sex, so they left the three pillows in a pile in front of the door and made their way to the hotel exit.

They crossed the road and leaned against the metal railing above South beach. The salty air, the blue ocean, and the distant horizon filled the three inlanders with a spirit of freedom.

Terry looked to his right, up the curving seafront. "Should we find our hotel and check in?" he suggested.

Len and Marvin followed Terry's gaze. "It's probably too early," Len said. "I'm hungry. Who feels like breakfast at that restaurant next to the hotel?" He read the sign on the yellow and blue billboard, *The Ritz Diner.*

The Ritz Diner was larger inside than expected, with booths around the walls and neatly spaced tables on the floor. Vacationing patrons occupied about a third of the seating: a few families, one elderly couple, but mostly young adults. Len led the way to a booth in the corner. The prices were right, the waitress friendly, and the coffee hot, and for the first time in thirty-six hours, the three friends relaxed and planned their day and the remainder of their vacation at a leisurely pace.

Situated on the seafront, opposite North beach, the Chateau was older and smaller than the Ritz. The business area and the hexagonal lobby were similar to those in the sister hotel, only the entertainment areas were different. Comparable to the music hall at the Ritz was a pub with a live band across the way from the reception desk, but the Chateau also had a number of smaller facilities leading off the central foyer, and at the entrance to one of these rooms was a poster that read:

For private parties contact management.

And in small print, the details:

Are you celebrating a special occasion?
Hire this facility for $50.00 per event.

You invite your guests, and we will provide the entertainment.
Appetizers
Discotheque
All drinks discounted 60%.
Speak to the receptionist on duty.

To the side of the poster, in a blue and yellow frame, was a typed announcement:

Tonight:
Happy Birthday, Herby Ellington.
It is with great pleasure that the management and staff of
The Chateau welcome all guests celebrating
Herby Ellington's twenty-first birthday.

Upon their arrival at the Chateau, the receptionist, an elderly plump woman, told Len, Terry, and Marvin that they would have to wait about thirty to forty-five minutes while the hotel staff readied their room.

After peeking into the pub and taking a quick tour of the hotel grounds, they returned to the foyer where they finally noticed Herby Ellington's birthday party announcement.

"How about that," Len said. "Do you think Herby Ellington knows that we are invited to his party?"

"Do you think Rick knows Herby Ellington?" Terry asked. "I've got a funny feeling this is going to be the most crowded party in Seaview. We haven't even checked into our hotel and we have been invited. Plus, we have already invited two others, Joyce and Gertrude."

The plump receptionist caught their attention. "Your room is ready, gentlemen. Fifteen to thirty minutes earlier than we expected."

After allocating the three beds and packing away their sparse belongings, they donned swimsuits, sandals, and T-shirts, put towels into a beach bag, and drove back to South beach.

A concrete stairway zigzagged from the edge of the sidewalk above all the way to the beach below. About halfway down and to the left of the stairs, a decorated concrete doorway led onto a flat open verandah with tables, chairs, a vendor selling ice-creams and soda-pops, and a magnificent view of the white sand and the open ocean. The three friends bought lemonades and leaned up against the railing, enjoying the view, searching for anyone they might recognize, and selecting a suitable spot to camp for the remainder of the day.

"It's cooler closer to the water," Len suggested.

Marvin was attracted to the boulders at the far north end of the sand. From the verandah above, the rocks appeared smooth and clean, with gentle slopes ascending about twenty feet above the sand and the water below. Besides, no other beach visitors had elected to camp on the boulders, so there was plenty of space to spread out and take in the sun. They headed for the boulders.

From close up, the walls of the boulder nearest the water were steeper than they expected, fun to climb, but not with paraphernalia in one's hands. About six feet off the ground, however, was a flat and comfortable shelf, and that was where the three elected to camp.

Within a few minutes, after staking a claim to their spot on the side of the boulder, they went for a swim in the sea, body surfing, diving under the waves, wrestling with each other, and rolling with the gentle tide.

At last, they took time to lie back on their beach towels, gaze up at the cloudless sky, close their eyes, and doze, or simply people watch from their elevated vantage point. The day was warm with hardly a breeze, and it did not take long for their brows to sweat and their mouths to parch.

"Who feels like another lemonade?" Len asked.

"Sounds good to me," Marvin said. "Who's going to get them?"

"I'll go," Len volunteered. "Tomorrow, we'll pack a cooler."

"Good idea," Terry agreed.

Len walked along the sea's edge, ankle deep in the water, until he came in line with the steps that led up to the verandah. Full of energy, he ran up towards the vendor and was about to go through the decorated concrete door when he realized that he had forgotten to bring money. The walk was not too far across the beach; still, he had not planned on making the journey twice. He started to turn back when he saw Gertrude coming down the stairs. Although she had the figure for a bikini, she had on a full-length white swimsuit and cotton scarlet shirt with buttons open all the way down the front. She carried a straw bag over her shoulder, and on her head, she wore a matching straw hat with a rim wide enough to shade down to her waist.

"Hi, Gertrude." *She looks gorgeous*, he thought.

"Hi . . ." she replied, taking a moment to recall his name, "Len"

He looked past her up the stairs. "Where's Joyce?" he asked, expecting the two girls to be together.

Gertrude misconstrued his question. *Where's your good-looking friend*, she heard. *It would be nicer to see her than it is to see you.* "She went with Colin for a ride up the coast."

"We're at the end of the beach, by the boulder." Len smiled. "Would you like to join us?" *Colin, the executive, who didn't budge from the top bunk. Who would have though that he, of all the guys, would have cracked a date with Joyce?*

"Sure. Thanks." *I hope Marvin is there.*

"Do me a favor, Gertrude," Len said, clearing his throat. "Could you lend me a dollar until we get back to the others? I came to buy drinks, but I left my money behind."

She laughed, shook her head, and took the straw beach bag off her shoulder.

She's still snubbing me, he thought.

I wonder if he would have invited me to sit with him and his friends if he didn't need to borrow money. She took out her purse and said, "Please get me a drink, too. Lots of ice."

At the campsite, Gertrude climbed onto the private rock-shelf by herself, found a comfortable seat-shaped projection against the side wall, and asked, "How's the Chateau? Better than the Ritz, I hope?"

"About the same," Marvin replied.

She sounds like a bit of a snob, Len thought. "Oh, yes," he said, reaching into the side pocket of the bag, searching for his wallet. "Thanks for the loan."

"The drinks are on me," Gertrude said, holding up a hand and making it quite clear that she was not going to accept the money. Then, remembering the previous night, she said, "Thanks for the pillows. We found them early this morning. You guys must have left before sunup."

"It's difficult to sleep in when you don't have a comfortable mattress," Terry said, laughing.

They finished their drinks, reminisced about the previous night, and then mulled over the advantages of living on the coast.

"Who wants another swim?" Len said. "Do you feel like a dip in the ocean?" he asked Gertrude separately.

"Sure." She briskly clapped her hands. "Let's go."

Len leaped off the shelf and onto the sand below. As a gentleman, he then reached up and offered Gertrude a hand, but she, too, chose to jump down by herself. On the ground, she whimpered gently and fell into Len's arms.

"What's the matter?" he asked. "Did you twist your ankle?"

"No." She sat down on the beach and inspected a cut in the sole of her foot. Somebody had dropped a broken Popsicle stick into the sand.

Len looked at the wound. "It's superficial and small; still, you don't want to get it infected."

Terry stood behind Len while Marvin remained on the shelf, looking down.

"Pass me a towel," Len said to Marvin. "And give me the melted ice from our drinking cups."

Len gently supported Gertrude's foot on a beach towel and cleaned the cut. He thought about drying it with another of the towels, but they all had too much sand in their fiber, so he reached up onto the shelf for his own T-shirt, dabbed the wound clean, and, without a second thought, tore the old shirt into make-shift strips that he used as bandages.

"You go ahead," Gertrude apologized. "I don't think I should swim in the sea with an open wound."

"Are you sure?" Marvin asked, climbing down from the shelf and edging toward the water.

As she twiddled her fingers as if to say, *Go on; go without me,* Marvin and Terry dashed toward the waves in anticipation of another enjoyable swim.

Len, however, remained with her. He laid out two towels on the sand against the boulder and bundled a third into a footstool to protect her bandaged wound from the sand.

Gertrude studied the concerned frown on Len's face. *He sure is a nerd,* she thought. *Staying behind with someone who can't join in the fun is a rare quality indeed, not seen in your average hunk or in anyone who fancies himself as a hunk.* She patted the towel next to her, inviting him to sit while scrutinizing his features. *Hazy gray eyes and a weak chin in a round face—nothing special at all, unworthy of a second look, and definitely not eye-catching. Yet, viewed as a whole, they mirror what I've already come to know about him . . . gentleness and perhaps a touch of sensitivity.*

"It must be nice to have college behind you," she said. "What are you going to do now?"

Len had been looking at Gertrude, but now he stared into the distance, closed his eyes, and said, "We did speak about it last night . . . quite a bit. Terry and I are going to med school, and Marvin is going to study engineering."

"I'm sorry," she apologized. "I'd forgotten . . . but I remember now."

"And you are going to become a teacher," Len continued, rubbing salt into the wound.

"I'm sorry," she repeated. "By the time you told us what you were going to do, we'd already had a few beers . . . I'm sorry."

"You're right," he whispered. "It is I who should apologize." He turned to face her and found her sitting forward, her body toward him, and he was uncertain whether she was truly apologetic or annoyed at his sarcasm. "I'm sorry. I didn't mean to sound angry. It's one of my shortcomings. I often make myself misunderstood. I seem to have quite a bad case of foot in mouth syndrome." He thought for a moment and, hearing himself sound stupid once more, tried to rescue himself by adding, "Sometimes."

"Thanks," Gertrude said. "Thanks for saying what you just said, because not paying attention or remembering is a shortcoming of mine."

Maybe she's not as big a snob as I thought. "It was nice last night," Len said, attempting to change the mood. "Wasn't it?"

He lay down flat on the towel, and out of the corner of his eye, he saw Gertrude relax, the brim of her hat scrunched against the sloping rock, cushioning the back of her head.

"So, what are you going to teach?" he asked.

"Math and Science," she replied. "I told you last night."

Len contorted his face into a painful grimace. "You did?" he asked. "When?"

"No," she laughed. "I don't think I mentioned what I was going to teach, but I got you good. Didn't I?"

The sun was well into its western descent. Most people on the water's edge were looking southward down the beach. Len scanned the crowd trying to ascertain what had caught everyone's attention when he saw Marvin and Terry with Bennie, Bernie, Rick, and six or seven other handsome young men and bikini-clad women.

Terry was shouting something and waving a hailing arm at Len and Gertrude. Len saw, but ignored his friend. Instead, he let his head fall flat onto the towel and gazed backward at the boulder rising up toward the sky. Within moments, however, Terry was standing over Len and panting, "Some fishermen caught a massive shark. We're going to have a look. Do you want to come?"

Len turned to his left. "How's your foot, Gertrude? Do you want to walk over?"

She raised her pleasantly surprised, well groomed, and dark brown eyebrows. "The foot feels fine, but I'm not going to walk on the beach until I have to go back to the hotel. You go see the shark," and she once more twiddled her *go on; go without me* fingers at Terry and Len.

I'd rather stay here with Gertrude, Len thought. *This is crazy. But I don't want to be too obvious.* "Okay," Len said, and he jumped up, dusted the seat of his swimsuit, and trotted after his friend, down toward the water and around the shrubbery at the far south bend of the beach.

As he disappeared from view, Gertrude reached up onto the rock shelf for her beach bag, found her pack of cigarettes, turned her towel to face the sea and the sun, lit up, and closed her eyes in idyllic solitude.

After a hot shower to take the sand out of his hair, the stiffness out of his muscles, and the sting from the sun out of his skin, Len selected the best shirt that he had thrown into his suitcase and the newer of his two pairs of blue jeans. Marvin and Terry both wore short pants and T-shirts. With nothing else on the agenda, they were going to Herby Ellington's birthday party, where they planned to join their friends from the Ritz and about half a dozen new acquaintances that they had met that day on the beach.

Herby Ellington's party was the best-attended event in Seaview.

The manageress on duty, a trim middle-aged woman in a dark skirt and white blouse, had to get two youthful yellow-shirted employees to open the partition into the next hall and convert the reception area into a veritable ballroom. Hors d'oeuvres were plentiful and discounted drinks flowed freely amongst the growing youthful crowd. The dance floor was packed with an assortment of strangers, only a few of who knew, or had even heard of, Herby Ellington before that night. Still, everyone was in high spirits, and the hotel manageress was so pleased with the numbers chalked up on the cash register that she transferred the live band from the sparsely crowded bar to Herby's party.

Marvin and Terry were dancing with an assortment of attractive and tanned women who were just as keen on meeting new faces as were the horde of rowdy young men in variable states of inebriation.

Len was sipping draught beer on a high stool at a tiny barroom table and speaking with a group of young men who seemed eager to participate fully, yet too nervous to approach the women of their choice. It was the niche and the company Len would seek out in any party; it fit right into his comfort pattern. That night, however, his heart was not in the predominantly raunchy, sometimes witty, and usually silly remarks; his mind was on Gertrude and his eyes were repeatedly on the entrance, through which he was willing her to walk.

Why is she late, he thought? Then, he remembered that Gertrude was coming with his other friends at the Ritz, and they had not yet arrived. He glanced at the clock on the wall. He had been at the party for over an hour and was beginning to tire of the tedious conversations and crude conduct that only yesterday he would have enjoyed. He stood to stretch his legs and perhaps get some fresh air in the hotel lobby, away from the smoke-filled party.

On his way to the exit, he heard a fanfare and turned to see three outrageous looking characters on the stage: One fellow in his early twenties, wearing a sleeveless black T-shirt and a red bandanna on his head, said nothing at all. He just stood to the side of the rattan chair, encouraging his two friends with his near-toothless smile that frequently broke out into a raucous laugh. On the opposite side of the chair was another uncouth looking man with a similar bandanna. This one, in his late thirties to early forties, was dressed in a sleeveless leather jacket that revealed a particularly hairy chest. He was the spokesman of the pack.

"Welcome everyone," he shouted, punching a rebellious fist high into the air.

As the guests settled down, he continued, "Is this a party, or what?"

Toward the front of the hall, close to the stage, a group of about eight bikers cheered energetically along with their toothless friend on the stage. But the applause was not fervent enough for the hairy speaker.

"Is this a party or what?" he again roared.

This time, the curious crowd applauded heartily in amused agreement.

"Well, it's my pleasure to welcome all of you here tonight."

The group of bikers around the stage led the crowd in cheering the speaker.

"Are we here to have a good time?" he shouted.

"Yes," replied the crowd, almost in perfect unison.

"Are we here to enjoy the fancy food and the cheap booze?"

But before the crowd could voice another round of enthusiastic agreement, the speaker raised his palms to silence his newfound fans and then smiled amicably and corrected himself. "Are we here to enjoy the fancy food and the *fine* booze?" he said, laughing.

There were a few creative responses, and the speaker waved a friendly hand in the direction of some of the more vocal people in the crowd.

"Are we going to celebrate with my pal, Herby? Are we going to help my pal and your pal, Herby Ellington, have the time of his life?"

"Yes," and "Yeah, Herby," and "Happy birthday, Herby," they shouted, raising glasses and bottles to toast the third man on the stage.

Herby Ellington, or the person posing as one Herby Ellington, was the size and shape of a professional sumo wrestler. He sat in the sagging rattan chair, his hands on his huge thighs and his belly protruding almost to his knees. While his head was bandanna-less and clean shaved, his face bore the stubble of about three days' growth. This night may have been in honor of Herby Ellington's twenty-first birthday, but the man on the rattan chair, turning to high-five his friend by his side, was closer to double that number of years, and no one seemed to notice or care.

"Happy birthday to you. Happy birthday to you . . ." the speaker led the crowd in singing, and the band waiting patiently behind the three guest on-stage performers spontaneously supplied the background music.

"We're happy for Herby and thankful to him for putting on this bash, and it's a shame that almost no one here remembered to buy him a gift," the speaker said. "As a token of our gratitude for this party, what do you say we at least put in a couple of bucks to cover the cost of the hotel?"

The people closest to the stage seemed to applaud the idea much more eagerly than those further back in the hall. The near-toothless gang member standing at Herby's side picked up an empty paint bucket, conveniently waiting at his feet, and passed it around. The number of people wearing red bandannas and sleeveless leather jackets seemed to have grown, and they took the lead in dropping donation dollars generously into the three or four buckets now making their way around the hall. The other hundred plus guests who, like Len, had received invitations by word of mouth felt obligated to follow the example of their hosts. Some felt really good about making their contributions, some dropped their money grudgingly into the bucket, while others, particularly those who tried to get away with donating low denomination coins instead of paper notes, felt intimidated by the bucket-bearing gang members, who would affront and embarrass—albeit in jest— anyone they considered miserly.

"Not exactly what I expected, but good fun," Len heard Joyce's voice speaking into his left ear.

"When did you arrive?" he asked.

"A few minutes ago, when that guy with the red handkerchief on his head began his big hoopla."

Len looked around the room. "Is Gertrude here?" he asked, unable to see her and concerned that she may not have made it. "Is her foot okay?"

"Her foot is fine," Joyce said, pointing toward the side of the stage where Gertrude stood laughing and chatting with the speaker of the pack, who seemed to be enjoying Gertrude's company as much as she was enjoying his.

Disappointment and jealousy left Len queasy in the pit of his gut. *I've been waiting for Gertrude for over an hour, and she probably hasn't even given me a second thought. When we left the beach and said we would see each other tonight, she was probably passing a casual remark while I thought we had a date. What an idiot I am.*

Len hated what he was seeing, but he could neither leave nor take his eyes off Gertrude together with the man he considered so crude. He also did not want to be seen staring, so he calmly strolled away from Joyce and found an open chair at one of the high bar tables, obliquely behind Gertrude, from where he watched her exchanging niceties with the speaker of the pack.

Len could not hear what they were saying; he could only guess. The speaker removed his red bandanna, then ran a hand over his neatly combed and expensively cut dark hair. He reached into the left top jacket pocket, found his pack of cigarettes, tapped it a few times, and, in a slick single stroke, pulled matches out of the opposite upper pocket and lit up. The speaker listened attentively to Gertrude and then suddenly mouthed a surprised *Oh*, gently nodded a polite *certainly*, and took out the pack again, this time for Gertrude.

She steadied his cigarette-holding hand, leaned over to light up, and inhaled a deep and satisfying lungful of smoke. They continued speaking together, smoking together, and laughing together at something that they found amusing about the drummer in the band.

Just as Len thought that he could tolerate this intimate scene no longer, Gertrude stubbed out her cigarette in an ashtray on the nearby table, shared one last amusing thought with her new friend, and turned to search the room.

Burning with curiosity, Len now made his way directly toward her. He thought about acting nonchalant, just in case he had truly misjudged her interest in him. But watching her with another man made her even more desirable in his eyes, and he decided to throw caution to the wind.

"Hello, Gertrude." He stopped a few feet away from her. She looked spectacular in her frilly white blouse and yellow skirt. "I've been looking forward to seeing you again."

"Hi, Len. Me too. This is really a crazy party, isn't it? If you can call it a party."

If she was looking forward to seeing me, she could have found me before speaking to that celebrity of the moment, he thought. Still, Len knew what he had to do. If he wanted to secure her interest, then he would have to give her a fun time. "Let's dance," he said, as casually as he could.

Terrific, Gertrude thought. *I hope he likes dancing as much as I do.* She took him by the elbow and led him onto the crowded small dance floor.

While the lead guitarist did a better than average impersonation of Chubby Checker, the band played their repertoire of Twist songs.

Gertrude was indeed having fun, dancing as well as the best dancers on the floor and performing for anyone who cared to admire her skills. "Do this," she would say to Len every now and then and show him a move done by some of the other dancers, the superior dancers.

"Want a beer?" he offered, as soon as he thought the time was right.

"Sure." She again held onto his arm as they walked up to the bar counter.

"Can you do the cha-cha?" she asked.

"No," Len answered, surprised at how easily the admission of this failing slipped off his tongue. "I've tried, but I'm not too good at it."

"I'll show you," she said, and Len was looking forward to learning the dance from her.

While on the floor, friends would bump into them, pass a few casual remarks, and move on. Len felt good. But it was not until Terry raised his what's-going-on-here eyebrows at Len and Gertrude, and Gertrude grinned and returned an it's-our-business shrug of her shoulder, that Len really felt comfortable. That was when he began to enjoy himself without worrying what she might have been thinking.

"Another beer?" he offered. "Or would you like something else to drink?"

"Gin and tonic."

He laughed at her request, and she smiled back, but she was even more receptive when he said, "They only have wine, beer, bourbon, scotch, and vodka at this party. We'll have to go to the pub to get your much needed gin and tonic."

In a quiet cubicle, Gertrude fiddled with the stirrer in her gin and tonic and Len sipped on another beer. "I saw you speaking to that guy who introduced the birthday boy," Len said, and immediately regretted raising the subject.

But Gertrude soon put his regrets to rest. "Why didn't you come and talk with us?" she asked, her face glowing with fervor at the prospect of telling her story. "Those guys are crazy. They have a motorbike club in Seaview and in some of the other coastal resorts around here." She took a sip of her drink and asked, "You realize that that fat guy on the cane chair wasn't really turning twenty-one, don't you?"

"Sure, and I'm not even certain if his name is Herby Ellington."

"No, that's his right name, but today isn't his birthday. Those guys just wanted to take advantage of the hotel's offer to supply the snacks and the cut-price drinks, so they declared it Herby's birthday. Then, they sent out open invitations by word of mouth to all the college kids on vacation here, bringing in the crowd."

"Why did they want to do that?"

"You saw what they did," Gertrude said, laughing. "That collection was all pre-planned. And Doug, that's the guy I was speaking with, the one wearing the jacket without sleeves, good looking isn't he," she interjected with a wink, "well, he reckons they'll make a profit of over a hundred dollars."

"That's not exactly honest," Len said. He thought about the collection and added, "Nor is it a tremendous amount of money."

"That's what I thought. But get this: you see that Herby Ellington, and the other guy on the stage next to him, not Doug, the one on the other side. Well, I don't know if you noticed, but they're a little slow."

Len thought for a moment. "I don't know about slow," he said. "To me, they looked rough."

"Don't be silly," Gertrude frowned at Len for not seeing things in the same light as she did. "Those bikers are just a regular bunch of fellows having a good time." She took another sip of her gin and tonic and stretched against the bottle green backing on her chair. "The money they collect isn't for themselves. They're not going to keep the profit. They, in fact, did pay out of their own pockets for the cost of the hotel. Doug told me that all they wanted was a bit of fun. 'We have a party, the college kids have a party, the hotel does a little extra business, Seaview becomes a popular place for a vacation, and something worthwhile is done to help the Herby Ellingtons of this world.' Doug claimed that his bikers were just the same as any other lodge or charitable institution in the big cities."

Len indeed felt foolish. And yet, he was not sure that Gertrude's opinion of the bikers was entirely accurate. He also felt confident that, given the chance, Doug might have been exaggerating the goodwill of his gang because he would have wanted to spend the evening with Gertrude. It was Gertrude who chose not to spend the evening with Doug. Len's earlier concerns were unfounded; all along, she had considered that they had a date. She was far less intense than Len was, but she viewed it as a date nevertheless. Len leaned against the backing of his chair and stared at the beautiful and exciting young woman sitting opposite him, and he felt flattered that she was actually enjoying the evening with him.

They finished their drinks, spoke for a while, and then Len asked, "Do you want to go back into the party, or would you prefer to do something else?"

She tilted her head coyly and suggested softly, "Let's go for a walk along the beachfront."

Len's heart started to race. They stood to leave, and he let her walk ahead.

Outside the hotel front door, he said, "I love the smell of the ocean."

"I wonder whether people living on the coast appreciate it as much as we do," she agreed.

"Probably not," Len answered. "It's the norm for people living here."

They crossed the road and began to walk uphill in a northerly direction, along the sidewalk that neither of them had previously been. Len wanted to hold her hand but was afraid she might consider him forward.

They passed two hotels and a few stores before they came to the summit of the rise. Here, there were no buildings, only a multicolored tiled floor that stretched out toward a protective railing above a sheer cliff. For a while, they stared down at the waves crashing against the rocks below.

Len glanced at Gertrude. Her eyes closed and her hair blowing freely in the breeze, she stood smiling happily and inhaling the fresh salty air. She was gorgeous. He turned to stare and felt warmth encompass his entire being. He wanted to hold her, even for a moment, but that was probably more than he could expect. Just being here with her stirred new and powerful emotions that he never knew he had.

Then, Gertrude opened her eyes and saw Len gazing at her, and he would not turn away. She, however, did glance downward, only briefly, before she stepped closer and smiled.

He kept on staring, so she once more looked away. But she then leaned up against his body, placed her hands around his waist, slowly closed her eyes, and brought her lips to his.

Len shuddered as he took her in his arms and held her. He could have cried with sheer joy as he made the kiss last. He would have done anything to have her forever, and he wanted to tell her what was in his heart, but he did not have the words to describe how he truly felt.

Yet, as their lips parted, he did speak, although clumsily, and he said exactly what he wanted her to hear. "Gertrude." He held her tightly. "I'm going to be here for two weeks. Please don't date anyone else. Go out only with me."

Gertrude gave a confused little laugh, but she suddenly saw the love in his heart. And she, too, wanted to be with him, so she kissed him again, and she did shed a few tears of joy.

This was the happiest moment of Len's life.

And, it was not until years later that he would come to realize it was the happiest moment he would ever know.

***

2005

Juliet the cat heard the garage door open. She hopped off Len Darshan's lap, waking him with an unintentional jolt to the groin, and ran to greet Gertrude.

Len rubbed the sleep out of his eyes, stretched the soreness out of his back, and bent over to pick up the magazine that had fallen onto the floor.

"You still up?" Gertrude asked, coming through the den.

Gertrude had early creases at the corners of her eyes, perhaps a hint of a paunch, or possibly not. Or maybe, she had begun to develop a bit of a belly but, being fastidious, took care of it before it could turn unattractive. Still, her elegance would never subside, and her hair, though cropped fashionably short, was the same red as it had always been—thanks to the exact color in a bottle.

Len fixed Gertrude in his intense gaze, then stood and walked over to take her hand.

"What?" she asked, puzzled by his stare and the unexpected attention.

Len could see she had aged, but that did not matter to him. She was the same beautiful woman he had always known. Tonight, however, with his awakened curiosity brought on by the consult with Ralph Carter, he had a burning question that he just had to get off his chest.

"Gertrude." After five years of dating and twenty-nine years of marriage, he raised the subject for the first time. "Do you remember our first kiss?"

CHAPTER THREE

Thrilled by the romance in the question, Gertrude smiled at Len and squeezed his hand in hers. Unfortunately, she was then forced to shake her head and admit, "Not really." She thought of guessing, but she could not recall that first kiss—so meaningful and memorable to her husband. She then sidestepped any embarrassment by suggesting, "We should go back to Seaview for a vacation, to see how it has changed."

In his usual practical way, Len replied, "I don't think Seaview will have changed. It's still a college resort town, not really for us. At our stage in life, it will probably have no appeal. It'll seem seedy." He then saw the same subtle signs of disappointment in his wife's eyes that he had seen so many times before, and he knew he had better compensate for his insensitivity, so he gently suggested, "Maybe we'll go to one of the better coastal resorts in that area. When we are there, we could take a trip to South beach, just to see the boulder where we spent those wonderful days together."

She smiled again, so he whispered, "It was a terrific vacation, wasn't it, Gertrude? I was thinking about it tonight when I dozed off."

"Tell me what you were thinking?" Gertrude asked, but before Len could answer, she offered, "Do you feel like a cup of hot chocolate?"

Len followed her into the kitchen. He found the chocolate mix in the cupboard, while she put the kettle on the stove to boil.

It's difficult to accept that she has forgotten our first kiss, Len thought as he watched her set the table with cups and saucers, plates and forks. *We may not be as like-minded as I believed.*

Then, Gertrude took out a leftover piece of lemon meringue pie, one of Len's favorite desserts, and he remembered, *Nice! She knows what I like. We may not always agree on everything, but we sure have grown closer and learned to understand each other. In the beginning, we may have had our differences. Perhaps that's why she can't recall our first date as clearly as I do. At that time, we were just getting to know each other. Still, I have been able to rely on her and trust her almost from the start.* Len grinned to himself. *Almost!*

"What is so amusing?" Gertrude asked, smiling in harmony with Len.

"I'm still thinking about the time when we started dating."

"So, you should be crying, not laughing," she joked.

"Do you remember your old boyfriend, Matt?"

"Yes. What about him?"

"Actually, I was thinking about the time I met him, the day you came home from Seaview."

"Oh, yes." Gertrude chuckled in recollection.

Len could not remember the exact details of the story. "You've told me in bits and pieces, but tell me again what happened at your parents' home that day."

Len and Matt actually knew each other from their days at East Yarwell High, a public school in one of the less affluent areas adjacent to Yarwell proper. Len went on to Jacobsburg State College, while Matt decided to enter his family's business. For a number of years, they each forgot that the other existed, until the day Gertrude came home from Seaview.

***

1971

Len, Marvin, and Terry left Seaview two days before Gertrude and Joyce.

Back home in Jacobsburg, Len was missing Gertrude, so at midday—the expected time of arrival—he went to meet her at the bus station.

Gertrude saw Len waiting and she waved excitedly, but she did not make her way directly to him; she first went to hug and kiss the middle-aged couple that had come to give her a ride.

"Mom, Dad." She waved Len closer. "This is Len, the one who's going to Jacobsburg University Medical School. Len, these are my parents. I told them about us."

"Pleased to meet you," Len said, unable to control the quiver in his voice or the blush on his face.

"We're going home for a bite," her father said to Len. "Why don't you join us? We live near the State College. I'm sure Gertrude already told you, but if you follow us, I'll show you exactly where."

"Thank you, sir. I'd love to."

Len missed the quick grimace on Gertrude's face.

Gertrude lived with her parents in a white stucco home with a colorful front yard and a white picket fence.

Gertrude's sister, Marlene, only eleven months Gertrude's junior, was waiting at the door. The girls had similar facial features and both were tall. The major difference between the two was Marlene's dark hair. She said hello to Len, but then could not wait to take Gertrude aside for a private word, as close sisters often do.

Eating turkey and pastrami sandwiches and drinking sodas and tea, Gertrude, her family, and Len spoke about the beaches, the hotels, the nightlife, and the people in Seaview and the surrounding coastal resorts. They all then went to sit on the verandah to enjoy the fresh air and the flowers in the front yard. That was when Gertrude said she was bushed and hinted that Len should leave.

Len felt disappointed, but not hurt, and asked Gertrude to walk him down the path in the middle of the front yard, and to his car. He wanted to spend a few minutes alone with her, to arrange to call her later, and perhaps to sneak in a few sweet words of love.

While they were dawdling between the rose beds, a yellow convertible pulled up in front of the house, and Matt stepped out and came through the gate.

"Hi, Matt," Len said. "I haven't seen you in a long time. How've you been doing?"

Slightly more insightful than his old school acquaintance, Matt was a little less cordial, but Len did not discern anything unusual. "Hello, Len . . . what you doing here?"

Before Len could answer, Marlene was by his side and saying, "Come with me for a moment into the study, Len. You're going to love this." Then, pulling him back toward the house, she turned around to explain, "Excuse us, Matt. I meant to show Len something, and I nearly forgot."

"What is it, Marlene?" Len asked.

She raised her eyebrows furtively and promised, "You'll see."

For someone who had, until this point, been quietly curious, Marlene certainly had a sudden change of demeanor. Still, once again, Len did not notice. He was in no hurry, and he was curious about whatever it was that Marlene wanted to show him.

In the dimly lit study, Marlene sat Len at her father's black leather chair in front of his burgundy leather desk. Len could appreciate the masculine fragrance of the books on the old wooden shelves, and the creaking sound of the floor under the worn woolen rug.

Marlene kneeled to open the solid door of a lower level cabinet. She took out three leather bound photograph albums and dropped them on the desk in front of Len.

"When I first started dating Matt," she said, matter-of-factly, "Gertrude showed him a collection of photos that were . . . how should I say . . ." She puckered her lips and gazed upward, searching for words. ". . . Particularly uncomplimentary to me." She paged through the top album until she came to the first picture she wanted. "I swore then that I'd do exactly the same to her. This is Gertrude at age five."

The picture was of a young girl with four missing front teeth, a patch over one eye, and scraggly red hair with a ribbon hanging loosely over her forehead.

Len grinned and asked, "What happened to her eye?"

"She was a bit of a tomboy, always getting hurt," Marlene said, turning the pages to find the next unflattering picture of her sister that she though Len might find amusing.

She came to one of a six-year-old Gertrude swinging by her legs from the limb of tree, her hands attempting unsuccessfully to prevent her dress from falling into her face. Marlene laughed. "This is one of my favorites."

Len chose rather to ask about a family picture on the opposite page. He turned the leaf for himself and scanned for pictures of Gertrude. He seemed to be enjoying the photo album tour, exactly what Marlene wanted, and she gave him leeway to continue perusing.

"How long have you been going out with Matt?" Len asked with his head still in the photo album.

"Quite some time now," Marlene replied, caught off guard by the question.

"He came to see you. Shouldn't you go to him?"

"Oh, he'll wait."

Len tried to get up after closing the cover to the first album, but Marlene managed to keep him in the study for about five or six more minutes while, in a feigned attempt to gain revenge, she found other uncomplimentary photographs of her sister.

"Matt wants his magazines back," Gertrude said from the study door. She came to relieve Marlene of her detaining-Len duties.

"Thanks. I'll get them for him."

For Len's benefit, Marlene pulled a tongue at her sister, as if to say, *I got you back.* Yet, as she passed Gertrude in the doorway, she offered a friendly wink, which suggested, *the plan seemed to work on my side. I enjoyed our trick, but you owe me one. How did it go with you?*

***

2005

Gertrude poured the two cups of hot chocolate and cut two liberal helpings of pie. "While Marlene had you in my father's study, she was worried you might have been thinking that she was a severe nut case. She's still not certain whether you were actually enjoying looking at those silly photographs of me or whether you were being just plain polite."

"I don't really remember what I was thinking, Gertrude, but I do remember sitting there in the study, so something must have made an impression. Maybe it was just the room itself. It was really cozy . . . in a man's sort of way."

"Yes," Gertrude agreed. "That room does remind me of my father. The rest of our house was my mom, but the study, definitely

Dad. Do you want some sweetener in your chocolate?" She offered the bowl with an assortment of colored sachets.

"No thanks. It's sweet enough." He picked up a forkful of pie, but hesitated before lifting it to his mouth. "I know Marlene pretended that Matt was her boyfriend, and I must agree it was a pretty smart plan, but what exactly were you saying to Matt when Marlene and I were in your father's study? What did you tell him I was doing at the house?"

Gertrude dabbed her lips with a paper napkin. "I told him that you had come to see Marlene, the same as Marlene told you. Only, I had an easier part to play. Matt could see that the two of you were off somewhere together. But you knew that, Len; we've spoken about it a few times, haven't we?"

"Why, Gertrude? Why did you tell him I was visiting Marlene?"

She placed her cup on the saucer. "What do you mean, why? I had two boyfriends visiting at the same time. It was a bit of a problem."

"I see," Len answered. "So when did you eventually let him know that I was your boyfriend? Funny, it has taken me thirty-three years to realize that you must have been seeing someone else at the same time you were seeing me."

Gertrude laughed at Len. "I don't believe that you're bothered by something that happened when we first met. He was on the scene before you, and I liked him, but you won."

"It's not really bothering me; I'm just curious why you've never told me that you were still dating him at the time I thought we were an item."

Gertrude clicked her tongue and shook her head in ludicrous disgust. "There's a right way and a wrong way to treat people, Len. Matt had been waiting for me to come home from my vacation. I couldn't embarrass or hurt him at that time. I can't recall when I told him that I wasn't going to be his girlfriend anymore. It was a long time ago, but I wasn't two-timing you."

Len took a long sip and then backpedaled. "I was just wondering why you didn't tell Matt at the time." *How can she say she wasn't two-timing me when she can't recall exactly when she let him go? In her own mind, she's probably telling the truth. I would never have given the matter a second thought if it weren't for Ralph Carter. Do I have the right to question every detail of her life before I came along? Probably not, and Gertrude is right; Matt was on the scene before I was, so she did owe him something, even if it was a gentle goodbye. Still, I'm not that big an idiot; if she cared for him, and she couldn't easily admit to him in front others that I was taking his place, then she must have met him in private. Had she called him on the phone to explain our relationship, she would have been quick to let me know. So, it had to be more than a brief call. I can picture the goodbye scene, with the tears and the kisses and the profound philosophy about love and pain. I know that it happened. What I don't know is whether she remembers the details. The point remains: if she hid something from me once, then how can I be sure she would not hide something from me again? It's not a matter of how long ago it happened; this is a matter of character.*

"How was your bridge game?" Len asked, changing the subject.

"We were coming second, until the last hand, then Jean messed up. We should have won, because the team in front of us also botched their hand. I didn't wait for the final score. If I hadn't left the studio then and there, I might have killed Jean."

"I thought you said that bridge is beginning to get on your nerves." Len got up to take his dish to the sink. "You remind me of golfers. They're always cursing the game, yet they keep going back for more."

"Golfers have no excuse. They don't have to play with Jean. Maybe I should change to golf." She stood next to the kitchen table, pretending to swing a club.

"Are you finished?" Len asked, while polishing off the large chunk of lemon meringue that Gertrude had set aside on her plate.

"Yes." She hardly ever criticized him about his weight, and he never questioned her about hers. She would ask him, parading nude in front of the full-length mirror in their bedroom, if he thought she had gained a few pounds, and he would examine her and then tell the truth, which was usually, "To me, you look fine."

Gertrude covered the small remaining piece of pie and was placing it back into the refrigerator when she remembered, "Oh, yes, I'm telling you now: in two weeks, I'm going out of town to play in a tournament. It's the last weekend of this month. On the Friday, Saturday, and Sunday. Is that okay?"

"Sure," Len said.

Gertrude was frequently going out of town to play bridge, and Len was always saying, "sure," but the day before she left, he could never recall her asking him. Tonight, however, he was paying attention, and for the first time, he did give the matter some thought.

"Don't forget," she warned. "There's going to be no food in this house for you."

She was always telling him that he would have to fare for himself, and to this he also never listened, because invariably she left enough food, cooked and ready for reheating in the microwave, to last Len the better part of a month.

"Whom are you going with?" he asked, as nonchalantly as he could, yet concerned that she might detect his curiosity.

"The girls asked me to play with them in the team game."

"Who?"

"Hillary, Talia, and someone else who you don't know."

Len was dying to ask the name of the "someone else who he didn't know," and normally he would have, if his enquiry reached this degree of inquisitiveness, which it rarely did. "What about Jean?" he asked instead.

Gertrude had a handful of bridge partners with whom she played regularly. At any given time, one of them could be having a bad streak, and when that happened, Gertrude was unforgiving.

"If Jean plays, I'm staying home."

"Can you earn points?"

Gertrude was a Gold Life Master and close to becoming a Diamond Life Master, an achievement that was far more meaningful to her husband than to her. She played the game for fun and for the mental stimulation. That she had amassed 4,860 points by winning major tournaments afforded her status in bridge circles, but this prestige held little meaning for Gertrude.

They tidied the kitchen and went together to the bedroom.

Len undressed, did his fifty sit-ups and fifty push-ups, which he performed religiously every night, and was in the shower before Gertrude. He washed his hair and, eyes closed, was enjoying the hot water rinsing the shampoo off his scalp and running down his entire body when he felt a draught of cold air as Gertrude came to join him in the large stall.

She gently nudged him out of the stream of water. "Let me get wet. Then you can have it back."

Len did not mind. While she let the force of the water splash onto her face, he stood behind her and washed her back. His hands could not work up much lather, so he used a washcloth. She reached back, took the soap from him, and, breaking her word, did not budge from the middle of the stream. Len wiped her neck and her sides. He then began to bathe her buttocks, but he dropped the cloth and continued to massage the shapely cheeks with his bare hands.

"That's nice," Gertrude said, and she took a step backwards to rub herself against him.

He turned her around and kissed her hard on the lips, his one hand still on her bottom, pulling her close.

She held him tightly while they kissed, but then drew away and asked him to pass the washcloth from the floor.

As Gertrude soaped herself, Len took a turn under the stream, rinsing the remaining suds from his hair, back, and legs. He then stepped out of the stall, dried off, put on a pair of boxer shorts, and hopped under the covers . . . waiting.

Gertrude took longer than Len expected. Through the open door to the bathroom, he could hear the hairdryer blowing.

Eventually, she came out wearing a loose nightshirt, and she, too, slipped into the bed.

Len moved closer to Gertrude, excited at the prospect of making blissful love. Her breath was fresh, her hair smelled like strawberries from the conditioner, and her thighs, where the nightshirt had pulled up, were soft and warm. He began lifting it even higher when Gertrude kissed him, this time gently, and said, "I'm sorry, Len. I'm tired. Can you wait until the morning?"

"I'd really like to do it now," Len said. "I'm in the mood." Even as he spoke, he knew that Gertrude had made up her mind.

"Sex wakes me up, and I won't be able to sleep all night."

"I can't understand that," he said. "I sleep so well after making love to you."

"Ask me early in the morning."

But Len would not want to approach her in the morning. In the morning, he would go to the early Synagogue service before work, and he did not want to be tired throughout the day. He placed his arm over her waist and moved as close as he could without prodding her inadvertently. She was a light sleeper, and if he woke her, she would have trouble dozing off again.

That night, it was Len who could not fall asleep. As he lay in bed, trying not to disturb Gertrude, his early arthritic changes in his knees and back came to visit, bringing with them the urge to move and turn. He shifted to his side of the mattress, but remained gazing at Gertrude's silhouette in the dull light of the night lamp in the plug next to the bathroom.

Married twenty-nine years, together for thirty-four. Len sat a little higher against the pillows. He wanted to examine her features. *To me, she has hardly changed. She remains a beautiful woman, and I, a most fortunate man. I'm certain that other men are attracted to her and have propositioned her. I'd like to believe that when they find out that she is married, they leave her alone. Perhaps share a few passing remarks, but then move on. I know this is true of most men. But what of the others, lecherous men with utter disregard for the sanctity of a woman's marriage . . . and there are plenty of them. Still, it takes two to tango, and I trust my Gertrude implicitly. No matter how persistent a man may be, the sharing of a private adventure also requires the woman's receptiveness. The little smile, the interesting conversation, and the invitation to share a few moments in the middle of a boring day, and before a woman knows it, a man trying to enchant her has her under his spell. Then, with a few drinks to ease the sense of guilt, no one can guess where the friendship may lead.*

But not my Gertrude, not now, not at this time in our lives or in our marriage. Although, what was it that I heard today about unsuspecting husbands? They never see it coming, and then, when it smacks them right between the eyes, they wonder how they could have been so blind. Is this the day of my awakening? Gertrude certainly has the freedom to fool around . . . if she wants.

Wide-awake and concerned, Len glanced at the clock on the pedestal. *1:30 in the morning. Stop being ridiculous, Len Darshan. I had better get some sleep, or I'll be a basket case in the office tomorrow. And yet, I may be the world's biggest idiot. I may be wearing the most tinted of rose-colored glasses. Because I managed to tuck away those earlier problems that we had in our marriage, it doesn't mean Gertrude, too, has been able to forget. She never reminds me of my stupidity, yet sometimes, I get the impression that it's always lingering in the back of her mind. I accepted full responsibility for my indiscretion. How long ago was it?* He made a quick calculation. *Twenty-five years, far longer than most marriages last today. I like to think that it was her fault. I'm certain she was just as much to blame . . . or maybe I am just hiding from the truth.*

The clock's minute column turned over a digit. *1:31 a.m. Stop it, Len Darshan, no more rationalizing. Your mind has not stopped churning a bunch of nonsense all day. Get some sleep. You should feel ashamed of yourself. Gertrude has done nothing wrong. What happened twenty-five years ago was your fault, and your fault only . . . not hers.*

CHAPTER FOUR

1971

The Seaview vacation turned Len's whole life around. All he could think about was his new steady girlfriend. He took her to the movies, sports events, the theater, and, of course, to bars, where he held onto her tightly, for fear one of the other young men should think she was alone. Len was not afraid that Gertrude would dump him; he just did not fancy the idea of having to defend his turf.

Needing extra cash, Len took a job in a liquor store. The work was easy and the pay was good. The only problem was that he could not be with Gertrude as much as he wanted. Still, he would call her at every opportunity, and he would sometimes manage to meet her during his lunch breaks. In the evenings, he would either spend time with her at her parents' home or otherwise continue to wine and dine her as well as he could.

Then, later at night, after they had parted company, the couple would speak on the phone into the wee hours about anything and everything. Len would tuck himself in the dark under the covers and pretend she was there with him.

Len knew he would never tire of Gertrude, and she felt the same about him.

Gertrude, too, wanted to contribute to the relationship, so on the fifth Saturday night after their return to Jacobsburg, she decided to have an intimate Seaview reunion. She invited Terry, Marvin, and Joyce, and to neatly round the numbers, her sister Marlene stayed home, too.

Everyone arrived early. The light was dim and the music was soft: The Lettermen, Nat King Cole, and, Len's favorite, Johnny Mathis. Chips and dip were waiting, and Marlene brought out two bottles of wine, a French pinot, and a Californian zinfandel, but just to make sure that the guests were perfectly comfortable, Gertrude had a cooler full of beers covered with shaved ice.

With Marlene's help, Gertrude served a fruit cocktail on a bed of ice, followed by a choice, actually a combination, of two entrées: beef in apricots and ox tongue in cherries. For dessert, they rounded off the meal with a sherry pudding, cappuccino, and crackers.

"Did you cook this?" Terry asked Gertrude.

She just grinned and stood to help Joyce take dirty dishes to the kitchen sink.

"Did she really cook this meal?" Terry turned to Marlene. "Best damn food I've had in a long time, probably the best I've eaten in my whole life."

"I had to help her," Marlene half lied. "Actually she did make it all by herself. I fetched, kept the kitchen sink neat, and tasted. It's the tasting that was most difficult, especially on the first trial run on Wednesday. She burned the beef, not a pretty sight, and even worse on the palate. But she is a good cook, isn't she?"

"You better marry her," Terry said to Len, who was sitting back and enjoying the praises of Gertrude. "Women who can cook like this are not easy to find. She'll definitely keep you happy in the cuisine department."

"I have been giving it some serious thought, even before I knew of this bonus talent," Len replied.

"Pretty serious, huh?" asked Marvin, sitting directly opposite Len and thinking that it didn't take Gertrude long to get her clutches into Len. He also wondered whether Len knew that she had made a move on him, before settling for Len.

Even Len could not miss the grimace on Marvin's face.

"Yes. Pretty serious."

The remainder of the evening they spent in the sitting room, talking about medical school, college, and the easy lifestyle of a schoolteacher. When everyone had had enough to drink, Marlene brought out her Bill Haley and His Comets record and grabbed Len to dance. Terry immediately got up to dance with Gertrude, and Marvin felt obligated to send Joyce a come-on-what-do-we-have-to-lose jerk of the head.

They danced a little, Marlene and Gertrude taught the others some fancy Latin American steps, they drank, laughed, and all in all had an excellent evening together.

Then, the others went home, and Marlene, wanting to leave her sister and Len some private time together, yawned and said, "Goodnight. I am going to bed. Gertrude made it nice, didn't she, Len?"

"Thanks for all the help, Marlene," Gertrude said.

"That's what little sisters are for."

Marlene was halfway out the doorway when Len asked her, "Why didn't you ask Matt tonight?"

Marlene slapped a hand over her grinning mouth, shut her lips extra tight, and kept on walking away.

"Did I say something wrong?" Len asked Gertrude.

"I don't think you can do any wrong," she replied.

"So what's happening with Marlene and Matt?"

"It doesn't look like it's going to last."

"Matt's an idiot. If I remember correctly, he was a bit dense at school, as well."

Gertrude laughed much louder than Len expected. He did not know why, but nor could he resist joining her.

The days of vacationing ended. Gertrude went back to study at Jacobsburg State College, which was near her home, and Len entered his first year at Jacobsburg University Medical School, a short westward commute from the college.

Len was disappointed that he had to leave his full time employment at the liquor store; he missed the cash. He did, however, continue to work weekends, and this earned him enough to take Gertrude out on Saturday nights and Sunday afternoons. Friday evenings, Len became a welcome regular at her family's dinner table, and gallivanting during the week had to take a backseat to study.

Len and Gertrude settled into their courses. Though neither of them reached their full academic potential, they both made passing grades. They did not skip classes, but whenever they had a few free hours, especially on either side of the midday lunch break, they would meet on the college campus grounds or in the cafés of the quaint district surrounding the University Medical School. On a few occasions, Gertrude surprised Len by attending one of his lecture classes, and when she did, no matter how hard he tried, understanding the material became near impossible. But perhaps Len's biggest study problem of all was his inability to completely expel Gertrude from his thoughts, for even at times when he was completely alone with his books, he could not always focus on the words.

Whenever the Medical School hosted a national or international lecture series, which it often did, Len always brought Gertrude, and when she went to college parties, she took Len with her. Everyone they knew recognized they were a close-knit couple. Of course, romance between young people was not an unusual phenomenon. Yet, while other relationships would last until they ended, Gertrude and Len's seemed to know no end at all.

***

1973

In the third year of Medical School, the emphasis shifted from the basic science of medicine to its clinical application, and the students moved across the road to the colossal high-rise maze known as *The Jacobsburg University Hospital.*

Old and worn gray stone steps led up to a main portal protected by a huge pair of lion statues. This imposing entrance may have afforded patients a modicum of confidence, but for the average third year medical student, it seemed to promise nothing less than strife and hard labor.

The entire class assembled in the main lecture hall on the second floor where, after a prolonged introduction to their clinical years, they were instructed to divide into teams of ten. Students understood that, for the next two years, the members of each of these teams would be eating, studying, complaining, and possibly

100

even crying together. Each team would grow into a recognizable unit, working in the same wards together and quizzing, advising, and teaching each other the skills and techniques that they were about to discover in the world of patient care.

Terry and Len found themselves in a team with three women students, Annie, Maria, and Ray, and five other men, Brad, Sammy, Joseph, Daniel, and Allan.

Annie and Maria were cousins who had been looking forward to attending medical school together ever since they were children, and Ray had teamed up with the pair early in first year.

Brad, Sammy, and Joseph were the three most observant Jews in the class. Their main interests seemed to be identifying medical specialties that would not require routine work on Saturdays and ensuring that their food approached the Kashruth requirements laid out in Jewish law.

Daniel and Allan seemed so unlike Brad, Sammy, and Joseph that Len and Terry wondered how the five ended up in the same team together. Because of their lighthearted demeanors, Daniel and Allan shared a conspicuous profile in the class: either or both usually arrived on Monday mornings with a hangover from a hectic weekend. They would often skip lectures in favor of an important sports event. Every Wednesday afternoon, they went to the horse racetrack forty miles north of town, where they worked as bookies, and on Mondays and Tuesdays, they would offer tips and take bets from their growing clientele at the University Medical School. They drove fancy sports cars and seemed forever flush, yet the entire class remembered clearly the Friday when

Allan needed five dollars to retrieve his laundry from the cleaners and earned the money by challenging everyone in the chemistry lab to chip in if he drank a beaker of his urine in a single swig.

The team began their clinical orientation in Professor Maynard's internal medical unit on the seventh floor. Patients' rooms stretched out along a lattice of corridors to the right and to the left. In the center of the unit, opposite the elevators, were the nurses' station, a kitchenette, and the doctors' lounge. On the one side of the elevators were the public bathrooms, and on the other, behind a glass window, was the students' study room. Furnished with about a dozen lightweight plastic chairs, a sturdy central butcher-block table, a blackboard and two cupboards at the front, and three well-worn leatherette couches around the walls, the medical students' room was comfortable, cozy, and practical.

Allan, thinning in the front of his straight dark hair, sat on one of the chairs opposite the cousins, Annie and Maria. Ray, a heavyset young woman, who looked like she might be the oldest in the team, stood at a corner of the butcher-block table scribbling notes on a pad, while Daniel, a thin and tall man with curly blonde hair and a slight droop of the left eyelid, slouched on the couch under the window to the vestibule.

"The senior resident is supposed to be here by now," said Brad, ambling slowly around the room and looking at his watch. He had an elongated face and cropped ginger hair sporting a beige and white knitted yarmulke held securely in place by two skinny clips.

"He'll probably be late. Residents are always busy," said his friend, Sammy, from one of the plastic chairs next to the table. Sammy was a slight man with a severe overbite, tinted gold-rimmed glasses, and a thick mop of pitch-black hair.

"While we wait, we should give ourselves a name," Ray suggested, standing authoritatively at the corner of the table, as though she had just convened the meeting.

"I'm okay with *Ray's Team*," Daniel mumbled, still slouching on the couch. "You're first to bring up the subject, so we should name our team after you."

"I don't want to be called Ray's Team," she argued.

"Why not? It sounds fine to me," Daniel said.

"What about *Daniel's Team*? That sounds even better," said Joseph, a large man, tall and fat, with a well-trimmed dark beard and thick-rimmed glasses. He was sitting on the couch next to Daniel, but leaned forward to look back at him, as though saying, *the ball is now in your court with the same problem. What do you say?*

Len, on another of the plastic chairs around the table, was afraid the situation was about to get ugly, and that the yet unnamed team was off to a bad start. He was going to suggest they put the team naming on hold when Allan, sitting next to him, laughed. "Don't be crazy, Joseph. Why would you want to draw that kind of unfavorable attention? The last name we want to call ourselves is *Daniel's* team."

"Maybe second last," said Terry from the couch opposite Joseph and Daniel. "I can't be one hundred percent certain, but *Allan's Team* may be even worse."

"We don't have to name our team right now," said Brad from the back of the room. "Let it ride. The right name will come looking for us when it's good and ready. And if we never have a nickname, it is also fine. We know who we are."

"We got to have a name," Ray said, now seated with one buttock cheek on the edge of the table. "But it doesn't have to be one of our names."

"How about the *Yeshiva Bochers*?" suggested Daniel from his position on the couch next to Joseph.

This time, Len thought Daniel had overstepped his mark. "What *exactly* do you mean by that?" he challenged, standing slowly and then walking menacingly over toward Daniel.

But before Daniel could answer, and before anyone else could intervene to maintain the peace, Annie, sitting next to her cousin Maria and believing she was merely reiterating Len's question, added in her strong Southern accent, "Yes. What does Yeshiva Bochers mean?"

Standing next to Annie, Brad looked down at her and explained, "A Yeshiva is a place of Jewish learning, and a bocher is a young man; actually, a young man who is eligible for marriage. Yeshiva Bochers is the term used for young men who are studying."

"Oh, and what is the word for a young woman?" she asked Brad. Annie had a peaches and cream complexion that seemed to blend right into her beige hair. With pixie features and a slight frame, she looked like a teenager, and, gazing up at Brad, she appeared as a student asking a question of her teacher.

"A bocherah," Brad answered. "A young woman would be called a bocherah."

"Then maybe we should call ourselves the Yeshiva Bochers and Bocherahs," she said without a hint of a smile. "Although that might be a little long . . . don't you think?"

Brad did not get a chance to reply, because into the study room walked a lanky young doctor with his stethoscope draped around his neck, his starched lab coat collar turned up in a fashion statement, and a blue yarmulke clipped onto his light brown hair. "Hello, everyone. I'm Dr. Scott Kaplansky. Welcome to Professor Maynard's unit. Today, I'm going to teach you a little about taking a medical history . . . nothing complicated, just the basic approach. Then, we'll go into the ward to speak to a few patients so that you can all get your feet wet. But before we get started, we need to take care of a few housekeeping notes. You are going to need to nominate a contact person in your team, someone to act as a liaison between you, the medical staff, the nursing staff, and a whole gamut of other people and staffs that you work with. That team representative will work closely with our unit secretary. Of course, your representative must have an efficient method of contacting everyone for scheduling changes or emergencies or allocation of duties, so besides word of mouth and the telephone, we have two notice boards for posting messages. You've probably already seen them; now get used to reading them. One is at the front of this room." He pointed backwards with his thumb. "And the other is in the lobby of the hospital, to your right as you come in. This one here," he said, again motioning over his shoulder, "applies only to you. The big one downstairs is for all clinical teams of students; therefore, you will need a name so that you can identify which messages are yours. Some groups use the name of their representatives, and that seems to work quite well. Other teams prefer to choose different names. We don't care what you call yourselves, but by the end of today, please let the secretary know who you are. She will get you a permanent spot on the board downstairs, and she'll post your messages."

He was about to continue when the other cousin, Maria, a pudgy little girl with pale yellow hair, deep blue eyes, and a button of a nose raised her hand and volunteered, in her deep Southern drawl, a voice even more accented than Annie's, "Dr. Kaplansky, we know what we want to be called, sir. We are the *Yeshiva Bochers*. We have already decided."

"What?" Dr. Kaplansky tried unsuccessfully to contain his laughter. "That sounds like a great name to me."

Despite their diverse backgrounds, the members of the Yeshiva Bochers knitted into a cohesive unit. During that short three-month stint in internal medicine, the students' study room became a home away from home. Not only were they mutually supportive in their learning, but they also felt comfortable bringing their personal and sometimes intimate problems to one or another member of the group, or to the group as a whole.

Their last day in that internal medicine rotation was a Friday, the day that Professor Maynard himself took the third year students on a ward round and teaching session. The professor allocated one student to each of ten pre-selected patients. They examined their patients and then assembled in the students' study to discuss their findings.

Two patients had been admitted to the hospital because of heart attacks, two had lung cancer, one throat cancer, and five had chronic lung disease with severe shortness of breath, bloating, and morbidly blue coloring of the skin.

As the students presented their allotted cases to the group, Professor Maynard remained uncharacteristically silent. Normally, he would seize upon a symptom and use it to drive home a lesson that he hoped would remain with his students for the remainder of their medical careers. That day, other than correcting one or two blatant mistakes, he allowed the students to have their say with a minimal of interference until the last student, Daniel, had completed his presentation.

The professor then stood before the blackboard, chalk in hand, and asked, "What did you notice about the patients that you examined today? What was the feature that they all had in common?" He looked at the ten faces listening intently and nominated, "Annie."

Annie thought for a moment and admitted, "I'm not quite sure what you mean by your question, sir," but then went on to comment, "They are all elderly or fairly elderly. They probably all have a poor long term prognosis."

"Good. I agree with your observations," Professor Maynard said. "What else?" He pointed to Joseph, who had allowed his beard to grow longer and thicker, and appeared quite a few years older than when he first arrived at the internal medicine unit.

"If we are searching for clinical features that they have in common, sir, then perhaps you may be referring to the fact that they are all short of breath."

"Good, although I am not certain whether Len's patient, the gentleman with the throat cancer, or the two patients with heart attacks were short of breath, but perhaps you are getting closer to the point that I wish to make. Anyone else?"

When no one volunteered, the professor once again nominated a student. "Allan."

"Were they all on oxygen, sir?"

"I believe you are correct, Allan." He looked around the room. "Anyone's patient not on oxygen?" he asked.

Len raised his hand. The patient with throat cancer did not have an oxygen mask.

"What we are searching for is a common etiological factor or common etiological factors," the professor added. "What is it in all these patients' histories that brought on their illnesses?" He again looked around the room and, this time, selected the student who had been earning the highest grades in the group. "Ginger." He called Brad by the pet name that had stuck.

As though he had known the answer all along, yet did not care to blurt it out, Brad replied, "Cigarettes, sir. They all smoke."

With an awkward grin that might have said, *you stole my thunder*, the professor nevertheless praised Brad with his most flattering comment. "Outstanding!" As he gazed slowly around the room, he added softly and emphatically, "Were it not for smoking, none of the patients you examined today would have been in the hospital. They would all be enjoying good health and a far longer life expectancy than they currently have."

Armed with graphic photographs, x-rays, statistics, and the ten practical examples that the students had encountered that very day, Professor Maynard went on to discuss the damaging components in cigarette smoke.

Over the years, the professor had developed a personal vendetta against the ills of cigarettes. True, this hatred was founded in clinical experience and scientific research, but his approach was beyond academic, it was emotional, and he made no effort to conceal his fervor. He knew that the medical students sitting before him would very soon be the health advisors of the population at large, and the professor wanted to create an army of soldiers to do battle with the wealthy tobacco companies. He realized that his students admired him and trusted his acumen, and in his war against the evils of cigarettes, he was prepared to exploit every bit of the student confidence he had earned. The students could not recognize the professor's passion as personal. They viewed that parting lecture as a legitimate component of the curriculum, and as they left their internal medicine rotation with an earnest desire to stamp out all the disease-producing enemies of humanity, tobacco assumed a prominent position at the pinnacle of the pile.

That Friday evening, Len was more pensive than usual. When Gertrude's mother asked him if he was not feeling well, he smiled cordially and, for a while, returned to his former lively self, but it did not take long for him to fall back into a quieter mood again.

It was not until the following night, at a restaurant, eating spaghetti before going to a movie, that he spoke about the concern that was weighing so heavily on his mind. Even then, it was not he who approached the subject; it was Gertrude who asked, "What's the matter, Len? You don't seem yourself. You seem down, like you are depressed or something. Is everything okay at school?" *He was quiet last night as well*, she thought. *I wonder if he has found someone else. Joyce said he wouldn't be able to keep his hands off the nurses at the hospital.*

Len continued to toy with his food. He did not want to anger her, yet he was about to impose his will upon her, and he realized that the conversation might blow up into an argument. "It's your smoking, Gertrude," he said as forcefully as he dared. "It bothers me a lot."

I suppose his concern about my smoking is preferable to his having another girlfriend, she thought. "You know that I smoke," she said. "Why the sudden concern?"

"I don't want you to smoke, because I love you, Gertrude."

"If you want, I won't smoke in front of you," she said, missing the point completely. "As it is, I hardly ever smoke in front of you."

"You have no idea how bad smoking is for your health. It'll kill you."

"It's my health. Besides, we are all going to die one day, so what's the difference what kills me."

"Not only will it shorten your life, it will make you unhealthy for years before you die. Please, Gertrude. I don't ask much of you. Please give it up. It's a bad habit that only gets worse with time."

"You knew I smoked when we started dating. I enjoy my cigarettes. You don't own me and you have no right asking me to quit. I didn't think you were one of those men who tells a woman what she must do. Smoking now . . . what's next?"

"Nothing is next. One day, I am going to marry you, Gertrude. I want us to have a long life together, and your habit is going to ruin everything."

"It's not my habit, as you put it, that's going to ruin everything, Len Darshan. It's bossy you."

"We're shouting, Gertrude. For argument sake, let us assume you're going to continue smoking. But let me tell you how it can affect your health."

Len spoke to Gertrude as rationally, yet as graphically and as simply as he could. He told her about various cancers, heart attacks, strokes, and the array of other lung diseases brought on by cigarettes.

She listened intently, asked pertinent questions, and challenged certain statistics, which she refused to believe.

He told her about Professor Maynard's lesson the previous day, and he described the suffering of the ten patients chosen to illustrate the professor's points.

She asked those patients' ages and argued that most people over fifty had a number of ailments, whether they smoked or not.

He would not accept that she was already addicted.

And she could not explain the pleasures of smoking.

Drained, depressed, and too late for the movie, they decided to go home.

Gertrude would not be bullied into quitting. She said that she understood Len's concern but could not comprehend his sudden change of attitude, and she was offended.

He said she was unreasonable and stubborn, and that her smoking was a deal breaker.

At her home, he parked the car next to the sidewalk, immediately hopped out, came around to politely open her door, and walked her to the front porch.

She neither invited him in nor kissed him goodnight.

Neither Len nor Gertrude were angry. It was unyielding pride that kept them from calling each other.

For two nights, Gertrude cried herself to sleep before deciding that it was time to send out word that she was no longer attached, to get on with her life, and to try forgetting Len.

Len was more passive about the breakup. He withdrew into himself and became even quieter than usual.

On the Monday morning, the Yeshiva Bochers were assigned to their new rotation in Professor Carson's surgical unit. Situated on the third floor of the hospital, the surgical unit had a similar layout to the internal medical unit on the seventh floor, and other than cane love seats in place of the leatherette couches, the students' study room was identical.

At first, Len's co-students thought that he just did not enjoy surgery, that he was missing the internal medicine unit. Why else would his demeanor have suffered such an abrupt change?

On Wednesday morning, thirty minutes before the ward round, Len was third to arrive in the students' room. Allan and Maria were already there, sitting on the love seat opposite the window that looked out across the vestibule and at the nurses' station. Although they were engrossed in what seemed a lighthearted yet compelling conversation, Len took out his Pediatric textbook to prepare for a lecture that afternoon. But Len could not concentrate on his work, nor could he help listening to their discussion.

"She's better looking than the blonde in Maynard's unit," Allan said.

"Which blonde?" Maria asked, staring at a group of nurses who were reading chart notes at the change of shift.

"Which blonde? Like you don't know. Elsie, the one I dated."

"Elsie wasn't good looking. She looked like a mouse."

"Come on, Maria . . . Elsie was good looking, and sexy, too. Admit it."

"She looked like a mouse, and that's why she dated you. I'm not saying she wasn't a nice girl, but that one is much better looking." Maria motioned surreptitiously with her head, as though the nurses might know they were being discussed.

"Do you think she'll go out with me?"

Maria gritted her teeth as though in serious contemplation. "No, Allan. That one is too good looking to go out with you."

"Maybe if you ask her for me." Allan nudged Maria's shoulder with his as he begged the sham favor.

"I'll have to lie," Maria said. "I'll have to lie quite a bit. And you must hide away in case she sees you. Otherwise, I don't think I'll be able to pull it off."

"Thanks, Maria. I'll owe you big for this one."

Brad was next to arrive. "Good," he said immediately to Len. "You look a little more like your old self. I was beginning to worry about you."

"Hey, Brad," Maria said. "We're eyeing the shikses at the nurses' station. You see the tall one standing up. The blonde. Do you think Allan will be able to crack a date with her?"

Brad shook his head at Allan, the instigator, as he spoke. "Shikse is not a nice word, Maria." He nevertheless then went on to ask, "Which one?" and immediately joined the other two in staring across the room and out the window.

Even Brad, serious Brad, knows how to have frivolous fun, Len thought. *I wonder if I could ever just let go like Allan and say whatever I felt, without making an idiot of myself. I was closer to that frame of mind when I had Gertrude. How I wish I'd never raised that smoking issue. Already, I miss her. She was right and I was wrong. She smoked when I first met her, so I had no right demanding she quit.*

"Morning, everyone." Terry came into the room, followed closely by Ray, Daniel, Sammy, and Joseph.

"How's it going?" Terry asked Len quietly as he sat on the chair next to his friend. "Have you called Gertrude yet?"

Len shook his head. "It's over. And probably a good thing, too."

"What the hell does that mean?"

Len actually smiled as he tried to play the role of an Allan. "Those nurses have been waiting too long." He pointed through the window. "It's about time I made myself available to them."

Terry laughed, not at Len's remark, but rather at the indignant expression on the tall good looking blonde's face as she noticed Len pointing her way and obviously speaking about her and her colleagues.

"I'll be fine," Len assured Terry.

"I'm sure you will," Terry replied, pensively.

But Terry was not sure that Len would be fine. He had never seen his friend so miserable, and he wanted to do something to help. Throughout that day, as in the past few days, Terry kept an eye on Len. Len moved about slower than usual and, other than the occasional spontaneous grimace of regret, wore the fixed facial features of depression.

In the afternoon, all third year students had to attend three formal classes in the Medical School main lecture hall across the road. Between the second and third lectures, Terry decided what had to be done. Just before the professor walked in, he said to Len, "There's something I want to show you."

"What?" Len asked.

"Not now, after the lecture. Be patient. You'll see."

There were a number of old and battered cars in the medical student parking lot, but the ugliest of all, a green hand-painted old Ford pickup with slanting fenders and an assortment of wheels, belonged to Terry.

In the passenger seat, with stiff springs pressing on his bottom, Len no longer asked where they were going, but rather how long it would take to get there.

"Not long," Terry replied, and it took but a few minutes for Len to realize where they were headed. He thought about objecting, but his heart would not listen to his mind, so his mouth remained tightly shut.

Terry's car spluttered up to the curb outside Gertrude's home. Without a word to Len, he jumped out and marched through the gate.

From the car, Len saw Gertrude's mother open the front door. She and Terry spoke briefly before she turned around to call Gertrude. Terry then accepted an invitation to step inside. He began wiping his feet on the welcome mat but never quite made it into the entrance hall. Gertrude, with her hair unkempt, barefoot, and wearing a bulky and stained sweat suit, came barging out the house. Her face was blotchy from tears; she was a mess, but to Len, she never looked more beautiful.

He managed to get out the car and close the door just in time to brace himself. For she threw her full weight into his open arms and kissed him with all the pent up passion that a few moments earlier she believed she never would spend.

"I hate you, Len Darshan," she said, but then withdrew from his arms, stared directly into his eyes, and confessed, "God alone knows how much I love you, Len Darshan."

His arm wound securely around her waist, Len and Gertrude walked up the path between the flowers toward the house. Gertrude's mother stood with her elbows pulled tightly against her heaving chest, her chin resting firmly on her laced fingers, and her tears streaming freely down her joyful cheeks. Next to her, Terry, too, was elated for his friends, and in addition to his delight, he was also tremendously relieved that his hasty plan had not backfired.

If their squabble had any effect at all, it probably served to draw Len and Gertrude even closer together. Len's friends were glad to have him back as his old quiet but content self, and Gertrude's friends at last realized that she was permanently removed from the circle of dating, that she was not available to anyone but Len.

Len and Gertrude were still extremely active, going out to parties, bars, and other gatherings. But unlike their friends, whose lives were hectic, Gertrude and Len led a cozy existence with a sobering aura of calm.

At the hospital, Len witnessed the bantering between the sexes and wondered what he was missing, but his interest was nothing more than mere inquisitiveness.

At college and then at her teachers' training courses, Gertrude understood clearly the motivations of young men, and she was content to discourage their advances.

Close friends said they began to favor each other, and everyone agreed that Len and Gertrude were a match made in heaven.

When alone, Gertrude would tell Len about the students she was teaching at East Yarwell High School, and Len would tell her of the more interesting facets of medicine. They were absorbed in each other and in each other's careers, and for them, the days did not hold enough hours.

At night, their favorite topics of discussion were their wedding and their marriage, and Len would take great delight in describing how he was going to give her the happiest life she could imagine. In return, she would tell him of the home she would run, of the meals she would prepare, and of the love that they would share.

During their conversations, every conceivable issue arose. When they spoke of their quarrel, he was always first to apologize, and when they spoke of smoking, she promised that she would quit both for her own health and to please him.

***

1975 to 1978.

On the day of his graduation from medical school, his diploma still rolled tightly in its cardboard tube, Len made his way directly to Gertrude's father to ask for her hand in marriage.

Ten months later, with Marlene as the Maid of Honor and Terry as the Best Man, Rabbi Irving Lathan married Gertrude and Len in the *New Yarwell Orthodox Synagogue.*

The couple stood under a prayer shawl supported at the corners by four wooden poles, each held up high by a young man: Daniel and Joseph to the right, and Sammy and Allan to the left. And whereas the law of marriage required two Torah observant witnesses, Len was proud to ask Brad to stand by the Rabbi's side.

It was a wedding that every guest had awaited, a match that promised to fulfill every hope of a perfect marriage.

Yarwell was a rolling suburb with the tallest hill on its southwestern corner known colloquially as Yarwell Mountain. Up this mountain wound a steep road toward the Yarwell water tower at its summit, and at the bottom of the road, built into the foothills of Yarwell Mountain, was a six-story high-rise apartment building, Tower Heights.

Gertrude and Len managed to rent an apartment at the back of the first floor of Tower Heights. It had a small kitchen, an entrance hall that Gertrude used as a dining room, one crowded bathroom, a huge bedroom, and a comfortable sitting room with a porch actually carved into the rock of Yarwell Mountain.

At the time of their moving in, Len and Gertrude had a new bedroom suite, which was a wedding gift from Gertrude's parents, and a top of the line stereo, bought with money they received as wedding gifts. The rest of their furniture they picked up either at garage sales or through newspaper advertisements for second-hand articles. They had everything they needed or wanted.

Len was a resident at the Jacobsburg University Hospital, about a mile and a half from Tower Heights, a comfortable walk in good weather, and Gertrude taught Science at East Yarwell High School, three to four miles from their home, so she drove their Volkswagen Beetle to work.

Although Len and Gertrude were first in their crowd to wed, shortly thereafter, and one by one, their friends, too, entered into the holy state of matrimony.

Marvin, who they had not been seeing too often and who Gertrude did not particularly like, moved out of state.

Joyce married a politician, George Ullman, and, to Gertrude's regret, had to leave the country when her husband was promoted to an Embassy in the Middle East.

At Terry's marriage to Melinda, Len was Best Man and Gertrude Matron of Honor. The two couples saw more and more of each other. Hardly a weekend went by when they did not go to a show, a club, or a restaurant together.

At Marlene's wedding, Gertrude was once again Matron of Honor, but Marlene's new husband, Larry, had a brother, Harold, who was bestowed the title of Best Man.

Larry and Marlene had been dating for about six months before he popped the question. Larry was about the same age as Len. He was an accountant in a successful firm and he was popular and friendly, so Gertrude and Len were confident that he would make a fine brother-in-law for them and a good husband for Marlene.

While dancing at Marlene and Larry's wedding reception, Gertrude asked Len, "When are you due for your next increase in salary?"

"If I stay at the hospital . . . in about eleven months," he answered. "I just got a raise last month . . . remember. But why do you ask? We're managing fine and saving most of your salary."

"Yes, but what if I were to stop working?"

"Why would you want to do that?" Len asked, but before she could reply, they bumped into Larry dancing with Marlene and smiling happily. Larry was about an inch shorter than Marlene, but it did not seem to bother either him or her. He had an open round face, similar to Len's face, and gray eyes, the same color as Len's eyes. Seen together, people who did not know them might have mistaken Len and Larry for brothers.

"Welcome to the family," Len said, attempting to add a little extra happiness to the couple's special day.

"Thank you," Larry replied. "I'm looking forward."

Marlene said nothing; she just smiled gratefully at Len, and the couples parted.

Although Marlene had dated a number of men in the past few years, Len's thoughts went back to the time he first met her, and he said to Gertrude, "I prefer Larry to Matt. I wonder whatever happened to Matt. I don't think he would have made a good brother-in-law. He wasn't as nice as Larry."

"How do you think we'll make out on your salary alone?" Gertrude asked again.

"I don't know," he answered and then said, "Does Marlene ever hear from Matt? Does he know she's getting married tonight?"

Gertrude stopped dancing. "I'll answer you if you answer me."

"Do you know what happened to Matt?"

She took his hand and led him off the dance floor and out into the foyer.

"Can I get you a drink?" he offered as they passed a bar, just outside the door.

"Any soft drink will do."

"No gin tonight?"

"A soft drink."

With that, the penny finally dropped, and Len beamed as he asked, "You're pregnant, aren't you?"

She nodded her head vigorously.

"Wow!" He took her into his arms and kissed her gently and happily. He was pleased that she would not drink alcohol when pregnant, and he assumed that meant she was responsible about cigarettes, as well.

Janet weighed six pounds, eleven ounces at birth.

Gertrude and Len continued living in their apartment in Tower Heights. It was a little crowded, but their bedroom was huge, so they partitioned off an area next to the window that looked out onto their porch for the baby. The decision to remain for a while in the inexpensive apartment would give them an opportunity to save for a deposit on a house. It would also free up any extra cash that Len might need, since he and Terry had decided to open a private primary care practice together.

Meanwhile, Gertrude stayed at home with the baby, and Len continued to work at the University Hospital.

Len could not wait to return to the apartment each day. He loved little Janet, and he treasured the atmosphere in his home. He would help Gertrude bathe the baby and prepare the evening meal. Then, while Gertrude sang the baby to sleep, he would do a few chores that might have mounted up during the day.

At last, they would enjoy their dinner, and then perhaps listen to some music on their stereo until it was time to go to bed, quietly so as not to wake Janet, and cuddle into a deep sleep.

Spring came around, the weather turned warmer, and Len bought two garden chairs and a small table so that they could enjoy their carved porch, the fresh air, and the view of Yarwell Mountain covered with wild blooms rising steeply toward the sky above. Now, in the evenings, they would make a point of sitting outside for a while and playing with Janet by the light of their bedroom and living room, adjacent to their porch.

Until one Sunday afternoon when they returned home from a drive in the country and a picnic by a lake in the State Park, and they found their garden furniture missing. The loss did not bother Len as much as the realization that his private porch, hidden from the world, was not as private or as safe as he had believed. He saw scratch marks where the thief or thieves had dropped down into the their property and stolen the table and chairs.

It had probably been some mischievous kids with nothing better to do. The point, however, was that the furniture was still new, and that someone had stolen it while they were away from home. Someone, a mischievous kid or not, had probably noticed the new furniture and returned to take it, which meant that that someone could have been watching them through the windows to their sitting room and bedroom. Yet, the porch seemed so secluded, so Len decided that if they were to continue living in the apartment, he had to see how the thief had entered their property and do whatever was necessary to render it more secure.

Len did not want to alarm Gertrude, so the next morning, a Monday, he woke a little earlier and left the apartment about ten minutes before his usual time.

He came out the front glass doors of the high rise, and instead of walking towards the hospital, he turned right, up the steep hill to the water tower. The sidewalk was narrow, with the sheer wall of Yarwell Mountain to his right and the road to his left. To climb onto Yarwell Mountain, Len had to go all the way to the water tower where access was easy. He would then come back along an easier trail on the mountain itself, downhill toward Tower Heights.

The view from the top was awe-inspiring. He spent a few moments recognizing some landmarks and deciding to show it to Gertrude the following weekend. He also understood why someone might want to spend some time here, climbing the smooth rocks and spying into private backyards down below.

126

Still, he was here to investigate the theft of his furniture and not to admire the vista, so he continued down the steep slope in the direction of Tower Heights. The climb was easy, along a well-worn path that led directly toward his apartment. He came right up to the edge above his private porch and, looking down, he immediately felt a wave of nausea—for here was a scene so upsetting that it was certain to affect the remainder of his life.

CHAPTER FIVE

2005

In the morning, Len conducted his first experiment to test his evolving but ridiculous theory. After a restless night, he got out of bed earlier than usual and went to the bathroom to make himself as appealing as he could. He showered, brushed his teeth and gargled, and sprayed a few puffs of men's cologne onto his neck and chest. He then returned to the bedroom, switched on his reading light, shuffled his wallet and watch, and, when she stirred, said, "Hi sweetheart, did you sleep okay?"

"Morning, Len. Do me a favor. Please turn off the light."

He did as she asked, but then walked around to her side of the bed and leaned over and kissed her, softly at first, but then with an open mouth and a sweep of his tongue over her lips, the way she liked it. When she said, "Mmm, that's nice," he slipped under the covers and caressed the small of her back while holding her passionately.

"All right," she whispered. Then, she pushed him gently away, lifted her nightgown, and offered, "This one's for you."

Satisfied and exhausted, Len wanted to hold Gertrude in his arms and fall back into a restful sleep, but it was time to get ready for the early morning Synagogue service. She, on the other hand, seemed invigorated and ready to start her day.

Together with the other men who had a need or desire to pray each day, Len donned his prayer shawl and phylacteries.

His mind was clear, but he could not concentrate on the words that he was uttering by rote; his thinking was fixated on the events of that morning. *Before I approached Gertrude, I didn't know how she was going to respond. I imagined she might rebuke me, as she did last night. Then, when we were making love, everything seemed so pleasant. Now, with no immediate need for physical gratification, I'm still not certain how she did respond. She knew I wanted to make love to her, and she allowed me, but is that all I really want from her? Do I want her to allow me? Do I want her favors? And when she told me, "this one's for you," she most certainly was doing me a favor. Do I want only her body, or do I want all of her as in days gone by?*

Len stood up with the others in the congregation, as those mourning for their recently departed relatives chanted, in unison, the liturgy, *Kaddish.* For a few sentences, he was able to turn his thoughts to matters holier than his latest obsession, but upon sitting, his mind again began to drift. *For her, sex seems a chore. She's always doing me a favor. She doesn't seem to find it as*

130

pleasurable as she once did. I wonder whether she enjoys it at all. Actually, that's not a fair question. She seems to enjoy making love . . . it is just less of a priority than it used to be. I suppose that is to be expected of a woman her age. On the other hand, my desire is almost as strong as ever. Men are different from women; they lose their libido less often. Even when they have erectile dysfunction, the libido commonly remains. Some even claim that they are as lustful in their advancing years as they were in their youth. But, that is men; what about women? What should I expect of Gertrude? How do other women her age feel about sex? Some women seem to lose their libido, although not all of them. In fact, as far as I'm aware, most of my middle-aged women patients retain their libido. When couples have sex problems, the man needs help far more often than does the woman. Except when the underlying issue is emotional, then, more commonly, it's the woman who needs help. Is it possible that Gertrude has some sort of a psychological problem?

They came to the solemn chanting of the Sovereignty of the Creator, and Len felt silently ashamed of his lack of devotion that day. Still, he could not avoid mulling over Gertrude's possible emotional issues. *If anyone is stable, strong, and level headed, and anything other than neurotic, it is Gertrude. If she has any psychological issues, I sure don't know what they might be, and after all our years together, I know her at least as well as she knows herself. No, Gertrude is the sanest and most levelheaded person I know. And yet, she does fit the profile. Maybe I am missing something.*

The congregation stood for the most important part of the morning service, the eighteen silent prayers. Determined to make amends for his daydreaming, Len closed his eyes to shut out all extraneous thought and moved his lips in unison with the meditation. For the opening two paragraphs, this technique worked, then he found himself concentrating more on the shutting out of unwelcome rumination rather than on the prayer itself, and finally, he could not resist answering the questions he had posed.

No, he thought. *I'm not missing anything now. Until today, I may have been missing a lot. Now, I can see clearly. And when I take two steps back to look at the way I've been able to read people's behaviors, I have not been too bad. I suppose for any doctor, understanding repeated behaviors becomes routine. Like every time I see a twelve-year-old-girl with makeup packed thick on her face, risqué underwear, and a rebellious attitude, I know she will soon be coming in with an unwanted pregnancy or a sexually transmitted disease. Funny how their mothers can't recognize it. Some mothers don't even see it after I council them about their daughters. They think their children are cute— innocent and cute. And yet my predictions are almost invariably right. Within a year or two, I have a crying adolescent and a family crisis on my hands. No, I think I've been too critical of myself . . . when I think about my skills in predicting outcomes of behavior patterns, I am probably as good as Terry. Yep, I can pretty much read what is going on. Like that fourteen-year-old boy who I diagnosed with oppositional defiant disorder . . . horrible kid. He killed a kitten in a microwave and had no remorse. His parents at least listened to my diagnosis and advice. They could see they had a problem. Yet, when I told them frankly that their son was going to end up in jail, that there was a strong likelihood that he would commit a violent crime, they thought I was exaggerating. And what was it . . . less than two years later that he did eventually kill someone.*

And now when I open my eyes and look at my own wife, again I don't like what I see: If some other guy had my story, I would bet better than even money that his wife was fooling around.

At the office, even as he tried to work, the irksome ponderings continued. But this did not divert his attention from his patients. Rather, Len added an additional facet to his treatment: for those patients with emotional problems—and there were many—Len delved deeper into their backgrounds, trying to uncover buried secrets that emerged in the disguise of physical and psychological illness. He knew that emotion was a major part of clinical medicine; his Psychiatrist colleagues often argued that its importance was underestimated. And now, with his added focus on the mental condition, he realized just how valid was their claim. Furthermore, as he considered the close relationship between physical health, emotion, and sexual behavior, he recognized that the early teachings of Sigmund Freud might have been spot on the mark. Unfortunately, most people hid their forbidden yet true sexuality captive in the deepest part of their souls. Then, when it did escape, it would run riot, doing its utmost to disrupt conformist lifestyles and stifled values. It took a trigger to set the sexual frustrations free. Sometimes, a person's unhappiness would search for the trigger, and sometimes, the trigger would sneak up to bite an otherwise content life that was holding the sexuality in check.

***

1978

All young Dr. Len Darshan really wanted was to find out whether he could build a protective fence around his porch in Tower Heights. Coming over the rise at the edge of Yarwell Mountain, he tried to imagine himself in the shoes of the furniture thief. How would he get down to the porch and then carry the table and chairs back up the steep slope?

Len expected to find his private little area empty, and he wondered whether he would be able to see through the glass windows into his sitting room and bedroom. But he was shocked at the sight awaiting him. For there, on the porch, was Gertrude, daydreaming and taking a break from her chores in the apartment and her duties with little Janet. Because the chairs had been stolen, she sat on the windowsill, a mug of coffee in her left hand, and a lit cigarette dangling loosely from her lips.

Gertrude brought her free right hand up to her mouth, grasped the cigarette between her index and middle fingers, and inhaled a gratifying lungful of smoke. She then switched hands to take a long sip of coffee, and as she tilted her head back, she saw him staring down at her. She knew he had been watching; she could tell from his slouch and frown. She felt immediately ashamed, not because of the smoking itself, but rather because she could sense his disappointment. She could not run away; there was nowhere to go.

Then, her shame turned to indignation. *Why should I be afraid of Len? I've done him no harm, yet he's looking at me as though I have committed the most egregious of sins. He's wondering*

134

whether I smoked throughout my pregnancy. When he asks, I may not even dignify his question with a reply. I have nothing to be ashamed of, and I should have nothing to hide. I'm actually glad he now knows that I still smoke.

Len could not know what she was thinking; yet, as he watched her defiant stare, his illusion of her perfection began to fade. All he could see was a woman with a grubby habit and a broken promise. From where he stood, he imagined he could detect her coarsened skin and damaged lungs. *Is smoking beginning to exact its toll on her appearance and health? How blind have I been?*

He then noticed the minor imperfections that had remained hidden from his consciousness all the years: the pointed chin and the smallish eyes and lips. The sudden realization that his beloved Gertrude was a mere mortal hurt Len deeply, and his mind could not believe what his eyes could clearly see. But more troubling than the mere physical revelation was the breach in trust. *She told me she wouldn't smoke, and she led me to believe that she had kept her word. I have been honest with her. How could she do this to me? If she lied to me about cigarettes, how can I believe anything else she tells me?*

Len turned slowly to make his way up the hill toward the water tower. He took one step but then looked back, possibly to ensure that this was not all a nightmare. And what he saw once more took him completely by surprise. For in her eyes welled tears of regret, and to her face returned the beauty he had always known, so Len opened his arms to beg of her, *why?* But Gertrude had no answer. She could only look away, cry freely, and run back into the security of their home.

At work, Len would not discuss his disappointment with his best friend, Terry. He was embarrassed about Gertrude's smoking, and he and Terry had other important matters on their minds: a private corporation had built a new hospital in the heart of Yarwell, and Terry and Len had signed a lease for a suite in the professional building attached to the main hospital.

Melinda Stein and Gertrude had been excitedly shopping for office furniture and wallpaper for the suite, while Terry and Len were more interested in the architectural efficiency and smooth patient flow.

Len believed that morning's episode was serious, and he did not know how it would end. But he also did not want to put a damper on Terry's zest, not at this time anyhow, not as they were about to move into their office, and not until his mind was settled and he had discussed the incident with Gertrude.

At home time, instead of hurrying to his wife and daughter, Len remained at University Hospital to round on his patients. He then went down to the medical records department on the first floor where he proceeded to dictate his outstanding discharge summaries and review the few queries that arose out of his medical charts.

By now, it was eight o'clock, and still Len did not feel like going home, so he went to spend some time in the little physicians' lounge adjacent to the records room.

He poured himself a cup of coffee, helped himself to one of the pastries laid on for doctors who might need something to eat during a long stint in the records department, sat in an armchair in the corner of the room, and picked up a medical journal.

A radio, which usually played popular music during the day, was tuned to a science-fiction station and was presenting a story called *Uncontactable*. Len did not intend to focus on the radio, but the adventure grabbed his attention, and he could not help listening to it in its entirety.

> *Futuristic explorers were on a mission to seek out and learn from any life forms in the galaxies.*
>
> *They came across a planet inhabited by intelligent life, almost humanoid in form, and they entered the phase of discrete observation to study aggression, relationships, and any other characteristics that the aliens might display.*
>
> *On this particular planet, the aliens were remarkably similar to Earthlings: they dressed in full-length robes, interacted with each other, lived in sheltered homes, used a form of rail transportation, and, to the explorers' delight, seemed to have a passive disposition. Yet, with all these characteristics, the explorers were forced to inform their base on Earth that they could not make contact—that the inhabitants were uncontactable.*
>
> *Commander Yadira Durbin, the woman in charge of all missions into space and heroine of the series, transported herself from the Earth base to the spaceship to*

137

investigate. She discovered that the exploring team had rendered an accurate account of the aliens. Arms, legs, torsos, and heads, a little smaller then humans, with pixie-like features and two distinct breeds—one with larger proboscises and the other with six digits instead of three on each hand, possibly the equivalent of males and females. The aliens had entered an era of technology: They had tiny receivers, used as telephones, attached to the front of the torsos, transporter devices for sending articles through space, and an elaborate rail system that approached every populated point in each of their vast centers of civilization. There were no other animal forms on the planet, but the atmosphere consisted of thirty percent oxygen and a seventy percent mixture of inert gasses, suitable to support both the resident alien life and the visiting human life, and superb for sprouting a variety of vegetation into perfect bloom. With pure water and an apparent absence of disease producing microbes, this planet seemed flawless— a colony of potential allies and a rest station in the galaxies—but for the single limiting factor: pace.

And Commander Durbin eventually had to agree with her scouts that the inhabitants of this otherwise ideal world indeed seemed uncontactable; the planet existed in a solar system similar to Earth's, with a number of planets rotating around a single central sun. But, whereas a day on Earth would last a mere twenty-four hours, this new planet rotated around its axis once every five years, and all movement and activity on the planet was proportionately slowed to the length of the day.

138

The visitors from Earth, moving at an incredibly rapid pace, relative to the aliens, were able to go about unnoticed. With a great deal of patience, they studied the aliens, their eating habits, their social interactions, their sluggish noises that they used as speech, their symbolic sculptures, and their level of technology.

Eventually, Commander Durbin felt the time had come to communicate. "Even if we learn their spoken language, still we cannot talk with them," she said to her gathering of seven officers.

"Unless we use some kind of recording device, slow our message down to their pace, and set it up at one of the train stations," suggested Captain Gregory Stokes, the leader of the scouting team. The captain was the person who first coined the term uncontactable, but he was not an arrogant man and was prepared to revisit the possibility of communicating with the aliens.

"Perhaps," Commander Durbin replied. She considered the idea and asked, "If we assume they have human intellect and emotion, how would they respond to a message from invisible visitors?"

"They may imagine it some sort of prank. But that is if they think the same as we do, which is an unreasonable assumption."

"Alternatively, we could decipher the symbols on their sculptures, which I am certain represent a form of writing

similar to our ancient Egyptian Hieroglyphics. Then, we could present our objectives and intentions in their script, and give them about a month, in their time, to respond."

"We would have our answer in about 150 years," Captain Stokes calculated. "Our grandchildren or great-grandchildren would have to come back here to see what these aliens had to say. Then, they could ask another few questions, and wait another 150 or so years for the reply."

The other officers nodded in agreement with their captain's assessment.

Commander Durbin summarized the situation. "We all accept that we cannot effectively communicate with the aliens in real time, that any correspondence will have to stretch over hundreds of years. However, it remains our duty to set the process in motion." She looked sternly at the seven officers surrounding her, ready to counter any objections, and when no one spoke, she continued, "Who knows what the future holds? This communication may be the exact stimulus that our scientists need to gain a better understanding of time. We'll need one team to work on a sound system and the alien language, and another to work on the alien script."

Commander Durbin wanted to adjourn the meeting, but Captain Stokes was still concerned. He held up both arms. "A moment please. We are forgetting one detail. We still don't know how they will accept a foreign presence. There are instances where, for a number of reasons, we may choose to chart and then bypass a civilization. These aliens, as the inhabitants of so many other uncomplicated civilizations we have encountered, may be a timid society, which will not tolerate an abrupt disruption of their simple routine. Or they may turn instinctively belligerent, especially considering that they have never encountered any other life form."

"Captain, you are right," the commander said. "Perhaps you and I should return to the planet's surface, to search for clues that might help us understand how they will react."

Armed with a small container of instruments, Commander Durbin and Captain Stokes beamed down to the planet. At what appeared to be a central train station, they wandered among a crowd of statue-like aliens, inspecting their features and poses, trying to gain an overall impression of how they would respond to stress and surprise. They walked up a soft but secure ramp into one of the trains, wherein they heard a drone of clicking whispers as the aliens communicated with sounds coming from two places in their bodies, small mouths at the junctions between their torsos and tiny chins, and protruding proboscises in the center of their round heads.

There were no seats on the train; in fact, Commander Durbin and Captain Stokes noted there were no seats or beds anywhere. If the aliens did sleep or rest, they did so in a standing position. The passengers stood a polite distance

141

from one another, so the two explorers were able to walk amongst them unhindered.

"For no good reason, we've assumed that those with six digits on each hand are female," Captain Stokes said. "We have not yet been able to find any younger or smaller specimens, so we do not believe that they procreate."

"They all seem exactly the same size, and other than the hands and proboscises, we can't tell any difference between the individuals—not a blemish or defect. Do you suppose that they reproduce in some sort of laboratory?"

"We have considered that possibility, Commander, but the team hasn't been able to locate any reproduction center. We're beginning to believe that there are a fixed number of aliens, and that they continue existing indefinitely. Where they originated is anyone's guess, and where they go if or when they die seems impossible to know; no cemeteries, crematoriums, or mausoleums to be found."

They walked up a spiral path and onto the roof, where they saw more aliens waiting patiently for the train to pull out of the station. In the center of this upper level, standing in front of a control panel, was one of the longer proboscis aliens who seemed to be the driver of the train. The passengers had given him a greater expanse of free space, probably for him to efficiently perform his job.

The two visiting humans watched as the driver transferred his hand from one control to another, a process that took fifteen minutes, yet a more rapid movement than any other they had witnessed.

They were about to walk down the ramp again, when Commander Durbin said, "I believe it is time for us to make our presence known."

Captain Stokes nodded. He knew that the aliens would more readily accept written or verbal messages if accompanied by recent visual contact.

They went to what appeared to be the back of the train and stood in front of three aliens facing approximately the same direction. Two had longer proboscises, males, and one had six digits per hand, a female.

Commander Durbin stepped closer than any human had been before. She looked carefully at one of the male alien's skin, smooth and pale lime in color with fine hair evenly distributed over all exposed parts. She was about to move onto the next alien, the other male, to examine and ascertain whether they were identical, which would lend support to the theory that they had been born in some type of laboratory, when she observed a subtle transformation taking place in the first alien's skin. Had she not been paying close scientific attention, she would never have noticed, but the alien's skin began to turn subtly more lemon in color. Commander Durbin took a magnifying glass out of the container of instruments and looked even closer. With the aid of the glass, she could make out a thin coating of transparent tiny scales. The coloring arose from a layer of swirling pigmentation just beneath the surface— not unlike human capillaries, only more homogeneous and with a freer flow. Again, she prepared to move on to examine the other male, and again, the first male's skin changed, this time closer to a leafy green color.

"Do you think he is reacting to our presence?" Commander Durbin asked.

"Perhaps," answered Captain Stokes as he examined the female of the trio. "But this one's skin is acting the same. Changing like a chameleon. We cannot detect the color variation from a distance. Hard to say what is happening."

Commander Durbin moved onto the other male and examined the skin. "I don't believe that they arose out of a laboratory, or at least not out of a single mold." She handed the magnifying glass to Captain Stokes. "The pattern of their fine hairs is not identical."

The captain examined the female's skin in different parts of her body. It continued to fluctuate between yellow and green. "Do you think they are aware of our presence?" he asked.

"I don't believe they have registered our visual images, yet. Although . . . we do not know the sensitivity of their receptiveness. We see that they react slowly, but they *may already have begun to perceive the light waves. The sound of our voices, too, must have impinged upon their hearing apparatuses; it seems to travel through this atmosphere at about the same rate it travels through Earth's."*

The captain nodded in agreement, but added, "They may have received our sound, but I'm not so sure that it has registered in the hearing centers of their brains, wherever those may be."

"Probably in their heads. Their organs of senses, as we know them, are most likely located close to their organs of perception, and they have noses or proboscises, mouths, and eyes."

Captain Stokes examined the alien's eyes. Two oval projections close together and directly above the proboscis, and with a transparent covering similar to a human conjunctiva. On closer inspection under the magnifying glass, these conjunctivae seemed to be made of scales that were even finer than were those over the rest of its body. Under this superficial layer were twenty-three small pupils—oval, slanting in various directions, and deep green in color. The captain compared the female's two eyes, one with the other, and then went on to examine the eyes of the two males. They were all the same with twenty-three pupils slanting in twenty-three matching directions. He then turned to the commander and said, "They have similar organs of perception to ours, but where are their equivalents of ears? They must surely have an organ to hear their own sounds."

Commander Durbin smiled as she pointed to the one male's neck, just below and behind the orifice that served as its mouth. "Look carefully at these indentations," she said. "They look like remnants of clefts, but they're surrounded by tiny megaphone-like protrusions, which lead me to believe that they are structured for capturing sound. Possibly ears in evolution, which argues against the theory of their origination in a laboratory. Left to evolve, these ears will collect sound much more efficiently than any other life form we have encountered. Their eyes, too, seem more efficient than ours. They probably already perceive a dimension beyond our comprehension, with a better interpretation of up or down or any angle in between."

"So what now, Commander?" Captain Stokes asked. "I have an irresistible urge to touch one of them."

"That's probably a bad idea, Captain, too much of an intrusion into their world. We have already sent sensory signals that will tell them of our presence on their planet. Perhaps we should remain here long enough to witness their reaction when they actually see us. That could be helpful; if their logic is in any way similar to ours, they'll put two and two together and better believe and understand our other modes of communication."

The commander and the captain stood directly in front of the trio of aliens.

"How long do you think it will take to get a reaction?" the captain asked.

"If we go with the theory that one of their days is equivalent to five of our years—based on the time it takes this planet to rotate around its axis—then they should react approximately 1,800 times slower than we do, which means that our half-hour will be the equivalent of a second to them. I think we should see something within the hour."

They waited and they watched, and the commander's estimation proved accurate, for after twenty-five minutes, the female responded: her eyes began to bulge further and further from her head, until they were supported by protruding stalks that gave them added mobility. The eyes then focused on the two intruders—a strange and probably frightening sight in her world of perfect order, if that is what the alien was capable of registering. And Commander Durbin and Captain Stokes soon came to believe that the alien's horror was far deeper than their meager human sensitivities would allow them to imagine. For over a mere five minutes—a fraction of a second in the alien's time— the gills at the sides of her neck ripped wide, lime green gas began to extrude into the air, and, with a series of soft popping sounds, reminiscent of a semi-automatic weapon, she began to deflate like a party balloon.

Captain Stokes stepped forward intuitively to do whatever he could to help the poor creature. But the wiser commander raised a restraining arm to hold him back. The damage was done, and even if they could rescue her, it would be a gross violation of their code of principles. They were the strangers, aliens in a world not their own, and they had no right to interfere more than they already had.

With a pitiful crackle and hiss, the creature uttered her last sound, and her covering scales lay motionless on the ground. But the crumbling did not cease, for her skin and her robe continued to disintegrate into a small pile of dust, and in the planet's gentle breeze, the remnants of the alien scattered gently into the air, until nothing of her remained.

Listening intently to the story, Len allowed his mind to run two distinct but parallel courses: while he could not completely forget his personal dilemma, he nevertheless managed to lend his support to the heroes of the radio adventure. And as the story began to unfold, he imagined that there was a hidden message meant especially for him: whereas the space explorers first saw the newfound planet as flawless, so had he seen his Gertrude in a similar light. Then in the story arose a problem, just as a problem had that very day arisen for him, and Len dreamed up a far greater connection than reasonably possible, even with the most favorable alignment of the stars.

Absorbed in the adventure, Len began to hope for a happy and simple ending, because if only Commander Durbin could solve her problem and make it go away, so Len imagined would his problem, too, find its own solution and go away. Len did not stop to consider that his personal preference for an amicable outcome at home lay largely in his own hands. The problem of mistrust had shown its ugly head, and he did not know how to make it disappear.

As Commander Durbin and Captain Stokes examined the aliens, Len again saw a parallel with his life. For when he watched his wife on their patio with the cigarette dangling from her mouth, she indeed took on an unexpected appearance, and in his mind, the connection strengthened.

Len kept telling himself that the game he was playing was all superstition; he knew quite clearly that it was ridiculous, yet he could not resist the pursuit. Then, as the female alien saw the two Earthlings, and her eyes began to change, Len recalled how Gertrude's eyes had changed as they welled with tears.

And the strongest connection of all, the alien's dependence upon a substance of smoke must surely have had some link to Gertrude's addiction to smoking.

Every now and then, as Len listened, he actually believed that the association had some basis. But Len was intelligent and sane, and he kept telling himself that he was merely exercising a common and creative facet of a normal human imagination. Still, he wanted that favorable finale. He wanted an omen to lean on and to offer him support. And when the alien came to a horrifying end, Len's heart sank as he foresaw ongoing strife in his relationship with Gertrude.

During the radio soft drink and soap commercials, Len thought about the central theme, the aliens' slow pace. At first, he could see no link to his life, but as he forced the issue, he began to imagine a connection with his slow realization that Gertrude may not have been all that he believed.

Still, this was all fictitious entertainment, which could have no relevance to the real world, so the end of the story was meaningless; it was time for Len go home and to face his personal life as the rational man he was.

The commercials ended and the conclusion of the play began.

Following the alien's drastic reaction to the human presence, the explorers felt compelled to leave the planet.

Back on Earth, Commander Durbin in her comfortable suite dictated a final log entry:

While the aliens may initially have looked and behaved like human beings, in reality they represent a curious life form, probably the most unusual I have encountered. Because of their unique makeup, we remain uncertain about their physiology and their mode of reproduction. We did discover, however, that they have a gaseous circulation, which apparently diffuses throughout their tissues and makes up an estimated ninety-five percent of their total body volume, not dissimilar to the role of water in humans and other creatures on Earth. We have also established that they live in a sophisticated and harmonious civilization that we cannot afford to ignore.

Therefore, although meaningful contact may only be feasible over a protracted period (probably thousands of years), we have decided to go forward with our project of monitoring the planet and its inhabitants. Captain Stokes has submitted a proposal that outlines a program of intermittent, unobtrusive visits, and our engineers are preparing to construct a space station for the express purpose of continuous observation.

With improved technologies, with better understanding of life forms in the galaxies, and with information gained from the new planet under observation—particularly a better understanding of their language—we are confident that our progeny will eventually devise a strategy for safe contact.

Commander Yadira Durbin.

With Commander Durbin's log turning the finale completely around and into a new message of optimism, Len Darshan found himself again assigning a mystical significance to the content of the story and grasping at an invisible ray of hope.

It was late, not too late for a hospital-based doctor to be coming home after work, but definitely too late for Len to be coming home after the tense moment with Gertrude that morning.

He thought to himself, *What should I say as I see her? Strange, I'm not nearly as annoyed as I thought I would be, nor as disappointed as I was this morning. She knows she let me down. She probably feels that she let herself down, too. At least, I think she must feel that she let herself down. Yet, if she were disappointed in herself, then why would she do what she is doing? She knows as well as anyone the damage of smoking. And she's a mother of a young child. She's probably feeling terrible right now. Maybe I should just do my best to make her feel better and sort out our differences later. Yes, that's probably the best way to handle it.*

But wait a minute . . . perhaps I should find out what's on her mind. Yes, that's probably an even better idea; I'll first listen to what she wants to tell me about this morning.

Len did not stop to consider that, for the first time, he was actually uncertain about how to handle his conversation with Gertrude. Previously, all he ever wanted was to be kind to her or to impress her, and now he was contemplating attitudes—both hers and his own.

He arrived at the front door, inserted his key into the lock, and went suddenly frail. All he now wanted was to get the tension out the way and go to bed. He took a deep breath and reached out for the knob, but before he could touch it, the door opened from the inside and there before him stood Gertrude.

CHAPTER SIX

2005

After another busy morning, this time with a greater than usual emphasis on psychological illnesses, Dr. Len Darshan went to his office to open the mail and take a midday break. Pharmaceutical representatives had not brought lunch, so he took a can of diet soda from the tiny refrigerator under his desk and a bag of potato chips from the bottom drawer of his credenza. He popped the lid off the drink, leaned back, took a sip, and closed his eyes. But he could not relax; his mind was still racing. *Is it possible that Gertrude has actually cheated on me? Until yesterday, the thought would never have crossed my mind. Does that mean I'm like all the other husbands—the last to know?*

He opened the bag of chips. *No, not Gertrude, the idea is ludicrous.*

He put two chips in his mouth and his hand back into the bag. *If I really want to get to the bottom of this nagging feeling, I had better do something about it.*

Although Len was alone, he shook his head in denial. Another sip and another mouthful of chips, and he grimaced in an effort to recall the name of a patient who had come in with a fractured hand about a week ago. *Little fellow. Persistent nasal allergies. Private detective. What was his name?*

Len pressed the *page* button on his phone and announced through the overhead, "Mary, please call Dr. Darshan's office."

A moment later, her voice sounded in his speakerphone. "Yes, sir."

"Mary, do you remember that man who came in early last week with a broken hand?"

"Last week? Fractured hand?"

"Yes. Or maybe the week before."

"Do you mean Nelson Underwood, the private dick?"

Len could hear Mary sniggering and could not help breaking into a smile himself. "If you are not too busy, would you bring his chart to my office?" Len asked.

Len remembered a conversation that he once had with Nelson Underwood, the slimy fellow, always dressed in black. Len had originally thought that detective work must have been exciting, like that seen in the television series *Columbo* and in other criminal investigations, fictitious and real. But Mr. Underwood soon put Len's mistaken impression to rest when he told him that over ninety percent of his clients were suspicious spouses and that most of his working hours were spent in the seat of his parked car watching and waiting for the suspect to meet with someone of the opposite sex.

"How many of the distrusting spouses are right?" Len had asked the private detective out of pure curiosity.

"Sometimes, the client pulls me off the case before I find the evidence," Mr. Underwood had replied. "Otherwise, most of the suspects are cheating. When a client has reason to suspect a husband or wife is unfaithful, usually there is a third person on the side."

As Mary came in with the chart, Len was murmuring to himself, "Usually there is a third person on the side."

"Thanks, Mary." Len took the chart from her, dropped it on top of the unopened mail on the desk, and stared at it.

"Are you feeling okay?" she asked sympathetically.

"I'm fine, thanks. Why?"

She shrugged her shoulders. "You seem a little preoccupied. That's all."

Len smiled appreciatively at Mary.

She turned to leave the room and close the door, as she had found it.

Len continued to stare at the chart on the desk. He thought again about Nelson Underwood, with his glistening buzz cut and ponytail, and instead of opening the chart, spun his chair to face his computer. He shuffled the mouse to illuminate the desktop on screen and clicked on the icon for the Internet.

Upon typing *Private Detective* in the line *Search the Web,* Len was not surprised at the large number of hits: advertisements for investigating fraud, missing persons, personal histories, and of course, matrimonial concerns.

Len searched for an individual detective or a private detective agency in Jacobsburg. When he found one, he began picturing himself in an interview with someone about as sleazy as Nelson Underwood, or perhaps someone who he knew, maybe another patient, or, worse still, someone who knew both Gertrude and him. This would not do, so he continued his search, this time for any information that might help individuals conduct their own investigation.

He came across an Internet address that advertised a number of electronic spying devices: hidden cameras, telephone bugs, and e-mail monitoring software. Len saved the page in his *favorites* column and continued his search. He found an interesting checklist for someone suspicious of infidelity: records of outgoing and incoming telephone numbers, credit card bills, and physical evidence of intimacy, like the one that left Len smiling—footprints on the ceiling of the car.

Then, Len found a product that promised better results than did any other, including the hiring of a private detective. It was easy to use and inexpensive, and the Internet commercial promised a discrete method of sale. The kit went by the name *A-fair-catch* and comprised two simple chemicals for detecting the presence of dried semen. With stirring phrases like *revolutionary product* and *utterly miraculous*, Len began to feel that this was what he needed, but it was not until reading the familiar words, *Don't be the last to know,* that he was completely sold.

As Len clicked the arrow on the final icon to make the purchase, he felt dirty. How could he retrieve his wife's underwear from the washing basket and then test it for another man's semen? He never dreamed his marriage would come to this. Still, he had to uncover the truth, even if this truth was nothing but a vague suspicion based on Gertrude's profile in a changing culture.

Not even Len fully realized how the smoking incident served to disrupt his absolute trust for Gertrude. He never did stop to seriously consider why she had returned to the habit of smoking or whether she, in fact, had quit at all. Or, most curious of all, her reasons for doing it behind his back.

Had he asked, and had she answered him truthfully, he would have heard that she knew how her smoking would disappoint him and how she did not want to lose him. Gertrude also knew Len would not accept the notion that she could not break the habit. Logic dictated that no one should smoke, and Len was incapable of siding against logic, especially since the medical evidence had never faltered. In all his years as a doctor, not once did he come across a single word in the literature that praised the calming effect of smoking.

Gertrude's smoking alone was not sufficient to disrupt their love. It would have taken a disagreement or incident far more profound. Still, the secretive smoking did enter into their marriage, and it did play a crucial role that neither of them may fully have grasped.

***

1978

Gertrude opened the door to their one-bedroom apartment. Her finger on her lips and her gaze at Len's feet planted on the welcome mat, she whispered, "Shh, Janet has just fallen asleep."

Len noticed her red eyes and brave front, and his heart melted. *So she smokes; what of it? She's still my wife and the mother of my child. I'll speak to her again about her habit, but not now. Later, when I'm rested and feel up to it.*

He stepped inside the door, kissed her gently on the forehead, and felt relieved that she, too, did not want a confrontation.

"Wash up and I'll warm the dinner: chicken fried steak." Gertrude had an endless variety of creative recipes, most of which she could whip up in a jiffy and each with a flavorful taste of its own.

"Thanks." Len tiptoed into the bedroom to peep into his little daughter's crib before taking off his jacket and then going to the bathroom. Back to the entrance-come-dining-room, where he helped himself to a glass of lemonade and then sat down to wait.

Through a quieter than usual dinner, during which both thought about the smoking issue, they spoke rather of mundane matters such as Len's workday, Gertrude's housekeeping and cooking, and Janet's milestones.

By the time the dishes were washed and the dining room tidied, it was nearly 10:30, and Len decided to relax a short while on the couch in front of the television. Gertrude came to join him, but they were both tired, so they showered and went to bed.

In the dark of the night, Len placed his hand on her breast and leaned over to kiss her. She, too, was glad that they had not quarreled, so she held him tightly, then rolled on top of him, and they made gentle love.

Once again, neither Gertrude nor Len could foresee the impact that that particular day and that particular act of lovemaking were having upon their lives.

Len with his rush of testosterone was as passionate as ever. He was able to enjoy the physical contact with a beautiful woman who wanted to give herself to him. In the back of his mind, however, remained the nagging disappointment, the impression that she had betrayed his ideals and his trust.

Whereas Len's passion did not wane, his love for the first time wavered, and he did not recognize it happening.

Gertrude, on the other hand, saw more clearly the feature of her husband that she had always known. Len the man, prepared to go out to work hard every day and to come home to her every night, because he loved her and because he loved their child. Despite her deceitfulness, he would return to her. Yet, while she loved him for who he was, she could not help but remember the very trait that she noticed the first time they met. She had seen him as boring and naive, as the unimpressive nerd that she had barely noticed that night in the Seaview Ritz.

It was not Gertrude's love; rather, it was her passion, which for the first time faltered.

They did eventually touch on Gertrude's smoking habit. She said she would try again to quit, but if she could not, she would not do it in front of him. She knew that he did not like it.

He continued to bombard her with medical facts and figures, information she already understood and accepted but which made little difference to her attitude. Unlike Len, Gertrude did not wear blinders; she recognized that human beings are destined to fall ill and die, and she was prepared to risk her longevity and health for the pleasures of today. Besides, she could see the great strides in medical progress, and she felt confident that the PhDs would one day come up with cures for all the ills of evil tobacco.

From the day it opened its doors, the new *Yarwell General Hospital* was busy and successful. The administrators did all they could to welcome patients and to make working conditions as pleasant as possible for the medical staff.

In return, the doctors felt an immediate allegiance and a desire to promote the hospital's reputation for quality care.

At the initial staff meeting, attended by twenty-nine physicians —all of whom had applied for clinical privileges—a formal medical staff was born.

Mr. Frederick Vansant, the bubbly thirty-two year old administrator of Yarwell General Hospital, opened the meeting with a slide show of the building while still under construction and a few upbeat remarks. He then went directly to legal requirements for the running of a hospital and, in particular, the role of the physicians in governing themselves. With a promise to supply all necessary secretarial and legal support, Mr. Vansant asked the physicians to select their new chief of staff.

There were grins and playful pointing, but no nominations.

Mr. Vansant smiled along with the crowd, gaining their acceptance and hoping to gain their future support. "Okay," he said, holding up his hands as though surrendering to the situation. "We all know that this is one of those thankless jobs with neither salary nor benefits, but we also know how important it is for all of us. For our continued success, we must set our structure in order. Who among you has served on the board of other hospitals? We could use your expertise. Even if you don't want to stand for chief of staff, still you could serve in one of the other positions. Can I see from a show of hands how many of you have administrative experience?"

Five hands went quickly up and down, but still no one volunteered for the job, nor did anyone nominate someone else. Until, Terry in the front row stood up and spoke. "Dr. Terrance Stein."

Mr. Vansant gave him the floor.

"Thank you, Mr. Vansant." Terry turned around to face his colleagues. "We all want Yarwell General Hospital to be successful, so we all have to do our bit. Today, the hospital is young with a bright future. Therefore, I feel it is fitting that we nominate a young and vibrant doctor with a bright future as chief of staff. I nominate my associate and friend, Dr. Len Darshan."

Len smiled wryly at Terry and then turned his gaze to the floral green carpet under his own feet.

"Thank you, Dr. Stein. Do you accept the nomination, Dr. Darshan?" Mr. Vansant asked.

Still in his seat, Len nodded.

"I move we close the floor to nominations," came a woman's voice from the back row.

"Second," the person sitting next to her.

"All in favor?" Mr. Vansant asked.

Every hand went up.

"Congratulations, Dr. Darshan."

Together with the applause, Mr. Vansant was on his way asking for nominations for the next position, chief of the department of surgery.

To Len's surprise, the chief of staff position carried more prestige than he had expected. All hospital employees recognized him and greeted him with a smile, and he enjoyed the newfound esteem. The position also occupied a great deal of his time, which kept him away from home. He would have to attend an average of one meeting a week, and they all took place at night. The meetings, however, were not stressful; they were sociable and relaxed with meals and liquor laid on. Len also had to interview each new physician applying for staff privileges, and because the physicians were busy during the day, Len would arrange to meet with them after office hours.

Len remembered clearly Mr. Vansant's message, that the office of chief of staff carried no salary. But the administrator was wrong about the benefits; the nursing staff were willing to offer Len special treatment. In Yarwell General, a private hospital, the hospital staff did their utmost to deliver excellent and courteous service to all patients and all physicians. Yet, Dr. Darshan was the chief of the medical staff, so they viewed him as the person at the top of the professional hierarchy and gave him that extra service that they deemed he deserved. From Maureen Redman, the administrative head of nursing, all the way down to the junior nurse on the late night shift, they all wanted to please the young and unassuming Dr. Darshan. And this was a benefit for both Len and for his patients. For whenever Len asked for anything, someone would scramble to get it for him, and whenever his patients needed help, they only had to ring that service bell once and an aide would be at the bedside.

Most of Len's patients were admitted to the first floor unit, general internal medicine, and he soon knew all the nurses who rotated through the seven a.m. to three p.m. shift. Their willingness to help left Len wondering at the difference between the nursing staff at The Jacobsburg University Hospital and the nurses here at Yarwell General. At Yarwell General, the day staff knew Len's likes, quirks, protocols, and preferred consultants. When one of his patients had a setback, the senior nurse on duty, or sometimes even the junior nurse attending the patient, knew precisely what Len would want done. While they had to put through the obligatory call to inform him of the problem, they were prepared to set the treatment in motion even before he gave the order. Sometimes, Len felt as though his hospital practice was on autopilot, moving along in the correct gear and at a comfortable pace. Provided the patient's medical problem was straightforward, Len could almost detect a friendly smile on the nurse's face at the other end of the phone line; when the setback was graver, he could sense her seriousness.

With all the added help, Len's reputation and practice thrived. This meant long hours at the office in addition to the duties at night, and although Len was energetic, the work began to take its toll.

On a night toward the end of his single-year term as chief of staff, the monthly therapeutics meeting had ended later than usual, and Len went to the internal medicine floor to look in on a patient.

In the compact nurses' station, the charts were kept in a rack against the back wall. The three night duty nurses were tidying the rooms, taking vital signs, giving prescribed sleeping medications, and tucking the patients in for what everyone hoped would be a peaceful sleep. Sitting at the desk was the charge nurse Maude Kimble, a petite woman in her late thirties, and speaking to Maude was Martha Saenz, the physical therapist.

"Evening, ladies." Len waved casually while searching the chart rack. "You're here late tonight, Martha. Why don't you let your patients get some sleep?"

"Some doctor wanted me to assess a patient, so here I am."

Len looked at his watch. "At 10:30?" he asked. "Couldn't it wait until the morning? Who called you in?"

"Dr. Stein," she remarked while nonchalantly returning her attention to the chart on the desk.

Len grimaced. "Oh my!"

Maude, the charge nurse, turned around to see how Len was reacting to the report about his friend.

Len found his patient's chart and walked towards the two women. "What was the problem?" he asked. "That doesn't sound

165

like Dr. Stein; he wouldn't call for a physical therapy consult in the middle of the night."

Martha laughed at Len's reaction to her harmless little prank. "I'm teasing," she said. "Dr. Stein did ask me to see the patient earlier this evening, but I was in the department, working with our new exercise equipment, and then I had to catch up with some reports . . . I try not to fall behind."

Len smiled at Martha's hoax and again looked at his watch. "You should go home, Martha," he said kindly. "You've had a long day. I saw you earlier, when I was doing my morning rounds."

"Then you must have a long day, too, Dr. Darshan."

Len looked more closely at Martha. He could appreciate her feisty confidence, and he could appreciate her good looks, too. She had smooth olive skin, glossy red lips, and fashionably teased black hair. Although she wore hospital scrubs, Len could not resist picturing her in flaring white skirts and with a carnation between her shiny white teeth, dancing a fiery flamenco, his childhood fantasy of a beautiful woman.

Len went to see his patient, an elderly woman in heart failure and with uncontrolled diabetes, to ensure that the treatment was going according to plan.

When he returned to the central station fifteen minutes later, it was time for the late night shift to take over, so six nurses were crowded around the main work desk, discussing the patients and changes in treatment plans. Martha, too, was still there, but she was at a smaller desk at the opposite side of the station next to the chart rack, completing reports.

Ready to make his own chart entry, Len flopped into the chair next to Martha. He raised his elbows, stretching the fatigue out of his shoulders, and then twisted his neck first to the left and then to the right, where Martha sat.

She shook her head. "You definitely look more exhausted than I feel." She stood, walked behind him, said, "Here, let me help you," and placed her hands on his tired shoulders.

Len could not resist, nor did he want to resist. *She's a professional therapist*, he told himself. *She's only going to help press the tension out of my aching muscles.*

Martha pulled down the top of Len's lab coat, locking his shoulders and arms, and then began to massage his upper neck, deeply and with hesitating pressure on the most taut and tender parts. Her experienced hands knew precisely where he hurt and how to soothe the pain gently away. Len could not help letting his head fall forward with a gentle groan. Then, he remembered the nursing staff, busy with their shift change. What would they think? But Martha took care of that concern, too. She casually turned around to Maud, said, "Here, I'm finished," and briefly interrupted her therapy to pass three charts across the narrow station. Her willingness to speak to the nurses in the middle of massaging Len's back and neck served to relegate the sensuous touching down to mere clinical contact.

She gently pummeled his shoulders and upper arms and then returned her fingertips to his spine, easing the tension and sending luxurious thrills to his neck and lower back. She patiently soothed his aching muscles, and he did not want her to stop. Eventually, however, after seven to eight idyllic minutes, he felt he should say something, lest the nurses begin to stare and wonder.

"Thank you. That was exactly what I needed." *I wonder whether she knows the magic in her hands.* He turned to face her, still standing behind his chair. She was smiling down at him, knowing exactly how much he had enjoyed her touch. And he knew that she knew. Not only could her hands deliver pleasure but they could also sense the pleasure they were delivering.

He wondered, *is she teasing me?* But her smile turned sober and she stared directly into his eyes, letting him know in no uncertain terms that she had even greater pleasures to offer.

Len felt uneasy. Before this night, he had not thought about Martha. He might have turned to sneak a look at her shapely figure as they passed in the corridors, but he had not seriously desired her. He was confused. Somewhere in the back of his mind, he knew that he was a handsome man with a modicum of esteem in the small world of Yarwell General Hospital, and that women must have found him attractive or even sexy. Yet, no one had made their feelings as clear as had Martha. Or had they? Perhaps they had, and he failed to notice. What was different tonight? Tonight, he did notice, and he relished the titillation. And all at once, Len realized the pleasures that he had sacrificed. Throughout his years as a medical student and as a resident, when his peers had been playing the field, he had remained true to his Gertrude. It was not her fault, but had he never met her, who knows what delights might have found their way into his stoic life?

But that was my choice, he told himself, *and I have had a better life than other men who have passed through any number of frivolous relationships - men like my old classmates Allan and Daniel, who would make a pass at whichever woman they found even the least bit attractive.*

Is that the truth, asked a deeper inner voice, *or are you kidding yourself? Did you just slip into the easy relationship with Gertrude because that was what you wanted, or were you too lazy or perhaps too afraid to face the world and sew your wild oats as a man with your looks and intellect should have done? Too late now! You'll never know any other women as stimulating and mysterious as Martha. But that was your choice, and you knew what you were choosing, so you should be satisfied.*

Len wanted to invite Martha for a late night coffee. He thought about it, and immediately felt ashamed of his thought. *Gertrude would never know . . . but I would, and I have to live with myself. I cannot do that to her. And yet, it would only be a harmless cup of coffee. I know Martha wants me to invite her. I could make it innocent, like a token of appreciation for the massage.*

He decided to do it, to take her to his favorite bistro across the road from the Jacobsburg University Hospital. As he stood from his chair, he meant to ask her . . . he even opened his mouth to speak . . . but he could not quite bring himself to throw out the invitation. Instead, he glanced at his watch and said, "It's getting late, isn't it?" Even as he spoke, he felt infantile. He sensed Martha was expecting that invitation, but he also knew she did not need it. She would merely turn her adventurous attention away from him and focus on someone else, someone who might be more interested.

While saying goodnight to the nursing staff, Len felt embarrassing pangs of inadequacy as he tried to guess what exactly Martha thought of him.

Over the following weeks, Len found himself thinking of Martha at all times of the day and night. While walking from his office to the main building of the hospital, he would hope to see her. In the corridors, he would actively search for her. At the nurses' station, he would casually ask for her, and while writing orders, he would make an added effort to consult her.

Then, while busy in the office, at a time when Len least expected to hear from her, she called.

"Dr. Darshan," she said. "About Mr. Perry, the patient with the neck injury. I think he's malingering."

Normally, Len would have been all business. He would have remembered the details of Mr. Perry's presentation and he would have had something constructive to offer, but taken aback by both the nature of the accusation and the sound of her voice, he asked, "Which patient is that?"

"Mr. Perry, the Workman's Compensation case."

"Oh yes. What makes you think he's malingering?"

"His strength and his range of motion are not consistent with an injury. They vary excessively during any single examination. He is also easily distracted from his pain."

Len desperately wanted to say something at a personal level, but Martha had called about a serious matter, and he had to address the problem at hand. "Has Mr. Perry responded to treatment?" he asked.

"I thought he was responding, but then it was like hitting a brick wall. It is possible that he was hurting when I first saw him. At that time, he was doing quite well. Over the last three treatments, however, he has not improved at all. And it seems like he is not trying to get better."

Without thinking it through, Len blurted, "If you massaged his neck the way you did mine the other night, by now he would have been cured." As the words left his mouth, Len wished he could jump into the phone and take them back, but it was too late, and all he could do was laugh, pretending it was an attempt at humor. After all, a bad joke was preferable to an unwelcome flirtation.

There was silence on the other side of the line, and Len considered apologizing for his forwardness, but then Martha said softly, "I'm glad you liked it."

"Oh yes, I did." His confidence fully restored, he knew he should return to the matter of the patient. "Tell you what: let Mr.

Perry make an appointment to see me, and I'll try to get to the bottom of this matter."

The following Saturday night was the anniversary of the inauguration of Yarwell General Hospital's medical board, and Mr. Frederick Vansant, the administrator, decided to throw the first of what he hoped would turn into an annual celebration to thank the outgoing officers for their service. The ball was held in the main hall of the Downtown Carlton Hotel.

Len bought a navy suit, a new white shirt, and a maroon and navy tie for the occasion. Naked from the waist up, he shaved in the magnifying mirror and combed his hair, neatly parted on the left, until he could not find a single strand out of place. He was certain that he would receive a special mention, maybe even be called up onto the podium to say a few words about the year gone by, and he wanted to look his best. Taking a final look at his reflection, he tried jutting his jaw to conceal the smallness of his chin, but he knew this technique was futile, so he turned his attention to his youthful clear skin and commanding gray eyes, and he felt quite proud of himself and his standing in the community. He pictured himself walking into the Carlton Hotel, Gertrude on his arm, and smiling at any number of people who would want to greet him and gain a moment or two of his valuable attention.

Strapping his watch to his wrist, he glanced at the time. "Gertrude," he called through the open bathroom door and into the corridor. "Are you nearly ready to go?"

When she did not reply, Len went to the bedroom where he found her sprawled on the duvet, her hose halfway up her legs and

172

the back of her arm draped protectively against her forehead. "What's the matter, sweetheart?" He rushed to kneel on the bed by her side.

"I'm not feeling too well."

"Do you hurt anywhere?" he asked, touching the backs of his fingers to her cheek.

"My whole body is aching. I've actually had mild muscle pains all day. I thought it was from playing with Janet in the park yesterday, and it would get better, but I'm feeling worse now."

"You're burning with fever," he said, and then slid on his knees back off the bed and went to the closet to fetch his little medical black bag.

Gertrude had a temperature of 102.4, enlarged glands in her neck, and white follicles on her tonsils. "You have tonsillitis, probably a streptococcal infection," he told her.

"I'm sorry," she said. "I know how important this party is for you, but I can't go."

"That's okay, sweetheart," he said sympathetically. "I'll call Terry and tell him to send my apologies."

Gertrude shot herself up onto the backs of her elbows. "No, Len. You must go without me. There's no point in your staying home."

"Will you be all right?"

She forced a smile and said, "Of course." But she did not give him the kiss on the cheek to go with the gesture. She was too weary to stand, and she believed she might pass the infection on to him.

"I have a few penicillin tablets," Len said. "Start with these and I'll pick up some more at the office tonight or tomorrow."

The doorbell rang.

"That's the baby sitter," Gertrude said. "You'd better pay her and tell her thanks, but we won't be needing her tonight."

Len quickly slipped on his new shirt, went to the front door, and then came back to finish dressing.

"Help me make up the couch in the den," Gertrude asked. "I don't want to make Janet or you sick."

When Len arrived fashionably late, he was not disappointed by the reception. Senior staff members and a number of doctors complimented him on his appearance or some other trivial matter, and many people did stop to ask him a question or two about the hospital. Terry had kept two seats for Len and Gertrude, and because Len arrived alone, one of the eight places at the table remained untaken.

While the band played background music and the waiters brought on an assortment of hors d'oeuvres, Mr. Frederick Vansant got up onto the stage to say a few words:

"Good evening, everyone. As the administration promised, this function is for you. It is our way of showing our appreciation for those men and women who worked so hard over the past year to make Yarwell General the success that it is. Without our medical staff, who are a force to be reckoned with anywhere in the whole wide world, we could never be what we are. Because this evening is for pleasure, and not for business, we have decided to cut the speeches down to the minimum: one . . . mine. Next week, at the Annual General Meeting, we will have plenty of time for speeches.

"I look forward to meeting your spouses and partners who are here tonight to help us celebrate, and I invite everyone to relax, have a good time, enjoy the food and drink, and dance to the music of *Splendid Seven*, the best band in all of Jacobsburg."

During Mr. Vansant's words of welcome, Martha Saenz made her appearance at the entrance to the hall. She was alone and waiting politely at the door, and everyone who did not have their eyes trained on the stage could not help but notice her. She had on a frilly white dress, which looked magnificent against her tanned skin and dark hair falling loosely around her shoulders.

Len wanted to invite her to sit at the open chair at his table. Most seats in the hall were already taken, and it would have been the polite and right thing to do. Still, he was also without a partner

175

and felt that his invitation would draw unnecessary attention, so he nudged Terry and suggested he ask Martha to join them.

Terry was sitting to Len's left, and Dr. Jewel Servance, the elderly hospital pathologist, to his right, and when Martha came to the table, Dr. Servance stood, offered his seat to Martha, and took the open seat on the other side of his wife, as though that was the natural thing to do.

"I just couldn't get out my apartment." Martha offered an unconvincing and unnecessary excuse for arriving late.

Melinda Stein said hello to Martha, and then Martha introduced herself to the other spouses who she had not yet met.

The band began to play, people began to talk, and Terry, wanting Martha to feel welcome, spoke with her. "How is the new therapeutic equipment working out?" he casually asked.

Len took a few bites of his appetizer and made small conversation with Mrs. Servance, a skinny woman with wrinkled skin who appeared old enough to be Dr. Servance's mother rather than his wife.

The waiters began to clear the tables of the hors d'oeuvre plates, the band livened the pace, and Terry and Melinda were first to peel off from the table and onto the dance floor. Dr. Servance and his elderly wife were next to leave their seats, which left Len, Martha, and opposite them, Maud Kimble, together with Maud's husband, Mel, a handsome young man with thick glasses who played the guitar in an amateur band and who was interested in speaking to the musicians in Splendid Seven. He asked Maud to dance, and immediately led her up to the edge of the stage where he could watch the fingers of the lead guitarist, and perhaps gain a few pointers.

Martha was looking down at the napkin on her lap. Her broad smile told Len that, although the situation might be embarrassing, she was pleasantly surprised to be alone with him.

"You look terrific, Martha," he said, savoring the sound of her name. "That dress really suits you."

"Thank you. You look nice too . . . in clothes."

"What!"

She giggled and placed a friendly hand on his arm. "You know what I mean, in a suit instead of a white lab coat."

He could not understand why he was getting such pleasure from her touch. "Would you like a drink?" he asked.

"I'd like to dance."

He stood to pull back her chair, and she turned to him and whispered, "Thank you, Len," as though she had always called him by his first name.

Len had become indifferent to dancing. It was merely a way to pass the evening in the company of friends. With Martha, however, the occasional closer frontal contact and the holding—formal as it had to be—lent sensuousness that launched shivers through his whole body. He wanted to dance with her, share the meal with her, and speak with her throughout the night. Yet, each moment had to be concealed in an aura of calm, for he could not allow anyone else at in the room to know what lay in his heart. And he knew that Martha felt about the same as he did. Every now and then, she would squeeze his hand and smile directly into his eyes. She would not conceal her pleasure as they brushed up close. Rather, she would offer a soft groan to tell him how much she enjoyed it.

At exactly 10:30, Len led Martha to a quiet corner of the dance floor, to the side of the band, and whispered, "Would you like to go somewhere else for a quiet drink?" He had no problem asking her. Over the past weeks, he had practiced the words and their timing at least a couple of dozen times in his mind. Only, he did not know how easily they would slide off his tongue, for until this night, he had the fear that she might refuse. Now, her gestures let him know that she would go with him wherever he wanted to go. All he had to do was ask.

Back at the table, Len sipped half a cup of cappuccino and then glanced at his watch, and said to Terry, "I think it's about time for me to head on home. I must see how Gertrude is doing and look in on the baby."

It was completely uncharacteristic; Len never told an intentional lie. Tonight, however, the components for dishonesty were in place: everyone at the table knew that Dr. Darshan's wife was ill in bed at home. As chief of staff, he had merely done his duty by attending the party, and he was quite right in leaving early.

Len's thoughts were on the adventure that lay ahead, so the excuse flowed freely, without inadvertent focus on the dishonesty.

Ten minutes later, Martha picked up her purse to leave, and again no one thought anything unusual. She had come alone, put in her appearance, and had no reason to remain.

CHAPTER SEVEN

2005

The A-fair-catch website advertised delivery within three days. While waiting for his order to arrive, Len could not approach Gertrude to make love; he did not want to find traces of his own ejaculate in her underwear. What would he do if he detected semen and was uncertain whether it was his or someone else's? Therefore, on the second night of waiting, in the comfort of his den at home and with Juliet purring gently on his lap, he returned to the product's Internet home page to investigate. Indeed, the manufacturers of A-fair-catch did caution the suspecting spouse against this very problem, and they advised abstinence for two days prior to testing. They also offered a second product, which could identify differences between the semen of individual men. The suspecting husband could test his own semen and then compare the results with that found in his wife's underwear. In this way, he could be certain whether the specimen in the panties came from someone else.

At eleven a.m. on Friday, day three after placing the order, Len asked Mary, his medical assistant, whether the mail had arrived.

The three examination rooms and the waiting room were full with patients, and Len was running behind schedule, so Mary stood staring at him for a curious moment before answering, "It gets here at 12:30." She thought about asking him whether she should watch out for a particular letter, but she also realized that it might be none of her business.

That day, Pharmaceutical representatives did bring in a kosher lunch. Usually, Len enjoyed the break, the opportunity to consult with Terry over one or two interesting medical problems, and the bits of up to date pharmaceutical information—even though biased in favor of the company paying for the food. But Len was anxious, eager to find his delivery of A-fair-catch, so he gobbled down the meal, had a few polite words with the representatives, and hurried back to his office. Sometimes Mary would open the envelopes, sometimes not, and Len wanted to get to the mail before she did. He did not know how the parcel would look, and he most certainly did not want anyone to find out what he had ordered. If Mary came across it before he did and understood what it was, she would probably say nothing. Perhaps she would look at him askew, perhaps not, but he would fall in her estimation—a situation he would rather avoid.

The mail was waiting on his desk, a tall pile that had lost its balance and toppled over. Len shuffled through the envelopes, set aside two medical journals and threw five others directly into the trash, and then fell disappointed into his chair. The parcel he was expecting had not arrived. Furthermore, the office would be closed for the weekend, so he had to wait until Monday. He felt strangely comforted, a reprieve for a few days; he was not really looking forward to snooping in the dirty laundry and fishing out Gertrude's panties.

The next morning, as on every Saturday morning, Len put on a dark suit and walked the half-mile to the Synagogue. He entered the vestibule and, instead of going straight ahead into the main sanctuary, he turned left down the corridor, passed the few kindergarten classrooms, and made his way to the library.

The eastern wall of the library had a built-in ornate cabinet that housed two Torah scrolls. Along the other three walls were floor to ceiling shelves, chock-a-block with books of all sizes and colors. In the front of the room, facing the Torah cabinet, were three neat rows of chairs. On weekdays, when attendance was low, the congregation would hold their services here instead of in the large sanctuary. Behind the rows of seats, in the middle of the room, was a large and shiny, oblong, mahogany table. And sitting at the far end of the table, engrossed in an open book, was Len's friend and colleague, Brad. Of all the members of the old clinical student group, only Terry, Brad, and Len remained in Jacobsburg.

"Good Shabbat, Ginger." Len walked up to shake Brad's hand. "Did you sleep here last night?"

"Ahh, good Shabbat, Len." Brad stood and held out his friendly hand. Yet, Len could see something was wrong. Brad was not smiling. Not that Len expected Brad to laugh at the silly "sleep here" remark, but Brad always had a smile for someone he knew.

183

"What's the matter?" Len asked.

Brad's eyes were red, as though he had not slept or, more likely, because he had been crying. His hair was thin and still cropped short, and the gray in the beard and on his head was rapidly supplanting the ginger. "Joseph died," he told Len.

Len shot a shocked hand over his mouth. "When? How?"

"He had a heart attack late yesterday afternoon. They didn't have time to bury him before Shabbat."

"I'm sorry," Len said.

Although Joseph had been practicing dermatology in a small town in the northeast, he and Brad had remained close friends and Len understood Brad's grief.

"The funeral will take place tomorrow," Brad said. "As soon as Shabbat is over I'm going to take a flight out."

Brad did not directly invite Len to join him in going to their friend's burial. He would not want to embarrass him if he could not make it. Yet, he clearly gave Len the opportunity to volunteer to tag along.

Two more men came into the library, followed by Rabbi Moishe Lathan, the son of the late Rabbi Irving Lathan, who had died soon after the birth of Len and Gertrude's daughter, Janet.

184

Rabbi Moishe Lathan was a slight man with thick glasses and a long black beard. He wore a black coat and, upon entering the library, he removed his black hat, revealing a black yarmulke over the crown of his prematurely balding head.

"Good Shabbat, everyone," the Rabbi said, and immediately went to a bookshelf at the back of the room to take out the dozen newly acquired books on ethics, with original text written by ancient sages and the extensive commentary by a prominent contemporary psychiatrist.

The seats around the mahogany table were soon filled, and latecomers had to borrow chairs from the three rows at the front of the library to sit and partake in the early Saturday lively discussion.

At five to nine, Rabbi Lathan shut his book and announced, "Time to move into the main sanctuary." The morning service was due to begin at nine a.m., sharp.

With a bang of his hand upon the lectern at the front of the Synagogue, the Rabbi began reciting the morning blessings.

Len and Brad sat in their regular seats next to each other in the middle of the Synagogue. Len knew clearly that he could not reach Brad's level of piety. While they would sit or stand, praying silently, participating in ceremonial procedure, or paying attention to a sermon, Len would periodically look Brad's way for inspiration. For Brad was always completely absorbed in the service and in prayer: He would often stand with eyes shut and with fingers clawed desperately begging for closer contact with his Creator. On this day, Brad was even more passionate than usual,

185

for as Len watched him out of the corner of an eye, he could see tears streaming down his cheeks, and Len knew that Brad was praying not for himself but for the soul of their friend, Joseph.

Len wanted to emulate Brad, but at this time of confusion, he continued to have difficulty focusing on the prayers. *I wonder whether Ginger has any dark secrets*, he thought. *Or, whether he has any secrets at all, or done things of which he is ashamed? I'm certain he could never entertain the sorts of ideas that I am having about Gertrude. But his wife, Lily, is nothing like Gertrude. Lily is active in the Synagogue and, other than that, seems to be a home person. She doesn't play cards or go out at night by herself. Still, what would Ginger do if he were in my shoes? Somehow, I cannot see him searching the Internet for A-fair-catch. And I cannot see him testing Lily's underwear for traces of another man's semen. He would speak to Lily, ask her directly about anything that was on his mind.* Len laughed to himself. *A fat lot of good that would do; of course, no one cheating would simply admit it, especially to the person being cheated. That's why spouses are the last to know. That's why we have private detectives and products like A-fair-catch. The question is not what would Ginger do? The question is what will I do if my suspicions prove true, and Gertrude is actually cheating?*

Len did manage to concentrate on the Rabbi's sermon and on most of the prayers too, and in-between he still had leeway to ask himself a compelling question, which he could not resist attempting to answer: *How will I tell Gertrude that I know? Of course, she'll deny any accusation that I may throw at her. She may turn indignant, probably start shouting. Then I'll do the test again in front of her eyes to prove that I really know the truth. But what if she still denies it . . . as she may.* Len shook his head. *No, she'll know that I know, and she'll have to give in. She may claim that the semen is mine.* Len smiled to himself. *That's why the makers of A-fair-catch have that other product to tell whom the semen came from. Maybe I should buy some before I start testing.* He thought about going back to the Internet site to put in another order. *Actually, I can wait until I first find the proof.*

Then what? What will I do when she realizes that I really do know? I'm not going to turn violent. That would be so undignified. That is not who I am . . . at least, I hope that's not who I am. I suppose the best way to look at it would be to ask myself what I really want. Should I leave Gertrude, or otherwise ask her to leave me? Is that what I really want? What if circumstances were reversed? What would Gertrude do? He nodded gently to himself as he honed in on the question. *That should be an easy one to answer. I have a good idea of how she would handle the situation.* He thought once more about the question, about his life with Gertrude, and how well he knew her, this time reflecting even deeper. *Or do I?*

***

1979

At the Annual General Meeting, attended by seventy-five physicians in the *Jamboree room* of the *Carlton Hotel*, Dr. Len Darshan called for nominations for the new chief of staff position in the upcoming year.

Mr. Vansant's was the first hand in the air. "I realize I'm not a member of the medical staff and therefore not allowed to nominate a candidate. Nor do I have a vote, but with your permission, I have something to say." He waited two or three seconds and accepted the silence as a token of the group's approval for him to go ahead. "I know I speak for the entire administrative staff when I say that I am proud to be associated with Yarwell General. It is not buildings that make a hospital; rather, it is the people. And at Yarwell, it's the quality and general camaraderie of the medical staff that combine to attract patients. With ever increasing specialization, it's important that doctors communicate with each other and work well together, and no where do we see a better model of cooperation between doctor and doctor, doctor and nurse, nurse and ancillary staff, care providers and administration, etcetera, etcetera, than here at our own hospital. This I know because I have worked elsewhere, in other hospitals. Most of you have also worked elsewhere, in other hospitals, and I am confident that you will agree"

Mr. Vansant was smart enough to realize that because Yarwell General was a new hospital, the mood was still in the youthful upbeat stage—no major malpractice lawsuits pending and a medical staff too untested to have discovered each other's shortcomings. Still, he was the administrator, and he used the atmosphere to cash in on his agenda: He wanted the geniality to feed on itself; he wanted his corporate superiors and members of the hospital board to view him as the architect of the amicable milieu, and he wanted to persuade Len to take the chair for another year.

"It all starts at the top," Mr. Vansant continued. "Good fortune doesn't just happen. It takes the driving force of willing workers under popular leadership. Therefore, I am suggesting someone in the hall request that Dr. Darshan accept the position of chief of the staff for another year."

Dr. Jewel Servance, the hospital pathologist, raised a hand and called, "I nominate Dr. Len Darshan for one more year."

Three or four voices called, "Second," and murmurs of approval sounded around the hall.

But Len held up a hand to halt the applause, stepped too close to the microphone, creating an irritating screech, and then spoke. "Thank you, Mr. Vansant, for those kind words, and thank you all for your vote of confidence. Unfortunately, however, I cannot accept the position for a second term. I have taken too much time away from my home. I may love Yarwell General, but my first love is my family: my wife and my baby girl. Perhaps I will serve another term at another time, but at this moment, they need me more than the hospital needs me. I thank you, but I must decline."

Another round of applause, this time with a few whistles and shouts of encouragement and approval.

Len was not completely off the hook. The hospital constitution required the outgoing chief of staff to serve another year on the board. The duties were few. The original board members created the position for two reasons: to ease the handing over of the baton to the next chief of staff, and to benefit from the outgoing chief's experience. Thus, Len remained on the board, he had to attend meetings, and Gertrude had no idea of Yarwell General's schedules.

Len still loved Gertrude dearly, but he could not resist Martha. Martha gave him something different. He could shout his love for Gertrude from the highest hilltops, but his passion for Martha had to remain a secret, a dark mystery hidden from all eyes and ears. He would, in fact, take her to restaurants or movies on the far south side of Jacobsburg, to areas where he did not fear bumping into people who might know him. And Len did not mind the clandestine nature of his intimacy with Martha at all. After his prudish youth, he found an excitement that outweighed even the most adventurous sexual fantasy he could imagine.

If word of his affair got out, the cloak-and-dagger element would be lost, and it would be just another shameful extramarital relationship. Yet, not everything remained in the dark. Len did manifest his emotion in the best of ways. He would smile easier, stick his chest out further, and walk with a slight skip in his step. Friends, colleagues, patients, and even Gertrude noticed his happy disposition, and they all liked him for it. In his own mind, Len came to believe that Martha had been sent to complete his life, both for him and for others around him.

Martha remained the perfect mistress. She was undemanding, discrete, and a boon to his ego. She wanted nothing from Len but his companionship and sex. Over the weeks and months, Len began to discuss anything with Martha, including Gertrude and Janet. Martha listened with a smile, asked pertinent questions sympathetically, and when Len complained about Janet's crying or

Gertrude's fatigue, Martha was quick to side with the other members of his family and virtually scold Len for his selfishness.

Then, he became confused. Although Martha was supposed to be his little escapade on the side, he wanted to spend more time with her than at home. In the quiet of the night, as he could hear Gertrude snoring gently and Janet occasionally moving in her cot behind the divider, he thought, *do I really love Martha more than I love Gertrude? With whom do I want to spend the remainder of my life? This cannot be happening to me. I never realized that I could love another woman more than I love Gertrude, but I also cannot deny my feelings. Yet, I cannot hurt Gertrude; I will not leave her.*

He heard Janet roll over, suck urgently on her pacifier, and then fall off into a deeper sleep again. *And how could I leave my Janet? Allow her to grow up without a father in her life. I won't do that to my daughter. But, what about my feelings? Am I to deny myself everything that I really want; the happiness that I have at last found?*

The situation did not require an immediate solution. Gertrude did not suspect anything—in fact, Len felt certain that no one suspected he was having an affair—and Martha remained undemanding. Len could continue this status quo indefinitely.

But, is that fair to Martha?

Weekends remained family time. Friday nights, they would have dinner at home or occasionally at Gertrude's parents; Saturday nights, Len and Gertrude would go out either alone or with other couples; and during the days, on the few occasions that they did not have plans, they would take Janet for drives and picnics or play in parks. Recently, however, their spare time was filled with another pursuit. Beginning to feel cramped in their one-bedroom apartment, they were busy hunting for a house.

Not too far from Yarwell General was a gated neighborhood with young families and nearby schools. On a Sunday, Jasper Schultz, the realtor, took Gertrude and Len to see five newly built homes. Gertrude was excited and loved everything she saw. Her questions revolved around the size of the yard, the layout of the kitchen, and the number of bedrooms. She foresaw two or three more children, at least one boy for Len, and a life filled with *happily ever after.*

Pushing Janet in the stroller from house to house and with Gertrude hanging on his arm, Len was more sedate. Gertrude assumed that his concerned frown reflected thoughts of the monthly mortgage, the taxes, and other added expenses, because all Len's questions seemed to revolve around price.

In the late afternoon, white clouds turned gray, a wind chilled the air, and Gertrude felt the first few drops of drizzle. "We had better get the baby indoors," she said to Jasper Schultz. "I love these houses and the neighborhood. Len and I will look at the floor plans, and we'll get back to you."

With Janet strapped safely in the baby chair, Len helped Gertrude into the passenger seat, put the stroller into the trunk, ran around to the driver's side of his new Cadillac, and managed to slam the door just as the heavens opened up.

Driving slowly in the narrow neighborhood roads, Len peered through the windscreen at the torrent and remarked, "I'll be glad to get home."

Gertrude was categorizing the information in the papers and pamphlets that Mr. Schultz had given her, trying to place the data in some sort of order for easier comparison. "If we go home, I'll be busy with Janet and cooking supper, you'll be on the phone to the hospital, and we won't get a chance to sit and discuss these houses. Let's go to the mall for coffee, Len. Don't you think that would be nice?"

The drumming of the rain on the car roof halted abruptly as they pulled into the mall's covered parking lot.

On their way through the pristine hallways, Gertrude stopped to gaze into the window of *Marketplace Stuff*, a trendy furniture store. "If we get the smaller four-bedroom house, don't you think a round table will go well in the open living-dining room area?" She held a pamphlet up against the store window for Len to visualize.

Trying to look interested, Len stroked his chin and grunted his "uh-ha" of approval.

Just off the food court was *Julie's Juvenile Jewelers*. Again, Gertrude could not resist window-shopping. Everything in her life seemed to be falling into place: Her daughter was thriving, her husband was succeeding, and she was looking forward to moving into a brand new home. "Look at that diamond tennis bracelet," she said, twisting her right hand around her left wrist, imagining she already owned it. "Marlene has one just like it." She edged her way around the corner of the window toward the entrance of the store and, still ogling the display, said, "What do you think of that necklace Len? The one with the emeralds and pearls, displayed around the mannequin neck; isn't it stunning?"

Len wanted to humor her by looking at the piece of jewelry. But, his eyes opened widely as he, too, could actually appreciate its magnificence, and he turned his attention to the price tag and thought, *not too expensive.*

Gertrude noticed his interest and then prodded him in the ribs with her elbow. "I don't need jewelry, Len," she said, laughing. "I can dream, but I know today is not the time to be buying a new necklace. Let's get some coffee and sit at a table." She led Len into the middle of the food court, dropped her papers on a table, and leaned over to take Janet out of her pushchair. "Should we get her some ice cream?" she asked Len.

Monday evening, Len called to tell Gertrude he would be late; he had another committee meeting.

As the valet drove his car to the parking lot, Martha took Len's elbow and looked up at the flashing sign above the restaurant. "I've never eaten here. I heard it's good."

Len was becoming more reckless. If people found out about his relationship with Martha, so be it. The issue might come to a head, and perhaps his life would turn along a happier path. Not that he was unhappy, but more and more he couldn't stand the thought of a future without his Martha.

"Welcome to The Boar and Beef," the maitre d' said. "A table for two?"

"I have a reservation . . . Dr. Darshan."

The maitre d' turned the page on his clipboard, fingered attentively down the list, and then looked up and smiled. "Ah yes, Dr. Darshan." He clicked his fingers at a passing hostess. "Table twenty-four."

"This way, sir."

They followed the hostess past a splashing fountain and to a dimly lit and intimate corner of the restaurant.

"Your waiter will be with you in a moment," the hostess said as she handed them two menus and a wine list.

Martha looked around at the plush green carpeting, the woman in the opposite corner playing gentle cords on her harp, and the interesting paintings on the walls, each depicting gluttonous characters partaking of sumptuous cuisine. "This place is really nice," she said, smiling contentedly.

Len leaned across the table and took her hand. "I'm glad you like it. I want it to be nice for you. I want everything to be nice for you, Martha." He looked down at the starched tablecloth and whispered, "You have no idea how I feel about you. I love you, Martha. I love you. And yet I'm not free to give you all I want to give you."

"Stop it, Len. I know how you feel; I feel the same about you. You mean much more to me than an evening in a fancy restaurant. You're the best thing that has ever happened to my life. And I understand your situation. So, why don't you just enjoy what we have without beating yourself to a pulp? You know it cannot last forever, and I know it cannot last forever, but I appreciate the time we have together. Why can't you do the same?" She reached across to place a pleading hand on his forearm. "Don't force anything, Len. Only, please be good to me as long as you can. That's all I ask. I don't ask for anything more, and I cannot expect anything more."

I could ask her to marry me here and now, Len thought. *Maybe I should.*

The words *I am going to ask Gertrude for a divorce* came to mind, but, being rational, he decided to tuck them away until he had the opportunity to mull over the consequences . . . one more time. And instead, he hinted about a life together by saying, "We don't know what the future holds, Martha, and whatever may happen, I know only one thing for sure, that I will love you forever."

Martha smiled at him and, swallowing her words, whispered, "I loved you from the first time I saw you, Len, and I know I cannot stop loving you."

Len sat back in his chair, placed his hand into his inside jacket pocket, and pulled out an oblong royal blue jewelry box. He placed it in front of her and leaned back to watch.

Martha bit her lower lip as she slowly turned back the lid. She then looked up at him and, with a palm on her pleasantly surprised cheek, whispered, "It's beautiful," and she stood to cross over to his side of the table and kiss him on the lips.

Len, too, got up and took the box from her. "Here, turn around. Let me put it on you."

He stepped behind her to fasten the clasp and looked at their reflection in an ornamental mirror along the back wall of the restaurant, while she ran her hand over the emeralds and pearls of the most gorgeous necklace she had ever seen.

Although he was preoccupied with thoughts of Martha, Len remained sexually attracted to Gertrude and continued to make love to her.

Gertrude, too, was preoccupied, but her thoughts were of their new home, which she longed to share with her husband and their growing family.

On the Tuesday night, Len was particularly quiet.

He must be having a problem at work, Gertrude thought. *It will probably be better if I let him sort it out for himself. If he wants my advice, he'll ask.*

How can I do this to Gertrude? She still loves me, and she thinks I love her the same as always.

Len tried to think of a gentle way of telling her that he loved another woman more than he loved her, but there was no gentle way. *She'll be devastated. It's sad that this should happen to her. Yet, it's also wrong for me to live a life of deceit. It's unfair to her and it's unfair to me. If I don't tell her, I'll grow to despise her . . . I know that is what will eventually happen. One day, we'll quarrel and I'll blame her for robbing me of the happiness that is today within my grasp. The quarrel may not even be her fault, nor will it be mine, but I'll blame her all the same. That undeniable force within the nature of man will drive me to resent her.*

Still uncertain of how to break the news to Gertrude, Len showered, brushed his teeth, and put on a pair of boxer shorts. He came into the bedroom and found Gertrude staring at their bed.

"I'm not certain how this suite will look in the new house," she said. "But I don't want to change it. It may upset my parents, and I've come to love it. It's our bed, Len. It's a part of us . . . isn't it?"

No matter how close Len had come to approaching the subject of a divorce, he could not speak about it that night, and he could never speak about it in their bedroom. He hoped that over the next few days, some tactful words would come to mind, some kind way in which he could let Gertrude understand that, although he did not hate her, he did not love her as deeply as he once had. He would also have to find a niche in time for this important discussion that he dreaded.

She noticed him staring intently and smiled at him.

In his mind, a smile before climbing into bed could only mean an invitation to make love. He smiled back, accepting the invitation, stepped closer, combed the falling red hair away from her cheeks with his fingers, and kissed her . . . tenderly at first and then with all the passion of expectation.

They fell onto the edge of the bed, kissed a little longer, and Len tugged at her nightgown, pulling it over her head.

She stripped him of his boxers, threw them onto the floor, and then cuddled closer.

Len kissed her neck and caressed her left breast.

She was groaning with pleasure, partly to please him, when suddenly he sat up, stared first at her surprised expression and then at the breast.

"What's the matter?" she asked, imagining she had done something wrong.

He knelt on both knees into the sinking mattress, and again felt her breast, this time with both hands and not a hint of passion. Back into the role of physician, he had detected an unexpected sign of pathology.

His transition sent a chill of fear through her entire being. She knew what he had found, so she brought her own hands up to her breast to feel the lump.

"What do you think it is?" she asked, hoping she would hear *it's nothing*, and knowing that no matter what she heard, Len had found reason for concern.

Len did not immediately reply. He leaned further over her to examine the opposite breast, not for another lump but rather for comparison.

With an all-knowing physician's nod and "mmm," he returned his attention to the left breast. Both Gertrude's breasts had diffuse nodularity, consistent with mild fibrocystic breast disease. But the mass situated above and medial to the left nipple was different to the general consistency of her breasts; it was harder and less mobile. Len tried to move it, hoping it would slip away and hide inside the connective tissue. This would indicate the possibility of a benign *fibroadenoma*. To his disappointment, it remained easily palpable, and in his mind's eye seemed even larger than when he first found it a moment ago.

Inadvertently, he shook his head.

At this gesture, Gertrude was afraid to ask again. She did not want to hear the word *cancer* uttered through his lips. She merely took another turn at feeling the tiny, unwelcome intruder into her body, and allowed a fearful flow of tears to trickle down her cheeks.

Len took her hand as kindly as he could, brushed his lips against her knuckles, leaned over to kiss her gently, and then offered the most comforting truth he could find. "I've never seen a breast malignancy in a woman your age. Not below thirty, and even below thirty-five, it's rare. You're only twenty-nine."

"Nearly thirty."

Now, it was Len's turn to shed a tear. *How unfair*, he thought. *She's still so childlike. If this tumor turns out to be a cancer, then all those dreams that she shared with me will be shattered. And, she may lose her life.* He closed his eyes and sighed. *Thank God I didn't tell her. Thank you, God, for not giving me the opportunity to tell her about Martha or to raise the subject of a divorce. That, together with this breast lump, would be too much for her to bear.*

He climbed off the bed to get his boxers. He was no longer in the mood for sex.

She watched as he had them half on, but she did not reach for her nightgown. Instead, she looked at him appealingly and asked, "Please, Len. Please make love to me. Tonight more than ever, love me, and then hold me through the night, so that I will know you are here. Don't stop now. Tonight, Len, I need you."

He squinted down at her, thought *how different are women from men,* and then climbed back onto the bed.

"The best thing we can do is send her to a surgeon to take care of the lump," Terry said to Len. "It's probably not malignant. She's too young. Step back and look at the situation objectively. If she were any other patient, you'd hardly give it a second thought."

201

The morning session was about to begin. The receptionist was pulling charts for the patients who had signed in, and the nurses were preparing the examination rooms. Len sat in one of the two patients' chairs in Terry's office, leaning forward over the desk, looking for comfort and sensible objective advice, which Terry ably supplied.

"Do you want me to take a look at her?" Terry offered. "Or do you think she'll feel embarrassed?"

"She's going to have to see a surgeon anyhow. I was thinking about Manuel Gomez. He is chief of surgery. I've been sending him a lot of my cases. What do you think?"

"Gwen Eschenbach. She's older and more experienced, and she has a special interest in breast cancer. Even though I'm still not convinced that Gertrude's lump is malignant . . . and neither are you." Terry stood up from his maroon leather chair and walked to the opposite side of the desk to place a comforting palm on Len's shoulder. "Use Gwen. Let me give her a call for you and get the biopsy set up. The sooner the better."

"Thanks, Terry," Len whimpered, appreciatively.

Dr. Eschenbach and four other specialists had converted a house, one block north of Yarwell General Hospital, into offices. They shared two receptionists and a waiting room, and coming off this common area, each doctor had a small separate suite. Wednesdays were Dr. Eschenbach's full operating day, on which she normally did not have patients scheduled in the office. For the wife of a colleague, however, she made an exception.

202

Dr. Eschenbach wore green scrubs. In her late fifties or early sixties, she stood about five-foot-three tall. Her close-cropped hair was pure gray; yet, more noticeable than her hair were her eyebrows. They, too, were gray. They might not have been so prominent had she trimmed them, but they were bushy and attracted the attention of anyone meeting her for the first time.

Len remained in the room during the examination, and Dr. Eschenbach directed most questions and remarks to him rather than to the patient, Gertrude. Then, with Gertrude still in a paper gown and sitting on the edge of the examination table, and Len on a stool in the corner, Dr. Eschenbach gave her clinical impression, which was essentially no different to Len's.

"We will need a biopsy," she said. "Usually in a woman your age, my suspicion is low, but this lump must come out."

Is she being extra cautious because I am a doctor's wife? Gertrude wondered. *If she would normally watch a lump in a woman my age, then why not watch mine?*

"Are we going to get a mammogram?" Len asked.

Dr. Eschenbach frowned. "I suppose we should. Not that I expect to get any information out of it, but we don't want to look back and regret not having done it."

Gertrude looked confused, so Dr. Eschenbach went on to explain. "In a woman your age, the breast tissue is so dense that malignancies don't show up. That's why we don't start routine mammograms before the age of thirty-five or forty."

"What'll happen if the lump is cancer?" Gertrude asked. "Len told me there are different kinds of treatment, but how do you decide? Will I wake up after the anesthetic without a breast?"

Dr. Eschenbach laughed condescendingly. "A few years ago, the pathologist would do a frozen section, that was to look at the specimen and make the diagnosis while the patient was under the anesthetic. If it was malignant, we made the decision there and then to go ahead with a mastectomy. Today, we wait for the definitive histology. We'll do only the biopsy, and then wake you up. If it's benign, that will be the end of the story, but if it's a cancer, we'll test to see some of its other characteristics. For example, the treatment may differ depending upon the exact size of the tumor, the type of cancer, whether lymph nodes are affected, and how the tumor reacts to the hormones in your body." She took Gertrude's hand, but looked once again at Len. "We may need to consult a medical oncologist and a radiation therapist." Then, looking back at Gertrude, she smiled apologetically. "Of course, sweetie, we all hope that it's benign, and there will be no need for any further treatment."

Gertrude grimaced. She did not like being called "sweetie." Dr. Eschenbach was pleasant enough, and Len said she was an expert in the field, but suddenly Gertrude felt that something was missing. She could not put her finger on the problem, but she lacked confidence in Dr. Eschenbach, and was not certain that she wanted this bushy browed and familiar little woman in charge of what might be a major illness.

Neither of them was hungry, and Gertrude was not in the mood for cooking, so together with little Janet, Len and Gertrude went for a pizza.

"I'm not that comfortable with Dr. Eschenbach," Gertrude told Len as she passed him a slice of pizza. "I know I'm only going by my gut feeling, but this may be cancer, and Dr. Eschenbach doesn't seem to have what I expected . . . the poise . . . or manner . . . or whatever."

"I've seen her work, and she has good surgical technique," he said, holding the limp piece of pizza without taking a bite. His heart was not in the meal. "You'll be in good hands."

"Shouldn't I go see someone else . . . get a second opinion?"

Len seemed confused. "Gertrude, you must have the biopsy. There is no other opinion at this time. Even in we found a surgeon who did not want to take it out, I wouldn't accept watching and waiting on this lump." He dropped the uneaten piece of pizza onto his plate and took her hands to kiss them tenderly.

Gertrude placed her forehead onto his knuckles and began to weep. Janet stared for a moment, then stretched her arms toward her mother and, sensing the depression, cried along with her parents.

At least I have Len, Gertrude thought. *He knows how I feel, and he's a doctor; he understands my medical condition. It would be much worse without him. I realize it's a cancer. Otherwise, why would everyone be telling me that this lump is so different to other lumps? I suppose I should sit back and let Len take charge.*

Len watched Gertrude trying unsuccessfully to hold back the tears that were upsetting their daughter. *Dear God, she looks pitiful. How could I leave her? I know that I'm not responsible for the tumor in her breast, but somehow, I feel it's my fault.* He shook his head, trying to rid himself of the daunting guilt. *There cannot be a connection, yet it's uncanny how on the very night I choose to speak about Martha, Gertrude comes up with this crisis. I feel that had Martha never entered my life, Gertrude would have been fine.*

Unable to eat, they boxed the pizza and went home, where neither of them could sleep. Gertrude was scared, concerned about the surgery, bodily disfigurement, and the possible loss of her life. Len was more anxious, eager to find out the exact pathological diagnosis, overcome the problem, and put the whole unfortunate experience far out of the way.

Thursday, Gertrude went to the hospital for the radiological, blood, and urine tests that Dr. Eschenbach had ordered, and Friday at seven a.m., she was first on the operating list.

"Wake up, Mrs. Darshan. Can you hear me? Take deep breaths."

The voice of the nurse, the slurp of the suction, and the smell of antiseptics filled Gertrude's senses, and at the foot of her bed, she saw her husband, Len, in coveralls, a surgical hat and mask, and tears streaming from his eyes. Gertrude knew the worst, and she was not surprised. She called to him, or thought she called to

206

him, but the powerful yet soothing urge to sleep overtook her effort to remain awake, and the next thing she knew, she was rousing once again, this time in a comfortable private hospital bed. Two huge floral arrangements were on the stand in front of the window: one with three-dozen red roses and a sprinkling of baby's breath and greenery, the other with a colorful variety and a blue teddy bear.

I did see Len crying, she recalled. *What does that mean? Obviously, it's a cancer, but we almost knew that. Is it worse than we expected? Can't be. A cancer is a cancer.*

She felt the urge to urinate and began to climb out of the bed when a young and plump nurse appeared out of nowhere, gently supported her at the edge of the mattress, and said, "We don't want to fall now, Mrs. Darshan. What is it that you need? Let me help you."

"Is my husband here?" she asked. "Dr. Len Darshan."

"I don't believe so." She smiled as if to say, *of course we all know your husband, Dr Len Darshan,* and then told Gertrude, "Dr. Eschenbach is at the nurses' station. She wanted to speak to you, but you were too drowsy. Meanwhile, you're not allowed out of bed by yourself."

After helping Gertrude to the bathroom and back, the nurse left, and within a few minutes, Dr. Eschenbach appeared, wearing a puckered brow, which brought her eyebrows closer together. She pushed a visitor's chair closer to the bedside, but remained standing as she said, "I'm sorry, sweetie. The lump was malignant . . . as we expected."

Gertrude already knew, but hearing the truth told was nonetheless shocking, and the words brought about a fresh batch of tears.

"So, where do we go from here, Doctor?"

"We'll probably do a lumpectomy, that is take out a wider area of breast tissue, and then have a six month course of radiation treatments. If the tumor is positive for estrogen receptors, then that will be all. I expect you to do very well."

Gertrude managed a polite smile. *That sounds simpler than I expected.* She thought for a moment and then asked, "What about the lymph nodes? Before the biopsy, you mentioned that you would have to find out whether the lymph nodes were involved."

"Quite right." Dr. Eschenbach leaned on her palms against the edge of the bed and explained as though it was a mere minor detail, "When we do the lumpectomy, we'll also remove axillary nodes for biopsy." She was about to continue to discuss the significance of spread of the cancer to the nodes when Len, together with Dr. Jewel Servance, the pathologist, walked through the open door of the room.

Len saw that Gertrude was awake and hurried to her side, leaned over her, and kissed her hard on the lips, not a passionate kiss nor a mere peck of greeting, more a kiss of support and concern, and once again Gertrude cried, this time tears of appreciation.

"Have you told her?" Len asked, turning to Dr. Eschenbach, who had stepped away from the bed, giving husband and wife space for togetherness at this crucial moment in her illness.

"We were outlining the probable treatment," Dr. Eschenbach said. "Of course, we'll discuss it in greater detail, but not now. Later, when Gertrude is fully alert."

Am I not alert? I feel alert, Gertrude thought.

"Dr. Servance says the frozen section showed *invasive lobular breast cancer*," Len said to the surgeon. "How does that affect us?"

"I treat it the same as a *ductal* lesion," Dr. Eschenbach replied. "And the prognosis is a little better than ductal."

"What does that mean?" Gertrude asked anyone willing to answer. "What is a ductal lesion, and what is invasive lobular cancer, the one that I have?"

"There are a number of different types of breast cancer," Dr. Eschenbach explained, "depending on the type of tissue from which they grow. Ductal tumors are by far the most common, about three quarters of the cases. Next in frequency is a toss up between adenocarcinoma, a bad one, which thank God you don't have, and lobular breast cancer, the type that you do have. And as I told your husband, lobular may have a better prognosis than ductal."

Hoping she had put her patient's mind to rest, Dr. Eschenbach smiled at Gertrude.

Gertrude looked to Len for acknowledgement of the explanation, and she felt a hint of encouragement knowing that her lesion was at least better than the other two common types of breast cancer. But even in her sedate state, she caught Dr. Servance's wince, a gesture she would not forget and which would have a profound effect upon her trust for her surgeon.

"Well, I must get back to the operating room," Dr Eschenbach apologized. "I'll return later to discharge you, Gertrude. You'll be able to go home today, and we'll give you an appointment to come to the office next week."

"I came to say hello and see how you are feeling," Dr. Servance said to Gertrude. His tone was kind and his concern seemed genuine, but more than this, he spoke to her as a person, and Gertrude took an instant liking to the elderly pathologist.

"Thank you for coming," Gertrude said, and she waited for Dr. Eschenbach to leave the room, before continuing. "What makes a lobular cancer different to other cancers? Why is it better than the most common type, ductal? I understand that they come from different tissues in the breast, but there must be other differences. What are they?"

Dr. Servance seemed suddenly uneasy. "I'm a pathologist," he explained. "There are some differences, but I'm sure that Dr. Eschenbach will go over them with you. She's much better than I am at clinical medicine. Let me rather leave the treatment to her. Meanwhile, I wish you a speedy recovery, and I do hope to see you again soon, Mrs. Darshan." He turned to shake Len's hand and left the room to return to the sanctuary of his laboratory.

Convinced that she was alert, Gertrude sat up in the bed and looked Len sternly in the eye. "I think Dr. Servance is less happy with a lobular cancer than Dr. Eschenbach seems to be," she said to him. "What is Dr. Eschenbach hiding?"

"Doctors don't hide things from their patients," Len said, laughing. "Sometimes doctors might disagree on minutiae, and patients might misinterpret this as a major difference of opinion and become confused. Dr. Servance sees disease from a different perspective to Dr. Eschenbach. He's a pathologist and she's a clinician, and he doesn't want to step on her toes."

Gertrude nodded as though understanding, but she remained curious and wanted to know why Dr. Servance seemed concerned, and although she felt she was beginning to nag, she asked, "So, how bad is lobular cancer, Len? And what exactly does *invasive* mean? It doesn't sound good."

He took on a professional air and sat in the chair that Dr. Eschenbach had pulled closer to the bed. "We pay more attention to the grade of malignancy as seen by the pathologist under the microscope, and the stage of the tumor, that is its size and degree to which it has spread. Invasive, as you probably guessed, means

211

that it has started to grow. If it hadn't, it would be called *in situ*, which would have been little more than a nuisance."

Gertrude began to feel a little easier. She leaned back and asked, this time in a more relaxed frame of mind, "Can lobular cancer grow bigger or spread more readily than ductal cancer?"

Len offered a comforting smile. "No, Gertrude, and I think it's generally less aggressive." Then, he, too, flinched in a manner similar to Dr. Servance. But Len was not intent on hiding those minutiae from her. "Lobular breast cancer does behave a little differently to ductal," he said. It's more likely to be *multicentric*."

She squinted. "What does that mean? Is it bad? It sounds bad. Is multicentric worse than invasive?"

He sucked air between his clenched teeth. "It means the tumor is more likely to pop up in different areas of the breast."

She remained silent for a short while and then said pensively, "That's bad."

"Not necessarily. I didn't say it's always muliticentic; I said it's more likely to be multicentric."

"Does that mean that other types of breast cancer can also be multicentric?"

Len felt a little uneasy. He understood the implications of multicentricity. He had been trained to think of breast cancer as a disease state rather than an isolated tumor, and he knew that

212

although treatment would have to be aimed first at the primary lesion, the condition would then be managed with chemotherapy, radiation, and hormonal therapy, and most important of all, with monitoring for the early detection of recurrence. Yet Gertrude, like any other patient being confronted with the horror of a malignant tumor, would want the cancer removed. If she were going to have an operation, she would want to shoot for immediate cure rather than prolonged management. So, Len tried to add perspective. "When we get the reports on the hormonal receptors, the final grade of the tumor, and the involvement of the glands, we'll formulate a comprehensive plan of management for you."

"And what about the other breast?" She looked with panicky eyes down at her chest.

Len again understood her fears. He stood up, took her left hand in his two, and answered as truthfully as he could. "Yes, there is a chance that lobular cancer can be present in both breasts."

She took her hand from his and began to palpate the right breast, searching for a lump that she and her physicians might have missed.

Len bent over to hold her. Whilst smothering her effort at self-examination with his chest, he kissed her caringly and whispered, "It's going to be all right, Gertrude," but the tears on her cheek were not from her eyes, they were from his.

Gertrude remained in a daze, astonished at the abrupt appearance of the cancer, and confused by the complexity of the condition and intricacies in treatment. She read Len's textbooks and went to him for explanations of tough sections. And she came to understand that, in some instances, patients with lobular cancer would undergo *bilateral mastectomies*. Doctors would not do this mutilating procedure when the tumor was low grade, but for lesions that were more aggressive, this was a reasonable option, and the patient herself often dictated the final decision. A predicament Gertrude understood clearly, for she, too, did not want to lose her breasts, nor did she want to gamble with her already threatened life.

Dr. Servance submitted his report. Not only was the histology discouraging, but the tumor was estrogen and progesterone receptor negative, which meant that no matter what surgery she had, she would need both radiation and chemotherapy, as well.

Len, too, was perplexed. Previously, he would rely on the evaluation by the specialist and input by the patient. Now, his role changed. He could not remain completely objective. Worse still, he felt guilt. Here was his wife pouring out her trusting heart to him, leaning on him for support, and he had betrayed her love.

He felt that his behavior had played a part in the evolution of her misfortune. Intellectually, he knew this was not so, yet every time he managed to expel the culpability from his thoughts, it would not go completely away. It would linger patiently in the shadows of his mind, waiting on an opportune moment to return and deal an added blow of blame.

With as open a mind as she could muster, Gertrude returned to Dr. Eschenbach. She hoped for some added enlightenment, an explanation that would settle the mounting confusion. Instead, the doctor would not entertain the idea of bilateral mastectomies. Not that Gertrude relished the idea of losing both breasts, but she wanted some degree of assurance that no cancer would be left behind.

"Unfortunately, there are no guarantees with this condition," Dr. Eschenbach apologized to Gertrude.

Len was supposed to have been with Gertrude, but he was delayed, and Dr. Eschenbach, running ahead of schedule, managed to take Gertrude early.

Perched at the foot of the examination couch, Gertrude then asked, "If the entire breast is removed, then surely the cancer is removed, too?"

"Unfortunately, it's not quite that simple," Dr. Eschenbach replied, gently shaking her head. "We may remove all the cancer, and still there is a chance of a recurrence. Hence, the adjuvant therapy, to remove any unfound residual and metastatic disease."

"But if cancer cells remain, surely the chance of a recurrence will be higher?"

Dr. Eschenbach frowned while searching for a comforting reply. "Most women will do anything to keep their breasts. Even take the added risk. Whereas you don't seem to want to accept the encouraging results of lumpectomy. Again, studies show equal survival between patient groups that have undergone lumpectomy, leaving them whole, versus mastectomy."

"I've read a little about the studies and spoken with Len about them, but I'm not certain that the results hold true for lobular cancers, Doctor. Women with invasive lobular cancers are having mastectomies. Some women end up having mastectomies, even with ductal cancer."

"Gertrude, unless the tumors are advanced, I've been doing very few mastectomies. I would really feel uncomfortable with anything more than a lumpectomy and lymph node resection in your case."

Gertrude remained silent. For once, Dr. Eschenbach sounded truly concerned, and Gertrude was about to go along with the doctor's recommendation, which was, after all, based upon years of experience. Gertrude also found relief at having explored the possibilities and concluded that she could keep her breasts.

Dr. Eschenbach, however, mistook Gertrude's pensiveness for ongoing uneasiness and suggested, "Perhaps you would feel comfortable with another opinion, Gertrude. This is a big decision and a second opinion is a reasonable option at this point. Why don't you think about it?"

At that moment, there was a gentle knock at the door. It opened a crack, and a nurse looked in. "Excuse me, Doctor, Mrs. Darshan's husband is here."

Len's head could be seen bobbing from side to side behind the nurse.

"Come in, Len," Dr. Eschenbach said.

As Len walked up to Gertrude's side, offering an encouraging smile, Dr. Eschenbach summarized the situation in clear and rapid doctor-to-doctor language, which let Gertrude realize that Dr. Eschenbach understood her dilemma and that her situation was not unique. "We were exploring Gertrude's risk tolerance."

Len turned up an enquiring palm. "And . . .?"

"Gertrude is informed and concerned," Dr. Eschenbach answered. "I'm uncomfortable doing a mastectomy or a bilateral mastectomy on her. I discussed the compelling favorable outcomes with lumpectomy, but Gertrude is still uneasy. Perhaps we should get a second opinion."

Len's round face blushed, afraid that his wife might have offended his colleague.

Dr. Eschenbach noticed his uneasiness and continued, "I can't say that a mastectomy is an unreasonable option with invasive lobular cancer. It's just not my recommended treatment. Still, who knows what future outcome data will show? If you want, I'll give you the names of some other surgeons with an interest in breast surgery."

Len felt embarrassed, and Gertrude felt strangely relieved. She never was comfortable with Dr. Eschenbach, and yet the doctor saw the uneasiness clearer than did the patient.

After a while, Len, too, had a sensation of freedom, for, with time to consider, he decided that Gertrude might have been better off under the care of his old mentor, Professor Carson, in the powerful institution, Jacobsburg University Hospital.

Impressively tall and slender, with mature gray hair combed neatly back, Professor Carson was everything that Gertrude expected in a senior doctor. Although she never actually heard Professor Carson saying, *Dr. Eschenbach, herself, could not tolerate losing her breasts, the emblem of her femininity*, Gertrude felt that somewhere in their conversation that supposition was conferred.

As authoritative and far more personable than Dr. Eschenbach, Professor Carson agreed that a bilateral mastectomy was a viable alternative and, in fact, the treatment of choice for invasive lobular carcinoma, especially for a woman as young as Gertrude.

Amazing how often the matter of age crops up, Gertrude thought. *First, I was too young to have breast cancer, and now because I am young I need surgery that is more radical.*

Jacobsburg University Hospital worked as a unit; the oncologist, the radiologist, the radiation therapist, the pathologist, and the surgeon all shared the same medical record and their notations were readily available to each other—another facet that conferred comfort to Gertrude.

The main waiting room outside the operating suite was L-shaped and huge, full of nooks and crannies, a mélange of tables and chairs, and two vending stations, each with a constant supply of free hot coffee and paper cups not quite thick enough to contain the heat. Gertrude's parents and her sister Marlene together with

218

husband Larry were there. Melinda, Terry's wife, had volunteered to babysit Janet, who was considered too young to come to the hospital.

Then, the wait. One disadvantage of the bigger hospital was lethargy. Although individuals may have been working under pressure, rushing from one place to the next and taking care of one emergency after another, the cumulative human machinery that ran the hospital barely ticked over.

An hour and a half after her scheduled starting time, an orderly eventually wheeled Gertrude from the holding area and into the operating room. By now, Gertrude was heavily sedated. She caught only a glimpse of the corridor filled with surgeons vigorously scrubbing their hands in water running from elbow-controlled faucets. She did see clearly the steel trolleys holding surgical instruments, and as a team of nurses and doctors conveyed her onto the operating table, the two huge overhead lamps staring brightly down burned a lasting impression in her tranquilized but troubled mind.

In the waiting room, Len stood for the tenth or eleventh time to stretch his legs and take a troubled short stroll. He saw Terry walking through the door. Terry had stolen a few precious moments out of the office to come and offer his valuable support. And together with Terry was Brad, the two men striding and deep in conversation. Brad noticed Len before Terry did, and he hurried forward to give his friend a firm handshake and shameless hug.

"Terry came in through the ER," Brad said. "I don't know what I could have done to help, you have had all the best doctors in

Jacobsburg on her case, but still, you should have told me earlier about Gertrude."

"I'm sorry, Ginger," Len said. "I would have called you, but everything has happened so fast, and my head has been in a spin. And you are wrong, you know. Seeing you here does help."

Brad shook Len's hand again, and then went forward to the family sitting around the table to have a short word with each of them in turn.

"How's she doing?" Terry asked. "Is the surgery almost done?"

"They only just took her in." Len smiled as he offered the redundant explanation, "You know how slow they are here."

Terry looked at his watch. "Let me go see the family, and then I'll have to get back to the office. Patients are already waiting."

Len waited as Terry and Brad spoke their words of encouragement and support for the family. Then, when Terry took off, Brad poured himself a cup of coffee and stood to the side with Len. "How is Gertrude taking it?" Brad asked.

"For her, too, it's all happening so fast. First the cancer and then the bilateral mastectomy."

Brad shook his concerned head. He considered asking whether the radical operation was necessary, but it was too late, the surgery was already underway, and he did not want to upset his already distraught friend. Meanwhile, he decided to read up on the topic and ask doctors in the surgical and oncology departments about the current treatment of choice for invasive lobular carcinoma in a woman Gertrude's age. He would also ask his fiancée, Lily, to prepare a meal or two to drop off at the Darshans' home. Gertrude would be in no mood for cooking for a few days

"Gertrude will be sleeping in the hospital," Brad said to Len. "Can Lily and I do anything to help you and the baby?"

Justifiably wrapped up in his own troubles, Len hardly noticed Brad's profound concern, and Brad, selflessly, did not care whether Len noticed or not.

"We'll probably go to my in-laws for a bite," Len said. "And they will keep Janet tonight."

Glad that Len had support, Brad glanced at the family sitting around the table and speaking amongst themselves. "I suppose I should also be getting back to work. The ER has been as busy as ever." He thought for a moment and then quietly asked, "What is Gertrude's Hebrew name?"

Len did not have to ask why Brad wanted to know Gertrude's Hebrew name; he understood that Brad was going to include her in his prayers for a speedy and complete recovery, and Len was grateful. Still, he did not immediately answer. Instead, he asked, "How often do you go to Synagogue?"

"I try to make it every morning and evening, as my work schedule allows." He smiled at Len and said, "That's why I chose emergency medicine. I never have to work Shabbat, and my hours are pretty flexible."

I should be the one praying for Gertrude, Len thought. *And while I'm at it, I suppose I should put in a few words to beg forgiveness for myself.*

Len told Brad Gertrude's first Hebrew name and then asked if he wanted her father's or her mother's first name, as well.

"Her mother's," Brad replied, pulling out a small notebook and pen. "When we pray for recovery from illness, we say the name of the person . . . son or daughter of . . . and then the name of the mother."

Intuitively, Len thought this made sense, but, for the first time, he realized how little he knew about the laws and customs of the Jewish religion.

"Do you think Gertrude would mind if I popped in to see her later today?" Brad asked.

"I think she would like that," Len replied, and he could not understand why he suddenly found himself battling to hold back tears.

Len watched Brad greet the family and make his way toward the door. But then he called, "Ginger, wait!" And he ran to catch up with his friend.

"What is it?" Brad asked; his brow wrinkled with a brand new dose of concern.

"Do you mind if I walk with you down to the ER?"

"Sure."

Len waved to the family and clearly mouthed, "I'll be back in a short while."

"What is it?" Brad again asked. "What's the matter, Len?"

They walked a short distance, heads down, and Len biting his lower lip, until he turned to Brad and asked, "How do I learn to pray properly, to *daven* like you?"

Brad broke into a short laugh and replied, "You're already over ninety percent there. Wanting to daven is the main obstacle, the rest is plain sailing."

"But I can hardly read Hebrew."

"Only a few people who come regularly to Synagogue are fluent," Brad explained, "And everyone is continually learning. It's a never-ending journey, and we are each at our own particular level along the way. Prayer and learning go hand in hand. But I understand what you are asking. When do you want to learn the basics of *davening?* Once you understand that—and I know it won't take long—we'll begin with one paragraph of one of the prayers, and slowly, slowly you'll also begin your journey along the path."

"How about tonight? Are you free?"

"No, not tonight, and not this week. I'm free, but you're not. Why don't you wait until Gertrude has settled down and will not mind you leaving her for an hour or two? However, if you want, I'll meet you at the Synagogue at six forty-five, and we'll go through the short afternoon and evening services together."

"Thanks, Brad. I'll see you then."

"Not if Gertrude needs you." As he shook Len's hand again, Brad said, "You had better get back to your in-laws."

As he returned to the surgical waiting room, Len felt a weight lift from his chest. *With Brad's help, I can make things right*, he thought. *I will make amends for my adultery.*

For the first time, he reflected on the nature of his crime. *I am an adulterer. That is one of the ten major sins of the bible.* And at a subliminal level, he began to hope: *If I do make amends, then this dreadful cancer, which I brought about, will have a much better chance of going away and leaving only its terrible scars. I heard somewhere that our God is supposed to be a merciful and forgiving God, who answers our prayers.*

CHAPTER EIGHT

2005

Monday went by and Tuesday went by with no trace of A-fair-catch in the mail. Len imagined that someone else in the office had found the delivery and, for a host of possible reasons, discarded it or returned it to the sender. It was on Wednesday afternoon that he decided to call or e-mail the website. He sat at his desk, brought up his search engine, and made his way through the Internet. But while he was waiting for the familiar home page, he noticed a square box, unopened, sitting on his credenza and labeled *Len Darshan, Personal.* There was no *Doctor Len Darshan* on the package, and more importantly, no clue about the contents or origin.

Len went to the nurses' station and asked Mary as casually as he possibly could, "What's happening, no patients at the moment?"

Mary pulled up the appointment schedule on the computer screen. "Fifteen minutes until the next appointment. Jennie Jensen says she is feeling much better and you told her to cancel if she didn't feel the need to return."

"That's right," Len said. "Let me try catch up with the prescription refills."

He returned to his office, closed the door, and hastily opened the parcel. The kit consisted of two small jars, a few pieces of blotting paper, two plastic pipettes, and a glossy pamphlet with simple instructions and a number of advertisements for other products that might be useful in investigating a spouse's fidelity— mostly technological devices, such as software for tracking e-mail and microchips for recording private telephone conversations.

Len read the instructions twice, thought about mixing the chemicals as directed, but decided against and placed everything back into the unmarked box. It was Wednesday and Gertrude had a regular bridge game scheduled every Wednesday night. He would thoroughly examine the contents of A-fair-catch when alone and in the comfort of his own home.

At this time, he did not consider the consequences; he did not know what he would do if his newfound suspicions proved true, nor did he contemplate what would happen if Gertrude found out he was spying on her. He had just stepped into the shoes of a real live detective and felt strangely exhilarated.

The afternoon patient load remained unusually low, and Len made it home in time for an early dinner together with Gertrude.

Then, as soon as he heard the garage door close and through the kitchen window saw Gertrude driving along the neighborhood road, he went to his car to retrieve his A-fair-catch.

He laid a few sheets of newspaper on the bathroom sink and then unpacked his precious paraphernalia. He once more read the pamphlet and then, item-by-item, read it again as he carried out the simple instructions.

Using the blue pipette, transfer ten cubic centimeters of fluid from the white jar to the blue jar . . .

Carefully, Len prepared his solutions without spilling a drop of fluid onto the protective newspaper. Then, repressing self-disgust, he went to the laundry, rummaged through the dirty clothing, and found two pairs of his wife's panties, one floral pink, the other briefer and plain white.

Back in the bathroom, he examined the crotch padding in the underwear and was curiously excited to find a small translucent area of what had to be dried-out bodily fluid in the white pair.

He ran his forefinger over the caked patch. This was definitely the remnant of a proteinaceous secretion.

Well, I'll be a monkey's uncle. Prepared as he may have been, Len still could not believe his senses. *She may fit the profile, and I have certainly been less attentive than a good husband should be, but this is incredible.*

He poured the few drops of clear liquid on the suspect stain, his head swimming with questions, scenarios, and uncertainties, most prominent of which was how he should react. *Somewhere in the back of my mind, I thought I should be violent. I seemed to focus on the other guy. Now with the problem in my lap, I see this is really between Gertrude and me. Ever since her mastectomy, she's been less responsive to me. I believed it was because she felt a loss of her femininity. Then, when she had the breast implants a year later, I thought she would feel better about herself, but still things never seemed to return to normal. I suppose my expectations were unreasonable. How could she return to her former self after such a mutilating operation? I tried to be sensitive to her wants. I didn't fondle her implanted breasts when we would make love.* Len dabbed the moistened area on the panties with one of the included pieces of blotting paper, and blew on it to help it dry quickly. *Maybe that was a mistake. Perhaps I should've been more open about her disfigurement. My ignoring the whole memory certainly didn't mean she was ignoring it. She may have seen my attitude as one of repulsion. And yet, her implants really look terrific. I never bothered to mention that flat-chested women who haven't had mastectomies often elect to have implants, and they're usually ecstatic with the results. Still, does my indifference to her implants give her the right to find a lover?* Len exhaled and glanced up toward the bathroom ceiling, in deep and honest reflection. *If she viewed my attitude as revulsion, then possibly it does. I wonder how long this has been going on behind my back. It seems like many years that she hasn't needed or craved my love. Now when I think about it, she's been indifferent ever since around the time of the mastectomy. I wonder whether she's had only one other lover or more than one. I really wonder when it all started.*

228

Len laid the piece of blotting paper flat, looked at the second hand on his watch, applied three drops of fluid from the red jar, and then waited for the blotting paper to turn violet. He had not made love to his wife for over a week; the positive test would prove what he already suspected, that she was unfaithful to him.

***

1980

Len put his heart and soul and every free moment he could find into the study and practice of his religion.

Gertrude thought Len was going through a phase, an attempt to be trendy, and she believed it was all Brad's doing. Len seemed intrigued with Brad's positive attitude towards life and had been spending more time with him recently. Len's newfound interest was rather sudden, but then this type of change of heart usually was, and Gertrude did not question him about it. She may have suspected that he had had a rude awakening when she developed cancer, but she could not have known of his pact with God, and Len certainly was not going to admit to her the complex reasoning behind his newfound religious zeal.

Len bought a new *prayer shawl* and set of *phylacteries* to participate properly in the rituals, and, with Brad's help, he learned to don these articles as nimbly as the most practiced members of the congregation, while uttering the appropriate blessings in both English and the language in the *siddur*, Hebrew. Like Brad, Len could not attend services as regularly as he would have liked. He often had to work both early and late, and from the get-go, he resolved that Gertrude and Janet would take priority over Synagogue. What is more, the new house was ready exactly one month after Gertrude's surgery, and moving in took up a large chunk of his time. He had not planned it, but fortunately, the house was within walking distance of the Synagogue. A fluke, maybe, yet Len viewed it as another omen, a convenient happenstance that would make it easier for him to become observant, for he would no longer have to drive to services on the Sabbath.

Learning was not drudgery; Len took pleasure in reading the Torah lessons, slowly and thoughtfully, searching for hidden meanings applicable to him and to his world. He was a welcome newcomer to beginners' philosophical studies on Tuesday evenings and to Torah classes on Saturday mornings before services. He listened diligently, asked thought provoking questions, and was soon a vocal contributor to the discussions. Whenever the conversation wandered into the realm of health and medical care, the regulars looked to Len for answers. They all soon discovered that he was the ex-chief of staff at Yarwell General, and that he had declined to serve a second term because of family commitments. Intelligent, well groomed, a family man, and a busy doctor, as well—what was not to like about Len?

Like the other members of the community, Len came to accept the teachings of the Torah as his absolute yardstick of morality. With his newly opened eyes, he could envision an even broader spectrum of moral values than he had previously known. Secular ethics had drifted so far from their source of origin that lawmakers had become obsessed with the separation of church and state. But, this did not seem to matter; the people of the Synagogue strove for a level of righteousness beyond the comprehension of the state.

Quietly, they upheld the commandments of the Torah and served their own consciences. And their doctrine would never clash with the lowly regulations of the land, because the Torah taught that one should follow the rules of the country in which one lived, as long as the courts were just, and American law remained largely reasonable, logical, and simple to obey.

Then, Len's diligence paid off in a manner he could never have dreamed. During the Tuesday evening class, the conversation drifted onto the topic of Abraham, the forefather of monotheism. Eleven men were sitting around the table in the library, listening to Rabbi Lathan speak about Abraham's two sons, Isaac and Ishmael, when Len was suddenly struck by a fact that he had always known.

"Excuse me, Rabbi." Leaning forward on his elbows and raising the pencil between his fingers to gain the rabbi's attention, Len said, "I have a problem with this concubine custom." He sat back in his chair and spoke to everyone in the class. "Maybe I'm missing something here, but why wasn't it considered wrong for Abraham to have a child with Hagar?"

As always, Rabbi Lathan took Len's question seriously, and he explained, "Abraham and Sarah were childless. This is why Sarah offered her maidservant to Abraham, so that they could have a son."

"Yes, Rabbi. I understand that, but I'm asking why no one ever brings up the question of Abraham's morality? He was married to Sarah. Surely he must have known that it was wrong to have a child with Hagar."

"Obviously, he did not consider it wrong, otherwise he wouldn't have had a child with her. And Sarah was helping her husband. She understood Abraham's need to have an offspring, and she was barren."

Sitting to the rabbi's right was Gerald, a middle-aged and balding man with an opaque left eye. Gerald shook his head and commented, "They sure don't make wives as generous as they used to."

Everyone, including the rabbi, enjoyed the little remark. everyone except Len, who waited patiently for the laughter to subside before again leaning forward in his chair and saying, "That's exactly what I mean."

"The point is that at the time of Abraham and Sarah, it was not wrong to have a concubine," the rabbi explained. "Interestingly, however, we see that after God grants Sarah a child in her old age, then jealousy does come into play. She then asks Abraham to send Hagar and Ishmael away. This is an important story with lessons to be learned. We read it every year on *Rosh Hashanah*."

"If Abraham could have a concubine, then why can't we have a concubine today?" Len asked. "Surely we should model our lives on a man as righteous as Abraham. And yet, we are not allowed to go out and find a girlfriend."

Rabbi Lathan flipped his hand casually into an offering palm, pouted his lower lip nonchalantly, and said, "Actually, there is no Torah law against having a girlfriend."

The rabbi did not mind the lesson straying from the differences between Isaac and Ishmael. There was no core curriculum, and he knew his students would learn more from involved discussion than passive listening. What he did not know was that Len had a sudden personal stake in the lesson being discussed. Nor did the rabbi notice anything unusual, for Len was often fervent in the classes.

Len wanted to quiz the Rabbi about the Torah laws pertaining to adultery, but before he could formulate his question, Gerald, the opaque-eyed man, raised a hand and said, "I don't know why we're jumping so hard on Abraham; what about his grandson, Jacob? He had two wives and two concubines."

"Now, Jacob married sisters," an old man at one corner of the table said. "That is against the Torah."

They all looked to Rabbi Lathan, but the rabbi, detecting a swelling eagerness in the young boy to his left, resisted clearing up the enigma and instead offered the floor to the boy. "Can you tell us why Jacob was able to marry the two sisters, Leah and Rachael?"

Len expected the boy to spin the story of how Jacob's father in law, Lathan, had made Jacob work seven years for Rachael and then tricked him into marrying Leah, but the boy, not more than a year past his *bar mitzvah*, answered simply, "Jacob lived before we received the Torah at Mount Sinai."

"Of course," the rabbi said. "In *Vayikra*, Leviticus 18, we read . . ." He reached over to pick up a *chumash*, the Torah in book

233

form, lying on the table and, before finding the correct page, quoted, "Do not perform the practice of the land of Egypt in which you dwelled; and do not perform the practice of Canaan to which I bring you, and do not follow their traditions." He replaced the book on the table and spoke directly to Len. "It then goes on to give the laws of forbidden relationships."

Len felt a twinge of self-consciousness. *Has the rabbi picked up on the reason for my special interest in the subject?* But, Len wanted direct clarification on the question, so, sounding as objective as he could, he said, "I thought a married man was not allowed to have a girlfriend. Isn't that adultery?" and wanting to bring academics into the discussion, added, "It's one of the Ten Commandments."

"Of course, adultery is forbidden," the rabbi was quick to reply, "and of course, a man should be faithful to his wife. But, by definition, the law of adultery applies only to the cohabitation with a married woman . . . a sin punishable by death, both the man and the woman."

"And if the man is single?" Gerald asked.

"If he has a relationship with a married woman, then that is the sin of adultery," the rabbi replied. "If the woman is properly married, according to our law, then both are guilty of adultery."

"But a single woman is allowed to have an affair with a married man?" It was Gerald again. He already knew the answer, but wanted to put the rabbi on the spot.

234

"There is no Torah prohibition," the rabbi answered without flinching.

If Len had any qualms about ethical guidance, this class put his mind to rest. The Torah laws met his needs, and his resolve to accept its direction was sealed: never would he doubt its wisdom; always would he accept its answers to his future dilemmas.

A huge part of the weight had been lifted from Len's conscience. He knew that intrinsically he was a good man and would never intentionally hurt another person, especially the innocent. And both Martha and Gertrude were innocent. Yet, Martha he had hurt deeply, and Gertrude he had treated unfairly. True, the damage was far less than he initially believed, but his slate was not clean.

After three days of agonizing, he went in the afternoon to the physical therapy department to speak with Martha. *Strange*, he thought, on his way over. *I haven't seen Martha for a long time. Maybe once, perhaps twice, since Gertrude was diagnosed, but I can't recall speaking to Martha. I know I didn't snub her; I would never have done that. But, what has happened to her? I always used to bump into her at the hospital.* He stopped in his tracks as the idea struck him. *Perhaps she has been avoiding me. Maybe she just wants to give me my space. She was always considerate. On the other hand, how would she even know about Gertrude's cancer? I don't think I told her. And yet, she must have found out. Almost everyone at Yarwell General knows.*

He arrived at the reception desk. No one was there, so he walked back into the department. A handsome young man, not much older than a teenager, came out of a treatment cubicle. "Oh, it's you, Dr. Darshan. What can I do for you?" He wore green scrubs and a white lab coat; otherwise, Len might not have known he was part of the professional staff.

Len pointed a thumb back over his shoulder and said, "There's no one at the desk so I came in."

"There are only two of us here at the moment," the young man explained. "Shelzie is setting up traction on the orthopedic floor, and I'm in the middle of a neck treatment."

"Oh," Len said disappointedly. "I was looking for Martha Saenz."

"Who?" The young man asked.

"Martha. Martha Saenz. She works here."

"Oh, yes. Martha. She left two months ago. I never knew her, because I'm new. I took her place."

So that's what happened, Len thought. *She must have left because of me. And I thought she was casual about our affair. Could take it or leave it. She let me know she loved me, but I didn't think she felt as passionate as I did. Seems I might have been wrong.*

"Do you know where Martha went?" Len asked the young man.

He shrugged his shoulders. "Apparently, she went home. Left Jacobsburg."

And I did this to her. I know she was happy working here. Hell! I was a bastard.

"I'd better get back to my patient," the young man apologized.

"Thanks." Len turned to go. He thought about leaving a message, to ask anyone in the department to send him Martha's home number, but he did not want to request such a personal favor of this young man who had only recently started to work here. *I'll get her number from administration*, Len thought. *Or, maybe she doesn't want me to call her. I need to give this matter some consideration.*

Len did give the matter some consideration, and by the time he arrived back at his office, he had decided it would be better if he did not open Martha's recent wound. Maybe later on down the line he might bump into her. Or, if he met someone who mentioned her name, perhaps then he would ask about her and maybe give her a call. There was no advantage to speaking with her now, not with the healing just underway. Later, yes, but not now.

Gertrude's wounds healed, and emotionally she was coping far better than anyone could have expected. Only, the chemotherapy left her nauseated, and for days after each treatment, she would wake up in the middle of the night vomiting. She was self-conscious about her flat chest and thinning hair, but she wore breast prostheses and took comfort in the knowledge that, soon after the treatments, her gorgeous red locks would return.

When incessant nausea prohibited her sleep, Len would sit up with her while they watched a late night movie on television. He would hold her and comfort her. He would assure her that he was more than satisfied with their one child, Janet—for after the radiation and chemotherapy she could have no more—and he would give her reason to fight to live.

She viewed these months of her life as a necessary part of the cure and was already planning to have breast implants.

Len was both sympathetic and proud of her. He wanted to do whatever he could to help, and he believed he was indeed helping her, because he felt certain that his prayers were being answered. On one or two occasions, as they sat up into the night, sipping cocoa and speaking frankly about their life together, he was tempted to reveal the reason he had turned toward religion. But Len was a superstitious man, and he thought that speaking about his pact with God might be divulging a secret and therefore bring Gertrude's excellent progress to an abrupt halt. He knew exactly what was required of him: everyday, he would have to wear his prayer shawl and phylacteries, and daven. Even when he could not make the services in the Synagogue, he would recite at least the minimal of the prescribed morning prayers at home. And there could be no end to this commitment, because while some malignancies might be declared cured after five cancer-free years, this was not so with all, and breast cancers were known to reappear after ten and twenty and sometimes more years of remission.

Gertrude's prescribed course of six chemotherapy treatments was coming to an end, and Len continued to feel satisfied . . . to a degree. He knew he would continue to do his part, and he would ensure that Gertrude go for her checkups, but something, which he could not quite identify, was still nagging at his thoughts. He did once raise the question of smoking, but he was not at all convinced that the habit had anything to do with Gertrude's cancer, and he was honest enough to tell her so.

The night before her final dose of chemotherapy, Len decided to take her out to a movie. He knew she was afraid of the treatment and would appreciate a distraction.

Then, on the way home, both were quieter than usual. Gertrude was thinking about the next day's inevitable nausea, and Len was pondering his own imperfections, and how they might affect the acceptance of his prayers. Also, when he glanced sympathetically out of the corner of his eye Gertrude's way, he felt guilt. *How could I have deceived her*, he thought for the umpteenth time. *How can I continue with this deceit on my mind? She deserves better.*

They pulled into the driveway. Len reached up to the visor and pressed the remote control to open the door, and his heart began to race. He drove slowly into the garage, turned off the engine, bit his lower lip, and then turned to Gertrude and said, "Gertrude, I've cheated on you."

She did not have to ask him to repeat what he had said. The words were clear and unmistakable. She could have been angry . . . she could have cried . . . she could have asked who, how often, since when, or is it serious, but she did not ask anything at all. As always, she said exactly what she felt.

"Not you, Len."

***

2005

"Not you, Len." From time to time, Len would remember Gertrude's words, her dejected tone, her sudden gloom, and then his own flash of regret. He saw his wife's utter disappointment, and he always understood that it was because he had let her down. He never considered any other basis for her abrupt response. It was plain to see. Until now, as he watched the seconds tick down on his test of her fidelity, and he realized the other possible reasoning behind her reaction. *Sure, she recognized me as a man of high moral standing, and she didn't expect me to betray her trust, but what else did she reveal by singling me out? What a fool I am. All those years I failed to see that she virtually expected other men to fool around, and she was disappointed when I turned out to be no better than the rest. Which means she had a far better understanding of men than I would have guessed, and that was twenty-five years ago. She was a beautiful woman then, and she's still a beautiful woman. Men must have found her attractive then, and I'm certain that middle-aged men find her beautiful now. In fact, even younger men must be attracted to her striking good looks. When I was younger, I was attracted to more mature women.*

Len glanced at the seconds ticking away on his wristwatch and then inspected the blotting paper for a change in color and compared it to the circle of violet on the accompanying glossy pamphlet.

Twelve seconds to go. *Now that I think of it, I must have been really blind. We spoke about my affair with Martha, but Gertrude never did go off the deep end. And that was when we were young and impetuous. It's strange that she did absolutely nothing to retaliate. I can't be certain, but she might have had her revenge by doing to me exactly what I did to her. Only, she remained hush about whatever she was doing.*

Forty-three, forty-four, forty-five. Time! Len compared the colors.

The blotting paper was more of a maroon than violet. Was the demonstration color a little too bright? Len was familiar with this litmus type of testing. In the office, he used similar kits to diagnose pregnancy and a number of different infections. When uncertain, he might wait a few extra seconds, and then get someone else's opinion. He read the instructions one more time. They were emphatic: if the blotting paper had not turned *violet* within the allotted forty-five seconds, then the test was negative.

He looked at the dilute area toward the edge of the test circle. It was now more than a minute since he had poured the drops of reagent, but perhaps the margin was closer to the violet. He was uncertain. So, he did what he would do in the office under similar circumstances. He repeated the test.

Again, the blotting paper turned maroon rather than violet. Len stared incredulously at the negative result. He was certain that

Gertrude was cheating on him. All the pieces of the puzzle seemed to fit, and yet his test failed to prove his theory.

With far less enthusiasm, he picked up the other pair of Gertrude's panties, the floral pink ones. The crotch area was softer, no suggestion of spilled semen. Still, the A-fair-catch literature said that the suspecting partner should estimate the most likely site where backflow might settle and test in that vicinity. Len did exactly as recommended by the literature, and once more waited the forty-five seconds.

Although Len had some degree of curiosity, he really viewed the pink pair of panties as a negative control, and when the blotting paper again turned a maroon color, validating the first two tests, he was disappointed but not surprised.

He felt a wave of relief. There would be no need for confrontation, and for a fleeting moment, his trust in Gertrude was restored.

He cleaned-up his workstation in the bathroom and hid the A-fair-catch kit in a distant upper corner of his closet.

With Juliet purring contently on his lap, he tried to watch the news on the den television, but his mind could not rest. *Perhaps that maroon did represent a positive test. Sometimes colorimetric results may vary when the reagents are old or contaminated, and who knows how careless the A-fair-catch manufacturers may be? I need to test a clean piece of blotting paper as a real negative control. Better still, I need both a positive and a negative. I suppose I'll have to use my own semen for the positive control.*

The question is: should I purposefully leave a stain on my own underwear when we next have intercourse, or should I collect a specimen when I'm alone. He gave the matter some consideration. *Probably better when I'm alone. I always wash off after sex. I don't want Gertrude to notice anything out of the ordinary, and I don't fancy not cleaning up. Or, I could use a cloth and keep it aside in my bathroom drawer.*

The commercial break on the television was taking longer than usual so, hoping to find something more captivating, he began clicking the remote to find another news channel. En route through the programs, he came across one of his favorite old movies, *Brigadoon*, and he settled on the sofa to watch.

Toward the end of the movie, Len heard the garage and then the laundry and kitchen doors open.

Gertrude came through to the den and looked first at the TV screen and then at Len.

"Still up?" She smiled at the tears streaming down his cheeks.

"Come sit next to me," Len said, patting the seat by his side.

Gertrude walked slowly sideways toward the couch, keeping one eye on the movie, while Len turned his attention to her. Something looked different. No radical change and not something bad, rather it was good, and Gertrude appeared more attractive than usual. She had on a brown blouse and a beige pair of slacks, again nothing special. She always went dressy casual to bridge. *My thinking about her probably nurtured my jealousies, and let my imagination run rife*, Len imagined.

She sat next to him on the couch, and he put his arm around her.

Or, the movie has put me into a romantic mood, he thought.

The reason did not seem to matter. He kissed her on the lips, and she cuddled closer. She did seem youthful and energetic and content to be with him, and he did not know why, so he asked, "What is it, Gertrude? You seem different."

She shrugged an unknowing shoulder under his arm. "Nothing's new."

He hugged her again and asked, "Have you lost weight? Are you on a diet? You seem a little lighter."

"You think so," she said, and stood up from the couch to look down at her figure. She then walked the few yards to the entrance hall mirror, turned side to side, and ran her hands over her belly and hips. "Come to think of it," she said to Len, who had turned his attention from the movie to his wife, "these slacks were a little tight, and now they seem to fit easier."

"You are looking good," he said ambling over. "But then, you always look good."

That night, after they made love, Len went to the bathroom, cleaned up, and then kept the washcloth in his drawer for later use. He had his semen specimen for his A-fair-catch positive control.

In truth, Len did not really want to uncover evidence that would prove Gertrude had a lover. He was approaching the mellow years of his life, in which adventure and excitement were more hardship than fun, and a rift in his marriage would not bring about passionate anger; it would bring misery alone. Younger couples seemed content hopping from one relationship to another. These days, many were actually avoiding the wedding canopy in the belief that permanence was unlikely. In contrast, maturing marriages were best left in their status quo. At work and in his social circles, Len had seen a number of longstanding marriages fall apart, and now with his suspicions about Gertrude growing, he seemed to remember more and more of those unhappy endings. It was all simply a sign of the times, and Len did not relish the thought of his marriage falling under the failed column of the often-quoted statistic.

Three and a half weeks went by, and Len managed to hold his suspicions at bay. After all, the initial testing proved negative, quelling his curiosity.

Then, on a Saturday, Gertrude said there was a major tournament at the local studio that night, and asked Len whether he minded if she played. As usual, Len said, "Sure, Gertrude. Go and have a good time." As usual, he stayed home and had a quiet evening, reading his medical journals and watching TV. And as had happened on a number of occasions in the past, Gertrude did not come home until 2:30 in the morning.

She tried to be as quiet as possible, and although Len was a deep sleeper, she woke him. He glanced at his bedside clock and was immediately concerned. Feigning mere inquisitiveness rather than revealing his suspicion, Len asked in a sleepy voice, "Why are you so late, Gertrude? Is anything wrong?"

"There was a midnight game," she explained. "Jean and I were having a good run, so we decided to stay. I would have called, but I didn't want to wake you. I figured you'd get me on my cell if you were worried."

After that, Len could not sleep well. *Seems I was right after all. She told me about those midnight games and I've always believed her. Now, I wonder if they are real.* He thought about the situation, the zest of the bridge players, how they oftentimes could not get enough of their game, so he accepted the late night entertainment as genuine. *Yet, do they put the extra games together on the spur of the moment?* He then remembered what Gertrude had told him earlier, that it was a major tournament. He felt like confronting her, like saying, *tournaments are organized events. How can you just add games?* But he did not waste his time asking, he could already hear her reply: *the midnight game wasn't a part of the tournament; it was only for fun.* Then, she would be alerted to his suspicion and become more discrete. *No, I'll have to find out the truth without questioning her. I still hope I'm wrong, but how can I be? Yet, I suppose Gertrude and Jean might have decided to stay for a midnight game. The guy who runs the studio . . . what's his name?* Len thought for a moment. *Blake . . . yes that's it . . . Blake. He seems like a pretty spontaneous type of person. I remember when he bought the business. Gertrude told*

246

me he left his steady job to take over the studio when the previous manager couldn't make a go of it. That was reckless. All the same, I suppose I shouldn't judge him; he seems to have turned the studio into a success. He even took on an assistant. I remember her. She was at the bridge club Christmas party. Nice woman. Mollie. That's right, Mollie. Good looking, too. Tall, with short blonde hair and freckles. She looks like a fun-seeker and much younger than she probably is. It's not too far fetched to imagine that after the tournament Mollie and Blake just threw in a late night party for their guests. Probably makes good sense in the entertainment business. Still, with this picture, I have no choice but to step up my scrutiny. I cannot continue to act like an ostrich.

After a restless night, Len woke up at the crack of dawn. He crept out of bed and remained perfectly still, listening to Gertrude's rhythmical and soft snoring. Then, certain she was still asleep, he tiptoed into the bathroom, gently closed the door, and switched on the lights.

Damn, they're not here, he thought, searching for Gertrude's panties. *She often just throws them on the floor after a late night.*

He turned off the lights and walked softly through the bedroom, hesitating to ensure she was still sound asleep, and then went to the laundry. On top of the pile of dirty washing were Gertrude's bra and panties. He began to feel nervous. How would he explain this to Gertrude if she were awake and see him walking around, carrying her underwear? So, he scrunched them into his hand and again returned to the bedroom and into his closet, where he took down his A-fair-catch kit. Then, he remembered the washcloth that he was keeping, the positive control, so he returned to the bathroom and went directly to his drawer. At last, he had what he needed.

Back in the closet, he set out his paraphernalia on the waist high middle shelf, applied the solvent solution to his washcloth and to the crotch area of Gertrude's panties, and then dabbed each specimen with a piece of blotting paper. Now, he had to wait for the paper to dry, but that did not matter; he could complete the test later.

Together with the washcloth, he replaced the A-fair-catch kit on the top shelf in the corner of his closet, and carefully left the two pieces of blotting on the middle shelf, the positive control to the rear and the sampling of Gertrude's panties nearer the front. He would have to remember, *positive on the wall side, test specimen toward the edge.*

He heard Gertrude stirring. He could hide the panties in one of his coat pockets, but he was anxious to get them back to the dirty laundry basket, so he switched off the lights in the closet, opened a crack in the door, and again stood perfectly still. Gertrude coughed . . . her smoker's early morning cough. She was awake. He could still leave the panties in the closet and retrieve them later, but he was obsessive and wanted them back in the laundry as soon as possible. Gertrude would often drop the dirty clothing into the washing machine first thing in the morning. She probably would not take stock of the items, but Len did not want to take that chance, so he again scrunched the panties in his hand, walked boldly through the bedroom, and said a carefree "good morning" as he passed her.

The panties back in the laundry, the specimens ready for the final testing, Len decided to go back to bed, catch up on his sleep, and once again consider how to approach Gertrude when the results turned out positive.

After forty-five minutes of delicious and much needed sleep, Len again awoke, this time to the shrill ring of his Sunday alarm clock.

Dressed in sneakers, a navy golf shirt, and khaki slacks, he was off to the Synagogue.

Sunday mornings were rather special; the prayer service took about thirty-five minutes and was followed by a leisurely breakfast of bagels, lox, eggs, juice, coffee, and trimming, and then a number of formal discussions and lectures—all over by 10:30 a.m.

It was the breakfast, usually sponsored by one of the congregants, in the hall behind the main sanctuary that Len liked the best, not the food but the heated impromptu debates. And this morning was no different to any other. Together with his Sunday clique of four, he sat at the first of three parallel trestle tables, discussing the topics carried over from the previous weeks and months: the American war in Iraq, the recent suicide bombings in Israel and now the rest of the world, and a new favorite, the nation of Islam.

"If ever we should be at war, the time is now," Gerald, now elderly and bald but with the same opaque left eye, said to Len and the others sitting at their corner of the table. All the years Len had known him, Gerald had been a calm person, until he lost a sister in

249

the spate of killings in the Middle East, whereupon he became passionately vocal. "I would like to go there myself to annihilate every last one of them, like they want to annihilate us. We're too soft. They are the worst enemy we have ever had."

"You can't compare them to the Nazis," said Irma, a plump middle-aged woman wearing a black headscarf.

"The only difference is that the Nazis were a dominant nation," Gerald hollered. "If these terrorists had their way, they wouldn't bother with mass graves and crematoriums, they would just push us directly into the sea . . . literally."

"Who exactly do you want to kill?" Len asked as calmly as he could. "There isn't a war at this time."

"Every Muslim. They want to kill us."

"Not every Muslim is bad," Irma replied. "Only a small minority are extremists. The average person over there probably wants the same as everyone else in the world—a decent living, safety, and happiness."

"What nonsense!" Gerald pushed his chair away from the table and threw up his indignant arms. "Those people over there are sending their family members to hell with bombs strapped to their backs. I wouldn't call that 'wanting safety and a decent living.' Would you?"

Irma would not be intimidated. "I wouldn't call suicide bombers 'average people.' Would you?"

"No, but the average Palestinian supports suicide bombing."

Instead of answering, Irma turned to Rabbi Lathan, who just happened to be walking past. "What do you think, Rabbi; what percentage of Muslims are terrorists?"

While Rabbi Lathan was the religious leader in the Synagogue, congregants commonly turned to him for advice in personal relationships and for an opinion in a number of topics, particularly history and politics. The rabbi was on his way to washing his hands and then pouring himself a cup of coffee, but he did not mind the intrusion. He stopped for a moment, shrugged his shoulders, and gave the honest answer, "I don't know."

Gerald jumped back into the debate, bringing Irma on track. "All right," he said. "Maybe not every Muslim, but most of them . . . and every Palestinian."

Now, Rabbi Lathan could read where this argument had come from, and he was curious about what these congregants had to say. He also felt obligated to throw a religious perspective into the discussion, so he pulled up a chair and said, "On Passover, we read in the Haggada that in every generation, someone will arise and seek our destruction, so why are you surprised?"

"Anti-Semitism has always been around, Rabbi," Len said. "And ever since independence in 1948, the State of Israel has not known peace, but terrorism is getting worse; factions amongst the Arabs seem to be growing more militant and desperate."

251

"They are all militant," Gerald threw in. "The Koran tells them to kill all the infidels, and anyone who is not a Muslim is an infidel."

"What exactly is an infidel?" asked Basil, the fourth person, in his South African accent. Basil was the youngest in the group, an immigrant of about fifteen years, who recently graduated as a Thoracic Surgeon.

"An unbeliever," answered Gerald. "The word infidel means an unbeliever. That is you, me, every Jew, and anyone else who is not a Muslim. According to the Koran, the Muslims have to kill every infidel, and it seems that the Palestinians are having a good go at it. *We* may not be at war, but *they* are."

"I have heard others who think the same as you," Basil said, shaking his head gently. "But Irma is right. It's not all Muslims. I have a whole bunch of colleagues from the Arab countries. I think most of them are Muslim, and they seem reasonable to me. I realize there are many radical crazies out there, but I don't see them. I must agree with Irma."

"You have no idea what those reasonable colleagues of yours are saying behind your back," Gerald said. "Those guys who flew the planes into the Twin Towers on 9/11 were living right here in America, together with other Americans, and no one suspected them of being 'radical crazies,' as you put it." He could hear himself going off the deep end, so he took a sip of coffee to calm down, but then trying to add impetus to his argument, asked, "Do you think I am wrong, Rabbi?"

While lifting his yarmulke out of the way with his left hand, Rabbi Lathan ran his right hand back over his head, and then leaned forward onto the table and spoke softly:

"There is no denying that the problem is terrible. And it is spreading. Perhaps the rest of the world is gaining an understanding of what it is like to live under the threat of terror, of how each bomb deals a horrific blow to any number of lives. You would think that they would now begin to throw their support behind Israel, but the opposite may be happening. Many people are actually blaming Israel for the problem, saying the Jews provoked the Arabs." He looked down at his laced fingers and then slowly raised his head again before continuing, "We may be militarily superior, but we are losing the propaganda war.

"As to the number of Muslims who might be considered radical, I am certain that it is not all of them, even though the number is great. Some estimates I have heard run around ten percent of practicing Muslims, some a lot higher. But even at ten percent, that is still more than double or treble the total number of Jews."

Gradually, Rabbi Lathan's words turned into a virtual chant, as though he was delivering a well-rehearsed speech.

"As with any reign of terror, it begins with one or perhaps a few extremists who manage to gain the support of a handful of prominent leaders in the community, and these leaders then disseminate the lie among the easily influenced. The longer it goes unchecked the more people believe it. First the people who live closer to the lie, then those further away, and eventually those who would actually oppose it. The question is: what is the lie?

"The lie is a matter of language. Although the Arabs arose from Ishmael, the son of Abraham and brother of Isaac, Islam as a monotheistic religion started with the preaching of Mohammed in the seventh century C.E. and grew out of Judaism and Christianity. Islam declares five prophets, Adam, Noah, Moses, Jesus, and their major prophet, Mohammed.

"English is precise; each word has an exact meaning. Not so with the Eastern languages. As with the Torah, which has been translated and interpreted many times over and which continues to be re-translated and re-interpreted, so, too, must the Koran be open to translation and interpretation. People who are both wise and evil can use the scriptures as a weapon in their arsenal. I don't know the ins and outs of the Koran, but I have read many passages, which may incite belligerence amongst susceptible Muslims and hatred amongst non-Muslims. So I now ask how accurate are the translations and interpretations, and what is the purpose of these passages that keep cropping up in e-mails, letters to editors, and, I am certain, in propaganda and classrooms on the other side, in the Muslim countries. Of all these provocative passages, the one most frequently quoted from the Koran, the one universally proclaimed by Muslim fanatics is, 'Death to the infidels,' and it has been chanted so long and so often that no one questions its meaning.

"My friends, herein rests the blatant deceit. The word *infidel* is exactly what it says—infidel. Infidel is the translation from the Arabic word *Kaffir*. Infidel is not an Arabic word that needs re-translation; it does not mean *unbeliever*, as is so widely accepted.

254

Infidel signifies infidelity. And infidelity to what? To Islam. An infidel, as denoted in the Koran, is a person who has broken his faith with Islam. This is the exact meaning of the Arabic word, *Kaffir*. This is the reason why the word *Kaffir*, without translation, has been used as a pejorative term.

"What do you know about the word *Kaffir*, Doctor," the Rabbi asked, as he noticed Basil smiling awkwardly."

Basil drummed his thumbs against the edge of the table. "In South Africa, it's a terrible thing to say," he answered tautly. "It's used as an insult to black people . . . the same as the N-word here."

"It occurs to me," Gerald said, "that the exact meaning of the word infidel is irrelevant. They call any non-Muslim an infidel, and then declare 'Death to the Infidels,' so semantics have no part to play in this quarrel."

"Ah! But semantics do," the Rabbi said, his index finger raised high. "The message is not to the belligerent fanatics— nothing anyone can say will get through to them—it is to the peace-loving Muslims, especially Imams and other leaders, who might be confused by all this violent propaganda."

"Imams and other leaders are not going to stand up to the belligerent fanatics," Gerald replied. "They are terrified they, too, will be labeled *infidel*."

"There, you have a point," Rabbi Lathan agreed. "Non-Muslims, they kill at random, but they will hone in on anyone they consider a traitor."

"An infidel," Basil corrected.

"Precisely," the rabbi agreed. "An infidel in its original sense is one of their own who they consider a traitor to whatever they declare acceptable. Like that Egyptian, Rashad Khalifa, who came to the United States. A committee of religious scholars from Saudi Arabia declared him an infidel, and hunted him down and had him killed somewhere in Arizona.

"That's like Salmon Rushdie, isn't it?" asked Irma.

"The Rushdie case is similar," the rabbi said. "Do you remember the name of his book?"

"That was *Satanic Verses*, wasn't it?" answered Irma.

"And what was it about?" the rabbi asked.

When faced with four blank stares, Rabbi Lathan said, "Rushdie was a secular Muslim from India, faced with two problems: Firstly, the Muslim fundamentalists did not appreciate the humor in his satirical work about Islam, and secondly, among the religious figures who he chose to criticize was the Ayatollah Khomeini. Rushdie called the fundamentalists *Thought Police* and said that they had taken over Islam. But his real problem was not with the group; it was with the Ayatollah Khomeini, who sentenced him to death for insulting Islam, the Koran, and Mohammed. The Ayatollah Khomeini called for the execution of anyone who insulted the Muslim sanctities. He also declared any zealous Muslim who died whilst doing this holy execution a martyr."

Satisfied that he had dealt with the questions, Rabbi Lathan went to pour himself a much-wanted cup of coffee.

Besides the rabbi's opinions, each of the others walked away with something else from the discussion. While Gerald believed intellectualizing could make no difference to the war against terror, Irma felt the rabbi had sided with her. Basil was intrigued by the origin of the derogatory word, Kaffir, and Len, who remained uncharacteristically quiet during the whole discussion, had heard an opinion that he did not like: traitors, considered despicable in anyone's language, were the same as infidels, and although he may not have committed adultery all those years ago, he was certainly guilty of infidelity. What is more, he was all but positive that Gertrude was guilty of the same offense now.

Anxious to uncover the truth, one way or the other, Len planned on testing the two waiting pieces of blotting paper as soon as possible. It was Sunday, and even if Gertrude had no plans, she was sure to leave the house at some time, so he would wait for the opportune moment.

But Len was in for an unexpected surprise.

CHAPTER NINE

Len thought nothing of the dark blue Chrysler parked in the street in front of the house. They were not expecting visitors, so the car probably belonged to the neighbors across the road.

He came in through the laundry and into the kitchen and was pleasantly surprised to find Janet, who had come to visit, and with her was Brian, Janet's boyfriend of two and a half years and roommate for the last six months. Len was not pleased with Janet's accommodation arrangements, but he felt helpless to intervene. As Gertrude told him, "Janet is an adult and that is the way of the world today."

Gertrude, Janet, and Brian were sitting around the table, eating doughnuts, drinking orange juice, and laughing, when Len arrived.

Gertrude and Brian turned silent, but Janet, now twenty-seven, jumped up and ran to give her father a big hug and a kiss on the cheek.

Something was afoot, and Len had little problem guessing what it might be. Janet and Brian had studied together in the Northeast and were now on faculty at the same university. Len and Gertrude had met Brian on a number of occasions, twice when they went to visit, and once, three months ago, when Brian had flown in with Janet. On every other occasion, the visits had been planned, so this one was indeed unusual.

"You look terrific," Len said to his daughter, playing along with this out of the ordinary Sunday morning visit.

Indeed, Janet did look terrific. She had her mother's height, trim figure, and features, but with a rounded chin and bright, big, brown eyes. Her hair was dark, as her father's hair had once been, and she wore it shoulder length, shining and loose.

"You, too, Daddy," Janet replied with a courteous smile, but then turned intense and added, "and Mom looks gorgeous. She says she hasn't been exercising more than usual and that she hasn't been on a special diet, but Brian and I find that hard to believe." She turned to Gertrude. "It's true, Mom. You're looking sensational."

Hearing these compliments about his wife were pleasing, but under the current circumstances, Len's mind also flashed to the two pieces of blotting paper on the shelf in his closet, waiting for their final stage of testing.

"Come sit, Len," Gertrude said. "Can I pour you a cup of coffee?"

Gertrude may have appeared more trim than on Janet's last visit, but this was understandable. She only managed to eat a third of a doughnut and left the remainder on the plate. She may not have been on any weight-losing plan, but she seemed to be eating less all the same.

"I'll help myself," Len said, and walked over to the percolator. "So . . . to what do we owe this pleasant surprise?"

Gertrude turned to Len impatiently. "Janet and Brian wouldn't tell me. They wanted to wait for you."

Oh hell! Len was having new thoughts about the purpose of the visit. *She's pregnant.*

Len sat opposite Brian and between Janet and Gertrude. He took a sip of his coffee and reached for a doughnut.

There was a moment's silence before Brian turned to his right, facing Gertrude, and said, "Janet and I love each other and we want to get married. I asked her last night. She said yes, and now I am asking you."

Janet moved over to stand behind Brian; Gertrude's broad smile reflected her approval; and Brian floundered an instant as he purposefully turned his gaze from Gertrude and toward Len, trying to recover from what he considered a faux pas, and added, "We flew in to ask your permission and blessing, Dr. Darshan."

Brian had curly blonde hair, cropped short, hazel eyes, and dimples in his cheeks when he smiled. But he was not smiling now. In the back of the mind was the possibility that Len might say no. Brian had not discussed this unlikely circumstance with Janet, but from what he had come to understand, her dad was somewhat of a religious fanatic . . . unpredictable and extra particular about his only daughter's choice for a husband. And now that he had inadvertently snubbed Janet's father by asking for her hand from her mother instead, Brian was expecting a negative reply, a tactful and logical reason to think more deeply about the engagement, but a refusal all the same. Until Len looked him straight in the eye and said, "I hope you will both be happy, and I expect you to take good care of her."

Brian's dimples returned. What had promised to be a quiet and restful day turned into a hectic morning and afternoon of phone calls to family and friends, people dropping by to visit and wish the young couple well, and dinner for a party of fifteen that evening at *Theo's*, Gertrude's current favorite restaurant in all of Jacobsburg.

Although Janet had left home for college nearly ten years ago, this day of her engagement to Brian marked a milestone in Gertrude's protracted empty nest syndrome. Gertrude had wanted a houseful of children, and because she was only able to have one, she had clung to her daughter.

Gertrude was vulnerable, had no one to turn to but her two-year-old daughter, the awful day Len dealt her that unexpected blow, the news that he had been seeing another woman. Gertrude believed then that Len would never cheat again, and she thought that time would heal her wound. After all, Len had volunteered the confession, and she knew he would do all he could to make amends. Still, she could not control her own resentment. She never spoke her anger to her daughter aloud, but often, just to relieve her frustrations, she would have a one-way silent dialogue with Janet. Some of these conversations she should have had with Len, but more often, they were about Len, some good and some confessional.

Len was largely correct about Gertrude's reasoning when she had said to him, "Not you, Len." She had viewed him as different, as a man less likely to go astray than other men. Even in her youth, Gertrude understood the nature and the sex drive of men, and she knew that they were frequently not to be trusted; this was one of the major reasons she had fallen in love with Len, and this was the major reason she was so deeply hurt. With time, the blow had softened, and although she did grow to trust him again, the damage was done. Gertrude knew she would always be able to trust Janet. Janet could not hurt her as Len had. In many ways, her daughter filled that void left by her husband, and in many ways, Gertrude felt more comfortable giving her daughter all the love that she had.

Gertrude was always there for her daughter. Throughout her school years, as Janet gathered a circle of friends, Gertrude gave her the space she needed, but mother and daughter remained best friends.

Gertrude never returned to the teaching profession; she remained a dedicated home keeper, mother, and wife. Still, she had many free hours in her days, so she found a suitable hobby, something mentally stimulating, the card game—bridge. Astute, sociable, patient, and willing to learn, Gertrude transformed first into a mediocre player and then, with time, into one of the major contenders in the local bridge club.

The bridge studio, adjacent to the freeway about a mile from Gertrude's home, was tucked away in a corner of a strip shopping center, between a dentist's office on one side and *The Gardens of Sicily*, a flamboyant restaurant with mediocre food and a popular bar, on the other.

Occasionally, socializing would continue beyond the last hand. Players would get together for postmortems of the more interesting cards dealt not only during that session but also from sessions past. Often, discussions would carry over from the club, onto the sidewalk, and into The Gardens of Sicily.

In the years before Janet left for college, Gertrude hardly ever played at night, and when she did, she was anxious to get home as early as possible. She never would wait for the final scores, even when she was in line to win valued bridge points or one of the token prizes.

When Janet eventually left home for college, bridge effectively filled the gap in Gertrude's life. Since only she and Len remained in the house, she felt less and less of a need to rush home. Len understood little about the game of bridge, and bridge was becoming Gertrude's major interest. She had a number of regular partners, and some of the better players in Jacobsburg often invited her to play in tournaments, either as their partner or as part of a team of four. Because she earned prestige and growing recognition in the world of bridge, she did not experience loneliness even in the years immediately after Janet's departure.

She loved the game and she loved hearing about interesting hands and the opinions and tactics of other leading players; she loved her world of bridge.

Gertrude and Janet remained in close contact through the phone and e-mail, and when Janet flew in from college, three or four times a year, bridge would be demoted to Gertrude's second priority. The remainder of the time, bridge was number one, and the people involved made up a harmonious society with a bonding interest. They were a large cohesive family. And while Gertrude may have liked some players a little less than she liked others, she found everyone generally acceptable.

***

1944 to 1953

Jon Yi, son of Elizabeth Morgan, was born and raised in one of the poorer neighborhoods of Liverpool, England. Although Jon had none of the finer things that money could offer, he did not miss them. He had a mother who loved him dearly and who saw to his continued happiness.

In the ninth year of Jon's life, a week before Christmas, Elizabeth Morgan took her son to the toy department of the downtown emporium, intent on giving him the finest treat she could afford: Jon was allowed to purchase any toy he fancied, up to the value of one pound.

Tears of joy welled in Elizabeth's eyes as Jon hesitated in awe at the entrance to the toy department. He did not believe in Santa, but that did not matter; the jolly man on the elevated throne under the Christmas tree surpassed his wildest expectations. And for the little girl sitting on his lap and for the children waiting in line to whisper wishes into his ear, he was as authentic as any Santa who had recently flown in from the North Pole.

But idle chatter with the store's imposter would have to wait; Jon had a more important matter on his mind. He knew it would be another year before he would again receive a brand new toy of his own choice, so the one he bought today should be carefully selected, not a toy of flitting pizzazz, like a kite or a model car, but rather something to offer enduring entertainment, like a croquet set or a challenging board game that he could play with his mother on cold wintry nights.

Elizabeth watched carefully as Jon set out to make his purchase. She knew he would not want to select something beyond the allotted budget, yet what Jon did not know was that Elizabeth was prepared to pay up to five shillings more if she detected he really fell in love with a particular toy. She also planned to buy one of his favorite treats—either ice cream or candyfloss—to celebrate the acquisition of whichever brand new article he would choose.

For nineteen shillings and nine pence, three pence less than the pound that Elizabeth was willing to spend, Jon found a cricket set with a wooden bat, a ball, and three plastic wickets with two bales. Now, Jon had time to dillydally around Santa, maybe speak of Christmas to some of the other children in the line, or perhaps tinker with the display toys that were far too expensive for anyone to buy.

They were on their way to the platform with the electric train when Jon suddenly felt a tug at his hand. Elizabeth's jaw fell limp and she stopped in her tracks when she saw the tall and elegant Taiwanese man in a dark suit and red tie wheeling his shopping basket in their direction.

"Chen," Elizabeth whispered, and she dropped Jon's hand to bring her own over her shocked mouth.

The man came closer, noticed Elizabeth's stare, looked away, but then turned to face her again as he strained to recall.

"Chen?" Elizabeth repeated. "Chen Yi?"

"Yes," the man replied, confusion still written all over his face.

"I am Elizabeth." She brought a palm to her chest, as though Chen might not know to whom she was referring. "Elizabeth Morgan."

The man ran his hand over his head of straight black hair, from his brow all the way back, and down his neck. He squinted at Elizabeth and then slowly remembered, "Ah, Elizabeth. Yes, Elizabeth." He spoke in short but clear staccato bursts, some not quite arriving at their complete pronunciation. He then smiled wryly and added, "We must get together, Elizabeth."

Speaking words of the utmost importance, Elizabeth then looked down at her son and announced cautiously, "This is Jon."

Chen extended a hand. "How you do, Jon." He again turned to Elizabeth and asked, "You married now?"

She laughed happily as though a tremendous weight had been lifted from her shoulders. "Heavens no." She then once more stared at Chen and repeated, "This is Jon. He is nine years old, Chen. This is Jon."

Chen now examined the boy by Elizabeth's side. Handsome, for sure, with features too soft for a European, yet not quite as elegant as those Chen noticed in Oriental children.

"How do you do, sir," Jon said, and Chen was surprised by the sophistication with just a hint of cockney in the boy's voice.

Not knowing what to expect, but tending toward a happy response, Elizabeth declared for the last time, "This is Jon, Chen. His name is Jon Yi."

The color drained from Chen's face, and he now seemed angry as he asked, "How did you know I would be here in this store, Elizabeth?" He then bent over to take hold of Jon's chin, jerked his face to the side, examined the profile briefly, and snapped, "Oh no, Elizabeth. Oh no, you can't pull this one on me." Chen then stood erect and with one last "Oh no!" he walked swiftly towards the door, leaving the shopping cart with a doll, a Superman costume, and a meccano set in the middle of the store isle.

He never knew his father, Chen Yi, a successful Taiwanese businessman, until the age of nine, and then, after the disappointing meeting, Jon did not care if he never saw him again.

Yet, Chen did give something of value to his son. When Jon sensed his father's affluence, he vowed that he, too, would one day be wealthy enough to give his mother everything that his father denied her, all that her gentle heart could desire.

***

November 2000

The regular Wednesday night bridge game meant as much to Jean as it did to Gertrude, possibly more, for whereas Gertrude still had her home and Len, Jean was childless and had lost her husband to the complications of diabetes. Other engagements were put on hold, and cruel weather, too, was no obstacle, just as it was no obstacle the wet and cold third Wednesday of November.

Gertrude and Jean arrived at the same time. They both wanted to share a few words, and so they opted to remain on the sidewalk under the awning for a smoke before entering the studio.

As Gertrude lit Jean's cigarette, protecting the lighter flame from the brisk breeze, Jean looked up and said, "Here comes that new fellow."

Gertrude turned around. A lanky man in a dark raincoat was walking their way. His forehead, wide set eyes, nose, lips, and chin seemed to blend in an uncanny yet attractive manner, making the man appear more youthful than his salt and pepper hair betrayed. He smiled cordially as he realized he was being discussed, and then, recognizing Jean, said, "Oh, hello. You were here on Monday, weren't you?"

Gertrude could see that the man had not remembered Jean's name. Jean was short and plump, with black hair also turning gray, but hers was unkempt and inconspicuous rather than groomed and elegant, as was the tall man's hair.

Jean was pleased that the man at least remembered her, and Gertrude could sense from Jean's sudden sprightliness that she wished he might have recognized her more readily.

"Jon," Jean proceeded to introduce the man. "This is my friend, Gertrude."

"Pleased to meet you, Gertrude," Jon said, offering his hand with a bow of the neck, a soft squint, and a friendly smile, which suggested that he might indeed be pleased to meet her. "What you ladies doing out here in the cold? Are you coming in to play?"

"Jean and I are finishing our smokes," Gertrude answered, making sure Jon heard Jean's name, in case had forgotten it. "Would you like one?"

Jon hesitated for a moment and then, to Gertrude's surprise, answered, "Sure. What are you smoking? I'm still trying to find an American cigarette that I like."

"Here, try one of these," Gertrude offered, reaching into her purse, and before Jon could reply, she said, "Is that really true? You are from Britain, aren't you? Are cigarettes that different over there?"

Jon laughed, took the cigarette, and let Gertrude light him up. He grimaced while inhaling the first puff, but then studied the brand name written just below the beige filter and said, "Hmm, not bad."

In the few minutes before going into the studio, Gertrude and Jean learned that Jon was a highly ranked British bridge player and that he owned a blossoming technology company, which had recently merged with a major American corporation with its head office right here in Jacobsburg. He would maintain his home in Liverpool, but for the foreseeable future, he would have to spend at least a third of his time in the USA, so he was searching for a suitable apartment. They did not discuss his marital status, but as they made their way into the studio and Jon went to speak with Blake, the owner, Jean whispered to Gertrude, "Did you notice he's not wearing a ring?"

Despite the miserable weather, the turn out was good. Wednesday nights always seemed to pull in a large crowd. People were over the hump, looking forward to the Friday, and anxious to break the monotony of the workweek.

Sixty-three players turned up, sixty-four including Blake, himself, who was to partner with Jon. This meant there would be sixteen tables and thirty-two teams, half of which would sit north south, and the other half east west. While the north south teams would remain stationary at their table, the east west teams would rotate around the room, playing two pre-dealt hands at each stop. This was the format, and looking around the room, the night promised some tough competition for all who came to play.

271

For Gertrude and Jean, playing north south, the hands were going well. They were bidding conservatively, communicating clearly, and raking in high scores, confident that they were contenders to take first place and perhaps win a point towards their Life Master ranking.

Then, with the final two hands left to play, Blake and Jon took the east west seats at Gertrude and Jean's table. Gertrude noticed Jean begin to fidget in her chair and tug at the collar of her paisley purple pullover.

All Gertrude could do was gently shake her head and hope that the presence of these two men, both far more handsome than any others in the studio, would not cloud her partner's thinking.

Each of the four players studied their cards.

Jean had the first call. "One club," she said, indicating that she had at least twelve points, a hand strong enough to open the bidding.

Jon, sitting to Jean's left, overcalled, "One spade."

"Pass." Gertrude, opposite Jean, had nothing to support her partner's bid.

"Two spades." Blake called, revealing limited strength, but with enough spade support for his partner.

The other three passed, ending the auction with Jon playing two spades.

Gertrude, to Jon's left, played the first card.

Then, Blake had to expose his hand for Jon to play and for all to see.

Gertrude was pleased; Blake's *dummy hand* seemed weaker than she had anticipated.

The first four or five tricks seemed promising, and Gertrude realized that she and Jean could prevent their opponents from winning the eight tricks needed to make their contract. Then, Jean, for no obvious reason, seemed to take an inordinate amount of time thinking; she could not accurately recall the cards previously played. Her rapidly dwindling hormones had drained from the matter of her brain, striking her temporarily dumb and defenseless and causing her to misplay, and she and Gertrude lost their opportunity to defeat the two-spade contract.

Gertrude was furious. Jean had given away the hand that would have clinched their overall win. To make matters worse, Gertrude thought she could detect Jon snigger, aware that he had been let off the hook. Still, she did not want to say anything hurtful or undignified, so she bit her lip and prepared to play the final hand of the evening.

Sitting in the north position, Gertrude studied her new set of thirteen cards:

♠A 9 7 6

♥A J

♦A 10 7 2

♣Q 5 2

Fifteen powerful points; this hand could bring in a high score, provided Jean had the necessary support.

At the other end of the table, Jean, with seventeen points in her hand, had similar thoughts.

♠K Q 8 5 2

♥K Q 9 7

♦3

♣A K 3

The bidding began, each player in turn nominating a suit together with strength, letting not only their partner but also the opposition understand the secrets of their hand. There could be no reading of subtle body signs, like a smile or a sweat, for total strength was not yet certain; it would depend upon the spread of the pack and the position of each card around the table. Furthermore, no one at the club would consider cheating. Any illegal signaling, such as a flicker of a finger or eye, any communication other than the few words of each bid would not cross anyone's mind. Bridge is a game with honor.

With strong bidding, Gertrude found herself in a contract of *seven no trumps* and eager for that fist glimpse of Jean's dummy hand.

Blake led with the King of diamonds, Jean revealed her cards, and Gertrude was satisfied with her contract. Being an expert, she calculated that she would probably win. Only two possible distributions of the cards could lead to her defeat; one she could overcome, the second she could not: if Jon sitting to her right had all of the four missing spades, she would go down. If Blake to her left had the four spades, although a lesser player would not make the contract, she could.

She won the first trick with the ace of diamonds, and she knew that she had eleven tricks off the top: one diamond, three clubs, four hearts, and three spades. What remained uncertain were the final two spade tricks; her first task was to carefully discover the distribution of the missing spades. Were she to return the lead to dummy and play the King of spades, she would lose if either Jon or Blake held all four missing spades. She therefore led the ace of spades from her own hand and watched the play unfold.

Blake followed with the three, she played the two from dummy, and lo and behold, Jon played the two of hearts; he had no spades. This meant that Blake still held the Jack, ten, and four. Her prudence paid off. By repeatedly bringing the lead back into her own hand, and playing spades through Blake, her dummy could beat whatever card Blake threw out, and she thereby won the hand.

The game complete, Blake had to jump up to help his assistant, Mollie, who had done an excellent job coordinating the evening's entertainment. That left Gertrude, Jean, and Jon at the table, with a number of regulars dropping by to welcome Jon to the club, compliment him on his game, and repeatedly ask the same questions: "Where are you from?"; "How long are you going to stay in Jacobsburg?"; and "What is your line of business?" Then, on their way out of the studio, they would remark that they hoped to see him again at bridge, soon.

The scores were in. Taking first place in the north south teams was the pair Gertrude and Jean, thanks in part to Gertrude's grand slam in the final hand. In first place east west were Jon and Blake, who were also, by a narrow margin, declared winners overall.

Jean grimaced, and Jon and Gertrude glanced her way, knowing that her single lapse had cost her and her partner the title for the evening and the single point toward Life Master ranking.

Still, it had been an exciting night's bridge, with many interesting hands, and even more potential strategies, both obvious and obscure.

The guests were filing out. Gertrude went to fetch her coat, and on her way to the cloakroom, stopped for a few words with Mollie, who was packing away the last few stacks of cards. Blake, too, had completed his duties and returned to the table to thank Jon for the game.

Jon, Blake, Mollie, Gertrude, and Jean were last to leave. Collars upturned and warm breath misting into the air, the others watched Blake turn the lock on the studio door.

"Goodnight, all." Gertrude was first to step off the curb.

"Call me tomorrow," Jean shouted to her.

Jon was next to peel off, but Blake, realizing that Jon knew few people in Jacobsburg and sensing that he might want to linger awhile before returning to his lonely hotel room, nodded toward the door of The Gardens of Sicily and suggested, "Do you feel like a night cap?"

"Sounds good to me," Jon agreed, while glancing directly at Mollie's friendly, freckled face, and Mollie accepted this as an invitation to tag along.

Mollie enjoyed the camaraderie, and always felt the more the merrier, so she called to Gertrude and Jean, both a few steps away, and the five of them made their way through the restaurant door and towards the bar

Fabio, the aging barman, waved a hand to them as they ambled up to the counter. Pointing first to Jean, he said, "Strawberry daiquiri," then to Mollie, "Piña colada," to Blake, "Draught on tap," and to Gertrude, "Hot chocolate; I'll send for some from the back." Fabio then hesitated before pointing to Jon and simply asking, "What'll it be?"

Jon looked at Gertrude and repeated, "Hot chocolate?"

Fabio probably understood Jon's question, but nevertheless misinterpreted, "Two hot chocolates."

"No," Jon interrupted, with a show of the hand. "I think I'll try your draught on tap. Is it dark?"

"The darkest, strongest, and tastiest in the mighty metropolis of Jacobsburg," Fabio said, one hand already on the lever of his draught tank, the other holding a twelve-ounce mug under the spout.

They took their drinks to the nearest table. The crowd in the main part of the restaurant had begun to dwindle, but the bar was still full. Three young men and a woman sat on stools at the end of the counter, and only two of the other eleven round tables were unoccupied.

"Good turnout tonight?" Fabio called to Blake.

"Pretty good," Blake answered, with a blasé salute of his beer mug.

After a moment's silence, Jean asked, "There was one board where east, the opener, held nine hearts to the Queen. How did you bid the hand, Jon?"

From there, the conversation flowed: strong opinions, a few contradictions, second and third thoughts about misplayed tricks, and plenty of laughs.

Jean was first to hold her empty glass aloft, pointing to it with the other hand. Within a matter of thirty seconds, Fabio had a daiquiri waiting on the counter, paper umbrella, cherry, and slice of orange on the rim for effect. Blake was next to need a refill. He walked up to the bar, but turned around to check on his new friend, Jon, and ask if he, too, was ready for another beer. They all had seconds and then thirds; only Gertrude did not ask for another cup of hot chocolate.

The conversation drifted to major bridge blunders and then to certain people who were losing their skills and others who probably had never found bridge skills in the first place.

Jon did not know the people under discussion, so he decided to stretch his legs, have a word with Fabio, and order a fourth beer. But Jon was a sensitive person. He noticed that Gertrude had been nursing her empty cup while the others continued to imbibe, so he asked Fabio to send to the kitchen for a refill for her, too.

Jon sat at a bar stool, sipping his drink and waiting. Then, when the hot chocolate arrived, he managed to gain Gertrude's attention and gesticulate an invitation to join him.

She appreciated his thought, and although she did not really care for a second cup, she also did not want to hurt his feelings, so she shook her head and accepted the offer, a little disappointed that it was not Jean on the receiving end of Jon's consideration.

He stood politely as she arrived, waited for her to get comfortable on her barstool, and then sat again, too.

"Talking about crucial mistakes," he said, nodding toward the other three at the table, "I must congratulate you on not losing your patience with Jean during that first game we played tonight. I didn't realize it at the time, but for a player of her caliber, she certainly did blunder."

Gertrude smiled to herself and said nothing.

"What?" he asked. "What did I say?"

With a toss of the head to clear a lock of red hair that had fallen over her eye, Gertrude admitted, "I've been known to be a lot less patient."

"Well, so far I haven't seen your impatient side." Jon seemed to forget the beer at his left elbow. "Perhaps Jean is your good friend, but we have all seen even good friends quarrel at the bridge table . . . haven't we?"

Gertrude laughed happily. She was beginning to enjoy Jon's company, and she, too, was not thinking about her drink, the cup of cooling chocolate. "Do you lose your patience with your bridge partners?"

At this question, Jon chuckled awkwardly. "I, too, have been known to lack tolerance for stupidity. And yet, I believe that anger is just one of the features that keep me coming back. I love the game; it stirs my juices and gives me one more reason to live."

"That sounds pretty morbid," said Gertrude somberly. "Are you depressed about something?"

"Not at all." But Jon returned his attention to his beer on the counter, and lifted the mug to take a long sip.

"Oh, forgive me." Gertrude placed an apologetic hand on Jon's forearm. "That was rude. I didn't mean to pry."

"No. It's my fault," Jon said. "And you are indeed astute. But I'm not surprised; anyone who plays the game of bridge as well as you do has got to be gifted with superior intelligence and insight."

"My remark was rude."

"Perhaps, but nevertheless true. Ever since my mother died, nine months ago, I've been feeling a bit down. She was the only family I had, and I miss her." Jon sighed, regaining his composure. "Still, she was old and she wasn't well. Her time had come and she passed peacefully. To tell you the truth, her passing was one of the reasons that led me to agree to my business merger. Otherwise, I could never have left her alone in Liverpool for such long periods."

Handsome, smart, wealthy, and sensitive too, Gertrude thought. *What a catch.* She then looked at the table where chubby-cheeked Jean sat talking with Mollie and Blake, and realized, *my good friend doesn't stand a chance.*

"I'm sorry about your mother," Gertrude said. "I hope everything works out well for you here in America, with your business and—"

"And the rest of my life." Jon laughed.

"Well, yes. The rest of your life."

Jon looked into Gertrude's steady stare. He really was growing fond of this woman. Her straight-forward honesty, her intelligence, and, of course, her tall and attractive figure. With four beers in his system providing all the courage his shy personality needed, he dropped his voice and whispered, "If you really mean that, you could help."

"How?" Gertrude asked inquisitively, yet also surreptitiously fishing for a compliment.

Jon decided to tread carefully. "For a start, I would love to play with you," he said, and when she did not immediately respond, he continued, "Bridge, that is."

"Of course, I would love to play with you."

Jon might have been misled by the fervor in Gertrude's immediate reply, but this pleased him all the same, so he decided to take the conversation a notch more intimate. "And perhaps after we play, you will allow me to buy you dinner?"

CHAPTER TEN

2005

Janet and her fiancé, Brian, remained in Jacobsburg for two days. Then, after they left, Gertrude's social schedule continued to overflow with arrangements that included Len. He would have to hurry home from work, maybe have time to clean up and change his shirt, and then go out with people who wanted to share in their joy.

It was not until the following Sunday night that the pace seemed to slow, and Len and Gertrude returned to their normal routine, which meant back to the bridge club for her and a peaceful night alone for him. Throughout the prolonged celebration of his daughter's engagement, Len had not forgotten the two pieces of blotting paper in his closet, waiting for the final few drops of A-fair-catch reagent to supply the answer to his question.

Once again, nervous about what he might find, Len did not rush to retrieve the blotting paper specimens. After he heard

Gertrude's car pull out the garage and the heavy electronic door roll shut, he took a soothing hot shower, put on comfortable slippers and a gown, and only then went to the closet, contemplating what he might find.

He retrieved the A-fair-catch kit from the top shelf and the waiting pieces of blotting paper from the middle shelf, where he had so carefully left them. The only problem was that, with the passage of time, he forgot which piece of paper was the positive control, with his own specimen of semen, and which one he had used to test the crotch of Gertrude's panties. But the disappointment was short-lived; it did not matter. One specimen had to be positive; two positive and matching results would supply the result he was seeking.

He was so excited about the test that he began to wonder which result he would prefer, a positive or a negative. *Don't be ridiculous*, he told himself, *of course I want a negative result. I don't want my life disrupted, and I don't want to confront Gertrude with evidence of her infidelity. After all this time, I still love her. Not that all encompassing infatuation that we once knew, but I do like having her around. She's really been a good wife . . . a far better wife than I a husband.*

With the pieces of blotting paper on the bathroom countertop and the reagent already drawn up in the dropper, Len considered abandoning the test, forgetting his obsession, forgetting the profile that so perfectly fit his wife, and forgetting the pieces of circumstantial evidence that had been flaunted under his nose. And Len would have been comfortable throwing the A-fair-catch kit into the garbage where it belonged, but he could not resist completing the test even if he tried.

His eye shifted to his propped up wristwatch and noted the second hand pass the twelve, and like a magnet, his hand let a few drops fall onto the first piece of blotting paper.

The paper turned the familiar maroon. Len began to think that the A-fair-catch website, together with all the people who staffed it, was one big fraud, and he had been taken. Even so, he could say nothing. It was not the type of product a person would want to make a fuss about or openly expose through a consumer advocate group. No one wanted to be a high profile customer of A-fair-catch.

He began to feel a sense of relief. He could say to himself that he had tried and that, so far, his effort had been unsuccessful. Meanwhile, he could take his time and consider where to go from here. Perhaps place his uncertainties on the backburner indefinitely.

Then, the color on the blotting paper began to change. It was gradual, just like the medical tests that Len used in the office, indistinct at first but slowly turning positive. He compared his specimen to the circle of violet on the pamphlet; the colors were identical. A-fair-catch actually did work. All that remained was to test the other piece of blotting paper.

He drew reagent into the pipette and let three drops fall onto the center of the second specimen: once again, the familiar maroon. He waited and stared, this time expecting the color to change as it had on the first piece of blotting paper. *The violet should emerge any moment*, he thought. But this specimen seemed stubborn. Slowly, he shifted his gaze to the watch, and he grimaced as he recalled that, in his haste, he had forgotten to mark the moment of applying the drops of reagent.

Despite the pamphlet's caution that the test would be invalid if the violet color appeared after the allotted forty-five seconds, he decided to ignore the time restraints. The center of the specimen remained maroon, but the rim, the part where the reagents were more dilute, may have transitioned toward violet. He compared the color on the rim of his specimen to the violet circle on the pamphlet. *Not as certain as the other specimen*, he thought, *in fact, not really a match at all.* He compared the two specimen results; one was positive, the other probably not.

With mixed emotions, he decided to accept the result as negative. He still did not have the proof he needed to confirm his suspicion about Gertrude, which was good; but his theory remained up in the air, and this Len found unsettling.

Anyhow, into the garbage went the two pieces of blotting paper, and he to the den to read his medical journal.

He had not completed a single paragraph when the thought came to mind. *Am I absolutely certain of the result, and which specimen gave the definite positive?* He could not rest, so he went to retrieve the specimens from the garbage and to his closet to find the washcloth with his semen specimen.

He knew the results even before he began retesting and, at the end of his experiment, had learned nothing new: the washcloth specimen tested positive for a second time. Also, while the forty-five second period had by now long passed, the color on the questionable specimen—the second that he had tested—remained a negative maroon. This piece of blotting paper must have represented the sampling from Gertrude's panties, and it appeared quite different to the other two positive controls.

At last, he could sit back with his journal in his hands and Julia on his lap. His eyelids began to sag, the magazine slipped out of his grip and slid down to the carpet, and his chin fell forward onto his chest.

Len was not certain whether it was the noise of his own snoring or the sudden thought that crossed his mind, but he awoke with a jolt. *The night that I went to get Gertrude's panties from the laundry basket, I was more concerned about being caught than about finding the correct panties, the ones she was wearing when she came home at 2:30 in the morning. I don't think she left them in the bathroom; I did look for them there. But who knows, maybe they were on the floor of her closet, or maybe they were in the laundry basket and I got hold of the wrong pair.*

He looked at his wristwatch. 10:45. Time to move into the bedroom. But before he climbed under the covers, Len went once more to his closet to inspect the kit of A-fair-catch. *Reagent enough for three or perhaps four more tests*, he thought. *That is, if the mixed chemicals do not deteriorate.*

Within ten to fifteen minutes, he heard the garage door open. The bedroom light was off, and Len did not say anything to her as she walked quietly through to the bathroom to take a shower.

He watched her tall silhouette with hair up in a towel as she returned dripping to the bedroom and then disappeared into her closet. After a short while, she emerged in her nightgown and tiptoed over to her side of the bed but then switched on the dull bedside lamp; she was not tired and wanted to read awhile.

"How was the game?" he asked.

"Hi, Len." She leaned over and gave him a peck on the forehead. "It was okay."

That sounds unenthusiastic, he thought. "Who did you play with, Jean?"

"No." Gertrude had her nose in her magazine.

"Did you win?"

"No, we came somewhere in the middle. I didn't wait for the final score."

Len was tired and did not register her uncharacteristic lack of disappointment at a less than excellent game. He rolled over onto his side, closed his eyes, and with his cheek buried in the pillow, muffling his speech, asked again, "Who'd you play with?"

She did not immediately reply, but then lowered her magazine onto the duvet and said softly, "Mollie."

"Oh! The tall blonde from the studio . . . that's nice."

"Yes." Gertrude leaned over and turned out the reading light. She then snuggled against Len, the curve of her body fitting neatly into his, and lay awake in the dark.

Over the following two weeks, Len's confusion would not settle. His curiosity was far from satisfied, and frustration drove him to reconsider hiring a private detective. To top it all, Gertrude appeared ever more beautiful in his eyes. This may have been in part due to his budding jealousies, but he was also certain that she had lost a few unwanted pounds in unwanted parts. He had no doubt that men were propositioning her. His only doubt was her response.

What would a private detective do? He wondered. *And how smart are the people who enter that line of work? What would I do if I were that detective? Is there such a place as detective school, or some sort of handbook?*

While he neither visited a bookstore nor browsed the Internet in search of the information he wanted, Len did mull over his scenario and, in his mind's eye, rehearsed an initial interview with a top-notch investigator:

I'm afraid you do have reason for concern, Dr. Darshan, especially in view of those late nights. Have you noticed a pattern? Does your wife stay out consistently any one night of the week?

Not really, Detective.

Perhaps the late nights appear in clusters. Is it possible that she is having an affair with someone who comes in from out of town periodically?

It's not only the nights that concern me, sir. I have no idea what she does or where she goes most days.

Well, do you have any suspects, Dr. Darshan? Perhaps a friend? It is likely that you have met the scoundrel at some time. Have you noticed her behavior change in any way when she is around one particular person?

This question Len pondered on a number of occasions. He really did not have any particular person in mind, and yet the imaginary detective's probe was legitimate. In his limited experience with patients who had marital problems, he had noticed that the spouse often had met the scoundrel.

I don't suspect any particular person, Detective. However, her social life seems to revolve around bridge, and on every occasion she comes home late, she has been playing cards.

That does narrow down the field, Dr. Darshan.

At first, Len was satisfied with the imaginary detective's deduction: this information did seem to narrow down the field. It was only after realizing that from the bridge players he had met he really had no suspect, that he modified the detective's reply:

We might not be dealing with a bridge player at all, Dr. Darshan. I am certain she often goes to the bridge studio, but perhaps she's not being honest with you on the nights she meets with her lover. Have you considered that she may be lying, using bridge as her alibi when she's actually meeting the other man?

Len hated the insinuation. Gertrude had been playing cards for so long and so often that her lying about these outings would mean he was still underestimating his own naiveté. He disliked the detective for pointing out his stupidity, and he disliked him for insulting Gertrude, and slowly the faceless detective began to take on the features of Nelson Underwood, the slimy detective with the vulgar ponytail, who Len disliked, as well.

Len never actually made the decision to follow the imaginary investigator's advice; he just did it: on a Thursday night, a night that Gertrude hardly ever played cards, Len found himself once again saying, "Goodnight, sweetheart. Enjoy your game."

He then poured a diet soda and settled into his armchair with a medical journal in his hands and Juliet on his lap, as usual. The only difference was that, on this occasion, Len did not shower and don the slippers and gown, as he otherwise might have.

His concentration wavered and he found himself reading the text a second and a third time, unable to retain the information. So he turned on the television to watch the news. Still, his mind churned and his thoughts kept returning to the fact that Gertrude had gone to play bridge on a Thursday night. He was not certain how common this was; over the years, he failed to pay close attention. Yet, it seemed that more often than not, Thursdays she would remain at home.

By ten o'clock, during the commercial before the main news headlines, he could tolerate the uncertainty no more, so he grabbed a light jacket and went directly to the garage. He turned the key in the ignition, shoved the gears into reverse, but then set the odometer to zero. If he knew the exact distance to the bridge studio, he could, in the future, sneak a glance at Gertrude's dashboard and then estimate whether she had traveled further than to the studio and back on any given suspicious night.

Seven to eight minutes later, Len turned off the freeway and into the strip center's parking lot. He scanned the cars. *Gertrude's white Lexus should be easy to spot*, he thought. *She always keeps it polished and shiny.* But the lot was full, and he could not immediately see it. He drove along the outskirts and through the rows of cars, and although he did pass one shiny white Lexus, it was not hers.

The main entrance to the bridge studio, in the obtuse angle at the middle of the shopping center, came directly off the sidewalk. Here, between the dentist's office on the one side and The Gardens of Sicily on the other, the bridge studio had no windows, only a single door that opened into a vestibule. On the inside, however, the studio was spacious, with a view of the rear drab concrete slab stretching back toward the dilapidated wooden fencing of the adjacent apartments.

From the main parking lot, Len drove past *The Shoe Boutique* at the one end of the center, and turned along a narrow road that took him around to the back. Here, hidden from the freeway, the air turned suddenly quieter and duller. Unlike the lighting mounted on the many poles in the front parking, the two rear spotlights at the ends of the building did little to banish the darkness. Cut into the middle of the concrete slab was an unkempt square of dirt that may once have served as a flower garden, but which today harbored only weeds and a single malnourished and scraggly pine tree. This back lot, parking for the overflow during the day, now hosted only about a dozen cars, most of which probably belonged to owners and employees working late into the night.

Len checked the suites and focused on the only one with visible activity: At the bend in the complex, with bright light shining through three picture windows, was the bridge studio. It was understandable that the studio would be intensely lit. While other businesses, such as The Gardens of Sicily next door, might prefer a cozier atmosphere, the bridge players needed the illumination to readily see the cards. Besides, the other stores focused their display to the front of the center, with the heavy traffic. Here at the back, most had only an occasional high window with opaque glass that served to aerate a bathroom or storeroom. The bridge studio, with its unique position, had no front display, only the entrance in the corner.

Len turned his attention to the studio: huddled around the back door—also built into the bend of the building—were four cars, one of which belonged to Gertrude.

So she is here, Len thought, *playing bridge just as she said.* Even so, he remained inquisitive: *With whom is she playing tonight? She didn't mention her partner's name.*

He dulled his headlights and then nosed his aging Lincoln against the curb, a few stores away from the studio.

Len sat in the car, thinking. *This is a bad idea. What will happen if I'm caught peeping into the window? If some old woman sees me and screams, and then the men rush out that back door to investigate, I don't think I could bear the embarrassment.*

He reached for the ignition key, ready to leave, but then realized that if he indeed was caught, he could always say he had come to fetch his wife after the game. He did not consider how he would explain himself to Gertrude; he would cross that bridge when and if he had to. He stepped out of the car and gently closed the door.

There shouldn't be a problem, he thought, remembering his basic physics. *While I will be able to see into the studio, they cannot see out into the dark.*

He walked passed the four cars to his left and the back studio door to his right, and toward the nearest window. He stopped a few feet away from the pane, from where he had a view into most of the room. The horizontal blinds were wide open, and he was right; he could see clearly the faces of the people sitting around the small square tables.

What a scruffy looking bunch, Len thought. *Like a gathering of hippies grown old.* He was actually not surprised. He never did have a favorable view of hippies, thought them irresponsible and a burden to society. Yet, overall, hippies were bright and many managed to graduate in whichever fields they chose. And these were the people who, in Len's opinion, would skip class to do meaningless things, like play bridge. Then, when some of them outgrew their wanton ways and actually turned into productive and prominent members of society, Len actually felt angry; he saw a great injustice inflicted upon the proper social order, as though the undeserving had triumphed over those he deemed more worthy.

On the occasions when he met Gertrude's card-playing friends socially, they seemed more kempt; the men would actually shave or trim their beards, and the women would dress up. Tonight, however, while at their craft, they reflected the aging card-playing time-wasters he expected. The women were more presentable than the men, but not up to the standard Len expected of people in a public gathering.

To Len's right, the building curved out of sight. Even his car, parked against the curb, was partially hidden from his view. To his left, the only other business with a significant back window was The Gardens of Sicily next door. Had he been a foot or two further from the pane, perhaps an inquisitive soul in a seat against the Italian restaurant's window might have noticed him, but from where he was standing, the angle was too great; he was confident that he could not be seen.

He remained staring into the bridge studio. The players were quiet and attentive.

Then, after a short while, the four people at a single table suddenly had a change of disposition. They shuffled in their seats, fiddled, spoke to one another, and passed the board of cards downstream to the adjacent table. This pattern spread to another table and another and another; until players spoke to others at different tables and stood to stretch their legs.

Meanwhile, freckle-faced Mollie walked between the three rows, apparently checking on the boards of cards and arranging and moving paraphernalia. The people playing east west moved upstream on to the next pair of north south teams, and while all this was happening, a fat woman in her fifties with an uncanny resemblance to the person Len had pictured as his whistle blower, walked directly toward the window through which he was gazing.

His heart thumped. His premonition was happening. The woman stared directly into his eyes. He turned to flee back to his car and speed away, but then the woman casually veered away from the window and reached her arm to open a door out of Len's view. His calculation was right; she could not see him at all. Fortified with this knowledge, he stepped even closer to the glass.

Mollie glanced at a clock on the wall and clapped her hands while making a brief announcement. The players began to settle down, Len heard the sound of a flushing toilet, and the fat woman reappeared and returned to a table to take her seat.

From his new position, closer to the windowpane, Len could now see Gertrude and Jean in a far corner. Jean had on jeans and a sloppy red T-shirt. Gertrude was wearing light blue slacks and a navy blouse and did not seem to fit in with the group. *It's not my imagination*, Len thought. *Gertrude is naturally sophisticated.*

Were she to have looked up, Gertrude would have been staring directly at him, but her eyes remained on her cards and the players at her table.

Len watched Gertrude for a while and then decided to steal a closer look at some of the other players: one person at each of the tables may have seemed less focused than the other three; this was the *dummy* player whose cards had been exposed. Yet, even this person was interested in the game at his or her table. The pattern was consistent and innocent, so Len decided to leave for home.

Paranoid! That's what I am . . . paranoid. Len actually began to walk away, but he turned for a last look, and something, or rather someone, caught his eye. Two tables away and facing Gertrude was a dummy player who seemed uninterested in his own game. He was a man who Len should immediately have noticed because of his apparent difference to the others. While his features were soft, like a successful professional who had led an easy life, his high cheekbones and wide set eyes lent his appearance an unusual strength—a masculine type of strength. He was exceptionally good-looking. What is more, his pencil moustache was trimmed and his graying hair groomed.

It did not take Len long to shut out all the other players in the room. The man would occasionally look down at the cards that his partner and opponents were playing, but the brunt of his attention was on Gertrude. Len turned his focus back to his wife's table. Everyone was attentive to the game. Even the woman playing in the dummy position seemed absorbed in each card played.

Is this my imagination? Len thought. He was no longer nervous about being discovered. He had to focus on the handsome man watching his wife and on his wife's response, if any. *No, this is not my imagination. That fellow is staring at Gertrude. True, his chair is facing hers, but his attention is consistent, definitely not casual, and not a coincidence.*

Meanwhile, Gertrude continued playing her game.

At the table closest to Len's window, the hand came to an end. The players began their traditional movement and stretch, laugh and talk, but unlike the previous break, they again started to play; the east west teams did not move on upstream to the next table. The format seemed to consist of two hands between each set of opponents. As the march of change continued throughout the room, Len could detect when the people at each table had completed the first game and began the bidding in the second.

The atmosphere settled. Everything was again the same, only a different set of dummy players. This time, Jean was playing the hand, which meant Gertrude was left with that modicum of freedom to concentrate or not, however she chose, and she did seem immersed in the play. Len continued to focus on her and the man two tables away. Everyone else in the room no longer mattered . . . only Gertrude and the handsome man.

Even if I did not know what I know, I would match Gertrude with that guy, Len thought. *Everyone else in the room seems so slovenly. Only Gertrude and that one man are groomed and good-looking.* The man had on a dark blazer over a crisp white crew neck shirt. *If she's involved with someone, I'll bet that's the guy . . . it has to be. No one else in the room fits the mold. More and more I'm beginning to trust my instincts, which may have lain dormant for years but have now awoken with a jolt. The question is: where do I go from here? Gut feelings and intuition are helpful, but they can take me only so far. While I'm pretty certain they are having an affair, I need more proof. I don't want to confront her; that will only bring up her guard. I could still hire a detective. Now it would be easy for him to gather the evidence I need.* Again, Len considered the Yellow Pages, the Internet, or finding someone through the local Police Department, but his thoughts kept returning to the slimy, pony-tailed Nelson Underwood, and he decided he could do a better job himself.

The bridge game continued. Nothing unusual until Gertrude took a turn at looking away from her table, and she was the only person in the room focusing on anything other than the game. She did not gaze immediately at Len's suspect; she allocated that direction to last. But when she eventually got there, she began to stare. Her eyes remained fixed on the suave man in the neatly pressed barathea blazer, as he played one trick, another, and a third, until he instinctively felt her stare, returned a smile, his only change in facial expression during the hand, and then went back to his game.

Wow! What more evidence do I need?

Until this time, Len had been trying to uncover Gertrude's relationship with another man. Now, his curiosity stepped up to the next level. *I wonder how long the two of them have been getting it on. Could Gertrude be planning to leave me? She must have given it some thought. And if my interpretation of their body language is correct, then that man wants her, too.*

He remembered how the man had stared unremittingly at Gertrude while she played her hand, and how she had first carefully checked to ensure that no one else was watching before turning her gaze to him. *Unless, that man is also married and they are merely enjoying an adventure.*

The thought of someone treating Gertrude as sport and the possibility that Gertrude might be looking to the other man as an outlet for her own frustrations irritated Len more than his original impression that she was involved in a serious relationship. *But, that cannot be. I've always been available for her. It is she who is unwilling at night before we go to sleep.* He reflected on his sex life with Gertrude and was rudely awakened to the clear reality: *She may be less willing to make love at night, but then I am hardly ever available in the mornings. Also, there is more to any marriage than sex. I know as well as anyone that women view a relationship in much broader terms than men do, and in truth, I have not been as attentive as I should have. Years ago, I couldn't do enough to please her, and now we don't seem to celebrate or go out together as often as we should. Could be largely due to her playing so much bridge; she would prefer a game of cards to an evening with me. And yet, I probably do share some of the blame . . . always running off to Synagogue, or Talmud discussions, or unimportant hospital meetings to rehash the same shortfalls that we have been ignoring for years. She doesn't say much about that. I wonder whether she would actually want to spend more time with me. I'm sure she knows what she wants, but do I know what I want? And at this point in our marriage, is the strength of our relationship really still up to me? How much sway do I still have? Confronting her with what I have seen tonight might very well serve to drive her away. Maybe I should just start courting her as I did when we were younger. If she has any thoughts of leaving me, I'm pretty sure I can win her back. Yet, I know me, and if I don't bring everything out into the open, I will harbor resentment. What should I do now?*

The card game behind the glass window came to an end. Players began to stroll around the room to single out opponents of the night for a quick word, a passionate gesture, a laugh, and, in one case, an exchange which Len gathered might have been quite irate. This time, the east west players did not move on to the next table, and no one passed the boards of cards in the opposite direction. Instead, some of the people turned to face the hidden side of the room, the part to Len's right and out of his line of vision, the section of the studio that had no rear windows.

Curious to see what was going on, Len moved to the next window to his left, from where he could see Blake, the owner of the studio, standing on a low platform and delivering some sort of speech or announcement. The final hand had been played, and the scores were now being tallied.

A gray and wrinkled man was first to use the bathroom to Len's right. He was followed by a woman and then a younger fat man. People were fetching their coats from the cloakroom, and a few began to leave.

Len turned to the parked cars and realized that soon one of the players would be coming through the back door. It was time for him to leave, too. He shifted his gaze for one last inspection of Gertrude and the handsome man. He needed to see what would happen at this crucial time, if anything.

The man was standing and concentrating on whatever Blake had to say. Although he had wandered to the back of the crowd, he did not have to shuffle or lift himself onto his toes; he was the tallest in the room and could easily see over the other peoples' heads. Gertrude, too, was looking in Blake's direction. She was a short distance from the tall man, leaning against the table on which she had been playing cards. Len considered getting into his car and driving to a concealed spot, perhaps behind the single pine tree. He wanted to see whether Gertrude would return directly to her white Lexus or perhaps go somewhere else first . . . together with the handsome man. He scanned the back parking lot and realized that there was nowhere for his Lincoln to hide. What is more, if Gertrude did drive directly home, he wanted to be there when she arrived. His options were few; he could not afford to be discovered, and the fat woman, who he had earlier pictured as his whistle blower, had her purse in her hand, a scarf around her neck, and was sidling toward the studio back door. Len would have to leave now if he did not want to be caught peeping into the game.

He took his first step, but then so did Gertrude, and she turned around and walked directly towards Len's suspect, the tall handsome man with the elegant hair and moustache. The man smiled happily and stood even taller as Gertrude walked directly up to him. Len almost expected this scenario, and yet he still could not control the wave of nausea in his gut and the thumping in his chest. Apparently, Gertrude was first to speak. The man did not reply. Instead, he placed a hand on her cheek and gazed directly into her eyes.

In front of all these people, Len thought. *This is even worse than I realized. Do they have no shame?*

Len wanted to remain, to see what would happen next. He expected the man to lean over and kiss Gertrude, and he expected Gertrude to welcome the kiss. This was more than Len could tolerate. He wanted to leave, and yet his feet remained glued to the floor, until he realized the fat whistle blower had disappeared from his view and had to be nearing the back door.

Len turned; he was right. The studio door between him and his Lincoln was slowly opening. He dropped his head and stepped away from the window. Whatever the fat woman might see, he did not want her to actually catch him in the act of spying. She turned to face him, and just as he had pictured, her eyes opened widely.

She made a quick calculation and instead of retreating into the studio, unwisely hurried toward her car, a battered black Nissan Sentra.

Len realized that the fat woman was more afraid of him than he was of her. *What an idiot*, he thought. *Were I a crook, I could easily catch up with her, snatch that purse, and be long gone before she could return to the studio. I hope she doesn't make such a poor decision if she ever encounters a violent criminal.*

He actually had to slow his pace to ensure that he did not arrive at her car before she drove off. Len considered returning to the studio window to see what was happening, but he did not want to push his luck. He also needed time to digest what he had seen and consider how to take his investigation to the next level. His immediate concern was to get home, and then to see how much longer it would take Gertrude to make the same journey.

Len sped through the neighborhood streets and into the safety of his garage. Forgetting to take note of the mileage, he hurried into the house, undressed, showered, and then hopped straight into bed, where his mind continued to race. *If she doesn't come home soon, it means she is with him. I wonder what they are up to now.* He glanced at the bedside clock, 11:13 p.m. *Assuming she waits for the final score, she shouldn't take more than fifteen minutes to arrive home. Maybe twenty minutes . . . twenty-five tops.*

Filled with anger and jealousy, Len could not keep his eyes from the clock. He went to the den to fetch a journal to read in bed, but that was impossible. He was unable to concentrate on a single sentence without his mind wandering back to Gertrude and her lover.

11:28 p.m., what will Gertrude think if she were to find me in the den, asleep on my armchair or watching TV? Nothing unusual. Then, why am I hiding here in this bed?

In the den, in front of the TV, he managed to concentrate on a news report of the most recent suicide bombing in Iraq; the horror and the newscaster's passionate comments were sufficient to subdue his own anxiety—for a short while. During the commercial break, however, he found himself slapping his own thigh, clicking his tongue, and speaking to himself about, *the cheek of that man who would dare to woo a married woman, and not just any married woman—Gertrude, my wife.*

11:45 p.m., 11:50, the news no longer held his interest and, accepting his worst fears that Gertrude was in the arms of her lover, Len eventually submitted to his own constant self-battering and returned to the bed, mentally exhausted.

Slowly, he began to doze, but when Gertrude eventually tiptoed into the house, he looked directly at the clock, 1:09 a.m., and his first thought, that Gertrude had been coming home at this late hour for more years than he could recall, jolted him back into full wakefulness.

Len pretended to be asleep. Through a narrow slit in one eye, he watched Gertrude remove a bracelet, earrings, and necklace, and place them on the dresser opposite the bed. As she went into the bathroom, Len groaned gently and rolled over as he imagined he would during a restless moment of dreaming. She disappeared from his view, and he heard shuffling as she undressed, loud swishing as she brushed her teeth, and a click of a closing glass door followed by a familiar gush as she turned on the shower and waited for the water to warm.

He glanced at the clock again. *Two hours*, he thought. *She took nearly two hours longer than I did in arriving home. That would be just about the right amount of time a couple would need to make love.* He rubbed a worried palm over his face and whispered, "Oh hell! I hope I'm wrong." *I may be wrong, but the odds weigh heavily that I am right. I can't ignore what I have seen.* He grunted a short groan of regret. *I would like everything to go back to the way it was. Life was so peaceful. I don't need this tension. More importantly, I don't need this uncertainty. Although, who am I kidding? I know what's going on. Only, I must collect some tangible proof. I should have taken a camera to the bridge studio. But how was I to know I would see her flirting with that fellow?*

He heard the shower door click open. After some pacing and sprucing, Gertrude came out of the bathroom and again crossed the bedroom floor, this time clad in a towel fastened around her upper chest and carrying a few articles of clothing. She walked down the passage and less than a minute later returned to the bedroom, entered her walk-in closet, emerged in pajamas, and without switching on the television or the reading light, got under the covers and closed her eyes to fall asleep.

Len understood exactly what Gertrude had just done. She had gone down to the laundry to drop off her dirty clothing. What troubled him was why. He did not stop to consider that she often did this. That she would sometimes leave her underwear lying on the bathroom floor until the next morning is what stuck in his mind.

She has something to hide, he thought. But with a moment's reflection, he realized that she had no reason to suspect that he was on to her. As far as he was aware, she had no way of knowing about A-fair-catch, no reason to hide her underwear.

He again stirred and turned to continue watching her, hoping she would not think him awake and start up a conversation; he wanted her fast asleep.

Gertrude must have been tired. Within a few minutes, she was perfectly still, and her breathing had a rhythmical and gentle snore.

Len waited, planning his strategy and giving her time to reach a deeper level of sleep. When he felt satisfied that she would not be easily disturbed, he rolled out of his side of the bed, quietly went to get his A-fair-catch kit, and then snuck down the corridor to the laundry. Here, he closed the door, switched on the light, and rummaged through the dirty clothing, making certain that he found all Gertrude's underwear and that he would not be testing an innocent specimen. There was only one pair of panties, and the crotch was moist with secretion, perhaps caking at the edge but fresh in the center, as expected.

Once again, he went to work. He did not bother with a positive control, he knew what color to expect and was certain that on this night the test would reveal the bright violet as in the accompanying pamphlet, expelling all doubt and forcing him to approach her. How he would handle the confrontation he was still not sure, but confront her he would. He had no choice in the matter. Anyway, the dilemma would be hers. She had brought this problem into their lives and she was the one who would have to supply answers and possible solutions. She would have to either leave him or apologize and beg his forgiveness. He did not really want a divorce; it would be ugly and inconvenient. But, if that is what she wanted, and that is what they eventually decided, he would do his part to make it as painless and swift as possible; the less he had to do with lawyers the better. If, on the other hand, she wanted to give up her suave bridge-playing boyfriend and stay, then he would not immediately give her his reply. As punishment, he would make her grovel for a few days, while he exaggerated his hurt.

The preparation of the blotting paper complete, he decided to wait a five full minutes by the clock. He did not want to spoil this specimen because of haste. He opened the laundry door, switched on the kitchen light, and went to see the time on the oven clock: 2:02 a.m. He pictured Gertrude waking, coming to the kitchen, and catching him at his work, but this did not bother him. He would not reply to her questioning until he had dropped the final reagent onto the blotting paper. There could be no more opportune a time to confront her with his foolproof evidence than now, while he still harbored remnants of anger.

He waited the allotted time, returned to the laundry, and checked to see that the specimen was reasonably dry and ready to be tested. Then, he once again stepped out of the laundry and went halfway down the corridor toward the bedroom to see if he had woken Gertrude. She was still fast asleep. This left him almost disappointed.

Never mind, he thought. *Perhaps it's better for me to give the situation a little more thought once I have the concrete evidence in hand.*

But that was not to be, for yet again, to Len's surprise, the specimen remained a stubborn maroon.

Guilt ridden, utterly convinced that the A-fair-catch was flawed, and curiously disappointed by the negative result, Len hid the A-fair-catch kit in his closet and returned to bed. In the morning, he would consider what next to do. He could not back away from the situation now, not after what he had witnessed.

But sleep did not come, and during his two further hours of wakefulness, he concluded that a proper private detective agency would be the way to go. Satisfied with this decision, and sensing that the weight of the task had been lifted from his chest, Len was eventually able to grab two hours.

The next day was a Friday. Len was both busy in the office and exhausted from lack of sleep. He knew he would do well by taking a few more days to locate a reputable agency rather than rush to select the first one listed in bold print in the Yellow Pages. Nelson Underwood, the slimy dick, was definitely not in the running.

Then came Friday night and the Sabbath, and Len did not want to think about a detective or about what he had seen at the bridge studio on the Thursday. Trying to forget, however, only served to maintain the images fresh in his thoughts. Still, he would do nothing about the dilemma until Sunday, when he planned to corner a lawyer at Synagogue, direct the conversation toward divorce, and try to find out the names of the better detective agencies.

Sunday morning arrived, but Len's planning came to an abrupt halt and in a manner he least expected.

CHAPTER ELEVEN

"I need to speak to you about something, Len. I didn't want to disturb you yesterday, on your Sabbath, but I think I might have a problem."

Len was in the bathroom, in his pajama shorts, leaning over the sink and shaving the last few stripes of foamy cream off his neck. *Oh oh! Here it comes, the confession.* He grabbed the towel from the railing to his left, dabbed his face, and wiped his hands. "What is it, Gertrude?" His heart was pounding. *It's not supposed to be like this. I thought I was the one who was going to broach the problem. I'm not quite ready.*

She moved closer to stand in the glow of the bright light bulbs around the rim of the mirror. "What do you see?" she asked, looking directly at him. "Do you notice anything?"

He stepped back to take in the bigger picture. It was early morning; she wore a nightgown, her hair was uncombed, and she had on no makeup. *What the heck does she want from me? Am I expected to notice that she is aging and that her needs are not being met? What is she planning?* "No. Nothing new. What am I supposed to see?"

"My eyes, Len. Look at my eyes. Are they yellow?

Suddenly, it was obvious. She indeed had a twinge of jaundice, a sign he would never have missed in the clinical setting of his office. He held her by the hips and turned her to face the line of lights. Then, he moved in front of her and placed a gentle hand to pull down on her left cheek, revealing more of the eye.

"Have you had any pain here?" he asked, prodding her upper belly.

"Not really, but I have been queasy."

This was not what Len wanted to hear. Painless jaundice was ominous, particularly when occurring together with weight loss, and Gertrude had been losing weight. Everyone thought it was becoming. Len and others close to her assumed she had been secretly dieting; they noticed she would often leave more food on the plate than she actually ate and attributed this to willpower. No one really believed her when she said she did not feel like finishing a tasty entrée or dessert.

Len's suspicions turned rapidly to dread, which Gertrude could read from his trembling weak chin.

"We're going to get to the bottom of this, sweetheart," Len said as he took Gertrude into his comforting arms. "I'm so sorry I didn't pay more attention to your weight loss. You seemed pleased and I didn't realize it could have been a problem."

"I've been losing weight because I haven't felt like eating," she said innocently.

He kissed her wet and salty cheek. "I'm sorry," he said, knowing she would hear an admission of neglect, yet secretly wanting her forgiveness for his suspicions, the belief that she might have been losing weight to please another man.

Anxiously, he moved to her right, placed one hand against the small of her back, and with the other attempted to palpate the organs in her abdomen. But her muscles were tense and he could detect no abnormality nor elicit any tenderness.

"You'll need a full examination, some blood work, and some imaging studies," he said to her. "Not today . . . tomorrow. You'll have to come to the office tomorrow."

"Are you going to take care of me?"

Len thought about the question. "Why not? Let's see what we find. There might be a gallstone, then I'll have to refer you to a surgeon." Len hoped for a gallstone, or perhaps a diagnosis of hepatitis or any other benign condition. At this time, he did not want to entertain the possibility of a malignancy, although with painless jaundice and weight loss, he knew this was high on the list of probabilities. "I'll do the preliminaries and we'll go from there."

"If I need a surgeon, can we use Professor Carson?"

Len smiled. "Professor Carson must be getting up there in age."

"But he still is a good surgeon, isn't he?"

"Sure, Gertrude. If you need a surgeon, and you're comfortable with Carson, we'll call him."

That Sunday morning, Len did not go to Synagogue. Instead, he devoted the day to Gertrude. He stayed home with her in the morning, took her to lunch, where she nibbled on a salad and ate half a slice of pecan pie for dessert, and when she receive a call from Jean, asking whether she wanted to play bridge that night, Len encouraged her to go, thinking the game would help alleviate her anxiety.

At home, with Juliet asleep by his feet, Len put through a call to Terry, who, as usual, lent a sympathetic ear, gave good advice, and then offered the help that Len desperately needed, as well. "You shouldn't take care of your own wife for this problem, Len," he said. "For minor stuff it's okay, but not when you are concerned that she might have a serious illness."

Len did not have to think twice about his partner's opinion. "You're right, Terry. So where should I go from here? Do you reckon I should send her straight to Carson? Gertrude said that if she needs surgery, she would like him to do it."

"Come along now, Len; we're not yet certain it is a surgical condition. We should treat Gertrude the same way we treat any other patient. Let's make the diagnosis or at least get her pointed in the right direction. If Gertrude doesn't mind, why don't I take a look at her tomorrow? I'll tell you both what I find."

"Thanks, Terry. I already feel a little better. I don't know what we'll uncover, but thanks for being there for us."

Len switched off the portable phone, placed it on the small table to his side, closed his eyes, and let his mind wander back to that morning. *Gertrude seemed so helpless, so frail and afraid. She came to me for help, and I'm glad I could offer the support she needed. She looked beautiful . . . and innocent, too, a different facet to the Gertrude I know. Has it been there all the time, and I was too blind to see, or did it take the fear of an impending catastrophe to waken her other side?*

When he recalled his effort to trap her, he felt ridden with guilt. He then thought about the last few weeks and months, and he remembered the interview with that patient who had come to him with his own marital problems. *What was his name? Carter. That's right . . . Ralph Carter. The man hasn't been back to the office. I wander what happened with his marriage. I suppose I should give him a call.*

Len chuckled to himself. *It was Ralph Carter who got me started. I couldn't understand why he wanted his wife back, and now I have come full circle. I realize how he didn't want to lose her. Gertrude and I are not really the same as Ralph and Elaine Carter, but now I can sympathize with his pain. Until this morning, I wasn't sure how I would react to her wanting to leave me. Who was I kidding? I don't want to lose her, and at this time, I'm*

315

definitely not going to desert or hurt her. It seems like I am the one who has been shocked into reality.

Drained from his emotional rollercoaster, Len decided to change into his pajamas and wait for Gertrude to come home. But before taking a hot shower, there was one task he had to do: he triple-wrapped the A-fair-catch kit in plastic grocery bags and buried it somewhere in the middle of the huge garbage can in the garage, ready for trash collection on Tuesday. He was still uncertain about the validity of the kit's results, but that no longer mattered; all he wanted was for Gertrude to be healthy and to guide their marriage happily toward their golden years.

On clinical examination, Terry agreed that Gertrude was indeed jaundiced, and he found an area of fullness in the right upper area of her abdomen, a mass that he did not want to believe represented a painless and swollen gallbladder, because this would virtually confirm Len's worst suspicions.

Terry had said he would treat Gertrude the same as he would any other patient, but with a little extra push and the mention of Len's name, the investigations were done and completed in less than half the time it would normally take. Within three days, Terry had the results of his laboratory tests, the ultrasound, and the state of the art *contrast-enhanced triple phase helical abdominal CT scan.* Gertrude had received the treatment of a celebrity, minus the inconvenience of an unnecessary hospital admission.

A week later, Len accompanied Gertrude to her two o'clock appointment with Professor Carson.

316

"Hello, Gertrude." The Professor offered a welcoming hand. "You look splendid." Then, in a more somber tone, he added, "Hard to believe you have this tumor. I've taken a look at the films together with our radiologist." Before she could reply, he turned to Len. "Not under these circumstances, but nice to see you again, Doctor."

"You are looking well, too, Professor," Len lied, glibly.

Once elegantly slender, the professor now had shoulders that were beginning to bend over his skinny frame, and but for a rim of gray hair, had a head that was shiny and bald.

The modest hospital clinic room had a battered desk, three patient chairs, and an examination area behind a folding screen. On one wall was a chalkboard with an indecipherable drawing, two x-ray-viewing boxes, and a number of poster-sized diagrams with ink markings left from previous explanations. Aware of the clinical findings, the professor nevertheless took a full medical history and performed a thorough physical examination, hoping to find some feature that might complete the picture and help establish a plan for optimal treatment. Len and Gertrude waited patiently while the professor jotted his notes in the manila file.

Professor Carson then looked up at Gertrude and rested his interlaced fingers on the desk. "As you know, you have a tumor of the head of your pancreas, which is almost certainly a cancer."

Gertrude's heart sank. She knew what she had, but she was nevertheless clinging to the hope that her trusted professor might have better news. She also watched his mannerisms for some token

317

of optimism, a smile, a higher pitch in tone, or a confident clap of the hands, but there were none. Instead, the professor stood, removed five preselected films from an x-ray cover lying on his desk, and hooked them into the holding clips of the viewing boxes.

"This is the pancreas," the professor explained, outlining the shape of the organ. "Here is the gallbladder, and here in the C-shaped bend of the duodenum is the tumor." He then subtly and subconsciously turned the focus of his address from Gertrude to Len. "There doesn't seem to be any extra-pancreatic disease, and the blood vessels, the portal vein confluence, here, the celiac axis, here, and the mesenteric vein, here, and artery, here, all seem patent. The liver is clear, and as far as we can tell, there is no lymph node involvement."

Professor Carson's demonstration helped Len distinguish the anatomical features and pathology, which he would not otherwise have been able to identify.

"This is good news," the professor said, bringing to Gertrude a faint glimmer of hope. "It means we may be able to shoot for a cure."

"What do you mean by 'may be able'?" Gertrude asked, alarmed by the sudden implication of her looming death.

Professor Carson noticed her alarm, but continued his blunt yet necessary explanation. "Not many patients survive a carcinoma of the pancreas. We only see about twenty-five percent of cases at a stage when they are still operable. The rest we offer appropriate palliative radio and chemotherapy together with surgery to alleviate discomfort. In your case, however, it seems that the tumor is resectable."

The professor moved over to a poster portraying the abdominal contents. "This is the stomach," he said, demonstrating the organ at the top of the belly. "Food travels from here, through the duodenum, and into the small intestines." Gertrude could now see clearly the C-shaped loop of duodenum cupped around the head of the pancreas, the site of her cancer.

"This green organ is the gallbladder," the professor continued, pointing to a small sac resting under the brown liver, which filled the right upper quadrant of the diagram. "Both pancreatic secretions from the pancreas and bile from the gallbladder normally drain into the duodenum through this little hole, called the *ampulla of Vater*. In your case, Gertrude, the cancer has begun to constrict the pancreatic duct and this bile duct coming from the gallbladder. The bile cannot drain into your duodenum, and bile contains the yellow pigment called *bilirubin*. That is why you are jaundiced, Gertrude, because you're retaining bilirubin."

Gertrude dropped her face into her cupped hands. She was pale with fear.

"Can I get you something, perhaps a glass of water?" the professor asked.

"No. I'll be just fine, Professor. Thank you for being so candid."

Len thought Professor Carson was more than candid; he thought he might have been harsh, certainly more blunt than either he or Terry were with their patients. Yet, now that the condition was well understood, all further discussion could be open and frank.

Len moved across to Gertrude, sat on the arm of her chair, and hugged her gently with one hand around her shoulders. "Do you feel comfortable going ahead with the surgery, Professor?" Len asked. "I thought you might first need further investigations."

Professor Carson returned to his chair on the other side of the desk and again rested his hands on the writing pad. "First off, Gertrude, please understand that I am not the best qualified man for the job. The procedure, known as a *Whipple's resection*, is quite specialized. It involves the removal of the head of the pancreas together with the duodenum and the gallbladder. In the best of hands, this surgery carries a five percent mortality. I will certainly be in on the case, but I must recommend that we consult Dr. Kallenbach. He is a bright young surgeon, who has an ongoing series of Whipple's resections, and his results are top notch, up there with the best in the world."

Both Len and Gertrude felt a wave of relief: Gertrude because of the professor's air of confidence in this surgeon, whose results were 'up there with the best in the world,' and Len because the perioperative mortality was down to a mere five percent.

"But to answer your question, Len," Professor Carson hesitated, looked from Len to Gertrude, then got up once more to return to the x-ray viewing screen, where he pointed to the film that best demonstrated the gallbladder. "Although you have not been feeling too ill, Gertrude, the first thing I want is to get Dr. Reddy, the head of our gastroenterology department, to position a *stent* that will reopen the flow into the duodenum. That mild nausea will disappear and you will regain your appetite. This will allow us to optimize your nutritional and medical status before the surgery." On his way back to his seat, he again spoke to Len. "And when Gertrude is under anesthesia, Dr. Kallenbach will want to do a laparoscopy to confirm the staging . . . make certain that the CT scan findings are accurate."

Len stood from the sidearm of Gertrude's chair, walked over to the films on the viewing screens, and with his inexperienced eye, tried to make out as much detail as he could. "What do you mean, Professor? Could the tumor have spread; are you saying it may not be operable?"

The professor shook his head gently. "The radiologist was pretty sure about this one. It's unlikely that Dr. Kallenbach will find anything unexpected. Still, on the off chance that the scan missed something, a laparoscopy is a good idea. Also, Dr. Kallenbach may want to make certain that we are, in fact, dealing with a cancer; he might want a biopsy."

They sat a moment in silence, the professor and Len staring at Gertrude, and she with her head bowed in deep thought. Gertrude then looked up and with a bare palm wiped a tear from her cheek. "Okay. So where do I go from here? Do I make an appointment with the gastroenterologist, Dr. Ready?"

Professor Carson nodded. "Helena, my secretary, will help you set it up."

Gertrude may have thought that the consultation had come to an end, but the professor was not quite finished. He fingered down a page in her chart, and then sat forward, his torso leaning over the desk. "There is something else we must discuss," he said. "How old were you when you had breast cancer . . . not yet thirty?"

"Twenty-nine," she answered, bewildered by his fervor.

"And you are Jewish. Do you know if you are of Ashkenazi descent?"

Len slapped a hand against his own forehead. He knew exactly what the professor was thinking, and was surprised that he had not seen the connection himself.

"Yes. My mother came for Poland and my father's parents were born in Germany," Gertrude answered.

"And you told me that they are both well. That's good, but this is your second bout with cancer, first breast, and now pancreas, both tumors that may be linked to genetic mutations. I would be amiss not to mention this observation. You don't have to do anything about it, but you may want to consider genetic counseling and testing."

Gertrude clapped both palms on her cheeks. "Oh my God! You mean I could have passed my cancers on to my daughter?"

"Breast cancer at the age of twenty-nine in an Ashkenazi Jew is suggestive of a mutation in a Breast Cancer gene, a *BRCA gene*." Professor Carson eased back into his chair. Discussing significant disease with any patient was never an easy task, which did not get any easier with experience and age. And the topic of a genetic mutation, an abnormality that could spell major illness and even early death to someone's precious child, was even more unpleasant to approach.

"I've heard about the BRCA gene." Gertrude spoke as calmly as she could. She had no alternative but to accept this added piece of unfortunate information, revealed at a time when her fighting spirit had already been dealt a series of major blows. "I don't know what to say, Professor. I don't want to have the gene, because I am afraid for my daughter . . . and for my sister, Marlene . . . and for her two teenage sons, Jeremy and Mike . . . and for my mother or father . . . I don't know which one. But, neither of my parents have cancer, and they are old. Doesn't that mean that, even if I have the gene and my daughter has it, that maybe she won't get cancer? I don't want to know, but I'm afraid of not knowing." She turned to Len and asked, "What should I say to Janet?"

"You have nothing concrete to say yet," Professor Carson interjected. "You may choose to speak to her about the possibility of a genetic disorder in the family, but until you are tested, you don't know whether you have one or not."

"If I speak to her, she may want to be tested."

"You will have to be tested first, Gertrude. You are the *index case*. If we find nothing abnormal in your genetic makeup, then all testing stops there. If we were to test your daughter, and her results were negative—as I hope they will be—then we still don't know whether you have a genetic mutation or not, and we won't know whether there would be any reason to council your sister."

"If I have the mutation, Professor, then what are the chances that my daughter has inherited it?"

"It depends which mutation we are speaking about. If you have one of the BRCA genes, then it's fifty-fifty that she will have it, too. It's inherited as a *Mendelian dominant*."

"Fifty percent," Gertrude repeated pensively. "That's high. I still don't want to know, but I think that maybe I should find out. If I have a mutation and Janet has it, too, can anything be done to protect her?"

"Nothing definitive. We cannot reverse the mutation. However, we will recommend more stringent monitoring for high incidence cancers and even discuss prophylactic surgery. Some people think this is the prudent route, while others prefer not knowing; they don't want to go through life burdened with the worry."

"What prophylactic surgery?" Gertrude asked, bothered by yet another consideration.

"Again, talking about the BRCA genes, the lifetime risk of breast cancer can run around eighty to ninety percent, and cancer of the ovary, about forty percent. With those odds, one might reasonably prefer an oophorectomy or even bilateral mastectomy before the cancer hits."

"And what about the removal of a pancreas?"

Professor Carson could not contain a friendly smile. "That is a reasonable question, Gertrude, however, we would never take out a healthy pancreas. We need it for our digestion and metabolism. Even in your case, we will remove only the cancerous part, the head of the pancreas, and leave the rest. Besides, the risk for pancreatic cancer is much lower, probably less than five percent." He thought for a moment and added, "Some doctors doubt any association between BRCA and pancreatic cancer. Most recognize an association with the BRCA 2 gene only."

Len leant over towards Gertrude. "I think we need a little time to think about the genetic testing," he said.

As Gertrude smiled at her husband, grateful for his support, her eyes regained their usual glow. She thanked Professor Carson, asked for one of his business cards, and stood to leave.

Gertrude had on an elegant beige slack suit over a black blouse, and she appeared stunning. If any woman had grown more attractive with time, it was Gertrude; hard for anyone to believe that she had a tumor growing in her belly or a genetic makeup prone to producing cancers.

As Len held open the door for her, she turned to the professor, standing behind his desk. "I think I will go for genetic testing. Will Helena help me with that appointment as well?"

"Yes, she will . . . if you like, Gertrude."

Len did not return to work that afternoon. He stayed home with Gertrude, spoke openly with her about the cancer, and even helped her prepare their dinner, which he realized she was preparing for his enjoyment only . . . and not hers.

The next day was a Thursday, and Len was the first person in the Synagogue. He wanted to arrive before early morning services and get Gertrude's name onto the rabbi's growing list of sick and often terminal people, his special *Mi Shebeirach list.* Saturdays, Mondays, Thursdays, and Religious Holidays, while the Torah was out of the arc, the rabbi would recite the names of congregants who were asking for God's help in a speedy and full recovery.

The next person through the door was not Rabbi Lathan; for Len, it was an even more welcome face.

"Shalom, Ginger." Elsewhere Len would have said *hello* or *hi* to Brad, only here in the Synagogue, *shalom* seemed to slip more easily over his tongue.

"How are you, Len?" Brad replied, and walked up to shake his hand.

"I am fine . . . physically, that is, but we have another problem, Ginger. It's Gertrude."

Brad listened intently as Len filled him in. It was Len, whose concentration was wandering, thinking how different this meeting would have been had he been telling Brad about his upcoming divorce instead of Gertrude's cancer. Even as he spoke, he could picture Brad evaluating Gertrude's infidelity, weighing it against her longstanding marriage to Len, and offering some creative advice on how to get everything back on track. He could not be certain, but that is how he imagined Brad would react. With the news of Gertrude's illness, however, he could virtually feel Brad's empathy—just as he would have predicted had he given the matter any forethought.

"When is she going to have her operation?" Brad asked.

"We'll meet with Dr. Reddy and Dr. Kallenbach tomorrow," Len said. "If you want, I'll let you know."

Brad looked quizzically at Len. "Of course I want to know."

Len should have expected no less an answer. Gertrude and Len's problem had become Brad's problem, too, and Brad would feel hurt if he could not share and perhaps lessen their pain.

Len could feel Brad's unique support and love. *Of course, he wants to know when Gertrude is going to have her surgery*, and Len's tears began immediately to flow. He could not understand what was happening, why he was experiencing this sudden burst of emotion. Particulars of Gertrude's predicament had passed a pinnacle, and other critical crossroads probably still lay ahead, but speaking of the trouble to a well-meaning friend should not normally have stirred up such a release.

Brad did not question Len's tears, for Brad was Brad. In his work with the severely ill, he frequently witnessed people cry, and he had no way of recognizing how his sincere sympathy was often the catalyst.

Brad placed a comforting hand on Len's arm and walked with him to his regular seat, where they both put on their prayer shawls and phylacteries, in readiness for the early morning blessings.

Before the service began, Len was too distraught to tell Rabbi Lathan about Gertrude. Instead, he had to wait until the Mi Shebeirach list was being recited and, at that time, walk up to the rabbi's side and speak Gertrude's name for the rabbi to repeat.

After graduating from medical school in India, Dr. Reddy immigrated to the United States, where he did his residency in internal medicine and then specialized in gastroenterology. He was a slight man with thick, dark hair that parted neatly on the right and swept back over both ears.

As he listened, he would occasionally tilt his head briskly to one side in agreement, instead of the more conventional up and down nod. He spoke to Gertrude about her condition, discussed alternate imaging techniques that might have been used in other major centers, but had no argument with the treatment she had so far received. In truth, while Professor Carson would value the senior gastroenterologist's opinion, Dr. Reddy had nothing extra to offer, other than his technical skill as an *endoscopist*. His function was to pass the endoscope down Gertrude's esophagus, through her stomach, and into the duodenum, where he would locate the ampulla of Vater, and continue his search into the ducts that drained from the pancreas and gallbladder. Perhaps he would biopsy any suspicious lesion en route, but the major goal was to position the stent and reopen the flow of secretion into the gut. The procedure was scheduled for the Monday, three days away.

From Dr. Reddy's outpatient clinic, Len and Gertrude went directly to meet with Dr. Kallenbach. He was far younger looking than Gertrude had expected, but his premature balding, trimmed mustache, and tall stature gave him an air of experience. Like Dr. Reddy, Dr Kallenbach, too, said that the findings were conclusive and that Professor Carson's recommendation for a Whipple procedure was appropriate. With all the doctors in agreement, any hopes that Gertrude might have had for a misdiagnosis were dwindling rapidly toward zero. Unlike Dr. Reddy, however, Dr. Kallenbach did not set a date for the laparoscopy and surgery; he wanted to reevaluate some of Gertrude's laboratory findings when she had the stent in place.

With two and a half hours to kill before the next appointment, a consultation with geneticist Dr. Eleanor Bush, Len and Gertrude left the hospital to go for lunch. Gertrude suggested *Uncle Mordechai's*, a kosher restaurant run by the Schititsky family, friends of Len and members of the same Synagogue.

About midway between the hospital and their home, they turned off the main highway, drove another half mile through a congested neighborhood, followed road signs around an almost180-degree broad curve, and came to the parking lot outside a pedestrian mall with artist galleries, T-shirt stores, ladies boutiques, Western bars, hair salons, a tattoo parlor, and a number of ethnic restaurants.

Made of smooth Jerusalem stone, and situated at the highest point in the mall, Uncle Mordechai's was readily visible. To get to its front door, however, guests would have to pass through a narrow winding passage with walls of stone on either side and a continuous tiny stream flowing down the middle.

Len and Gertrude chose a small round table next to a window with a view overlooking the mall below. A boy, no more than nine or perhaps ten, dressed in jeans, a white apron, an evening shirt with a red bowtie, and a yarmulke on his head came to take their order. He almost handed a menu to Len before Gertrude, but quickly corrected his mistake and said, "Good afternoon. My name is Jordan, and I will be your waiter today."

Gertrude smiled in amusement, not so much at their waiter's youth, but more at his apparent confidence.

"Can I get you something to drink: soda, a bottle of wine?"

"Iced tea," Gertrude replied.

"I'll have the same," Len said.

"Two iced teas."

The boy turned to fill the order, but Len stopped him. "Just a minute, Jordan."

"Yes, sir." He was ready to write whatever Len wanted to request.

"You're Jordan Schititsky . . . Mark's son, aren't you?"

The boy dropped his notepad and pencil bearing hands, and his eyes turned into joyful, proud slits. "Yes, sir. That's my dad."

"Is your father here?"

"No, sir. He will be back in a short while. Jose, the head waiter, is in charge while Dad's away."

Len nodded, and the youth once more turned to fetch the iced teas.

Len and Gertrude scanned the menus while at the same time looking down onto the cobblestone walkway below their window.

In the bright light of day, Gertrude's eyes seemed even more tinged than before, and for the second time, Len wondered why he had not been first to notice.

"Sweetheart," he asked out of pure curiosity. "How long have you been feeling poorly? When did the nausea first occur?"

Gertrude shrugged her shoulders. "Probably two to three months, but it was gradual, Len. Could have been even longer than that."

"And the jaundice. When did you first find the yellow in your eyes? Was it the Saturday, the day before you told me? You said

331

you didn't want to trouble me on the Sabbath, so I presume you must have known for at least a day . . . or maybe two."

"A couple of days. On Friday, you were out the house before I woke up, and when I saw you that night, it was already Sabbath, after dark, and so I decided to wait until Sunday morning. I also wasn't absolutely certain about the jaundice; I was not the first to notice it."

"Who did first notice it?"

"Someone at bridge."

"A nurse or a doctor?" Len asked with a hint of jealousy for the person's acumen.

"A man, who was staring into my eyes," Gertrude teased, oblivious to Len's recent suspicions.

"A good looking man?" Len asked, playing along.

Elbows on the table, chin resting on clasped hands, Gertrude thought about Len's question. She then held up a wait-a-moment finger and began to rummage through her handbag. Wherever she went, Gertrude was never without material pertaining to bridge, and today was no exception. She had brought a copy of the district weekly publication to read in the waiting rooms, should there have been a delay in any of her appointments. The magazine had articles of interest to bridge players: discussions of interesting hands, upcoming events, the latest rankings, and the results of recent competitions. Gertrude's name and photograph often appeared when she had won or placed in one of the larger tournaments, and she would show the articles to Len. Today, however, it was not her picture she wanted to find, it was the picture of the man who first noticed her jaundice.

Paging through the magazine, she was searching for a photo she had seen earlier. Len, scooting closer, had his neck bent, trying to read over her shoulder, when Jordan Schititsky returned with a pushcart carrying their rolls, butter, and their drinks. The other waiters would bring the food and drinks to the tables, carrying dishes in their hands, or, if the order was large, balanced up an arm, but Jordan was not yet mature enough to be that coordinated; without the cart, he would probable drop and break too many of his father's plates.

"Have you decided what you would like to eat?" Jordan took half a step back, eager to jot down their order.

Gertrude knew what she wanted, but she nevertheless lifted the single laminated menu page, pointed to the item with a finger, and said, "I'll have the chopped herring plate, please."

Jordan's face dropped. "We don't have the chopped herring today," he said, apologetically.

"Oh." Gertrude gazed at the menu, turned it over to the opposite side, and continued her search, whereupon young Jordan offered, "I have a whitefish plate, today. I can recommend it. It's excellent."

Gertrude lifted a palm to hide her smiling lips. "Good. I think I'll try your whitefish plate."

"Thank you." Jordan turned to Len. "And for you, sir. What can I get you?"

"Do you have grilled snapper today?" Len asked.

"I do. How would you like it cooked, sir?"

"Medium."

"Very well, sir. One whitefish plate and one medium Mordechai's grilled snapper," Jordan read off his notepad, and then hurried with his cart in front of him to turn in the order.

Gertrude giggled as she watched their little waiter disappear behind other seated customers, enjoying their midday meal. Then, she turned a few more pages of her magazine, tilted it to face Len, and pointed to a picture. "This is the guy who saw the yellow color in my eyes."

Len stared, barely able to hide his surprise. The smooth features, the elegant moustache; yes, it was the man he had seen flirting with Gertrude at the studio, and yes, he was handsome, and yes, he had been looking into her eyes, and yes, Len had not ruled him out as Gertrude's lover. It all made sense, except for one facet: why would Gertrude be showing him this picture? *Surely, she would want his very existence kept hidden from me. Unless, she is toying with the notion that I might have some inkling into her infidelity with this man, in which case she is testing whether her secret is still secure.* Len looked up at Gertrude, and she was indeed staring at him. *She's studying my reaction to the picture,* he thought. *At this critical juncture in her life, she might be having a change of heart, wanting to return home to me, and how else can she put all doubt to rest, other than by flaunting his picture in front of me.*

"What is it, Len? Do you know Jon?"

"His name is Jon, is it?" Len asked. "Jon who?"

"Jon Yi."

"Jon Yi. Really? Where's he from?"

"England, actually. He travels back and forth, but spends most of his time here in Jacobsburg. You looked like you may have recognized him."

Len shook his head. He could still vividly visualize the events that had played out in front of his eyes as he watched through that bridge studio window. He had detected a special relationship between Gertrude and this fellow, Jon Yi. Gertrude had admitted that it was a man, who had been staring into her eyes; there was even a hint of the amorous in her admission, so why should he now be surprised that it was Jon Yi who first noticed the tinge? Len wanted desperately to know more, yet he did not want to hurt Gertrude . . . not now . . . not with the abundance of bad news raining down all about her. Still, if he kept smiling, he could ask whatever he wanted. If she remained inclined to tread daringly close to the truth, he might even learn more than she actually intended to reveal.

"He is good looking, isn't he?" Len said.

"The women at bridge seem to think so."

"And this is the guy who was looking into your eyes?" Len remained smiling and even dared to give Gertrude a naughty wink.

"Oh, please," was all Gertrude felt necessary to reply.

"Well, he was looking into your eyes, wasn't he? And you must have been looking back, otherwise how would he have been able to notice?"

Gertrude giggled and shook her head.

"You got a little crush on the guy?"

Gertrude rapped her knuckles on the table. "Believe me, Len, after twenty-nine years of marriage to you, I've had enough. I would never allow myself another crush . . . not for any other man."

"That's because you know I'm the best, and you could only head downhill from here."

"I wouldn't say that."

"Really? So who's better than me?" Len asked, and then recklessly threw in, "And how do you know?"

Fists on her hips, Gertrude said, "I don't know who, Len, but you haven't been easy." She turned suddenly sullen and added, "Although, you have been terrific these last two weeks. Thanks, Len. Thank you for your support."

This was not what Len wanted, not while the conversation was progressing in such a relaxed mood. If they continued in the vein of Gertrude's serious remark, he would lose this opportunity to find out more about this fellow, Jon Yi.

He took a sip of the iced tea, reached across the table, and picked up the bridge magazine. After staring with a furrowed brow at the photo of Jon Yi, Len lifted his gaze to Gertrude, but then dropped it back down to the magazine again.

"What?" Gertrude asked.

But Len said nothing. He just continued to scrutinize the picture in the magazine until Gertrude again asked, "What's the matter? Why are you so taken up by that picture?"

"Who's better looking," Len eventually asked, "Jon Yi or me?"

She rolled her eyes to say *that was a ridiculous question*, and in case Len could not fully understand, she also added, "You don't stand a chance."

Len knew she was teasing, but he also understood that Gertrude appreciated the man's good looks. "So you find him more attractive than me," he reiterated, trying to look hurt.

"You may not believe this Len, but I find many men more attractive than you."

"Yes, but we are not talking about many men, we're talking about this man, the one who was staring into your eyes," Len said, still smiling, as though playing a childish game. "I think you have a hidden crush on him."

"No, I don't," Gertrude said emphatically. "Although, he did once have a crush on me."

The cat was at last out the bag. Len now knew for sure that Gertrude had not gone untouched by all those hormonal urges floating freely around the bridge studio and the rest of the bridge world. He also accepted that his analysis of Jon Yi's body language must have been right on the mark, that this man was attracted to Gertrude. Who now could know what happened during those weekends at major tournaments away from home? When one person had a crush, and the other knew about it, then one of the two must have raised the topic of emotions. And if the one was handsome, skilled, and suave, an icon for all the women in the room, who knows where a little wine, friendly conversation, and hero worship could lead?

"You want to tell me about the crush he had on you?" Len asked, expecting a creative story and ready to pick at the edges for the truth.

"Don't be ridiculous," was all Gertrude chose to answer.

Len was not taken aback by her retort. He also would not be sidetracked. *I saw what I saw two Thursdays ago, and I want to know more.* "Does Jon Yi still fancy you; do I have some competition?"

When Gertrude did not immediately reply, Len understood she was searching for the best way to spin her tale. He waited for her to speak, but Gertrude's was not the voice he heard.

"Here we go. Whitefish for the lady, and snapper for the gentleman." Jordan Schititsky arrived with his loaded cart. He reached over the table and placed the orders carefully in front of his two customers. "Anything else I can get you? You seem to be doing okay with your iced tea."

"No thanks," Len replied while picking up his napkin, shaking out the folds, and laying it on his lap.

As Jordan maneuvered his cart, still carrying sodas and bread for other customers, Len stared at his plate and remarked, "Looks good, doesn't it?"

But Gertrude did not immediately feel like eating. She leaned forward on her elbows and asked, "What exactly do you want to know, Len?" She seemed indignant, but not quite insulted. If Len was correct in his assessment, she was acting exactly the way *she* believed she should act. Only the anger was missing.

339

Len was ready; he had brought the conversation to the precise point he wanted it to be. Knife and fork in his hands, all set to attack his meal, he feigned surprise. "What do *I* want? I don't know. You tell me that you and this good looking Jon Yi fellow are gazing into each other's eyes, you even show me his picture, and you expect me not to be interested? What do *you* want of me? If you don't want to talk about it, that's okay. We can talk about something else."

She had to reflect on what had transpired between them, and it seemed that Len had offered an accurate rendition.

"All right." Unaware of Len's suspicions, she felt she did owe him an explanation about Jon Yi. *I really do enjoy my freedom*, she thought, *yet I also want to maintain my marriage to Len*. "Just over a week ago, I was playing bridge against Jon. The hand was fairly complex and I didn't know whether to finesse. Because I was taking a little longer than usual, Jon and everyone else at the table turned to watch me. I actually thought Jon was becoming irate, I could see it in his face. Then, he saw the color in my eyes. I know that was when he first noticed; I could see his abrupt change in expression. Something was disturbing him. Neither of us could say anything at the time, we were in the middle of a hand, but we both understood that something needed to be addressed once the hand was over."

That may actually have happened, Len thought. *Why would she have made it up? Gertrude is basically honest. Even in the years she was smoking behind my back, I don't recall her telling me that she didn't smoke. She may have skirted the truth, like a politician diverting attention from an explosive disagreement, but she never would utter a blatant lie. Still, I know that more must have been going on between Gertrude and Jon.* "He must be very astute, this Jon guy," Len said. "One quick glance and he knew."

"I asked Jean to look at my eyes, but she couldn't see anything wrong, so I decided I would leave it until I could ask you."

"Why didn't you take a look in a mirror?"

"I did, and I wasn't sure." Gertrude gave a little laugh. "I also wondered whether the yellowness would affect my vision, so a few hands later, when I was dummy, I tried looking around the room at everything white to see if it would appear yellow, and for anything blue, to see if it would turn green. You know that yellow on blue gives green, don't you? But my vision seemed normal. My only reason for concern was the yellow that Jon had seen. He suggested I have it checked out." She shrugged her shoulders, thinking about what Jon had told her. "A little later, however, he seemed less certain about the color. Either he changed his mind or he was sorry for upsetting me."

"Why do you say that?"

"When the game was over, I asked him to look more carefully, and he did. He made me turn my eyes sideways and examined the whites carefully. That was when he said that he also couldn't be sure. We were not 'gazing into each other's eyes,' as you put it. I suppose I should be thankful to him; he was right. Who knows how much longer I would have gone undiagnosed if it wasn't for him."

The part where Jon made Gertrude turn her eyes sideways caught Len's attention. He felt certain that he had actually witnessed the event through the bridge studio window. He remembered Gertrude walking up to Jon, and he touching her cheek. What Len interpreted as a token of affection could also have been the pulling down of an eyelid to examine more readily the color. What is more, Len recalled that this was precisely what he had done on the Sunday morning in their bathroom, when he wanted to reveal more of Gertrude's eye.

Could everything be much simpler than I thought, that Gertrude is true to me, as I always believed, that all my suspicions are unfounded, that I totally misread an innocent encounter, that the person who first found her jaundice just so happens to be a handsome man? Logical as this seemed, Len still could not accept it, not after discovering that Jon actually had done something to strike up a relationship with Gertrude. And yet, he knew Gertrude was telling the truth. Everything seemed to fit the scene that he had witnessed. She had explained away the supporting evidence for his suspicions, and this without even being aware that he had been conducting his own private investigation. Len was relieved. With Gertrude's unexpected illness, he didn't need the extra concern about her fidelity. What he wanted at this juncture was to steer the conversation in another direction, put the episode of Jon Yi behind them, enjoy their weekday lunch together, something they should have done much more frequently over the years, and, of course, prepare to return to the hospital for the third consultation of the day.

Unlike the visits to Dr. Reddy and Dr. Kallenbach, the consultation with the geneticist, Dr. Eleanor Bush, proved anything

342

but routine. Dr. Bush was as tall and as slim as Gertrude, and about the same age, too, but that was where the similarities ended. Her forehead was too long, her chin too short, and she wore steel wire reading spectacles balanced on the tip of her hooked and narrow nose. Before Gertrude took her seat on the patients' side of the desk, she was discretely deciphering the cosmetics, coiffure, and surgery needed for Dr. Bush's extreme makeover.

"I've seen your medical history," Dr. Bush said. "I don't know how far you've thought this through. You have compelling evidence for a genetic mutation, and you may or you may not want to be tested."

"I do want to be tested," Gertrude replied, surprised that this was not going to be a swift discussion before beckoning a nurse with a tourniquet and syringe to sample her blood.

"First off, we must understand that a lot of people are going to be affected by the decision," Dr. Bush said. "This is not the kind of test you do only for yourself. It may change the lives of your close relatives. Have you decided who you would have to tell if the results were positive for an inherited mutation that may be responsible for your cancers?"

Although Dr. Bush did not want to talk Gertrude out of genetic testing, she also did not want her in a situation that she might regret. "We may believe we know how others think and what they want, but we can't always be certain."

"Surely people want to know if they're at added risk for cancer," Gertrude said. "Professor Carson outlined steps that people can take to prevent it."

"Yes . . . people!" Dr. Bush actually smiled as she considered how to tell Gertrude that people, particularly young people, feel they are invincible. "Confronted with an immediate threat, most patients will do what they must to ward off discomfort and disease, but as the threat becomes more distant, so does the concern. People know what is hazardous to their health, yet they continue to smoke, drink too much, exercise too little, and generally invite illness into their lives. And that is toward the better end of the personality spectrum; we have been talking about average, so-called *normal* people. Those who are anxious about their health do much worse when they come across a seed that may lead to their death. They may obsess to the point where they allow it to take hold of their lives. Hypochondriasis is far more common than we would like to believe."

"Surely people are entitled to know about their added risks and then make a decision for themselves. I don't think I have the right to impose my values on others." Gertrude felt like saying that *we don't have the right to play the role of a god,* but she did not want to sound insulting.

"Of course you're right in all you say, but we must learn from experience. Before we bring information into others' lives, the least we can do is ensure that it will not ruin them. What I want is for you to be aware of the potential hardship that knowledge of this seed can bring, and please understand that as long as a person with a gene mutation remains unaffected, that gene is merely a seed."

"A very special seed, which can grow and lead to death."

"A very special seed, because we can identify it. We are all born with many seeds that will lead to our deaths. Most of us have seeds for a cardiovascular death, and yet only some of us do what we can to hold it at bay. The difference between a specific seed and the whole array is that at this particular time in our quest for understanding, knowledge of a single seed with a potentially dire outcome may be devastating to one's emotional being, as well."

Dr. Bush went on to discuss personality traits, focusing on the traits in Gertrude's family, particularly those of her daughter, Janet. She spoke about the possible genetic mutations that Gertrude might have, particularly the BRCA 1 and 2 genes, and the chances that others close to her could be harboring the same problem, information that Gertrude already understood. She did not impose her opinion on Gertrude; she merely guided her through the thought process toward Gertrude's own conclusions, clarifying preconceived notions and correcting wrong assumptions.

At the end of the day, Gertrude had her blood drawn for genetic testing, and Dr. Bush handed her a pamphlet, which covered the information they had discussed.

Throughout the consultation, Len remained quietly attentive. He had nothing to add to Dr. Bush's advice or to Gertrude's decision. All they could do now was wait for the results and pray that she did not harbor a BRCA gene; although, they both realized that if not *this* gene, then the culprit could still lie somewhere else in Gertrude's genetic makeup, waiting to surface again in Janet or in other offspring down the line.

Driving home, Len felt about as satisfied as he could under the circumstances. They had tied up a few major uncertainties, and now they had to follow the prescribed course. There remained, however, a few nagging details yet to be explained, not about Gertrude's illness but about her relationship with Jon Yi. As they drove in silence, Len actually decided against asking about Jon. Nor did he want to ask her anything else. They were both exhausted, and her eyelids were half-closed. He actually thought he would allow her to doze off, and then without fully realizing, he found himself blurting a question.

"You said you didn't want to upset me on the Sabbath, Gertrude, but surely you realized how important jaundice can be?"

She blinked twice, surfacing from a daydream about the endoscopy tube passing down her throat. "Actually, no. I imagined I was ill in some way, but not like this. I thought more in terms of an infection or gallstones . . . not a cancer. Also, I looked at my eyes a few times, and I still wasn't sure."

"So if you didn't ask me on the Sabbath, why not on the Saturday night, when Sabbath was over?"

She nodded gently to herself, recalling. "To tell you the truth, Len, you seemed tired or in a bad mood. If you remember, you were in bed early on Saturday night, so I let you rest."

Again, Gertrude had an answer to his question. He had been preoccupied and tired, unable to expel the thought of his wife with another man, and still fatigued from the lack of sleep on that Thursday.

Len chose to forgo his other question. It would only upset Gertrude and cast suspicion on his otherwise seemingly innocent interest. The reason she had not come home until after one a.m. would have to wait; at this stage, he did not care what she had been doing for the two hours after the Thursday night bridge game had ended. Besides, with her accounting for all his concerns, Len felt certain she would have yet another logical excuse; although, what that might be, he could not guess.

CHAPTER TWELVE

Gertrude had considered the endoscopy a first phase in the definitive treatment of her cancer. As she came around from the sedation, she was amazed at how she suffered no discomfort. She may even have begun to feel better. Len had told her the procedure would be a breeze, and he was right. This all served to boost her confidence and courage, and she even allowed herself the luxury of an occasional moment of optimism. The only negative was that Dr. Reddy had obtained a small biopsy, and by the Wednesday, two days after the procedure, the report confirmed that the tumor was indeed malignant, an *adenocarcinoma* of the pancreas.

The following Monday, a week after the endoscopy, Gertrude received more news, both good and bad: her blood tests showed a remarkable improvement. This did not surprise her; she had not felt as well in a long time. The insidiousness of the cancer had helped hide the sickness from her recognition, until Jon Yi noticed the jaundice. Dr. Kallenbach was pleased. He scheduled the surgery for the following week, Wednesday, nine days later.

Then, there was the other report, equally expected but utterly unwanted: Dr. Bush was explicit and solemn. "Your tests confirm a BRCA 2 mutation. This is the most logical result, because only the BRCA 2 has shown an association with pancreatic cancer, not the BRCA 1. As you know, Gertrude, this means you are also at risk for ovarian cancer."

"What are the chances?" Gertrude asked.

Len, sitting supportively by her side, knew about the increased incidence of ovarian cancer, but he was not sure of the exact added risk.

"Forty percent."

"What would you recommend?"

"At this time, nothing. Take care of the pancreas. Later, we may decide on a prophylactic ooforectomy."

Dr. Bush may or may not have been sensitive to the encouraging information she had given. "Later" meant there indeed might be a *later*. It also meant that whatever might happen to Janet, there would be treatment available.

"What would you recommend for my daughter?" Gertrude asked, stealing a quick glance at Len, but turning back to Dr. Bush for the answer.

"At this time, your daughter has a fifty percent chance of carrying the gene, and so does your sister, Marlene. We can be certain that one of your parents has it, too. I prepared a letter that you may want to hand to each of them. It explains the statistical chances of their having the gene and then goes on to outline the associated risks. Each person should be informed. Then, whoever wishes can come for testing."

Gertrude realized more clearly than before that Marlene might not want to have the genetic testing or counseling. Marlene had not yet been affected and, as such, could cling to the belief that she did not carry the gene. Furthermore, at this stage and time, her sons, Jeremy and Mike, each had only a twenty-five percent chance of carrying the mutation. And if they did, although at added risk, they nevertheless had a far lesser chance of developing a cancer than did a similarly affected woman. If the boys were to marry and have daughters, then the chance of passing on the gene would again be diluted by half, and at twelve and a half percent, the threat was close to the overall incidence for breast cancer, for which women undergo annual mammograms and monthly self examinations anyhow. It was all a game of statistics, as was the inevitability of contracting one or another serious illness. So why torture one's emotions by honing in on a single possibility? Yes, Marlene might want to hang onto her hope that she had not inherited the mutation. Yet, if she opted against testing, then she would still have to live with an awareness of the BRCA 2 threat to herself.

They spoke a little about genetic engineering, but expectations for a cure were not yet even a speck on the horizon. The best anyone could do was to undergo frequent testing and perhaps prophylactic surgery before the cancer took hold in any threatened organs.

Of everyone at significant risk, only Janet opted for testing. Not unexpectedly, this was what Dr. Bush anticipated. She had done nothing to influence those involved; yet, experience had given her foresight into peoples' decisions.

Thursday, six days before Gertrude's scheduled surgery, as Len said goodbye on his way to the morning Synagogue service, he also mentioned that the hospital internal medicine department was holding its quarterly meeting that night. "I don't think I'll be going," he said. "I'd rather be home with you."

While Gertrude was feeling better and better, she had also been spending an inordinate amount of time indoors, moping. "Why don't you go to your meeting?" she suggested. "I wouldn't mind an evening at the bridge studio. I could use a little distraction."

He turned to look at her, seated at the kitchen table and sipping a cup of morning tea. She was radiant. *Strange how one's outer appearance reflects the inner body chemistry and organ function*, he thought. Her cheeks had already begun to fill and her skin had regained some of its youthful luster, features which no one had noticed decline.

"Okay. I'll see you tonight."

Len's workday was routine and the departmental meeting boring. He was driving home with no interest in his radio talk show host, who was babbling about offensive remarks uttered by some no-name political figure regarding an equally unknown politician in the opposite party. He was thinking about Gertrude, how well she was looking and how worried she must have been feeling. He had taken to wanting to please her, a trait he had lost over the years. Perhaps this was a subconscious desire to make amends for his mistrust that had surfaced on the heels of her second cancer. He took his eyes off the road to change the station. At that moment, he heard a screech of tires followed by the honk of a horn sounding angrily at him for swerving out of his lane. Len regained his bearing and noticed he was close to the exit for the bridge studio. Without a second thought, he headed down the ramp. He would surprise Gertrude, maybe take her somewhere for dessert. The dinner at the hospital meeting had been scrumptious for other doctors, but not for Len. He would not eat the *traif* meat; he had one of the vegetarian plates that the administration provided for those with various dietary restrictions. The problem was, he had grown tired of the same green arrangement from the same nearby restaurant always looking up at him as he opened the lid of the Styrofoam box.

He glanced at his watch as he pulled into the front parking lot of the shopping center. *10:05, I'm probably a little too early.*

He grimaced, recalling his last visit, when he had come to spy on his wife rather than please her with a surprise date. He thought about going to the entrance of the studio, peeking in, and asking whoever came to the front vestibule how much longer the game would take. He did not want to call from his cell phone to hers; this might disturb her game and her concentration. Before parking his car, he drove up and down the rows of parked cars, looking for Gertrude's white Lexus. While he did not believe he was still spying on her, he nevertheless found himself questioning his own motivation behind this search. There were plenty of open spots in the front parking lot, yet he could not find her car. Realizing that she had arrived earlier in the evening, when the stores might have been busier, he drove to the end of the lot, past *The Shoe Boutique,* and around to the back parking lot, for the second time. Here were a few cars, just as he suspected there might be, and this time Gertrude's Lexus was the one parked closest to The Gardens of Sicily, in fact, directly behind the window through which he had watched her, Jon Yi, and the other players on his previous visit.

Len changed his mind. Instead of going to the front door, he decided to park, look through a window again, and try to gauge how much longer they would have to play. If he went to the front vestibule and told whomever that he was her husband waiting for her, he would spoil the surprise.

The blinds to the studio were once again open. Len stood on the sidewalk, watching the players who were deep in concentration. Even the dummy players at each table seemed interested. Somehow, this time he felt less nervous. If anyone wanted to know, he would simply tell the truth, that he was waiting for his wife.

There she was, at a table third from the window, absorbed in the game and seemingly having a good time. Recalling his caution on the previous visit, he confirmed that no one could possibly see him from one of the stores around the bend in the building to his right. To his left, he again noticed the back window of The Gardens of Sicily, angled obliquely and virtually obscured from his line of vision. Confident that his secret was secure, he felt a sense of relief. He then sniggered to himself, realizing that he had no way of gauging how much longer the game might last. He could not hear through the window and there was no bulletin board indicating the number of hands remaining.

Deciding to revert to his first plan, he turned to head back to his car. As he walked passed Gertrude's Lexus, however, he noticed that the line of vision from the window of The Gardens of Sicily was far more direct. What is more, the white Lexus bathed in the light from the studio window could probably be readily seen from the restaurant's dulled interior. He again changed his mind. He would go to the restaurant, find a seat with a view of Gertrude's car, have a beer or cup of coffee, and wait the twenty to thirty minutes until, in his estimation, the bridge game would be over.

Fabio's bar in the front of the restaurant was crowded. He glanced up at Len coming through the door, quickly calculated he would have to seat him at one of the two empty stools near the entrance, and was then disappointed when Len turned to make his way into the near empty restaurant at the back.

"For one?" A short waiter dressed in a white shirt with a gaudy green and red tie held up an index finger.

"Yes," Len nodded.

The waiter gestured toward a private booth near the front of the restaurant, but Len shook his head and asked, "Do you mind if I sit over there, at that small round table on the other side?"

"No problem. As you please."

Sitting close to the window, Len had a clear view of Gertrude's white Lexus. He was also pleased to notice that, even with his nose against the pane, he could not see into the bridge studio next door, nor could he see the sidewalk where he had stood watching the players a month ago. In the other direction, across the floor of the restaurant and through the glass front, he had a panoramic view of the sidewalk and main parking lot, not very attractive, but interesting for those who enjoyed people watching.

Len could relax. He would now wait until he saw the first few people leaving the bridge studio and then hurry next door to find and surprise Gertrude. He was going to either bring her back to The Gardens of Sicily or take her to some other dessert place nearby; he had not definitely decided. But he was certain that either way she would be pleased. He felt good about himself and his decision to take that off ramp to the bridge studio. With all the unpleasantness Gertrude was going through, she could use a pleasant surprise, no matter how small.

The same short waiter gave Len a few moments to settle into his chosen spot before he came by. "What can I get you to drink?" he asked, placing a menu, a napkin, and cutlery on the bare wooden table and apparently expecting an immediate answer.

Len would have wanted a minute or two to peruse the menu, particularly the selection of drinks, but feeling pressured to place an order, he said, "A cup of coffee, please," and in case the waiter intended asking whether Len wanted anything to go with the coffee, he went on to explain, "I'm waiting for someone to join me."

Cheesecake with strawberries, crème brûlée, tiramisu, rum bread pudding: all Len's favorites were right there to be had. That settled it; he would encourage Gertrude to return with him to The Gardens of Sicily. The ambiance in this near empty restaurant left much to be desired, but Len did not notice. All he wanted was to share a few moments with Gertrude in an environment other than home, speaking about something other than her cancer.

Two or three cars moved slowly through the parking lot, the occasional pedestrian passed before the restaurant front window, and three women stopped to inspect plates of food being served to a couple. One of the three pointed through the glass at something of interest to her two friends. They all seemed to be in agreement about whatever had caught their interest, and they, too, moved on.

The waiter brought Len's coffee. "Anything else I can get for you, sir?"

"Not at the moment, but how is your bread pudding; is it moist?"

"It's very good, one of my favorite items on the menu."

"Good. I'll probably have some a little later."

He added sweetener and cream, and took a sip. Nothing was stirring through the back window, so Len again turned his attention to the front. Two older women were stepping off the sidewalk and onto the street. They spoke a few words and then each went their own way. A man in a leather lumber jacket hesitated to light a cigarette, and he, too, moved on to a nearby car. Five women and two men were eagerly debating something while standing partly on the sidewalk and partly on the car lot. Two more men stopped to join this group, have their say about some apparent dispute, and then they all dispersed. Perhaps it was all happening too soon, before Len was fully ready. Only when he saw three cars reversing from the back curb and driving away did he realize that most or all of the people he had been watching had come out of the bridge club, and that the game had already ended. Len was not too concerned. He knew he had not missed Gertrude; her car was still waiting in the beam of light coming from the studio window. Also, for some unfounded reason, he believed she was a perpetual straggler, a regular among the last to leave the studio, which, for her, had become a home away from home.

He decided to get up, just as he had planned. Perhaps he should tell the waiter he would be returning shortly. On second thoughts, the restaurant was not full and no one would really care. Besides, he had already mentioned he was going to be joined by someone else.

One or two more sips of the coffee while it was hot. It was good— full flavor with a rich aroma. He hoped the desserts in the restaurant would be equally tasty. He decided to take the cup with him, sip as he went, and then return to the same table. He was growing fond of this position in the restaurant with a panoramic view of the lively shopping center and the private outlook over the stark rear lot.

Halfway up onto his feet, he noticed a beam of light passing on the far side of the white Lexus; the back door to the studio had opened and closed. Curious about whether the person coming out would be Gertrude or someone else, he remained staring out the window. If he remembered correctly, there were four cars behind the studio when he arrived, perhaps five . . . he was not certain. Then, he had seen three leave, so maybe Gertrude's was the last car in the back lot. No matter how he angled his line of vision, he could not see any other cars parked around the bend in the building. If he did not want to miss her, he would have to hurry through the studio and out the back door to stop her. Or, he could wait to see whether this was, in fact, Gertrude, and if it was, he could merely call her cellular phone before she drove off. He stood with the cup of coffee in his hand, trying to decide.

She appeared, coming around the front of her car, purse slung over a shoulder, clicking the remote with her other hand, and seemingly deep in thought.

Len cussed under his breath; now he was certain he had miscalculated. He could never catch her before she would drive off. Still, he had the other option, the cellular phone. He reached for the phone in the clip at his right hip. Anxious to get through to her before she pulled out of the lot, he opted to use two hands, but the other had the coffee; he would have to set it down. Clumsily, he missed the center of the saucer, and the cup tippled over. He jumped back, but still the hot liquid caught the right leg of his pants and both shoes. Len grabbed the napkin to mop up the spilled coffee. He straightened the cup and cleaned the tabletop. Outside, Gertrude had not yet opened the door to her car. Len's shoes would have to wait. Something or rather someone distracted Gertrude. Len watched her drop the car keys with the remote control back into her purse. He could not hear what she was saying but she was speaking with someone out of Len's view. He had his hand on his cell phone, but decided against calling. Why, he was not certain; maybe he was curious about what he might see. Perhaps his recent spying had whetted his voyeuristic appetite. The other person came into view. It was only Mollie, the woman from the studio. The blonde with the freckles, about as tall as Gertrude and with an equally alluring figure. Len opened the flip top to his phone, but then looked up, and something outside convinced him to again put the call on hold: It was Mollie. She had stepped closer to Gertrude and had a persuading hand on Gertrude's elbow. Perhaps Len should have been concerned for his wife's safety, but he was not. In no way was Mollie's hand menacing. It was a soft touch, friendly and enticing. Both women turned their gazes downward toward their shoes and the concrete floor, and from behind his window, Len continued to watch.

"I'm so sorry, Gertrude. You know I would never mean to hurt you . . . not you," Mollie said.

"I know." Gertrude placed an understanding and comforting hand over Mollie's, and gently massaged the fingers. "It's just that I'm scared, and Len has been so supportive. I can't help thinking that these are his true colors. All his selfishness over the years, all the insensitivity, everything that I told you about may mean nothing at all. I confided in you, and in no one else, because of how I feel about you. You know that, don't you?"

"And haven't I always been there for you? I didn't mean to suggest you shouldn't accept his support; I just don't want to see you hurt again. You can lean on any sympathetic shoulder you want, only I wish that shoulder were mine." Mollie placed her free hand under Gertrude's chin and gazed directly into her eyes. "I

360

want so much to do whatever I can to help you over this hurdle. I never meant to love you, and now I'm frustrated because I do. If I were in Len's place, I, too, wouldn't leave your side for a moment. It's not easy for me, hiding my love in case someone finds out. If it were up to me, I would shout it from the highest mountains. I understand that you still have feelings for your husband, and I have grown to accept that. But you must understand that every time he does any little thing that hurts you, it hurts me, too. When I warned you to be careful, it was because I am afraid for you. I wasn't trying to be hateful to Len. It's not him who I care about; it's you. Please don't be angry with me, Gertrude, not now. I cannot forgive myself if you don't forgive me. I couldn't forgive myself for hurting you at any time, but especially not now."

"I'm sorry, too. It's you who should forgive me." For a second time, Gertrude cast her eyes downward, perhaps trying to conceal the tears.

But Mollie would not allow her. She let go of Gertrude's elbow, held her face gently in both hands, and moved closer to kiss her softly on the lips.

Gertrude allowed her tears to flow. She pulled away for a brief moment to check the studio door and window, and then one hand around the small of Mollie's trim waist, the other running through Mollie's short blonde hair, pulled their bodies together. Mollie did not care to check for their privacy; she returned the embrace, the passionate kiss on the mouth, and dropped a hand onto Gertrude's buttocks to draw her even closer.

361

Their lips eventually parted, and while panting passionately, Mollie asked, "Will you come home with me tonight? Please."

"Only for a short while." Gertrude replied.

Len still had the cellular phone in his hands, ready to dial. He watched Gertrude remove the remote from her purse, lock the Lexus again, and then walk with Mollie around the bend in the building. He did not know what to do next. He thought he felt hurt, but the emotion had not yet had sufficient time to settle in. Should he call her anyway? And if so, why? What would he say? He did not want her to know that he had come to take her for dessert and a drink. Nor did he want her to know what he had witnessed, for both her sake and his. He did not know why he did not want her to know; it was still an emotion without reason, and the painless pounding throughout his being was doing its utmost to retain the confusion. Still undecided, he saw a yellow sports car reverse from the hidden side of the curb. Len could make out the blonde hair of the woman driving and the red of the passenger sitting uncomfortably close. As the car pulled away, Len replaced his cell phone into the clip on his belt, and silently left The Gardens of Sicily.

Gertrude arrived home around midnight. Len said nothing to her. He did not even bother to check the time.

The following day and night, his mind and his body functioned like a conditioned robot, emotions not surfacing. Whatever he might have expected, this was not it, and try as he may, he could not shake the confusion.

Saturday morning, as usual, Len awoke early and was in Synagogue before the morning class was scheduled to begin. In the library, waiting for others to arrive, he opened a chumash and searched the index for laws on homosexuality. He thought he knew what he would find; he had attended classes on illicit sexual relations on a few occasions. But now, with a personal interest, he wanted to read it again, study the commentary, and see how it applied to him and to Gertrude. He went to Leviticus 18 and skimmed through the laws of sexual immorality until he came to verse twenty-two:

Thou shall not lie with mankind as with womankind.

Len read the law a few times and then reviewed the commentary. Leviticus 18: 22 was quite explicit about male homosexuality, but there was no reference to a similar transgression by women. The chumash went on to describe the prohibition of intercourse with an animal, both man with a female animal and woman with a male animal. He read Leviticus 18 in its entirety, just to be certain, and the law seemed clear: there was no prohibition of lesbianism. Furthermore, it would be ludicrous to believe either that the Almighty would expect us to assume that such a law applied or that Moses had inadvertently omitted it. The laws of sexual intercourse all seemed to have one common component—the emission of sperm. The list was complete, and Gertrude's relationship with Mollie did not transgress any commandment.

What did this mean? Len had taken it upon himself to accept the Torah as his only guide for morality. He could not help feeling that Gertrude was committing a grave transgression, but a transgression against whom or what. He was the only hurt party. Apparently, she had not broken the laws of his religion, so what could or should this matter?

There in the Synagogue library, sitting all alone, he actually felt an air of smugness. He had been right all along. His intuition, although late to awaken, was spot on target . . . or at least close. He knew Gertrude had been cheating, but he did not suspect it was with another woman.

He glanced up at the clock on the wall, 7:55, and no one else had yet arrived for the eight a.m. class. *So, Gertrude is having an affair with another woman, Mollie,* he thought. *Somehow, this doesn't hurt as much as it would if she had been with another man. I'm glad that it was not with Jon Yi. I wonder why. Probably because she said he is better looking than I am. That's right. That's why it would hurt. From my perspective, her affair with a man would be more of an insult. Her attraction for another woman is different; the fault lies with her, not with me. Were she dating a man, one might reasonably claim that I had failed, that I must have let her down.*

With a pleasant "Good Shabbat, Len" and a hearty handshake, next to arrive was Brad.

"Good Shabbat, Ginger." Len now hoped the other students would take their time. He could use a few minutes alone with his friend, to pick his brain and get a perspective that he had come to admire. Of course, Len did not want to tell Brad what he had discovered, that Gertrude was having an affair with another woman. He would have to use some other approach to rope his friend into the discussion.

"What do you think about this same sex marriage that is all over the news?" Len asked.

Taking a chair opposite his friend, Brad opened and then shut his hands in a non-committal gesture. "They have a point. If they are living together, then I suppose it is reasonable that they be allowed the same legal rights as a married couple."

"Yes, but what do you think of the morality of a homosexual marriage, and homosexuality in general?"

"Of course the Torah forbids it," Brad said with a condescending smile. "But they are living together anyhow. If the state does not legalize their marriages, then they're breaking two laws: the law of the state and the law of God. Whereas, if it is legalized, then they are breaking only one."

"Do you mean that? Don't you think the laws of the state should follow the rules of morality? Aren't we supposed to be responsible for each other?"

"Naturally, we are responsible for each other. But do you know how many people are doing things that they should not be doing, terrible things to other people, things that you and I would not dream of doing?" Brad shrugged his shoulders. "Taking responsibility for the whole world can get tiring, and what people do with their sex lives is right down near the bottom of my list of priorities."

"Legalizing whatever may be wrong is no great solution," Len said sarcastically. The conversation was not going as Len had planned. He wanted to speak about the difference between male and female homosexuality and was nowhere near the topic. Still, he was pleased with Brad's understanding outlook, pleased but not surprised. Brad had long been a role model for Len, and now Brad had inadvertently brought to Len the impetus to do what he really wanted, forgive Gertrude in her hour of need and win back all of her affection.

"Before you came in, I was reading in Leviticus about the laws of forbidden sexual relations." Len was surprised at how unforced his attempt to direct the conversation sounded. He was also surprised when Brad turned abruptly solemn, reached a friendly hand across the table, and completely changed the subject. "Gertrude's surgery is on Wednesday. How is she is holding up, Len?"

Len felt ashamed. He had meant to keep Brad in the loop and probably would have, had his mind not been jam-packed with all sorts of other concerns. He considered apologizing, but instead followed Brad's lead and also turned more serious. "She seems confident, Ginger. Dr Reddy's biopsy confirmed the malignancy, but her labs have really improved. Her color is good and she has even put on a few pounds."

Brad had more to ask about Gertrude but was interrupted by Rabbi Lathan coming into the library. After all-round shaloms and wishes for a good Shabbat, Len was pleased when Brad actually returned to the topic of homosexual relationships. Only, Brad was asking a question that he must previously have given some thought, a question that had arisen out of intellectual curiosity. "Tell me, Rabbi," he said. "Len and I were discussing these new laws about homosexual marriage. From a Jewish perspective, non-Jews are *not* obligated to follow the laws in Leviticus, yet they are subject to the seven Noahide Laws, which include laws of sexual immorality. Which way is it for them? Are they subject to certain laws that were received at Sinai, or not?"

Rabbi Lathan nodded cautiously, realizing that Brad's question might be loaded. "As you know, any non-Jew who follows the Noahide laws is considered righteous," he said. "The Noahide laws are extracted from Genesis and apply to all of humanity; only Jews are obligated to obey the rest of the Torah laws. But as with most laws, the Noahide laws may need clarification, and when we look specifically at the Noahide prohibition against sexual immorality, we can find the clarification in *Vayikra 18*, Leviticus 18, and we accept that this Noahide law forbids sodomy, adultery, incest, and male homosexuality."

There it was again. Rabbi Lathan was specific about homosexuality: forbidden to men, and nothing said about women. Len was pleased, and so was Brad: Len because he could forgive Gertrude, without deviating from his own ethical yardstick, and Brad because he knew exactly what he wanted to ask next. "But tell me, Rabbi." Brad stroked his beard, considering how to phrase his rhetorical question. "Although the Torah is silent on lesbianism, is it not forbidden in our Code of Law?"

The question got Len's attention. He knew Brad and now realized that lesbianism must have been forbidden, just as Brad implied. Len was content with the words in the Torah, but now he had to hear how and why this ruling had been made.

It was already a minute past eight and other men had started to trickle into the library. Rabbi Lathan did not want to leave Brad's question unanswered, so he told the new arrivals that he had been asked about the laws pertaining to lesbianism, and went on to explain. "Around about three hundred C.E., almost two thousand years after we received the Torah at Mount Sinai, the question arose as to whether or not a woman who had committed an act of lesbianism should be considered a harlot. This was not about seeking punishment for these women; it was a practical consideration, because a priest, or *Cohen,* was not permitted to marry a harlot, that is, a single woman who had had casual sexual intercourse with a single man. So, was a sexual encounter between two women to be considered the same as between a man and a woman?" The rabbi waited a few seconds for the question to sink in. "And our rabbis were not in agreement on the issue. One opinion was that women who rubbed their genitalia together were ineligible to marry a Cohen, while another opinion referred to the act as mere lewdness, and not intercourse, and therefore did not render the women ineligible."

The rabbi smiled at Brad and said, "As you can see, this was an in-house problem, which did not extend to non-Jews." He then swept his eyes over the growing number of students in the class, now filling every chair at the table and a few in the beginnings of a second row behind. "Enter Maimonides, about 850 years later. And he draws our attention to the same section of *Vayikra,* in which we read: *Do not perform the practice of the land of Egypt in which you dwelled; and do not perform the practice of Canaan to which I bring you, and do not follow their traditions.* What does this mean?"

Len had first heard the passage when he was trying to glean insight into his own extramarital affair with Martha Saenz. How uncanny that the rabbi should use the same quotation again, at this particular time, now twenty-five years later.

"What does this mean?" the rabbi repeated. "Or, more specifically, what did Maimonides take it to mean in the context of lesbian relationships?"

When no one else could come up with an answer, Brad, who had instigated the discussion, offered the obvious explanation. "It seems that Egyptian or Canaanite women would indulge in lesbianism."

"Mainonides was actually referring to ancient Egypt, where they apparently practiced same sex marriage. To answer your question, Brad, it was because of Maimonides' authority that this ruling was introduced into the *Shulchan Aruch*, our Code of Law."

"Does that mean that women are not allowed to marry or does it mean that lesbianism is forbidden?" Len asked, trying to cling to the rabbi's exact wording as protection for Gertrude against any wrongdoing.

"That is a good question, Len. The term marriage was used, yet Maimonides also said it was forbidden for women to intertwine; all lesbianism is prohibited." Then, as though the rabbi could read Len's mind, he went on to explain, "And what about a

369

married woman having a lesbian affair with another woman? Although this act is forbidden, it is not considered adultery. And because it is not mentioned in the Torah, therefore there is no prescribed punishment. The woman may remain married to her husband. If deemed appropriate, however, the Jewish courts may impose a punishment."

"What kind of punishment?" the voice came from someone in the second row of seats, somewhere behind Brad.

"Flogging!" Rabbi Lathan shrugged his shoulders and raised his blameless hands as though asking forgiveness for mentioning such a barbaric punishment in the light of contemporary American standards. "Maimonides also said that a husband should do what he can to prevent a wife from committing the act of lesbianism."

Hoping for guidance on the matter, Len wanted to ask how the husband should break off the affair between the wife and the other woman. Short of taking his wife to the Jewish courts and seeking a sentence of flogging, what could a husband do? Before he could articulate his question, however, Brad asked the Rabbi in both words and tone of finality, "So what was Maimonides' opinion: can a lesbian marry a Cohen or not?"

"Because there was no intercourse, she is permitted to marry a Cohen."

The rabbi looked up at the clock. "Open your books to page 212. Will those of you who do not have a book please share with someone who has? Brad, please read for us. We are on the second paragraph from the top of the page."

370

Once again, Len had trouble focusing on the Synagogue service. Throughout the prayers, the songs, and particularly the rabbi's sermon, other considerations were spinning around his thoughts.

He wondered at the appropriateness of the Torah, at the leniency for those who were fundamentally moral. And he considered both Gertrude and himself in the moral category. Despite the fact that they had both strayed from their fidelity, neither of them had broken a Torah Law. He wondered how the Rabbi would have explained what a husband should do to break off the wife's affair with another woman. He also pictured at least a few men offering the obvious advice to *divorce the bitch*, and he wondered whether he would not have done exactly that, had Gertrude not been so vulnerable; Len felt particularly righteous about that thought. He still did not know what would happen on the other side of Gertrude's surgery, when she recovered and regained her strength, and when she would one day be declared cured. He felt a chill run down his back as he realized that the threat of a recurrence of the cancer and of death would remain hovering over her head for years to come. What he had to do was first support her over the immediate hurdle and then decide how to continue supporting her down the stretch. Then, there was always the possibility that Gertrude would approach him and confess to her relationship with Mollie. He did not know how he would react if she were to ask for the divorce. There was also the chance that Mollie had not been the only woman in Gertrude's love life. But Len quickly discounted that likelihood, not because it was impossible, but because it would raise so many other new considerations: instead of having to contend with only one other

371

person, he would have to watch out for a more promiscuous lifestyle and view any other good looking women with suspicion as they entered Gertrude's circle of friends. There was one other possibility, which Len began to consider. *Is it feasible that I am again wrong? Could I be mistaken about what I saw through that window of The Gardens of Sicily? I was almost certain that she was having an affair with that Jon Yi fellow, and yet I was wrong about that. I misinterpreted what I had seen once; I could have misinterpreted again.*

Len shook his head as he recalled the closeness of their bodies as Gertrude and Mollie had kissed and rubbed their pelvises in their passionate embrace. *No*, he had to admit to himself. *This time, I am not wrong.*

CHAPTER THIRTEEN

Wednesday morning, Gertrude was admitted into a private room in the surgical section of the Jacobsburg University Hospital.

An overweight, slow moving, and soft speaking ward clerk spent three quarters of an hour at the bedside, questioning Gertrude and ensuring that her watch, clothing, and jewelry were securely stored.

"What time am I going in?" Gertrude asked the clerk.

After a brief silence, during which the clerk had to search her recollection to discover that she did not have that information, she eventually and pleasantly answered, "I'll go find out."

Fifteen minutes later, the clerk returned. "Dr. Kallenbach is scheduled to begin operating at two o'clock," she said. "You are second on the list. The nurse in charge says that you will be going in at about three to four this afternoon.

By mid-morning, Gertrude was thoroughly bored. Dr. Reddy had been by to see her, but that was a short courtesy visit during his morning business rounds.

A frail old man working as a volunteer in the kitchen brought a lunch tray, and Gertrude had to explain that she was due to have a major operation, that she was on *nil per mouth*. After checking and confirming that Gertrude was correct, the old man returned with a yellow sticker that he placed over the head of Gertrude's bed.

Shortly thereafter, an attractive young woman in a white lab coat introduced herself as Eve, a third year medical student assigned to Gertrude. At first, Eve appeared apprehensive; her voice had a quiver and her hands a mild tremor. She was probably intimidated by Gertrude's dominating composure, evident even in a hospital bed and while wearing a nightdress. But, thankful for the company, Gertrude was both pleasant and cooperative, so toward the end of the visit, the conversation flowed easily and Gertrude was able to teach the young student about BRCA mutations commonly seen in Ashkenazi Jews.

They said goodbye, but fifteen minutes later, Eve returned, this time with eight other students and the familiar figure of Professor Carson in tow.

The professor had a few friendly whispered words with Gertrude and then asked if she would not mind being used as a patient on his teaching round.

Gertrude agreed.

Eve presented Gertrude's case, two other students asked a few questions, and then the professor gave a short lecture on the presentations of pancreatic cancer.

Gertrude understood clearly most of what the professor said; she had suffered the symptoms. Only the part about *hypercoagulability* she had not previously heard or read. At that time, she did not ask; she did not want to disrupt the professor's teaching or the students' learning.

At one o'clock sharp, when the ward round ended and the medical students left for their lunch break, Professor Carson remained with Gertrude.

"You're looking very well," he said to her. "That in itself is a good sign."

"You will be with me at my operation, won't you?" Gertrude asked, sounding somewhere between pleading and commanding.

"Of course. I said I would and I shall. I'll be in the operating room next door to Dr. Kallenbach. I'll see you when you come down. He will do the laparoscopy on his own, and then I'll scrub with him." He gave her hand a comforting pet. "Are you ready?"

"Yes. I thought that by now my operation would have been over."

"Won't be long," he assured her, looking at his watch. "Is there anything else you need?"

375

"Not really."

"Good."

"Although, I do have a question."

"What is it, Gertrude? I'll answer if I can."

"You were telling the students about the tendency to clot, you called it 'hypercoagulability.' What was that all about?"

"Okay." He stroked a hand over his head and then all the way down the back of his neck. Gertrude was not certain, but the question may have made him feel uneasy. "Pancreatic cancer can be an evasive condition, so we must therefore be on the alert, thinking about it when it may not be overtly obvious. In your case, you had weight loss and jaundice, classical signs, but in other patients, the condition may not be so easy to recognize. One of its features is its influence on coagulation. So, when a patient presents for no rhyme or reason with a clot, we must keep certain conditions in mind, including some cancers and particularly an adenocarcinoma of the pancreas. That's all."

Gertrude's forehead wrinkled in thought. "Why does that happen?" she asked. "How does the cancer make someone's blood clot? Can it happen to me?"

The professor could see that Gertrude was concerned, so he pulled one of the three visitors' chairs up to the side of her bed and sat with a relaxing sigh, letting her believe that he had all the time in the world for her. The room was pleasant, considering it was a public hospital. A large window with bright yellow drapes overlooked the street below and the medical school across the way. There was a sleeper couch and a small table with two more visitors' chairs, all three upholstered in the same yellow material as the drapes.

"As you well know, Gertrude, blood is a lot more than merely red-colored water." The professor spoke in general terms, as though discussing a point of interest rather than addressing Gertrude's fear. "Blood contains cells, enzymes, hormones, minerals, and thousands of life sustaining chemical and nutritional factors that it transports throughout the body. Its consistency is also dynamic. Normally, it flows, but under certain circumstances, it must coagulate. Otherwise, each time we cut ourselves, we'd bleed to death. As you may also know, we all have a number of factors that are responsible for this coagulation, or clotting, or as we call it under normal circumstances, hemostasis. Each of these coagulation factors exists in an inactive state, until our body calls upon one of them to activate the defense mechanism against a bleed. What happens next is that the activated factor activates the next in line which activates the next and so on and so forth, until the system comes to the end of its *cascade* and converts *fibrinogen* into *fibrin*, which then hardens into the plug in whichever place it is needed. If one of these factors is missing or defective, then of course the system will fail. Perhaps the best-known example of this type of illness would be *hemophilia*. You know of hemophilia, don't you?"

"That was the bleeding disorder of the Russian royal family."

"That's right. The men in the Russian royal family inherited a defect in one of the coagulation factors. Actually, it was *factor eight*, and their coagulation was defective. Patients with this and other coagulation problems may bruise easily and bleed."

"But that is the opposite type of problem to hypercoagulability, the condition you were talking to the students about, Professor."

The professor smiled, still attempting to put her at ease. "Of course, a bleeding disorder is the reverse of a coagulation disorder," he said. "Now, imagine what will happen if a coagulating factor becomes activated when it is not needed, then we will have just that, the opposite, abnormal and unwelcome coagulation. And there are a number of conditions that bring about this unwanted activation of a coagulation factor. We see it in patients with massive trauma, or infections with sepsis, or sometimes in patients with certain cancers, like pancreatic adenocarcinoma. And to answer your question, patients with tumors may release a substance called *tissue factor*, which sets the coagulation cascade into action."

The professor shrugged his shoulders and closed his eyes as if to suggest that the discussion was going into more detail than he intended. Still, she had asked, and if she wanted to understand, then he would have to continue.

"Sometimes, the clots break down while the coagulation cascade is still in process. Under these conditions, patients will use up their clotting factors and they, too, will develop a bleeding problem. We say they are consuming the factors, and we call it a *consumptive coagulopathy*."

"I still don't understand what kicks the clotting process into action, what makes the tumor put out that tissue factor," Gertrude said. "Can it still happen in me? I know blood clots can be bad; is there anything that I should be doing to prevent it?"

"Hopefully it won't happen to you," the professor said. "And you are doing what you must to prevent it; you're having the tumor removed. Also, we will get you moving as soon as possible after the surgery. Lying in bed can be dangerous."

"Good." Gertrude seemed relieved, but ensuring she understood, she asked once more, "So if the cancer is removed, then I'll be okay?"

"You should be." Again, the professor smiled, this time to himself. He was puzzled by Gertrude's unwarranted fear of a complication that she did not have.

On his way out of Gertrude's room, Professor Carson passed Len carrying a huge bouquet and coming in. They exchanged greetings and then the professor excused himself, saying he had to get to the operating room.

Earlier that day, after seeing that Gertrude was comfortable in the hospital, Len had returned to the office to tie up some loose ends. Now, as the time for her operation drew closer, he was there to hold her hand.

Soon after Len's arrival, a nurse anesthetist came to hang an intravenous line. She also gave Gertrude a dose of tranquilizer, which seemed to have more effect than anticipated, and Gertrude had trouble staying awake. When she heard Len say, "It's all right, sweetheart . . . close your eyes . . . I'll sit here with you," she allowed her consciousness to drift into a comfortable and carefree slumber.

She saw Len staring out the window, and she remembered asking him the time. She did not, however, recall his reply; she either forgot what he said or fell immediately asleep before he told her. Then, she heard a knock at her door and saw Len stand aside while a deliveryman brought in a huge bouquet and placed it on the table. She did not see the man leave. Upon arousing again, there were four floral arrangements, three on the table and one on the windowsill. Gertrude did not remember them being delivered, nor did she know when her mother and father had arrived or whether she had greeted them when they had.

She felt a shuffling of her bed and heard someone count, "One, two, three," and she felt herself being hoisted from her mattress and across onto a gurney. Following an abrupt bump as the gurney swung out her room, Gertrude recalled a pleasant ride through the hospital halls with a few sharp turns and a few smooth changes in pace, and then another restful sleep.

She should have had a degree of reassurance as she opened her eyes and saw Professor Carson leaning over her and asking once more, "Are you ready? We'll take good care of you," yet the kind words were superfluous; the preoperative medication left her with no fear. She noticed that the professor was wearing green scrubs and a protective hair cover, so she understood that she must have been in the holding area of the operation suite, and calculated that she was therefore alert.

But the smugness did not last. Restful sleep once more encompassed her entire body until she again felt herself being transported from the gurney.

Now, she lay on a hard surface, a circle of five bright lights shining down on her belly, and nurses and doctors working calmly in the room. Everything about her was shiny silver, hospital green, or sterile white. She tasted a metallic chemical at the back of her throat, she once again noticed the face of Professor Carson, the colors and lights overhead mingled and swirled, and then she heard the thumping sound of a mechanical pump and a nurse's voice calling, "Can you hear me? The operation is over, Mrs. Darshan. You can wake up now."

Gertrude felt a catheter retreating from her mouth. She opened her eyes to find herself in the recovery room with gurneys to the right and gurneys to the left and gurneys opposite. The haziness was familiar; she had felt the same sensation twenty-five years earlier, as she awoke from the surgeries for her breasts.

"Am I okay?" she asked. "Did Dr. Kallenbach get the cancer?"

"You are fine, sweetie. Take deep breaths now. Come on. Deep breaths." Then, more distantly, Gertrude heard, "She's awake," as the nurse spoke to someone else in close proximity.

Again, a relaxed sleep, surprisingly painless considering the magnitude of the surgery she had undergone, but not completely without sequelae: as Gertrude drifted between levels of awareness, she could sense nausea brought about by the anesthetic and analgesic medications.

Gertrude opened her eyes to find herself in a cubicle, walled on three sides and a door and huge window on the fourth, to her right. Beyond the pane of glass was a central island of workspace with writing stations, central monitors, and readily available crash carts with medications and equipment. Gertrude felt more alert than she had during her earlier arousals, and she was fascinated by the busyness of the nurses, writing notes in charts, speaking on phones to outside doctors, and circulating between a number of other cubicles. At the end of the unit, above a line of storage closets, was a narrow and horizontal window to the outside world. At first, Gertrude thought that the weather had turned threatening, that clouds must have been blotting out the sunshine, for only a short recollection ago, she had looked past Len standing before the yellow drapes and seen a bright and optimistic day. It took a few moments to register that the weather had not changed; rather, dusk was settling over Jacobsburg, and she had missed virtually half a day.

The door to her cubicle opened and in came one of the nurses together with Dr. Kallenbach. He looked at Gertrude. She felt certain he must have noticed that her eyes were open, but still he said nothing. He bent over to examine the contents of a plastic bag hanging over the railing at the side of her bed, and then he turned his gaze toward the monitor overhead, beeping softly and recording squiggly patterns. The nurse, too, seemed to ignore

Gertrude. She made a minor adjustment to the stopcock valve of the intravenous line, checked the leads attached to Gertrude's chest, and then tidied a corner of the covers.

"How much drainage from the wound?" Dr. Kallenbach asked the nurse.

"She arrived here with that bag," she replied.

"Good." Finally, he turned his attention to Gertrude. He had on scrubs, a stethoscope dangling around his neck, and a surgical hat. With his baldness covered, he seemed younger. "Your operation went well," he said. "I spoke with your family in the waiting room. You are probably still more sedated than you realize, so I'll speak with you tomorrow." He turned to the nurse. "We can let her husband in for a while. Not too long, though."

The nurse gave a tiny nod, just enough to let Dr Kallenbach understand that as soon as he left, she would call Len in to visit, that the visit would be appropriately short, and that no one else from Gertrude's family would be allowed into the ICU.

Dr. Kallenbach then asked Gertrude to sit forward. Supporting her with one hand, he maneuvered the earpieces of his stethoscope into place with the other, and then listened to her lungs. He helped her ease back down onto her bed and uttered a two-syllable grunt of approval.

The nurse then once more tidied the top sheet with corners tucked firmly under the mattress.

Len looked concerned as he came around the door and into Gertrude's cubicle. He hurried over and kissed her on the forehead. "The doctors seem pleased," he said. "I spoke with Dr. Kallenbach and with Professor Carson. Do you hurt?"

"No. No pain at all."

"Oh, that's right. You have a *spinal*."

"Where are my flowers?"

"They are on the surgical floor. No flowers allowed in the ICU."

"Who were they from?"

"I'm surprised you remember. You seemed to have fallen asleep after the sedation. Marlene sent a pot plant, I brought one arrangement, and the other two were from your bridge club."

"Who from bridge?" she asked.

"Jean sent one bouquet, and the other was from the club itself."

"The club itself?"

Len could see that Gertrude was fishing, and he knew what she was fishing for. Although he would feel uneasy mentioning the names on the card, Gertrude wanted to know, so he said,

"Blake . . ." and studied Gertrude for any change in facial expression.

Gertrude said nothing. She waited for an instant, and then gazed disappointedly downward.

"And Mollie . . ." Len continued. "They sent a terrific arrangement."

Gertrude gave a satisfied sigh. She closed her bleary eyes and a contented smile found its way onto her exhausted lips, and Len understood that her feelings for Mollie were even deeper than he imagined.

When Gertrude next awoke, she was alone. A dull night-light lent minimal visibility to her cubicle, and the horizontal window to the outside revealed a sky of pure black. There were fewer nurses, six in all, and they seemed less animated than were the others on the day shift, until one nurse stood from her seat and spoke earnestly to others around her.

Through the shut door and soundproof glass, Gertrude could not hear what was being said, but suddenly, the pace changed. Two nurses rushed into the cubicle directly opposite Gertrude's, one hurried to fetch some equipment from a closet under the horizontal window, one wheeled a cart into the cubicle, and the final two nurses sat with phones to their ears. Less than a minute later, a doctor together with another nurse, probably the nursing supervisor, came through to the front door of the unit and ran directly to the cubicle with the commotion. About two minutes after their arrival, a second doctor arrived.

Consideration for the other patients' sleep was suddenly less of a priority; lights in the active cubicle were shining brightly and nurses were hurrying instead of tiptoeing throughout the unit.

The hullabaloo continued for over half an hour until one of the doctors came out and shook his head. He stood next to the central island with hands on his hips and said something to a nurse, who then returned to a phone.

A woman arrived, her hair a mess and wearing a track suit. She spoke a short while with the doctor standing in the central workspace, and then borrowed his stethoscope and went into the cubicle. Gertrude deduced that this last woman to arrive must have been a senior consultant or, more likely, the patient's personal physician.

After a short while, the other hospital-based physician came out, followed by two nurses and the personal physician. The team stood in an informal circle discussing, nodding agreement, rubbing forlorn palms over fatigued faces and heads, and occasionally returning into the cubicle or referring to a chart that lay open on a desktop in the central island.

Finally, two other nurses came out the cubicle and turned down the bright light.

The hospital-based physicians waved goodbye, and the unit-based nurses returned to their posts, which left the nursing supervisor and the personal physician, who sat together on chairs at a desk and continued discussing the case.

About thirty to thirty-five minutes later, the patient's family arrived. An elderly wife was crying incessantly into cupped palms, while a younger daughter clung to her elbow, and a man, either a son or son-in-law, followed a few steps behind.

The personal physician stood to greet the family. She bent over toward the shorter wife, spoke a few words, and then stood upright and said something to the two younger family members. When the wife continued to weep, the physician again stooped and moved closer, this time with a comforting arm around the elderly woman's shoulders. The wife eventually said something to the physician, who then held the woman's hands in her own and spoke to the cluster of family members. They remained talking quietly, all eyes of the nursing staff turned politely away. The younger woman and the man seemed to be asking a few questions, but the physician was the one with most to convey. Eventually, they walked together toward the darkened cubicle. At this juncture, the nursing supervisor joined them, switched on the light, and the five people went in.

Gertrude was not certain, but she thought she could hear a wailing issue from the cubicle, whereupon the physician appeared through the cubicle door, and said something to one of the nurses, who promptly went to a refrigerator to fetch a paper cup with water.

After only a short while in the cubicle, they all came out. The physician said a few more words and then handed the family to the nursing supervisor.

Fifteen minutes later, the family and the nursing supervisor left the ICU together, and the nurses began to move around the floor and look in on other patients.

Gertrude lay awake wondering, not so much about the deceased patient in the cubicle across the way, but rather about herself. The sooner she would get out of the ICU the better. This was a place for the severely ill, for people who needed intensive nursing care. ICU was by definition a dangerous place to be.

Dawn and a dull gray sky through the narrow horizontal window brought a degree of optimism into the ICU. For those on the road to recovery, another day alive meant another day closer to discharge into the outside world, a place and a state often better appreciated after release from this halfway home to death.

The late night staff was still on duty when Doctor Kallenbach arrived for his morning rounds. In a gray suit and red tie partially hidden behind his trusted stethoscope, he appeared rested and ready for another long day's work. No one could have guessed that his phone had woken him twice from a deep sleep and that he had returned to the hospital from 2:00 to 3:30 a.m.

"Morning, Mrs. Darshan." He stood before her, all business, no smile, neck bent, and hands clasped in front of his abdomen, and Gertrude felt certain that the doctor was scrutinizing her for a myriad of clinical signs. "Do you have any pain?" he asked.

"A few creaks in my muscles, and the tube is beginning to irritate my throat, but my tummy feels fine."

"Good." He looked up at the overhead monitors and squatted to see the plastic bags attached to the railing of her bed. He then examined her chest and back, and pulled back the covers to palpate her legs. "We are going to get you up and into a chair as soon as possible. Meanwhile, I want you to wiggle your toes and tense the muscles in your legs whenever you remember. We must keep the circulation moving. After any operation, we can get a venous thrombosis."

Dr. Kallenbach helped Gertrude roll onto her side and inspected the catheter inserted into her spine. "We're going to leave this epidural anesthesia for three days," he said. "If you still feel some pain in your abdomen after we remove it, we will give you a morphine drip that you'll be able to self monitor. A nurse will show you how."

He left her abdomen for last. He palpated gently around the sides and the lower part of her belly and then worked his way up and toward the middle, over the operation area. Then he auscultated for sounds, and not surprisingly, there were none. It would take a few days for the involuntary muscles in the wall of her intestines to kick in and begin propelling any contents down through the bowels. "These are drains," he said, pointing to two tubes exiting under the dressings and making their way to the plastic bags attached to the side of her bed railing. "As you know, we removed part of your pancreas and part of the adjoining intestine. At the site where we reconnected everything back together, there might be some secretion or even be a bit of leakage. These drains will draw off that fluid."

"When will you take this tube out of my nose?"

389

"As soon as your intestines regain some activity, which will be in about two days." He pointed to the bottle almost filled with green secretions. "This is what we have suctioned out of that tube, so far. If we don't remove this stuff, it will sit there and distend your gut, which will hamper your recovery. When the volume drops to below four-hundred milliliters in a twenty-four hour period, we'll talk about removing that tube."

Gertrude lay in her bed and nodded. She realized that her hair was a mess and her face must have looked terrible, probably blotchy, perhaps even wrinkled around the eyes. She decided that, as soon as possible, she would clean up, brush her hair, and put on makeup, if the nurses would allow.

The doctor left, and Gertrude watched the ICU activity through her window. When the morning shift came on duty, most nurses sat around a desk, learning about the changes that had occurred overnight.

The same frail old man that Gertrude had seen the previous day wheeled in a breakfast trolley, and someone dressed in a dark suit came to remove the corpse from the cubicle across the way.

A tall blond nurse in her early to late forties introduced herself as Nancy. "I'll be taking care of you today," she said, while measuring Gertrude's blood pressure. "You must tell me if there is anything you need."

"I feel grimy. Can I brush my teeth?"

"That'll be okay, but try not to swallow the water. We'll be giving you a bed bath in a short while, and then we will help you into a chair. Do you feel up to it?"

"Yes, and can I put on a little base and lipstick?"

Nancy laughed as she detached the bottle with the green intestinal secretions. "I'm glad you ask. That's always a sign that you are well on the way to recovery. I'll have to inspect your makeup before we allow you to use it, but I'm certain there will be no problem. And if there is, we can always get some other brand."

"Where are my things?"

Nancy remained silent for a short while as she charted her findings on a sheet of paper attached to a clipboard. "Over there in the corner," she eventually replied, pointing to a narrow locker.

By eight o'clock, Nancy had completed taking the vital signs and administering medications to other patients, and she returned to Gertrude as she had said she would. With some difficulty, she and another nurse managed to get Gertrude out of the bed and into a comfortable chair. Nancy helped Gertrude with her makeup and then, after asking permission, proceeded to brush the knots out of her hair. The surgery might have saved Gertrude's life, and the post operative care was certainly necessary for her recovery, but the tending and pampering did more to make her feel whole than any medication or treatment.

In the short time they spent together, Gertrude grew fond of Nancy. And she could sense that Nancy felt the same about her.

Nancy may have been doing her duty, but she had gone beyond the job description of a nurse. Sharing and comparing a frivolous common interest like cosmetics, their emotions touched. But the relationship would not blossom; Nancy was a professional, and Gertrude a passing patient.

Nancy put Gertrude's things away and left the cubicle with a warm smile.

With little to do and at a milestone in her life, Gertrude was left thinking, *I'm not surprised that we are getting along so well. This is nothing new. It merely proves what I already know, that I find it easier to identify with women than with men.* She peered through her window at Nancy speaking to one of the other nurses. *Nancy actually reminds me of Mollie. Maybe that's why I like her. But the reason does not matter. The stone cold fact is that I prefer women to men. I am more comfortable with most women than I am with my husband, Len; in fact, especially more comfortable than I am with Len. I don't find this disappointing or even puzzling. What is puzzling is why more women do not feel the same as I do. After all, whenever women get together with a group of friends, they seem to relax. Often, they pour their hearts out. And what do they mostly talk about? Men. Those women who do not have a man seem to spend a great deal of energy trying to capture one, while many who do have one spend almost an equal amount of energy complaining about him. And to whom do they complain? To other women. Of course, there are happily married couples, but they are not as plentiful as one would like to think. And I cannot help suspecting that the women in those apparently happy relationships are making compromise after compromise to keep their relationship on an even keel. That is the world of men and women, or at least, that is the world as I see it.*

Gertrude was not always that way. She, too, was once interested in capturing a mate of the opposite sex, but after the sizzle left her marriage and she no longer saw life through rose-colored glasses, disappointment and apathy remained with her for many years—the years she would devote to her daughter and then to bridge. Then came the other blow. In her comfortable hospital chair, Gertrude closed her eyes and remembered that wintry night when her tedious indifference turned to utter disillusionment.

* * *

November 2000

She felt insulted. No one meant to insult her, but that made it even worse. In wanting to get closer to Gertrude, Jon Yi had inadvertently dealt her integrity a severe blow:

Gertrude had begun to admire Jon as an outstanding card player and as someone who cared about others. Any man who would build his own life around his ailing mother deserved a special kind of respect. Had Gertrude not placed him on such a pinnacle, then probably nothing in her life would have changed. She would have plodded along, accepting men as men and women as the other people in the world.

As they sat together at the bar in The Gardens of Sicily, Jon seemed lonely, a man who could use a friend and perhaps a woman in his life. Gertrude did not have much hope that he would turn his

393

attention to Jean. After all, they were worlds apart. Jean was far too coarse for a man as genteel as Jon.

Gertrude felt flattered when Jon offered to play bridge with her. True, he was new in town and needed a few partners, but he was a superior player, and that he should choose her was a compliment.

In those moments when they were arranging to play cards together, Gertrude also pictured herself helping Jon settle in. She certainly noticed his good looks, but that did not make him any less or any more a decent person. She also may have been attracted to his good looks, but that, too, had nothing to do with her respect for him.

It happened as soon as tentative arrangements to play cards had been made, for the very next words out of Jon's mouth made Gertrude lose all respect for him. How, at that point in their relationship, could Jon have invited her out on a date? Gertrude did not hear the friendly invitation that Jon had tried to convey. What she heard was that he did not care at all for her skills as a bridge player, and that all he wanted was to get her into his bed. And if a man the caliber of Jon Yi could see a woman only as a sex object, then how could she expect more of other lesser men?

Sitting on that bar stool, Gertrude suddenly stiffened and pulled her arm away from his space.

"What?" Jon asked, believing he had trespassed into some Anglo-American cultural barrier.

Gertrude shook her incredulous head. "I think we should go back to the others," she said, and she slid off her stool and returned to Jean, Blake, and Mollie, all a little intoxicated and all having a good laugh about one or other happening earlier that evening in the bridge studio. Jon picked up his beer and Gertrude's hot chocolate and followed.

At the table, Jon smiled self-consciously and Gertrude tried to appear interested in the frolicsome conversation, while each devoted the lion's share of their energy to avoiding the other's eyes.

Jean and Blake, sitting diagonally opposite each other, continued teasing. Only Mollie noticed that something must have gone awry. She said nothing but maintained a vigilant watch on Gertrude and Jon to ensure that her suspicions were correct. Sure enough, their dispositions had changed. Both were more subdued than before their little tête-à-tête. Jon was more fidgety than he had been all night, and Gertrude was either angry or glum. Normally, Mollie would have been able to tell the difference; as a card player, she could read body language. Tonight, however, she had more than usual to drink, and her intuition may have been dulled.

After a short while, Gertrude stood abruptly and, while grabbing her coat, apologized with a forced smile for having to break up the party. Mollie could now tell that Gertrude was upset. She was eager to lend Gertrude a shoulder; she may also have been a little curious, so she offered the excuse that it was getting late and said goodnight, too.

Under different circumstances, the other three would have left, as well. However, Jon was eager to see a distance between himself and Gertrude, and Blake was still playing host to Jon, so they remained seated, and Jean, the fifth person at the table, was only too delighted to be the only remaining woman with these two handsome men.

In the parking lot, Mollie caught up to Gertrude. She took her by the arm, walked with her, and said as sympathetically as she could, "You seem upset, and I don't like to see you this way. How can I make you better?"

At first, Gertrude was taken aback. She and Mollie were friendly enough, but neither had been the other's confidant. "It's nothing," she said, but then inadvertently let the truth be known by continuing, "It's probably me."

"Probably not," Mollie whispered, sobering quickly in the cold night air and finding herself in a more intimate situation than she would normally have chosen.

"You're right," Gertrude agreed. "Probably not." She shuddered from both the cold and the pent up frustration. Then, she smiled at Mollie. "Was I that obvious? I mean, how could you tell that I was angry with Jon?"

"He's a man, isn't he?" Mollie rubbed her cold hands together and then tucked them tightly under each opposite arm.

By now, they had reached Gertrude's car. Gertrude looked back toward The Gardens of Sicily to see whether the others had come out and then opened the driver's door. "He's probably quite decent," she said. "I'm sure he doesn't even know what he did."

Mollie scrunched her nose and peered at Gertrude as if to say, *What does that mean, and what did he do?*

"Come on," Gertrude said, closing the front door, opening the back, and urging Mollie in. "I'm not certain what he did, but I'm not going to stand out here in the cold speaking about it. I'll tell you what happened, and you tell me if I'm being ridiculous."

Inside the car, it was still cold. But they shivered and huddled and spoke about Jon Yi, and then about men, mostly about good-looking men, and about men's obsession with sex.

Mollie said she could understand why Gertrude felt insulted by Jon Yi, but that was the way men were. An inroad towards intimacy was the objective of virtually every man's conversation with any good looking and eligible woman.

"But I'm not eligible," Gertrude protested.

"But you are good looking," Mollie replied with a contagious and naughty giggle.

While skirting some daring issues, it became apparent that of the two women, Mollie might have been worldlier. Therefore, Gertrude was asking most questions, and it did not take long for her to ask the one that had long been on her mind. "Are you in a relationship with Blake?"

"Oh, no!" Mollie giggled into her left palm.

"Well, do you have a boyfriend? Or more than one?"

"I was once married, but for a very short time."

"Hard to believe that you don't have someone special. A beautiful woman like you must be fighting them off."

"Why, thank you," Mollie said, offering Gertrude her profile while brushing her short blond hair with a palm, and again laughing pleasantly.

The car was becoming warmer and cozier. It reminded Gertrude of her youth and of the nights she and her sister would cuddle in the same bed, pretending the babysitter watching TV in the den was about to change into a flesh eating monster and come to devour them. It reminded her of hiding under the covers with Joyce or some other friend in a sleepover and talking of topics secretive, mischievous, and, of course, scary. And Mollie was the perfect catalyst for such memories. She was fun loving, and she was ready to listen, and more important than these, she had freckles. The freckles made Gertrude feel safe, like she was back in her youth and talking with a friendly child. Gertrude must have known other women with freckles, but they kept them constantly covered with makeup. No one flaunted them, as did Mollie; other women did not seem as fond of their youthful freckles as did Mollie.

Gertrude could not forget that snug evening in the back seat of her car, and from that time forward, Mollie reminded her of everything warm and snug. And when she had issues that were upsetting or depressing, while she might speak of them to Len, it was to Mollie that she would pour out her heart.

***

Jacobsburg hospital, 2005.

Len arrived for the early visiting hours, which lasted from 9:00 to 9:30 a.m. He asked her twice how she was feeling and four times whether she had any pain. More importantly, he remarked how good she looked. She enjoyed the attention and tried her best to appear upbeat, but she was fatigued. The Whipple's operation was taking its toll, and she had difficulty keeping her eyes open. Again, as before her surgery, she dozed off in front of him, and when she opened her eyes, he was gone. Unlike before the surgery, however, this time she dreamed. And not surprisingly, it was about the matter on her mind—her operation: She could see Dr. Kallenbach and Professor Carson standing on opposite sides of the surgical table, masked and gowned, and working meticulously together. No words were said, only an occasional grunt and nod to convey what they wanted of each other. The overhead circle of five lights shone brightly into her open eyes, so she asked the professor whether he could lean over to protect her from the glare.

"Of course, Gertrude," the professor said. "You know I'll do anything to make you feel better," and he did as she asked.

In her dream, Gertrude could see her own face, smiling, and she could hear her own thoughts reflecting the relief of her body as the two surgeons removed the ominous tumor. She did not see their hands as they worked deep in her belly, but she could sense that their effort was *top notch, up there with the best in the world.* The words *top notch, up there with the best in the world* reverberated in her dream, the same words that the professor had used when first recommending Dr. Kallenbach, and that was all she could recall when she awoke.

Her dream was not far from the truth: The surgeons indeed needed a minimum of verbal communication. With their combined experience and the fact that the professor had been Dr. Kallenbach's mentor, it was as though their minds blended into a single thought process commanding their four cooperative hands. Dr. Kallenbach undertook the major part of the surgery, but Professor Carson understood his every move, giving him maximal exposure, performing any dissection that was easier from his vantage point, and uncomplainingly carrying out the menial tasks required of a surgical assistant.

The entire operation involved hundreds of individual steps: cutting through different tissues, mobilizing the various parts, stopping hemorrhage from the many blood vessels that had to be bypassed, and then repair of the organs. To attach the cut-off end of pancreas into the inner cavity of the gut, Dr Kallenbach first lined up the two structures. Then, he began with the posterior or under part of the *anastomosis*, carefully inserting the stitches one at a time. He tied each knot firmly but left the strings long. When he had completed this half of the connection, he held all the loose strings taught, and Professor Carson trimmed the long ends to an even quarter inch length, like a hairdresser cutting a girl's fringe. Except, either the professor angled the scissors for a brief moment or otherwise Dr. Kallenbach was pulling too hard: whatever the reason, they left the strings on a stitch in the corner of the anastomosis too short, almost flush with the knot. Both doctors noticed this imprecision. They stared briefly at this corner suture with its short ends; Dr. Kallenbach even tugged on the tissues in either direction, testing the strength of the connection at that point. Then, without a word, they accepted it as good enough and proceeded to the ventral or front part of the anastomosis.

The major part of the operation complete, Dr. Kallenbach positioned the two drains, and they closed Gertrude's abdomen.

At 9:45 a.m., Professor Carson popped in to say hello and to tell Gertrude how satisfied he was with the surgery. He, too, examined the overhead monitors and the parameters recorded in her chart. Gertrude was always pleased to see the professor. His openness and his standing in the medical community never failed to fill her with a new wave of confidence, and his friendly demeanor always made her feel special.

"Is there anything else we can do?" Professor Carson once again offered, his hand already on the doorknob.

"Yes," Gertrude replied. "I'm tired. Would you ask the nurse to help me back into bed?"

Deep within her belly, tiny capillaries were slowly growing into the operation site, bringing fluid, nutrients, oxygen, and cells of inflammation, all the necessary ingredients for her body to heal. Her intestinal muscles were beginning to recover and the internal sutures were comfortable and moist. And the knot in that one suture with no tags lost some of its tension and began to work its way loose.

Nancy and a colleague came into Gertrude's cubicle. Careful that the drains should not pull and that the catheters should not hurt, the two nurses helped Gertrude from the chair and back into the bed. Yet, cautious as they might have been, there was still that inevitable, unwanted heave, and as Gertrude fell limp against the pillows, her internal organs jolted and that suspect knot popped open. Had this happened a week later, the anastomosis would have been healed and no fluid would have escaped, but it was only her second day post-surgery, and pancreatic secretion found its way out of the lumen and into a niche, hidden from both drains.

Back in the bed, Gertrude felt stronger and alert. She could not see everything that was happening in the ICU, but from what she could gather, five patients were discharged and two admitted through the course of the morning. Doctors would come and go. They remained varying lengths of time, and often would get together with colleagues to discuss one or another case. Gertrude would have liked to hear their conversations, not because she was interested in what they were saying, but rather because she was curious about their demeanors and attitudes as they made major decisions on people's lives.

At midday, the central floor almost cleared; suddenly, only two nurses remained, and Gertrude wondered where everyone had gone. Then, she heard two thumps on the wall and she realized the patient in the cubicle next door was in serious trouble. Like the man last night across the way, the condition of someone a few feet away had turned critical, and doctors and nurses were fighting to keep that person alive. One or two staff members hurried by her window and others came into the ICU from outside, but no one remained in her line of view.

The commotion settled, and the ICU returned to its normal pace. When Nancy next came in, Gertrude asked what had happened, and Nancy told her that this time they were successful, that the patient, a seventy-four year old woman, would live.

The doctor responsible for the seventy-four year old woman's recovery walked over to a desk at the central island, and Gertrude was pleased to recognize the long jaw and the graying ginger of Brad. The ICU nurses had called for a doctor from the emergency room, and Brad had come to help.

Gertrude watched as Brad sat writing in a chart and then dictating into the phone. When he had completed his entries, he studied the patient list on a clipboard, and then looked around until his eyes came to rest on Gertrude's cubicle.

He came over to speak with her and to wish her well. He also told her that at the beginning of each work day, he would pull up computer records of patients he had treated and of other patients who the ER thought might possibly be needing urgent care, particularly those in the ICU. The information was readily available, so he would be following her progress, if she did not mind.

As she thanked him for his interest, she knew that Brad was a man of his word and that she would indeed have another pair of trained eyes overlooking her case.

At two, five, and eight p.m., for half an hour on each occasion, Gertrude received visitors, two at a time. She managed to stay awake all afternoon, and by nine that night, she was exhausted, and other than the irritation from the nasogastric tube, she had a restful sleep.

The next day was a Friday, and Dr. Kallenbach was again pleased with her condition. The nasogastric tube would have to remain, but he removed the epidural and the bladder catheters.

Two tubes less made it easier to get into and out of the chair, and Gertrude felt confident that all was what it should be. When she began to feel pain in her belly, she was not surprised or even disappointed. Dr. Kallenbach had warned her that this might happen. She was given a morphine drip with a hand-held control to self-administer narcotic as she felt the need. Into the night, however, the pain got worse, and this she did not expect. Dr. Kallenbach had told her that with the passage of time, everything should improve.

By morning, she was drenched with sweat and had a temperature of 102.

Professor Carson was in to see her before Dr. Kallenbach. He took the initiative and ordered blood and urine tests, x-rays, and a new CT scan of the abdomen.

By midday, the results were in and both her surgeons were there to tell her that she had developed an abscess in the area behind the pancreatic-duodenal anastomosis.

"This is unfortunate," Dr Kallenbach said, standing with the professor at the foot of Gertrude's bed. "Normally, we expect the drains to remove any excess fluid that might accumulate, but sometimes we get a small pocket that becomes infected and we need another drain."

When Gertrude said nothing, he answered the question that he was almost anticipating. "You won't need another operation," he said. "We'll be able to insert the new drain in the x-ray department, while watching on an imaging screen."

With appropriate antibiotics and the abscess drained, Gertrude felt much better and everyone believed she was again on her way to recovery. What they could not see, however, was a trickle of pancreatic secretion making its way into tiny capillaries and venules, and thence flowing to larger veins and distributing itself throughout her circulation.

Gertrude awoke early Sunday morning, her fever gone, the pain tolerable, but with a new brand of weakness. She placed her hands on the dressings over her belly and was surprised at the moisture. *Something must have come loose*, she thought. *Probably the new drain. Instead of drawing the fluid into that bag at the side of my bed, it's spilling over the wound dressings.* She rang the call bell.

A new nurse, someone Gertrude had not previously met, came to attend to her.

"Good morning, Mrs. Darshan." The young nurse was short with a plump, round face. "My name is Lee. How are you feeling today?"

"There seems to be a bit of a mess on my bandages."

Lee switched on the overhead neon light and pulled back the covers. She was asking how Gertrude had slept, but stopped before ending the question and uttered a soft, "Oh dear!"

"What is it?" Gertrude asked.

"You seem to be bleeding."

Gertrude looked down at her abdomen. The dressings were soaked and her hands and the sheets were covered with bright red blood.

Lee put on latex gloves and began to remove the bandages. She had not called for help, but another nurse came into the cubicle to give a hand. Blood seemed to be leaking through the surgical incision and around the three drains. The nurses dried and cleaned the wounds and then reapplied dressings and put in an urgent call to Dr. Kallenbach.

It was strange to see Dr. Kallenbach in jeans and a T-shirt, but then Gertrude realized that he had arrived at the hospital in less than twenty minutes, and he was probably woken from a sleep. While Dr. Kallenbach seemed perpetually serious, on this occasion, he was even more perturbed than usual. In addition to his usual examination, he asked for a bright light to see her mouth and throat, he looked carefully at her fingers and toes, and he turned her in all directions to inspect every square inch of her skin. He then stroked his chin and looked at her sternly. "We may have a bit of a problem," he admitted, "with the clotting mechanism in your blood."

Gertrude went suddenly even paler. What she had discussed with Professor Carson in theory was becoming a reality.

"We are going to take some blood samples to evaluate the status of your clotting system, and we're also going to reexamine to see if we are missing any other possible cause for this condition."

"Isn't the cancer the cause?" Gertrude asked.

"It could be the cancer or the abscess that we drained yesterday, or even both. But we must do another scan to make sure that nothing else is happening in your belly, and we must look elsewhere, as well." He placed a hand on her shoulder, an unusually compassionate gesture for him. "As soon as we have taken the blood specimens, we'll begin treatment by replacing ingredients that are being depleted, like platelets and certain factors in plasma."

"Are the clotting factors in my blood being consumed?" Gertrude asked, already knowing the answer.

"Yes. That seems to be the problem," the doctor replied, surprised that she should ask so sophisticated a question.

"Am I going to die?" she asked, tears trickling from both eyes.

He looked her directly in the face and said, "The condition is serious, but we will turn it around." He then added as though it were an afterthought, "I'm also going to get a consultation with our hematologist. Things can become tricky, and we might need an expert in the field."

Dr. Kallenbach left Gertrude's cubicle, spoke a few words to Lee, the nurse on duty, and then went to the phone to make a call.

In his mid-forties, of average height and average build, there was nothing particularly distinctive about Dr. Mercer. He wore a white shirt and gray slacks on this Sunday morning, and his personality seemed about as bland as the rest of him.

"You are basically right, Mrs. Darshan." Dr. Mercer did not add to Gertrude's understanding or contradict it when she asked whether coagulating factors had found their way into her blood and were destroying her normal clotting mechanism. Dr. Mercer was more intent on evaluating Gertrude's diseased coagulation system than explaining it, and his attitude showed. And at this stage, Gertrude did not mind. Her understanding of the complexities would matter little to her chance of survival, and she was glad to have "an expert in the field" on her case. Besides, Gertrude was feeling incredibly weak. Despite the blood and blood products flowing through the IV and into her veins, she remained anemic from the bleeding.

Unlike the other physicians on the case, Dr. Mercer took his own blood samples from Gertrude. He then excused himself, and

Gertrude could only guess that he was taking them directly to the hospital laboratory for further testing.

At mid-morning, Professor Carson arrived. Although he had referred her to other doctors who he thought more qualified than himself, Gertrude felt confident that his mere presence would make everything better.

This time, she was wrong. Although the professor remained kind and concerned, all he could do was confirm what she already knew and what he had already told her, that tissue factor and perhaps other extrinsic factors had set into motion the coagulation cascade, and that unwanted clotting was taking place within her circulatory system. The professor held her hand as he spoke, staring at her fingers rather than into her eyes.

"I don't understand," she said. "I know that I am bleeding because my coagulation factors are being used up. But what is happening to those clots? Are they all being broken down immediately? I don't know whether it is worse to bleed or for my blood to remain clotted inside my body."

Professor Carson at last lifted his gaze to look at her. Perhaps he had given her too much information, and now she was beginning to panic. But her panic was warranted, because her perception was correct. He again looked down, and this time all he could do was to continue staring, for he knew that she would soon see what he had discovered, and she would grasp the gravity for herself.

Gertrude followed the professor's stare with her own. She saw her hand resting loosely in his, and she was uncertain. But then she slowly turned her wrist until she could see her palm, and her heart and hopes sank, for at the tip of the middle finger was a tiny patch of black. With the pulp of her thumb, she tried in vain to rub the color away, and she was once again surprised, this time by the painful sensation in the spot of dying skin.

They remained in silence, Gertrude not wanting to ask what she already knew, and Professor Carson seeing no value in repeating what he had already said. Dr. Mercer was an experienced hematologist and if anyone could halt the vicious cycle, it was he. It was also Dr. Mercer who broke the tension by arriving to reevaluate Gertrude's condition.

"Hello, Professor. Morning, Mrs. Darshan." Dr. Mercer seemed more personable when with his colleagues, but not much.

"Good morning, Dr. Mercer." The professor smiled and stood to shake the doctor's hand. "I saw your *DIC* lab reports. Thanks for helping out."

"Yes. You were right about the diagnosis," he said, ready to discuss the findings with the professor. "At this juncture, we must continue replacing the clotting factors."

Professor Carson wanted to ask the hematologist about the balance between two critical enzymes, *thrombin* and *plasmin*, which would determine the *thrombotic* or *bleeding* tendency, but Gertrude, hearing a new term, and concerned about its implication, first asked, "What is meant by the DIC lab reports, Professor?"

Happy to be able to speak to her without imparting new or unfavorable news, the professor explained, "DIC is the condition that you have, *disseminated intravascular coagulation.*"

Remaining inside the cubicle with Gertrude, the two doctors shuffled a short distance from her bed and continued to discuss her case, speaking too softly for her to comprehend. From time to time, however, one or another man would turn briefly toward Gertrude and squint or grimace ever so slightly, and unbeknown to them, each gesture sent added despondency into their ailing but astute patient. Then, Dr. Mercer and Professor Carson strolled back to Gertrude's side, and while the hematologist began to adjust the rate of flow from the three bags delivering life-sustaining ingredients into her veins, the professor sat to speak with her. He once again discussed DIC and her ongoing treatment. He also assured her that he would continue to follow along with Dr. Mercer and Dr. Kallenbach, only, this time, he did not ask whether there was anything else he could do for her.

Gertrude missed the professor's customary offer. She believed his omission signified bleakness, and that he had little else to add for both her comfort and her medical care.

Outside the door to the ICU, and at the end of a curving corridor was the ICU waiting room. With a number of televisions, a bathroom, vending machines, and two stations with coffee percolators and paper cups, the administration did as much as could be expected of a state hospital to keep visitors content. On Sunday afternoons, at the unit nurses' discretion, visiting time was extended to one full hour, from two to three p.m., but still only two visitors at a time.

Normally, only close family members would come to see patients in the ICU. Friends would usually wait until sick people were discharged to the general units before visiting. On this day, however, two of Gertrude's bridge pals, Jean and Mollie, were hoping to spend a few minutes with her. When Len saw Mollie, he did not know how to react. He thought he should be angry, but he was not. He actually felt a strange respect for her effort to visit Gertrude, and he knew he did not want to make a scene.

At two p.m. exactly, when Len and Janet went in to visit Gertrude, Lee, the nurse, was completing her change of dressings. Len caught a glimpse of Gertrude's abdomen, at the purple hue in the macerated tissue around the moist surgical wounds, and his hopes for her recovery began to fade. He had seen a number of patients with DIC, and most of them would survive, but their chances always depended on the severity of the disease, and Gertrude's case seemed severe. Nevertheless, he did his best to remain upbeat, believing that optimism could only help and pessimism would harm. Len also did not want to unduly upset their daughter, Janet.

By about 2:20, Len could see that Gertrude was beginning to tire, so he asked her if she wanted to close her eyes.

"No," she said. "I'll sleep after my visitors leave."

"Your mom and dad are in the waiting room," Len said. "I'll tell them to come in." He thought for a brief moment, and then added, "Mollie and Jean are here, too."

This time, Len tried to ignore any zeal that Gertrude might show at the mention of Mollie's name. He also had a hard time fighting back tears as he pictured his broken father and mother-in-law, who had aged over the past few days as their daughter lay fighting for her life.

As Gertrude's parents sat with their daughter, they asked the usual questions that visitors ask of a patient. "How are you feeling? Do you have pain? What do the doctors say?" Then, they sat mostly in silence, holding her hand and communicating their hurt and sorrow and the despair that Len had tried so hard to avoid. Lee came in during their visit, and they stood back to allow her to do her work, which was to adjust the leads to a monitor overhead. With an air of authority beyond her years and with a smile of a passing business acquaintance, Lee then introduced herself. When she left the room, Gertrude and her parents had something else to talk about: the nursing in general, which was what they wanted to discuss, anything about the hospital or about her care. But all three dared not venture within the rim of the real issue, Gertrude's dismal prognosis and its consequences.

With ten more stringent visiting minutes remaining, Gertrude studied the love in her parents' faces and may even have felt guilty about the heartbreak she was bringing into what should have been their golden years. Her mother was battling to hold back tears, so to break the silence that had again found its way into the cubicle, Gertrude asked, "Who else is in the waiting room?"

"Two of your friends, Jean and another tall woman," her father whispered." I think she said her name is Mollie." He then looked across at his wife, stood, leaned over towards her, and continued in the same subdued voice, "Come, let's give them a chance to visit."

From the moment they sat at either side of Gertrude's bed, Jean could not control her tears. "You must hurry back to the bridge studio; I haven't won a hand without you," she said, trying to make as light of the situation as she could, believing that it would help Gertrude feel better.

Gertrude, on the other hand, suddenly realized what a major part she had been playing in Jean's life. On the two or three times had they gone any place other than bridge together, Jean would always seem elated. Gertrude had accepted this as Jean's normal jubilant self. Only now, with the tears streaming down her cheeks, did Gertrude reflect more deeply on Jean's otherwise dull existence.

The three spoke about people in the bridge studio and about the party to celebrate Blake's achieving Diamond Life Master, and Mollie and Jean remembered the names of friends who had asked them to bring regards and wishes for a speedy recovery. Throughout the conversation, every so often, Jean would contort her face, trying unsuccessfully to hold back tears, until Gertrude had to offer her the box of Kleenex from a drawer and try to console her.

Nurses began to move more noticeably around the floor, bringing out medication trolleys, looking in on patients, and tidying rooms; the clock on the wall registered the hour of three.

Jean made her way to the exit, but Mollie wanted to steal a moment alone with Gertrude.

Mollie stood close to the right side of Gertrude's bed. She wore no makeup. She was a beautiful woman and did not need any. Nor did she need words to tell Gertrude what was in her heart. Her eyes spoke all she wanted to say. And for the first time during the precious visiting hour, a tear found its way into Gertrude's eye.

"I must look a mess," Gertrude confessed.

"Yes, you do." Mollie laughed softly, and reached her fingers to brush away a few loose strands of Gertrude's red hair. Then, she leaned over to kiss Gertrude tenderly, first on the brow and then on the lips. They stood apart, but Gertrude could not let go of Mollies' hand, which she took to caress her own cheek.

By now, it was past three o'clock, and Lee came into the cubicle to busy herself and to let it be known that Mollie was the only remaining visitor in the ICU.

Bearable but persistent pain was beginning to gnaw at every point in Gertrude's body. She dimmed the overhead lights and fell into a blessed, dreamless sleep. While she rested, Dr. Mercer adjusted the rate and proportions of platelets and plasma flowing into her veins. But factors in Gertrude's blood had taken on an evil life of their own, with an insatiable hunger for whichever products

Dr. Mercer offered. The disease process raged relentlessly ahead, gobbling up and spitting out critical enzymes, rendering coagulation impotent while paradoxically threatening the blood supply to every organ in her body.

Dr. Mercer was an expert; he had treated DIC many times before, and he knew what had to be done. The risk was high, but without halting the cascade, his patient would surely die. He had no choice.

He wrote the order for *heparin*, a drug normally used to *thin* the blood by *preventing* the clotting process.

Dr. Mercer then went into Gertrude's cubicle to tell her what he was doing. He knew that she could understand, and he felt that he owed her the truth about her condition and the reasoning behind his decision.

But Gertrude was sleeping, and the right to a peaceful rest he owed her, too, so he stood for a short while, staring at her face.

Dr. Mercer was by nature a shy man who did not enjoy conversation, as did many of his colleagues. This did not mean he was any less compassionate than they were. Gertrude seemed so helpless against this dreadful disease, which she was probably not going to survive. Then, he noticed a patch of darkness on her cheek, and realized that the skin was losing its blood supply. It was in the process of dying, no different to the rest of her organs, only more visible. Satisfied with his decision about the heparin, Dr. Mercer tiptoed out the cubicle.

Other than a few gentle and necessary interruptions by the nursing staff, Gertrude slept through the remainder of the afternoon and that night.

Monday morning, my sixth day in the ICU. Double what I expected. Gertrude inspected her right hand, hoping for a miracle, but the area of dead tissue was even larger than before. The entire middle finger was now purple, except the tip, which was pure black. She knew the digit was lost. What is more, the thumb was beginning to sting and to follow the same pattern of distal darkening. She looked at the other hand and was relieved to discover that it still appeared normal. Then, she swirled her tongue in her mouth. It felt moister than it had for days and she believed the nasogastric suction was in some way leaking. So, Gertrude reached into the drawer for a tissue. She wiped her lips and tongue, but moisture remained in her mouth, and when she looked down into her hand, the tissue was covered with bright red blood. She pressed the call button.

Nancy was back on duty. She seemed genuinely happy to see Gertrude and did not flinch as she calmly inspected Gertrude's mouth. Nancy then instructed her on the use of a mouthwash and examined her again, before deciding to put through a call to one of the doctors.

It was 5:30 in the morning. Dr. Kallenbach was on his way to the hospital, but Dr. Mercer was already there. Within a few minutes, he was standing with Nancy in front of Gertrude. He was still wearing gray slacks and a white shirt, but they were scruffy, and his beard had a day's worth of growth. Gertrude suspected that he might have stayed overnight in the hospital on her account. Dr.

Mercer did a brief exam, but he believed the cause and any possible cure for Gertrude's problems lay entirely in blood specimens rather than coarse physical findings. He also seemed unperturbed by the slow ooze from Gertrude's throat. "We have replaced two to three times her total blood volume," he explained to Nancy. "*Where* she bleeds doesn't matter; attaining hemostasis is our only concern."

Gertrude's pain continued to increase, and she was developing a fever. She also realized that her thinking was becoming clouded, but this was almost a blessing. She knew the doctors were in a race against time, and she did not want to contemplate the stakes.

First Dr. Kallenbach came by and then Professor Carson. Each examined Gertrude's hand and mouth, and Nancy showed them both the early *necrosis* around the surgical wound. The professor thought for a while and then said that he would speak to Dr. Kallenbach about cutting away the dead tissue, which could be exacerbating the problem. Other than this frightening remark, both surgeons were deferring Gertrude's care to the hematologist.

At nine a.m., Gertrude had visitors, her husband and daughter, both upbeat as they came into the cubicle.

"Good news!" Len said, his fervor tapering off as he noticed her lethargy and the patch of dead skin on her cheek. "How you feeling?" he then asked, sympathetically.

Gertrude managed a smile and attempted to hold out a welcoming hand, but her right shoulder would not obey. *Stiff from lying in the bed,* she thought. *It'll work itself loose.* Still, she wanted to show her love, so she reached over with the other arm.

"Mom, we were at Dr. Bush this morning, and my tests are negative. I don't have the BRCA gene."

Len was smiling and nodding his head in agreement with their daughter. Even at this critical time in Gertrude's illness, he could not contain his happiness.

And Gertrude felt the same. She sighed deeply and offered an immediate prayer in the best manner she could. "Oh, thank you, God. Thank you, God." She closed her eyes and slowly repeated, "Thank you, God." Given the choice, she would gladly accept her current situation. *If I am to die, then I die in peace, knowing that I did not pass on the accursed genetic mutation to Janet.*

Gertrude looked from Janet to Len and back to Janet again, and she realized how important were these two people in her life. She thanked God once more, this time silently, and vowed to bring her tiny family closer together. How she would do this, she did not know, and whether she would survive to contemplate a method, she seriously doubted. But one thing she realized for certain, that she no longer wanted to deceive her husband.

She tried to reach out to embrace her daughter and husband, to bring them both closer into her arms, to reflect the emotions in her heart. As she attempted to sit forward, she instead found herself rolling toward the right. Her shoulder had not worked its way loose. If anything, it was weaker. And her right leg failed to gain traction against the mattress.

"I can't move my one side," she said to Len, horror in her eyes.

I am having a stroke, she realized. Her major focus was one of surprise, not on the weakness but rather on the lack of headache, something that she would intuitively have expected.

Janet clasped a hand over her mouth and stared at her mother.

Len, too, felt helpless. He pictured a clot or perhaps a bleed spreading in Gertrude's brain and believed that nothing could be done. He nevertheless remained calm and told Janet to fetch a nurse.

Alone with her husband, Gertrude felt herself drowning in regret. If she were to die, she wanted to go with a clear conscience. She felt an urge to confess, and for the first time in her life, she gave thought to others who, nearing their end, felt a similar urge. *Perhaps Len won't understand, but it's a chance I am willing to take; it's a chance I have to take.*

"Len." She stared nervously at the ceiling. "There is something I have to tell you."

"What is it?" Len asked, tears filling his eyes.

"It's about me. I've done something that you'll think terrible and that I now regret. I'm so sorry. If you can't forgive me, I'll understand."

420

He took her lame hand, but then set it down carefully lest he should hurt the necrotic finger and thumb. "You don't have to say anything. I already know. And it's I who should be begging your forgiveness. I am the one to blame."

She looked at him quizzically. "No. You cannot know what I have to tell you," she started to say. "There has been someone else—"

He put a finger to her lips. "I already found out. You don't have to say anything more. Only, please forgive me. Give me a second chance to show you how much I care for you. You mean everything to me."

Gertrude, too, began to cry, but hers were tears of joy. *Len is more forgiving than I would ever have dreamed, which must mean that he loves me more than I knew. Or maybe he doesn't really know about Mollie and me. Maybe he has something else in mind. I must be certain.* "There had been someone else, Len."

She was about to continue, but once again, Len interrupted. "Yes, I know. She was here yesterday." Len wanted to spare Gertrude the ordeal of mentioning Mollie's name. He also did not care to hear the name spoken aloud. "I don't know how long you have been seeing each other, but it doesn't matter. It is my fault. I'm sorry, Gertrude, for not letting you know how much I love you."

Janet came back into the cubicle, together with Nancy.

"Excuse me, Dr. Darshan," Nancy said, concern written all over her face, yet maintaining respect for Len as a physician and as the husband of the patient.

"What is it, Mrs. Darshan?" Nancy pulled back the bedcovers to waist level and slid her hand under Gertrude's forearm, lending it support. "Can you move your hand?"

Gertrude stared at her flail limb. She was trying to do as Nancy had asked, but her hand and arm would not respond.

Nancy then drew the covers all the way down and asked, "Can you move your legs?"

Gertrude managed to lift her left foot and leg, but the right remained frozen; it merely bobbed with the motion of the mattress.

Nancy stepped to the door of the cubicle, twiddled her index finger clockwise, and then held up a clenched fist to her ear. Her colleague immediately got onto the phone.

Throughout the hospital came the overhead announcement, "Code yellow in unit one," and the voice repeated the cryptic message, "Code yellow in unit one."

A nurse on duty in the Emergency Room answered the ringing phone. "One moment," she said and then looked to the doctors' dictating desk. "We have a *change of status* in ICU."

Brad completed his sentence, dialed zero one one, to place his note on hold, and crossed over to take the other phone.

"Yes . . . which cubicle number . . . that's Mrs. Darshan. I'll be right up."

But Brad did not rush directly to the ICU as he may have intimated. Instead, he returned to his seat at the dictating desk and logged onto the hospital computer, and only after studying Gertrude's latest laboratory reports did he leave to attend to her.

"Can you feel my fingers as I touch your arm?" Nancy asked Gertrude.

Len and Janet were standing to the side of the cubicle against the window. Len knew better than to interfere. He also understood the seriousness of the situation, that, at best, Gertrude was in the throes of a major stroke, and that he could not halt the acute process, that no one could halt or reverse the process.

"I can fingers . . ." *I want to tell her that although I can feel her fingers, it is not a normal sensation. It's dull, like feeling through nylon hose. What are those words? I have lost my words.* "The nylon . . . are fingers . . . not," Gertrude stuttered. Then she clucked her tongue in frustration, lifted her neck to look past Nancy, and uttered a thought that was ready and waiting in the depths of her mind, words that were not new, words that did not take an effort to formulate. "Thank you, my darling. I love you, Len. I will love you forever."

Len pressed the back of his fist tightly against his mouth, fighting to hold back tears. Janet did not even try; she wept into her palms and went to stand just outside the cubicle, lest she further upset her dying mother.

Competent as she was, Nancy was willing a doctor to come into the ICU and take charge. She began checking the vital signs. The blood pressure was dropping, pulse racing, and breathing was turning erratic.

Again, Nancy went to the door of the cubicle. She once more gestured the dial of a phone, and she mouthed the word "blue."

"Code blue in unit one." This time, the overhead voice may have been a little more hurried. "Code blue in unit one."

Out of habit, Brad quickened his pace.

On his arrival in the ICU, he was breathing hard. He offered Len only the briefest acknowledgement, and went directly to Gertrude's side to examine her heart and lungs and evaluate her level of consciousness.

"You can stay if you want," he said to Len. "I would advise you to leave."

Nurses were already in the cubicle with all the resuscitation medications and the defibrillator, waiting on Brad's instruction.

Brad returned to Gertrude. Her breathing was labored, her eyes were closed, and she was unresponsive, but the monitor overhead still registered a strong heartbeat.

Brad looked through the cubicle window to see Len and Janet on their way out the ICU door. He again tested Gertrude's sensation and muscle tone. Her breathing stopped, but again began to race.

One nurse was tearing open a paper bag filled with sterilized instruments. Two others remained staring at Brad, and waiting. But all Brad did was to stand straight and stroke a concerned hand over his mouth and beard. He gestured the nurses to wait, and everyone in the cubicle exhaled pent up tension and stood in still silence.

Along the curving corridor, Len could not accept what was happening. *This is my worst nightmare*, he thought. *Over so many years, I didn't appreciate how much I need her. What will I do without her?*

Inside the waiting room, Len and Janet sat holding hands.

In the ICU, the nurses slowly dispersed, leaving only Nancy and Brad watching Gertrude's breathing fade and resume, with longer pauses and less and less struggle, until she fought no more and until the squiggles on the monitor came to rest on a straight base line.

Nancy looked approvingly at Brad, who went to examine his patient and friend one last time.

Only three people were in the waiting room. Brad sat on a chair opposite Janet and Len. He offered them all the support that a friend could give, and more than this, he told them the truth about Gertrude, that in her final moments she had passed on in peace.

Brad knew there was nothing else to do, except sit with them and listen if they wished to talk.

Father and daughter wept bitterly, Janet at the loss of a mother, Len at the loss of a wife, and both at the loss of a best friend. Len could not imagine a future without her, and stranger than this, try as he may, he could not remember his life before her. Before he met Gertrude, there was nothing in his life worth remembering.

But greater than his loss was his regret. How he wished he could travel back to Seaview, to the year 1971, not to relive what had already passed, but rather to nurture what could have been. Heaven upon Earth was within his grasp, and were it not for a handful of poor choices, he could have arrived at this dreadful moment with no regrets at all.

Printed in the United States
215261BV00002B/25/P

9 781606 937792